MW01172528

A SAFE PLACE TO DIE

WRACK AND RUIN

BOOK 2

OTTO SCHAFER

SOUND EYE PRESS

Published in 2024

ISBN 9798990705005 (hardback)
ISBN 9798990705012 (paperback)
ISBN 9798986076096 (ebook)

Cover design and illustrations by Rafido @99Designs
Editing by The Blue Garret

Sound Eye Press
www.ottoschafer.com

For the nurses of the world—

In the face of unimaginable challenges, your tireless dedication, selfless care, and often thankless efforts stand as a beacon of hope and resilience. This book, set in a world of chaos and survival, is inspired by your unwavering commitment to saving lives and providing comfort.

Thank you for being the true heroes, not just in my story, but in everyday life.

CONTENTS

CHAPTER 1
DEAD-DEAD

ZOE SHIVERED as she squinted against the wind blasting through the busted windshield of the church bus. Jagged shards of glass edged its border, leaving nothing to protect her from the red rain and the alien parasite it carried – the one that made people sick. With the carnage of her neighborhood and burning home a couple miles behind her, she turned right onto Dee-Mac Road.

Zoe's eyes flicked up to the oversized rearview mirror mounted to the ceiling. Thankfully, bus mirrors weren't mounted to the windshield because hers was pretty much destroyed. Only a few seats back, Oliver was sitting upright, leaning against the side of the bus. He was still unconscious and pale as death from all the blood he'd lost. She'd found him lying prone behind what was left of their house, with an undead woman covered in burn wounds chewing on his shoe. He'd been damn lucky he hadn't become zombie food.

Zoe lifted herself in her seat so she could see Jurnee, the six-year-old Oliver had brought home when all this madness started. The little girl was hugging herself as she snuggled for warmth between Oliver and Louie, their blue-nose pit bull, who now sat facing the undead man in the aisle – the one responsible for destroying her only barrier of safety. Louie probably wasn't sure if the dead man was going to stay dead, but Zoe knew that with a bullet in his brain, he was dead-dead. Was "dead-dead" a term she had just created? If so, she was going to have to keep using it because apparently, thanks to the red rain, they were now living in a world where the dead refused to die – a world where the rain made zombies real.

As if to punctuate her fear, thunder rumbled across the quickly reddening sky, a prelude to infection. The last several days flashed through her mind, a kaleidoscope of images straight from a nightmare, and it all started with the red rain.

The destruction of the asteroid responsible for this madness had unleashed an alien parasite into the atmosphere. As rust-colored rain poured from the sky, the parasite it carried fell to Earth. She'd seen it for herself, studied it under a microscope with her naked eyes as it grew at an exponential rate. Those caught in the rain became infected with the parasite. What followed was madness – worse than madness.

Straight away, Oliver had called them zombies, but as a registered nurse about to earn her nurse practitioner credential, she'd been in denial. The dead simply couldn't come back to life. She'd been so sure these people were sick, and if she could figure out what was causing it she could help them. Maybe even save them. Now she knew better. Once the infected died, they became zombies by the very definition of the word. Instinctively, she reached for the .357 on her hip, brushing the pistol's grip with her hand.

Oliver's plan had been to travel the fifteen or so miles to the church he'd stopped at with Jurnee on his way home, stock up on food, and then head to the farmhouse a few more miles up the road from the church. But her view from the busted windshield told her that to get to the church, she would have to turn west, heading directly towards the bank of red storm clouds that roiled like a cauldron of doom.

She crossed the Mackinaw River and climbed the steep hill ascending from the river valley as fast as she could make the bus go.

The engine roared like an angry T-Rex. *Come on!* she screamed inside.

Another mile down, and she knew her turn onto Broadway Road would be coming up on her left. Squeezing the wheel white-knuckle tight, she tried to make a decision that could be the difference between life and death. Should she turn west onto Broadway Road and pray she could make it to the church before the sky let loose, or continue north and try to find more immediate shelter?

Zoe's anxiety was rising by the second. Whatever she decided, it was up to her now. They were all depending on her.

I'm sorry, Oliver. She blew past her turn, continuing north on Dee-Mac Road. *What now?* she thought, knowing this decision had only bought her time. Eventually, the storm would overtake them. She needed shelter, and she needed it fast.

Zoe passed a sedan pulled onto the shoulder. It had been coming from the other way. She couldn't say why the driver had pulled off, how long the car had sat there, or why the driver's door was standing open. But she had a feeling, and that feeling was telling her to keep going, that this wasn't the shelter they needed. If the car wouldn't start, they'd be stranded inside, sitting ducks for the undead until the rain stopped.

Something splatted on the hood. "Oh god! No!" Was that a sprinkle? She wasn't sure. Was it starting to rain? To her left, a long driveway led past a farmhouse, ending at a huge red barn. "Hold on, Jurnee!"

Without another thought, she yanked the wheel hard, turning the bus into the driveway of the small farmhouse. She cut the corner too fast and too sharp, and the driver's-side rear wheels dipped into the ditch, bouncing the back of the bus up into the air.

Jurnee screamed.

The small brick ranch house flashed by in a blur as Zoe aimed the bus at the set of weather-faded barn doors.

As the bus smashed through the doors, Zoe let go of the steering wheel, throwing her arms in front of her face. Instinctively, she slammed on the brakes. Something scraped across her forearm.

The wheels locked up, but the bus continued forward, finally halting with the sound of crunching metal.

The sudden jolt threw Zoe into the steering wheel, a guttural grunt escaping her as the force of impact pushed the air from her lungs. "Ugh," she moaned, lifting her head.

In front of the buckled hood of the bus, an old green tractor stood like a mighty oak tree, unmoving. She might as well have slammed the bus into the Incredible Hulk. "Jur... Jurnee?" she called, looking around.

From outside a voice called, "Who's in there? You come on out now!"

Zoe's heart stalled. Once again, her eyes found the oversized mirror still hanging from the ceiling, though it was all out of whack now. She pushed a piece of red barnwood off her lap and looked back over her shoulder, but she didn't see anyone. "Jurnee!" she whispered urgently. "Where are you?"

"Back here," came the girl's tiny voice. "I'm okay, but Oliver fell on the floor."

Louie barked.

"I got a gun!"

Zoe heard the telltale warning of a pump-action shotgun. Through one of the bus windows, she glimpsed an older man with grey whiskers, wearing a flannel shirt, blue jean bibs, and a green John Deere ball cap. He was creeping low along the passenger side of the bus, approaching the door with his shotgun held at the ready.

"Jurnee, listen to me," she whispered. "Hide under the seat until I tell you to come out!" Zoe held up her hands and stood, unable to determine if the man was infected. He was talking, so he obviously wasn't one of the undead, but that didn't mean he wasn't sick – and with sickness came insanity.

From what Zoe had been able to ascertain, if someone was infected, the parasite took control of their mind – how, she wasn't sure. Perhaps some chemical venom like the zombie wasp used. However it worked, it triggered insatiable hunger in the victim. But not hunger for a cheeseburger, hunger for something much worse – human brain matter. At this stage, the victim still had use of all motor functions, including speech and the ability to use a shotgun. In some ways, they were scarier than the undead. The only way to kill infected – to make them truly dead-dead – was to destroy their brain. Any other fatal injury and the parasite would somehow bring them back – make them undead... make them... zombies.

As Zoe knew all too well by now, the next moments would tell her if this man had all his faculties or if he were infected and a slave to the parasite controlling him.

She spun in a slow circle, her hands still held up, fighting the urge to draw the .357 from her hip holster. "I'm sorry, but the rain. My windshield was broken."

"Rain? There ain't no rain!" the man shouted.

Zoe turned to the side to hide the fact she had a gun on her hip. She peered out the window, trying to see the man's eyes, but the bill of his cap shielded them from her view.

She'd learned back at the Bloomridge courthouse to always check the eyes. Bleeding eyes and severe cravings were the first signs of infection. Though even if he wasn't infected, he wasn't likely to be happy; she'd destroyed the man's barn doors and smashed a bus into his tractor. What if he made an assumption that *she* was infected? *Shit.*

The man peeked around the corner of the broken bus door. "I see you up there! By god! You wrecked my whole damn barn! I ought to just shoot you where you stand!"

"Please, I... I had no choice! I'm not infected! I was worried about the rain!"

Louie barked out a warning, followed by a deep growl. Zoe's right hand slowly dropped towards her hip, towards the gun she didn't want to draw.

"Lady, I'll shoot that damn dog if it comes at me!" the man shouted, his eyes going wide.

Zoe saw his eyes then. She saw them clear as crystal. The man's eyes were normal.

"He won't! I promise." She turned and motioned to Louie, who now stood in the aisle. Just behind the dog, Oliver's unconscious body lay sprawled halfway into the aisle. Jurnee's little round face topped with two afro puffs peeked out. Her eyes were wide. The poor thing looked terrified. Zoe looked Jurnee in the eyes and waved her back with a one-handed motion, "Stay, Louie." But she wasn't looking at the dog.

Jurnee's little head nodded up and down in understanding, and she vanished back behind the seat.

"Thought I heard you talking to someone a moment ago. You alone up there?" the man asked, his voice laced with suspicion.

"Yes," she lied. "Other than my dog, and a couple dead men that were infected."

Even though this man didn't seem to be showing signs of infection, Zoe wasn't willing to take any chances, not yet. Plus, she still had to worry about the other concern. Infected or not, he had a gun pointed at her.

The man took a cautious step forward, coming into full view. He was wiry, lean and fit, probably in his late forties, but his grey whiskers made him look older. He squinted up at her, trying to gauge the situation.

"Well then, you alright?" he asked, his eyes scanning her for any signs of deceit.

"Just a little banged up," Zoe replied, trying to keep her voice steady.

The man leaned in, trying to see up into the bus. "Do you mind if I come up?" he asked, his voice cautious yet firm.

"No. I don't mind, but my dog might go nuts if you do. My name is Zoe, and I just live down the road. Just outside Mackinaw. Thing is, our house was overrun with... um, well, sick people, and it caught fire. We had to make a run for it. Is it okay if I just come down? I can explain everything," she said, trying to sound both friendly and desperate.

The man nodded slowly, his expression softening a bit. "Well, Zoe, sounds like you had a hell of a day. My name is Trent. This is my farm."

From outside the barn came a voice, high and worried. "Trent! Trent, what happened? For heaven's sake, are you alright?"

"And that is the voice of my lovely wife, Minnie." Trent turned his head but didn't lower the shotgun. "I think so, hun! Give me a minute!"

"Well, whatever's happened, you best get in the house before it rains, and you get stuck in the barn!" the woman shouted.

"She isn't wrong – it's gonna cut loose any minute," said Trent.

"Right. That's why I wrecked into your barn. My windshield was smashed, and I was afraid..." Zoe motioned towards the busted windshield.

Trent lowered the shotgun, holding it with one hand as he lifted his hat by the bill and rubbed his balding head. "You sure did a number on my barn. I would have preferred you just knocked on the door."

"I... I thought it had started to sprinkle," she said, feeling embarrassed.

"Why don't you come on down and let's get you in the house. We'll get you something hot to drink and Minnie can tend to that scrape on your arm. Then we'll go from there. That sound alright?"

Zoe gave a slight smile and nodded. Still, she held back from telling Trent about Jurnee and Oliver. She needed to be sure. "Thank you, Trent. That sounds good. Let me just leash my dog so he doesn't follow me and I'll come right down."

"Do hurry. We don't want to be stuck out here when the rain lets loose."

Zoe turned and hurried down the aisle, kneeling next to Oliver and Jurnee. "Jurnee, I need to go inside and make sure everything is okay, then I'll come back. Stay here with Oliver and Louie, okay? I'm counting on you."

Jurnee nodded, her little eyes welling up.

"It's going to be okay. Be brave, and I'll be right back. You have Louie and Princess. And Ollie has you." She gave the little girl the brightest smile she could.

Jurnee did not smile but pulled her doll, Princess, onto her lap and nodded again, wiping her eyes on her sleeve.

"Trent! What in the hell are you doing out there?"

"Sorry, I'm coming!" Zoe stood and hurried back to a waiting Trent. She hesitated for half a beat and then descended the stairs onto the hard dirt floor.

"Don't worry about Minnie. She's just worried is all," Trent said, his eyes falling to Zoe's side arm. "Um, listen. I'm gonna take you into my home, but it ain't gonna go over well with Minnie you having a gun on your hip. And if I'm being honest, it isn't just Minnie. It would make me feel a whole lot better if you left that here. I promise you can have it back after we get to know you and figure out a plan."

Zoe hesitated. She didn't want to leave her gun. She wanted to protest. To try and reassure him it was only for her safety, only to protect her from the sick. But he wasn't sick, and if this Minnie was sick, she would have certainly attacked Trent by now. Plus, she was a stranger, being invited into his home. Wouldn't she ask the same?

Minnie's voice called out again. "Trent, for Pete's sake!"

Trent kept his eyes trained on Zoe. His eyebrows were lifted as if to say, *What's it going to be?* He turned his head and called back towards the house. "Dammit, Minnie, hold your horses! We're coming out now!"

Zoe drew the .357 from her holster and set it down atop a workbench. She turned back to Trent, took in a deep breath, and nodded.

Trent smiled, showing tobacco-stained teeth. "Alrighty then, this way."

CHAPTER 2
MINNIE

ZOE FELT her anxiety rise as she stepped out of the barn to cross a gravel driveway where a sidewalk led to the back of the brick house. High above, the cloud-stuffed sky was pregnant, ready to birth monsters. She'd been under the sky a few times since the asteroid but never when the threat of rain was so certain.

A woman who Zoe assumed was Minnie held open an aluminum screen door. Her expression was etched with a concern that must have matched Zoe's own. Like Trent, this woman appeared to be in her late forties. Her dishwater-blond hair was pulled into a messy bun, and she wore colorful nurse's scrubs with a butterfly print. The prospect that this woman worked in the medical field gave Zoe an instant, if only slight, bit of relief.

Zoe forced a smile as she entered the back porch behind Trent. "Thank you."

"You're welcome, dear," the woman said, before turning to Trent. "What the hell took you so long? You know what happens if you get caught in the rain!"

"For Christ's sake, Mins. Let the poor girl get all the way in the door before you start in on me." Trent leaned his shotgun against the wall and stepped past Zoe to click the lock on the screen door.

"I can't do this again – and I can't do it by myself! Think of the children!"

Trent looked suddenly serious. "Don't you dare. You know that's all I think about!"

Zoe suddenly felt very out of place; diverting her eyes from the couple, she scanned the closed-in back porch. At one end, several bicycles hung neatly. Below the bikes were a couple of skateboards and a pile of shoes. Clearly, children lived here. Zoe wondered where they were.

"I swear it's like you're trying to get yourself killed! Just look out there." Minnie pointed through the glass window of the screen door. Red-tinted spots dotted the sidewalk they had just traveled, and more were falling.

Zoe's heart quickened. *Think of the children.* Jurnee was out there alone. Well, not alone. She had Louie and she knew, no matter what, to never go into the rain.

Silently she prayed that the rain would pass quickly and that, by the time it had, she could tell Trent and Minnie the truth. Surely they'd understand why she'd held back about Jurnee and Oliver. She had to make sure they were safe.

Trent flicked his hands up and down his body. "Look at us, Mins. Not a drop on us. We're here and we're safe. Now let's get off this porch and get this lady some of that special tea of yours."

Minnie narrowed her eyes and pointed at Trent's cap. "Take off that hat before you set one foot in this kitchen, mister." She turned to Zoe, her face lighting up with a smile. "Forgive me, what's your name, hun?" she asked expectantly.

Zoe held out her hand. "Zoe."

"Zoe," Minnie repeated, taking Zoe's hand in hers.

The older woman smiled now, and Zoe saw it. The swelling in Minnie's face and the black around her eyes. It was like the woman hadn't had a good night's sleep in days, and she'd clearly been crying. It was a stark reminder – Zoe and her family weren't going through this alone. The asteroid and what it brought with it had changed the world.

Minnie squeezed Zoe's hand. "But I swear, he just doesn't think!"

"I understand, and I'm sorry for showing up like this. Truly I am."

Minnie waved off the apology, motioning her towards a door that appeared to lead into the kitchen. "Nonsense. People don't smash buses into barns for no good reason. Come in and tell me all about it."

Zoe followed, pulling the door to the kitchen shut behind her.

"Oh, just leave it open, dear. The screen door to the porch is locked and, besides, it will be good to let some fresh air into the kitchen."

In the kitchen, Minnie motioned Zoe to sit at the island as she rounded the other side and placed a stainless-steel teapot on the stove. She turned the knob, the igniter clicked twice, and flame blossomed. "Warm tea coming right up."

The kitchen smelled of fresh coffee and pumpkin spice and was larger than Zoe expected. Across the kitchen, a coffeepot percolated, while on the island a three-wick candle burned bright. The kitchen must have been recently updated with its white cabinets and quartz countertops. The floor was a stylish tile that looked like a black hardwood but wasn't. The place had a modern charm as if pulled right from the pages of *Better Homes and Gardens* magazine.

As Zoe watched Minnie prepare the tea, a sense of relief washed over her. Finally, she'd found others to compare notes with. And even better, judging by her outfit, Minnie appeared to be in the medical field.

Trent lifted the coffeepot, poured himself a cup, and crossed back around the island, taking the chair next to Zoe. Truth was, she'd rather have a cup of that coffee than tea, but at this point anything warm sounded good, and she didn't want to be rude. After all, Trent and Minnie were being incredibly gracious to someone who'd just damaged their property.

Glancing towards the kitchen window, she could see the rain was coming down hard now. She shouldn't be sitting here about to enjoy a cup of hot tea. Jurnee was out there. What if she didn't listen? What if she panicked and came looking for her? She needed to hurry this along and tell them about Jurnee and Oliver. Then she could shout over to the barn and tell Jurnee everything was going to be okay and to stay put.

"Zoe?"

Zoe gasped. "Oh, sorry... I..."

Minnie followed Zoe's gaze to the kitchen window. "Don't worry. The rain can't hurt you in here."

Trent pointed in the direction of the barn. "She wasn't alone on the bus."

Minnie's eyebrows rose.

Zoe felt her heart stop.

"She has a dog with her. I'm sure that's what it is. You're worried about your pup?"

Now was her chance to tell the truth. "Louie, yeah, I... well, yes. But—"

"Well, don't. You leashed him up. He can't get into the rain, and you know what?"

Zoe shook her head.

Trent gave her a comforting smile. "I don't think the rain makes animals sick like it does us. Four days this has been going on, and I ain't noticed any issues with the chickens or cows."

Minnie, her back to Zoe, now fished around in a cabinet, retrieving a couple coffee cups, tea bags, and some honey. "Trent is right. I'm a home healthcare nurse. Well, I was before all this started. You see, this parasite. It doesn't affect animals, only people."

Zoe brightened. "You figured out it was a parasite too? But how?"

Minnie's expression fell and her eyes welled. "One of our children... she... well, we were able to restrain her. I sedated her..."

The teapot whistled.

Minnie turned away and busied herself making Zoe's tea.

"Oh my god. I'm so sorry, Minnie." She instantly had a million questions that she couldn't bring herself to ask.

Trent cleared his throat. "Janis was our only girl and the big sister to our twin boys. Two days ago, Minnie removed what she thinks is a parasite from the back of Janis's neck." Trent closed his eyes and drew in a steadying breath. "She died less than a minute later."

Minnie's shoulders sagged, and Zoe felt her own eyes welling up.

The woman took a steadying breath, placed two steaming cups of tea down on the island, and sat across from her.

The silence lingered as Zoe's mind reeled at the revelation that Minnie had removed a parasite from the back of their daughter's neck.

Minnie blew on her cup of tea and then broke the silence. "Zoe, enough about this medical stuff – tell us about you and how you ended up in our barn."

Zoe nodded and took a careful sip of her own tea, a flavorful spiced chai.

"You like it? I ordered it all the way from the UK."

"Mmm, yes. It's very nice." But she wasn't ready to move on – not yet. "The barn, of course – well, I live just down the road in Mackinaw, and I'm in school finishing up the nurse practitioner program at Bloomridge College."

Minnie gasped and clasped her hands together. "Really? An NP? Oh, that's fantastic."

Zoe nodded. "Thank you. I was able to get a look at a few blood samples and determine that after the parasite was exposed to the atmosphere, it died. That's why we don't get infected walking through wet grass or simply breathing in the air. As near as I can tell, the parasites die when they get exposed to anything outside of the rain they're contained in, unless it comes directly into contact with humans. I have to ask – how did you know to remove it from your daughter's neck?"

Minnie's eyes glanced over to Trent. The look was one begging for strength.

Trent reached across the counter and gave his wife's hand a squeeze.

"She developed a large knot on the back of her neck beneath the skin, just below the cerebellum. You haven't seen this?"

Zoe pulled another long sip of tea and shook her head.

"Well, that doesn't surprise me – it only became noticeable on Janis after the second day of infection."

"I tell you, Mins, this is all the goddamn government. Some scheme to thin the population." Trent slapped his hand down on the counter. "Probably never was an asteroid. All government lies!"

Minnie glared across the counter. "Trent! Calm down! You're going to scare the poor girl half to death."

"It's fine. Really." Oddly, Trent's outburst didn't scare her. And she hadn't even jumped at the noise of his hand slamming on the counter. Maybe she was more tired than she thought. "How large was the..." She forgot what she was going to ask. Frowning, she glanced back to the window. Jurnee. She'd better tell them.

Minnie sipped from her own cup. "How large was what, dear? The parasite?"

Zoe nodded. "Yes... when you removed it?"

"Four inches. It was awful. Full of sharp teeth and long tentacles." Minnie shivered. "I have it saved in an old mason jar – later, I'll show you."

"Hell of a thing," Trent muttered.

Zoe looked over at Trent, but his face was fuzzy. She blinked, trying to bring him into focus. "There's something... something... I need to... It's about the bus..."

No one spoke for a long moment. The silence seemed to stretch on and on. Wasn't she about to tell them something?

Minnie smiled. "It's okay, Zoe. Take your time. Have some more tea."

"What?" She heard herself say the word, but it came out all wrong. Lifting the teacup towards her mouth, she stopped and looked down.

"Sorry, dear, but I barely understood what you said? You want to tell me about the bus in the barn?"

Zoe blinked, feeling her eyes slowly close and then open.

The cup of tea slipped from her hand, crashing onto the counter.

She glanced past Trent to a closed door across the room. "Where... where... are...?" Her tongue felt too big, too slow in her mouth. "The... twins?" She tried to lift her arm to point at the door, but either her arm wasn't lifting or she couldn't feel it... She definitely couldn't feel it.

CHAPTER 3
TERRY'S STRIPES

"PLEASE WAKE UP, OLIVER."

Oliver's eyes fluttered open as blurry images filled his vision. "Zoe," he croaked.

Someone was shaking him. He tried to move and instantly regretted it. Pain shot down his back, and his left arm, which he realized was pinned beneath him, ached to be freed. Trying to twist, he bent his knee. "Ahhh god!" A new pain racked his foot. He sucked in a sharp breath and his nostrils filled with the smell of smoke. His home was burning down! Zombies! Zombies were closing in! "Zoe!" he moaned again as a flaming zombie crawled atop his feet and bit down on his shoe!

Something wet and coarse swiped his cheek. The zombies... the zombies were eating his face.

Oliver kicked his feet, his right shoe crashing into something solid. "Gahaahha!" he screamed, sparks igniting in his vision. He clenched his jaw and nearly pissed himself.

"It's just Louie, Oliver," a tiny voice whispered. "But you better be quiet. Zoe said we needed to be quiet until she made sure it was safe."

Oliver swallowed, his eyes slowly coming into focus. "Jurnee." He tried again to turn over, slower this time. It took a hell of an effort, but he finally managed to roll onto his back and free his left arm.

Next to him, Louie let out a small whine and lay down. He realized he was lying on the floor of the bus between the seats, one leg sticking out in the aisle and the other twisted beneath the seat. As he looked up, a little round face with two puffs of hair stared down at him from atop the bus seat. Jurnee looked frightened, and he could tell she'd been crying.

Oliver had no memory of how he'd gotten on the bus or why he was on the floor. The last thing he remembered, he'd just blown up their home. He was lying in his backyard in the grass, and burning zombies were about to eat him. How did he get here? And where was here anyway?

"Jurnee, where is Zoe?"

"She went with the man who was yelling to make sure it was safe."

"What? What man?" Oliver pushed a palm against the floor of the bus and tried to sit up. The world spun and once again his vision blurred. "Oh, god."

"You have a bad owie, Oliver. Please be careful. I really don't want you to go back to sleep. Louie and I are scared." The little girl's hand appeared and reached towards him. She patted his shoulder. "Will you hold my hand?"

He took her little hand in his. A bad owie. That had to be the pain he was feeling in his back. His foot hurt too, but that wasn't new. A few days ago, he ran a nail through it, and it was still sore as hell, but the pain in his back was definitely not good. But there was something else. He felt weak. Extremely weak. "Jurnee, it's... it's going to be okay. Do you know how long I slept? Do you know what happened to me?"

"You got glass in your back, Oliver. I helped Zoe fix it. But..."

"Glass in my back," he repeated.

"Um-hm. I never saw so much blood. And I got to help make it stop. I held the bandage on and pushed real hard. See, if you push real hard it might make the bleeding stop. Then Zoe pinched it and put... um... Terry's stripes on it. I don't know who Terry is, but he makes really good tape that's kind of like stitches but without the needle. You know, I would be super scared if I had to have stitches. If I ever get an owie that needs stitches, I'm going to ask if I can have some of Terry's stripes."

Carefully, he moved his right shoulder. He could feel it then, not just pain but a wound in his back. Oliver understood too that Terry's stripes were Steri-Strips, and Zoe had used them to close his wound. Steri-Strips were a common tool in the nursing profession, often used to repair skin tears and lacerations. He remembered Zoe talking about some of the skin tears she'd treated back when she'd worked at the nursing home. He must have lost a lot of blood. That's why he felt so weak.

In the quiet, he heard something he hadn't noticed before. Rain.

"Jurnee, how long has Zoe been gone?"

Jurnee looked up towards the ceiling. "Well, I didn't count, but even if I had I don't think I could count for as long as she's been gone."

That wasn't helpful. Could be minutes, could be an hour. "You said the man Zoe went with was yelling. Do you know what he said? Do you know why he was yelling?"

"I think he was mad that we crashed his barn."

Crashed his barn? Zoe drove the bus into the man's barn? Oliver turned his head, trying to see up and out the bus windows, but it was no use. All he could see from the floor was that there wasn't much light coming in, and he didn't see rain, but he could sure as hell hear it. He had to get up.

Letting go of Jurnee's hand, he said, "I want to come sit up there with you." Carefully, he pushed himself into a sitting position. It took some time and effort and it hurt like hell, but he managed to get there without passing out. Once he was sitting up, he used the back of the seat in front of him and his left arm to slowly get his feet under him. He stood, but only long enough to pivot into the bus seat next to Jurnee.

Everything spun and darkness closed in, blotting out his peripheral vision. For a brief moment he thought he might black out again, but the tunnel widened and the world steadied.

"Are you okay?" Jurnee asked.

He was in fact not okay, but he nodded anyway, forcing a smile that must have looked like an angry grimace because the little girl frowned back at him with a look of worry too grim for a six-year-old. At least he was sitting up in the seat and, despite the pain, he was conscious.

He could now see they were in fact in a barn. Carefully, he looked out the rear of the bus, which was just inside the large barn. Beyond the broken doors, a long driveway stretched out to a road that ran crossways. Through the tinted rain he could see another road on the opposite side, leading in the opposite direction. He didn't recognize where they were. He played out the path he'd taken to work every day for the past several years and couldn't place it along the route to the church. But something else caught his eye. Near the back of the bus, a man's body lay in a crumpled heap. How did that get here? He could ask Jurnee but thought maybe he shouldn't. He turned back to the front of the bus. The windshield was completely smashed in – did that happen before the crash or during?

Jurnee scooted over and pressed herself into Oliver's side. "Come up here with us, Louie."

Louie obeyed, jumping up into the seat next to Jurnee and lying down.

Oliver looked down at the little girl. "Hey, kid, that must have been quite a crash into the barn."

"It was! You flopped right off the seat and I screamed!"

"But you're okay?"

Jurnee nodded. "Uh-huh."

"And was Zoe okay when she left with the man?"

"She seemed okay. She asked me to stay here and hide with you and Louie until she made sure it was safe."

"And the man, was he still yelling when they left?"

"Um... nuh-uh. They were just talking. Well... there was a woman calling for them to get inside before it rained and she seemed really mad."

For whatever reason, Zoe didn't tell this man about Jurnee or him. So either the man was infected or something else gave Zoe pause. But if he was infected, she wouldn't have gone with him. She had her gun. She would have shot him before being taken hostage by an infected, and why would she tell Jurnee she was going to make sure it was safe? He was overthinking this. She must have gone inside to make sure it was okay. She probably told them by now that he and Jurnee were out here, but it started raining and they couldn't get back in here to get them until it stopped. Maybe, if he could get over by the doors, he could yell over to the house.

First he needed to take inventory. He felt at his waist, knowing he'd had the 9mil tucked in his waistband when he left the basement, but he must have lost it in the yard. Damn, he'd loved that gun. Luckily, his shoulder holster still held the .45. He drew the gun, released the magazine, and found it was empty. Double damn. He didn't think he could reach his ankle without getting dizzy, but if worse came to worse, he had his little .22 deuce-deuce boot gun strapped to his ankle.

Carefully he leaned out, scanning down the aisle. He was looking for two things. His shotgun and that duffle bag of ammo. He knew he'd gotten at least as far as his backyard with both.

Glancing around, he didn't see the shotgun, but sticking out from beneath the seat he saw his old gym bag. Well, that was something. Now he just needed to get to it, get his gun reloaded, and make his way over to the barn door. Then he'd go from there.

He gripped the back of the seat with his left hand and prepared to pull himself up.

A blood-curdling scream cut through the pitter-patter of the rain.

"Zoe!" Pain be damned, Oliver bolted upright and lurched into the aisle. "Stay here!" he growled through a clenched jaw of gritted teeth in the direction of Jurnee. Head swimming, he tried to steady himself using the seat as he took one step, then another. The bus spun around him as sparks ignited from the corners of eyes. "No!" he growled. Another step, and the starburst turned to dark shadow.

He staggered down the aisle, stumbling down the bus stairs. Dizzy, with the world out of focus, he missed the last step, and his lower back scraped across the bottom step as he collapsed onto his hands and knees.

He moaned, feeling it all as his vision blurred. Fueled only by adrenaline and the love for his wife, Oliver stood, blinking, his legs shaking. Straight ahead, atop the dusty workbench, something shiny caught his eye. He blinked again and frowned. It was Zoe's nickel-plated .357. She didn't even have her gun! He staggered towards the doors and the deluge awaiting him beyond, not caring about the pain or the rain or becoming infected or undead. Zoe needed him! The one thing, the only thing in this whole godforsaken world worth dying for needed him, and by god he was going. He'd die ten times over, if it meant she would live, because without her, there was nothing to live for. She was everything. She was life! "I'm coming, Zo!"

Once he hit the rain he'd have at least fifteen minutes to save her from whatever the fuck was happening. Fifteen minutes before he turned. It would be enough. It had to be.

Dots of light flashed in the corners of his eyes.

Still he moved forward.

Something wet soaked his back. The rain. He must be in the rain.

He stumbled.

Darkness brought his vision to an ever-tightening tunnel. "No! Do not fail her! I forbid it. Do not..."

Another step, and all that remained of his vision closed in like an old tube TV blinking off.

Oliver felt himself falling, but he couldn't control it.

Felt himself hitting the ground, but he couldn't brace for it.

Felt himself slipping away, but he couldn't stop it.

The last thing Oliver felt wasn't the pain of his bodily wounds; it was the pain of his failure.

Then once again, he was gone.

CHAPTER 4
RUG BURN

ZOE FELT herself tip sideways off the chair, and though she couldn't do anything to stop it, she managed, for whatever good it was, to scream with all she had.

Hands cradled her, staying her fall.

"I got you," Trent said, easing her down to the tile.

"What... what's happening?" She managed to say the words, but it was like talking with a mouth full of oatmeal.

Minnie rounded the counter and looked down at her. "Ketamine. You being a nurse yourself, I'm sure you're familiar with the drug."

She was familiar. Minnie had given her a powerful anesthetic commonly known for its use as a date rape drug. How much of that tea had she drunk? She was so confused. Why? Why had they done this?

"Hmmm," Minnie hummed. "I don't think she drank much, but the damn coffee cup shattered. Should I get an injection ready just in case?"

Trent shook his head, grabbing Zoe by the wrists. "Let's just get it done. I've got her. Get the door."

Zoe twisted her head back as the door to the next room swung open. She gasped sharply, not at what she saw in the next room but at the stench. The drug had dulled her motor skills, but it had done nothing to dull her sense of smell. It wasn't overwhelming, but it was there – the putrid stink of death. "No!" she managed as Trent jerked her by the wrists hard enough she felt like her arms might pull from their sockets.

As Trent dragged Zoe across the threshold, Minnie looked down, her face doleful. "Wait just a sec, hun."

Trent stopped, let go of Zoe's wrists, stood upright, and stretched his back.

Minnie knelt down. "I am sorry, Zoe. Truly I am. I think if this horrible thing hadn't happened and we met under different circumstances, we could have been friends. And for that I feel bad, really I do, but there is nothing I wouldn't do for my boys."

"No! No pleash!" she slurred.

Trent pulled Zoe into the next room. The kitchen door swung shut behind them, not latching but springing in past the threshold like a tavern door – *swoosh-swoosh, swoosh-swoosh,* before settling into place.

Zoe felt the carpet rubbing against her clothes, burning her backside as the friction built. The ceiling was white and stamped in a fan-like pattern. She passed below a ceiling fan that was spinning slowly, or maybe quickly. She blinked. "Where 're... take mmm..." she tried to ask but the words were too hard to form.

Trent paused, and the tug on her arms eased.

Zoe's head tipped to the side, showing her a floor of beige carpet. A flower-patterned couch sat in the distance. In front of the couch stood an IV stand with a half-empty bag hanging from the hooks. Next to the stand was some kind of table covered in a white, blood-soaked sheet. A long coffee table perhaps? Trent pulled again, Zoe's shoulder sockets stretched, and she slid. A pile of white towels crusted in brown blood entered her vision and then passed as she was dragged deeper into the house. The room disappeared, and suddenly she was very close to the wall. A hallway – she was in a hallway.

The next time Trent stopped pulling, she was in front of a closed door. From beyond the door, Zoe heard something. Something between a moan and a cry – something pained.

When Trent pushed open the door, the smell of rot engulfed Zoe and, despite her medical training, overwhelmed her senses, eliciting a gag as vomit spewed up her throat.

"Wait! She's going to asphyxiate. Let me turn her." Minnie rolled her onto her left side, and Zoe coughed out a mouthful of vomit onto the carpet.

She was now staring down a dark stairwell into what she knew must be a basement. Wait. How did she get here? And where was here? Her head felt so fuzzy.

Below, shadows stirred.

She blinked, trying to focus on what was happening, clarity returning in a wave. Oh that's right – she was poisoned by these freaking nutjobs.

She tried to speak. "No... No... Please!"

Minnie's face came back into view. "Trent, try not to let her head bounce off the stairs when you take her down."

Trent stepped over Zoe. "I don't see why it matters."

"Because you weren't careful with the last one, and I don't think Jack liked that so much!"

Zoe felt the man's rough hands wrap around her wrists again. "Well now, Mins, I'm not so sure about that. The last one died before the boys got to her, and you damn well know it wasn't from her hitting her head."

"Just what are you saying?"

"I'm just saying you might have given that Katie girl too much."

"You shot her in the stomach – I had to give her something! She was screaming bloody murder! Besides, it was the first time! You expect me to be good at this?"

Trent backed down two steps and heaved Zoe onto the stairs. "I'm sorry. Of course not. And there's no point in arguing. I'll be careful. Besides, it didn't stop the boys from getting what they needed, right? Hey, get the light, would you?"

Zoe's head flopped back, but before her head hit the step, she felt Trent's arm come in from underneath, cradling her neck as he slid his hands under her arms.

Minnie flipped the light switch.

A single bulb lit above the stairs, pushing back the darkness. The woman in the butterfly scrub top peered past Zoe and down into the basement. "Jack! Gene! Mom and Dad have something for you!"

Zoe pressed her head back, craning her neck to see what waited below. Upside down as her view was, she needed to see! She twisted and tried to fight, but her body wouldn't cooperate. She caught one quick glimpse of stairs that led to a landing, but beyond the upside-down world, shadows swallowed it all, hiding whatever horror awaited her.

Trent pulled. "No use fighting now."

Zoe's feet thumped numbly atop the next step. Down she went – another step, then another.

"Boys! Do you hear me? We've brought you something!"

Thump! Another step.

"Trent, don't you go all the way down there. Toss her now, you hear me?"

"First you want me to be careful, then you want me to throw her? They can't reach me unless I step off the landing. I made sure of that when I chained them up."

From somewhere deep in the bowels of the basement, low, guttural moans filled the stairwell, like two alley cats in a standoff.

Minnie began to sob. "I only wish Janis were here. She could be down here with her brothers. If only I'd known!"

Trent pulled once more, and again Zoe felt her body slip downward two more steps.

"Now ain't the time for this, Mins. Let's just get this—"

"Dad?" A quiet voice called from the darkness.

"Jack? Jack, I got something for you and Gene. Just like I promised I would."

Another voice now. "Oh, Dad," it moaned, but quickly rose to a scream. "Dad, I'm so fucking hungry!"

CHAPTER 5

YOU KNOW BETTER, OLIVER!

"OLIVER!" Jurnee called as she watched him disappear down the stairs of the bus. But Oliver didn't answer. Beside her, Louie whined. Jurnee set Princess down and stood on the seat to peer out the back of the bus.

Oliver wobbled into view. Watching him through the window reminded her of her sixth birthday. Her mom and dad got her a bouncy house, not to keep but just for her birthday party. She wished she could have kept it, though. She would have bounced every day until bedtime, and when she got older she would have just bounced and never gone to bed.

That day, her dad was about to leave to go to his big airplane carrier. He said it was so big you could land a plane on top of it. She'd never seen a boat that big, and she really didn't understand why you'd need a boat to carry a plane! Planes can fly! Anyway, he got in the bouncy house with her. They bounced and laughed, her dad chasing her from one side to the other, wobbling and falling the whole way. Her dad said he couldn't stop wobbling, and she remembered giggling so hard because "wobbling" was a funny word.

But Oliver wasn't having fun, and she wasn't having fun either. Something was wrong. There was a scream that sounded like Zoe.

Jurnee was scared. Louie was scared too, but she thought he might be braver than she was. Probably because he had such big teeth. If she had teeth like he had, she would be brave. But she only had plain old little girl teeth, and Princess didn't have any teeth at all! Well, maybe she did, but since she never opened her mouth, Jurnee couldn't be sure. "It's okay, Louie. Oliver is going to get Zoe. We just have to wait here and be brave, okay?"

Jurnee looked past Oliver through the busted-up barn doors. The red rain was really coming down now. Hey, wait a minute! Oliver couldn't go out there in the rain! He knew better. But something told Jurnee that was exactly what he was going to do! He was wobbling right for the busted-up doors, and he wasn't stopping! "No, Oliver! Don't go in the rain! You know better, Oliver!" she shouted, yelling as loud as she could.

Louie barked.

Oliver was only a few steps away when he slowed and then fell down face first onto the dirt floor.

Jurnee gasped. She watched him lying there on his stomach, just inside the door. "Louie, c'mon. Oliver is too close to the doors! He might get wet!" She picked up Princess, jumped down off the seat, and ran down the aisle to the big steps leading off the bus, with Louie on her heels.

She paused at the steps and looked down onto the dirt floor of the barn. She didn't even have shoes on, just her Mickey Mouse socks. Her heart raced in her chest. "Don't be scared, guys, Oliver needs us," she said, sounding way braver than she felt.

Jurnee jumped down one step and then the next until she landed on the dirt floor. She stood there frozen in place as she observed these new surroundings. For the first time since she met Oliver and Zoe, she'd disobeyed what they'd ask her to do. Her mom had always told her to be on her best behavior around other grown-ups, but she was sure this time she'd understand. A thought occurred to her then. She didn't mean to think it, but it just sorta popped into her head. It was the day Oliver had found her. They were on their way home from

Gran's house. "Oh, no," she whispered. There was a big crash of noise, and glass broke. She went upside down and her mom screamed.

She shook her head, not wanting to remember that. Not wanting to ever remember that.

Louie jumped off the last step, stopped at her side, and whined.

Carefully, she looked left towards the back of the barn where the biggest tractor she'd ever seen stood – almost to the ceiling! Quickly, she looked away because it was really dark back there.

In front of her, a riding lawn mower sat near the wall, surrounded by other grown-up stuff. It smelled weird too. Like her dad's greasy hands after he'd been in the garage working on his motorcycle. A long workbench had all kinds of stuff on it, and big metal tools were hanging on the wall above it. Under the workbench was really dark too. Just then, a shadow moved, she was sure it did! She did *not* like this place. "It's okay, Louie. I know you're scared," she whispered. "Follow me."

Jurnee turned to her right and ran towards the back of the bus, not looking left or right – especially not looking left! Instead, she kept her eyes on the barn doors and the light ahead.

When she rounded the back of the bus, there was Oliver, lying just a couple feet away from the door. Where he fell was dry and the rain hadn't gotten him, but his back was wet with fresh blood. "Oh no!"

Jurnee grabbed Oliver's ankle and pulled.

Oliver moaned, "Zoe!"

"Wake up, Oliver!" What if the rain leaked inside or the wind blew it in?

But Oliver didn't open his eyes.

"Come on, Louie! We gotta pull him back so the rain doesn't get him!"

Louie cocked his head to the side, peered out into the rain towards the house, and howled.

Jurnee stopped pulling on Oliver's ankle and stood, realizing there was no way she could move him. She followed Louie's gaze towards the screen door of the house, and she knew what she needed to do. Stepping in front of Louie, she faced him, placing a hand on each side of the pit bull's cheeks, and looked him square in the eyes. Then, in her most grown-up voice, she said, "Look at me, Louie."

Louie flopped his tongue out.

"Zoe needs help, and you can go in the rain! I can't but you can! You have to because Oliver needs help too. I have to go back to the bus and get Terry's Stripes for Oliver's back." The thought of going back into the bus was scary, but Oliver's back was still bleeding. "Do you understand? You have to go get Zoe! Go, Louie! Find Zoe! Go!"

The pit bull barked in response, causing Jurnee to jerk her hands back and jump.

"Whoa!" She pressed her lips tight, narrowed her eyes, and pointed into the rain. "Go! Find Zoe!" she ordered.

CHAPTER 6
CHAINS AND BRAINS

THE VOICES CALLING up from the darkness confirmed Zoe's worst fear. She was about to be eaten alive. Now she realized that it wouldn't be the undead eating her but the infected living. Not that being fed to one was better than the other. The realization sent a terrifying burst of dread down Zoe's spine. But the fear also sent a burst of adrenaline through her veins, and she somehow managed to grab hold of the wooden stair, gripping the board with all she had, desperate to hang on.

One of the boys called out again. "Dad! This dog chain is hurting me. Don't you even care?"

"Now, Jack, you're sick is all. We can't have you roaming around until we get this figured."

Glen's voice, angrier: "Can't have us roaming around! I'm going to get out of this collar, and when I do I'm going to empty your fucking head!"

Above her near the top of the stairs, Minnie sobbed quietly.

A chain dragged across the concrete floor, getting closer to the stairs. "Shut up, you whore! You think I don't know you're there, Mother? You think I can't smell you? Smell your brains?"

With a final grunt, Trent pulled Zoe onto the concrete floor at the bottom of the stairs.

Two boys stood not three feet away, silhouetted in shadow. Both lunged forward, chains rattling until they pulled taut. Zoe slammed her eyes shut, reflexively anticipating the boys' hands grabbing her and the pain of teeth to follow. She wanted to pray but couldn't find words. She wanted Oliver but knew he wasn't coming. He wouldn't come bursting through the door like with the neighbor. This time, she couldn't fight back, and no one was coming.

When she didn't feel the boys' hands, she forced herself to look. Trent was stepping over her, pressing his back to the wall. In front of her, the two boys had reached the end of their chains and were illuminated by the stairwell light. Their blackened and bruised hands, crusted in old blood, were outstretched just out of reach... but only just.

"Gene? My boy, I know you don't mean any of that. You're just sick is all. And that makes you this way. But can't you see your mother and I love you both so very much? Can't you see there's nothing we wouldn't do for you?"

Behind her, Zoe felt Trent's hands on her back, preparing to roll her towards the boys.

The teens reached and hissed; their lips were split and crusted in blood, their cheeks stained in crimson trails from infected eyes. Blackened veins showed through pale skin that looked rice paper thin. A red rash circled their necks, the skin rubbed raw by the chains that bound them. The boys' clothes were bloodied too and their black hair was oily and disheveled.

One turned and knelt, picking up a hammer. Why in the fuck did he have a hammer?

"Crack her skull, Jack! It hurts so bad! We need it! We need it!"

Jack held up the hammer for a swing. "Push her here! Push her to me, Daddy!"

"Yes! Then bring Mom down! You hear me, Mother! I smell

you!" Gene shouted, his fingers tucked into the chain collar as he jerked at it with frustration.

Zoe tried to push herself back, to not let Trent roll her over, but she wasn't strong enough. She was on her side now, palm planted on the cold concrete, trying desperately to resist, but her arm buckled.

From upstairs, a loud crash of breaking glass cut through the sounds of the moaning teens.

Minnie shouted from the top of the stairs, "Trent!"

"What the hell? Someone got in! Zombies!" Trent let go of Zoe and jolted upright.

Jack stretched out and swung the hammer.

Zoe pushed herself off her side, tipping onto her back.

The head of the hammer cracked down into the concrete an inch from her ear. Concrete particles peppered the side of her face.

"Get her! Get her!" Gene cried.

Trent started up the stairs.

Jack reached, stretching his arm all the way out towards Zoe, the claw of the hammer extended, his blackened tongue poking out of the corner of his cracked lips. The claw raked her shoulder, hooking her shirt. "I got you now," he giggled as he pulled the hammer back towards himself and Zoe along with it.

At the top of the stairs, Minnie screamed and fell backwards into Trent as he ascended the stairs – both of them were falling now.

Trent's head thunked hard against the step. Minnie bent wrongly as her own shoulder bit into a step with a sickening crunch.

Zoe screamed, managing to somehow pull her knees up towards her chest just as Trent landed on her.

Minnie fell to the side, landing atop Jack's outstretched arm, breaking his hold on the hammer.

"Mother! Oh, thank you."

Minnie was screaming. "No! Trent! Help me! Oh god, my shoulder. I broke my collarbone! Help me! Please!"

Blood leaked from Trent's head onto Zoe's face. She tried to push him off, but her arms felt like they were full of lead.

From the top of the stairs came a deep growl, and for a split second Zoe thought a zombie was coming down the steps. But she knew that growl and the bark that followed. Adrenaline surged through her again. "Louie!"

Trent squirmed atop her, trying to get up. "Ugh! Minnie," he moaned.

Faster than Zoe could comprehend, Jack found the hammer once more and swung, cracking Minnie over the head. He swung wildly, again and again.

"Minnie!" Trent cried. "No, Jack! That's your mother, for god's sake!"

Stairwell light illuminated the hammer as Jack drew it high over his head.

Zoe could see a chunk of Minnie's hair and scalp wedged into the claw of the hammer.

Jack laughed. "I've been waiting for you, Mother!"

The woman squealed inhumanly as Jack struck her over and over.

Trent rolled off Zoe and towards Jack. "Stop this! Stop this right now!" He grabbed Minnie, desperate to pull her away from the boy, when Gene sprang, leaping onto his father's back and wrapping his legs and arms around the man.

Zoe knew this was her moment to escape, but she couldn't get her legs and arms to cooperate. Still, she managed to press herself back against the wall.

Louie was beside her now, barking at the commotion and ready to pounce.

Her mouth still felt weird, but words were coming easier now. "No, Louie. Heel!"

Louie positioned himself between Zoe and the deadly commotion.

Zoe tried to sound encouraging despite the brutality of what was happening a few feet away. "Good boy, Louie. Stay."

Gene bit into the back of Trent's lower neck, releasing a fountain of viscous blood.

Jack laughed, going back to work on his mother's head with the hammer.

Trent spun towards her, his son clinging to him with his legs wrapped around his father's thighs and his arms clenched around his shoulders as he bit him over and over, trying to force his father to the floor.

As Trent surged forward for the stairs, the chain around Gene's neck tightened, jerking the boy's head back and forcing his body to follow.

"What have you boys done?" the frantic man cried out, his hand doing very little to stanch the blood oozing from his neck wound.

Louie wasted no time locking his jaws around the man's lower calf.

Trent screamed, falling onto the stairs, blocking Zoe's only means of escape.

Louie jerked and shook the man's leg like a rag doll. "Stop, dear god! Please!"

Zoe pushed herself up into a sitting position. Whether because of the passing of time or the surge of adrenaline, she felt less confused and more in control of her faculties.

Despite her dizziness, Zoe managed to use the wall and get to her feet. If the world was a drunken blur before, it was a spinning top now and she thought she might puke. On the basement floor, Jack and Gene no longer paid attention to her or their father. Instead they scooped handfuls of grey matter into their mouths, their cheeks puffing out with the contents of their mother's head.

"Louie. Heel," Zoe ordered. Instantly, Louie released Trent's leg.

The world around Zoe steadied slightly as she focused on Trent, the only one standing between her and a way out of this nightmare. But Trent wasn't looking at her; he was looking at his boys as they ate his dead wife.

Trent was bleeding to death, and Zoe knew it – maybe Trent

knew it too. Tears spilled down his cheeks. "We gave you boys everything, and this is what you do!"

Gene stopped then, looking dead into his father's eyes, and swallowed. "Not everything. Not all of it. Come back... Father."

"Look what you've done," Trent moaned.

Gene wiped his mouth on his sleeve. "You don't get it. You don't understand how much this hurts!"

"Killing your own mother should hurt!"

Gene voiced something between a laugh and cry. "No, Father! The hunger. The hunger never stops!"

Trent's gaze turned to the discarded hammer lying next to his dead wife. Now that her head had been cracked open like a chestnut, the boys' only focus was eating. Then for the first time since this all went wrong, he looked at Zoe. "I could have stopped this. I could have put them down when they'd become infected." Trent's face was twisted in some strange combination of agony and confusion. "But how? They were my children!"

Louie, not liking Trent's tone, growled a warning that said, *Try it and I'll rip your balls off.*

Zoe stood on unsteady legs, leaning heavily against the wall, just out of reach of the boys with Louie between her and the man who'd brought her here. "I'm leaving," she said in a flat tone.

Trent only nodded, his gaze falling back to his two children and then the hammer. He closed his eyes, drawing in a deep breath and then letting it out. When he opened his eyes, his expression was one of fixed conviction. A decision had just been made.

Zoe reached down, held Louie by his leather collar, and nodded to the man. She knew what came next.

Blood-soaked, with only one working leg, Trent dove past Louie, landing belly down on the concrete basement floor. He scrambled forward, reaching for the hammer.

"Go, Louie! Up!" Zoe ordered, letting go of the dog's collar.

Louie barked and ran up the stairs, turning at the top to wait for Zoe.

Falling down onto her hands and knees, Zoe scrambled on all fours up and out of the basement. Leaving the screams and sounds of bones crunching behind.

CHAPTER 7
LOST AND FOUND

ZOE LOOKED right and then left. Her memory of how she'd been brought to the basement was fuzzy, leaving her unsure which way to go. Left felt like the right way. She steadied herself by dragging her hand along the wall. A picture frame fell and cracked with a pop as it hit the floor. She couldn't help but glance down at the smiling family dressed in their Sunday best. The twins sat side by side, hands folded in their laps; their sister stood next to them, and Minnie and Trent were behind the three kids. Trent had his hand on one of the boys' shoulders and his other around Minnie. They looked so happy, and maybe they had been, but now... Now the girl, Janis, was dead and her brothers were in the basement killing and eating their parents.

Slapping a palm on the kitchen door, Zoe pushed through. The door swung inward, smacking into the kitchen wall. Bile surged up, burning the back of her throat as she crossed the kitchen just in time to vomit into the sink. Whether the nausea was from the drug or what had just taken place in the basement she wasn't sure, but she had never been so certain she was going to die. She turned on the faucet, cupped her hands, and splashed water onto her face. The cold water helped, and her vision was almost back to normal.

Heart still racing, she made her way onto the porch, where what was left of the screen door hung in a ruin of twisted aluminum, ripped screen, and broken glass. She pushed the broken door aside and looked down at Louie. He still hadn't left her side. "Thank you, Louie."

Louie licked her hand, barked, and ran out into the driveway.

Outside, the clouds were thinning, allowing scarlet rays of light to pierce the veil of red. Satisfied it was no longer raining, she changed her focus to the barn. The sight stole her breath, and somehow her already pounding heart kicked into overdrive. "Oliver!"

Confused, Zoe ran across the gravel on unsteady feet. Just inside the barn, Jurnee sat next to Oliver with the first aid kit sitting next to her. The top was open and bloody gauze lay discarded next to it.

Kneeling faster than she meant to, Zoe fell onto her ass next to the little girl. "Jurnee! What happened?"

"We heard you scream! Oliver was going to go into the rain even though I yelled for him not to, but then he fell down. Terry's Stripes didn't hold his owie shut, so I sent Louie to find you while I went to get more!"

"You sent Louie to find me," she repeated in disbelief.

The little girl's eyes filled with tears as her head bobbed up and down. "First, I pushed real hard like you showed me. Then, I put some more Terry's Stripes on his owie but they aren't sticking like when you did it!" Jurnee started to cry then. "Am I in trouble?"

Zoe assessed Oliver's back. His shirt was pulled open where she'd torn it when she and Jurnee patched him up the first time. But the shirt was wet with fresh blood. There was a new scrape across his back that had torn loose the Steri-Strips Zoe had put in place. Judging from the blood all over Jurnee's hands, she had pressed on his back, but probably not long enough to stop the bleeding. And judging from all the bloody gauze on the ground, Jurnee had wiped his back too. But with the blood still flowing, the new Steri-Strips hadn't stuck.

"In trouble? Why would you think that?"

"For not staying on the bus? But I was scared. And Oliver fell down!" She threw herself into Zoe's arms, buried her face in her shoulder, and sobbed.

"It's okay. You didn't do anything wrong. If it hadn't been for you..." She trailed off, not wanting to voice the horror of what would have become of her if not for Louie – if not for this brave little girl sending Louie to find her. "Hey, it's okay."

"No. No, it's not okay! I think my mom is... is gone forever." Jurnee cried harder, her little body shaking uncontrollably in Zoe's arms. "I thought you and Oliver might be gone too!"

Zoe had no idea what she was supposed to say to a six-year-old who had just voiced what she must have known for the last four days. Jurnee's mother had died in the crash Sam and Oliver pulled her from. Zoe began to cry too, hugging the little girl back as tight as she dared.

Once Zoe started, she couldn't stop. The weight of it all. It was too much. She said the only thing she could. "I know. I know, and I'm sorry."

On the ground, Oliver moaned, "Zo! Zoe I'm coming!" Somehow, he started to push himself up onto his hands and knees.

Louie barked.

"Oliver, I'm here. It's okay!" she said, placing a hand on his lower back.

He collapsed back onto his belly and rolled onto his side facing her, eyes blinking. "Zo? I heard you scream. What's happened? Why are you two crying? Are... are you okay?"

"Shh," she said, rocking Jurnee in her arms. "It's okay, Ollie. Just take it easy. Don't try to move. You were stabbed by a shard of glass. Your back wound has opened up and you've lost a lot of blood."

Jurnee pushed herself back and wiped her nose on her sleeve. "Oliver, you were going to go in the rain! Why would you do that? You know better!"

Zoe was taken slightly aback by the sudden scolding from Jurnee. "Jurnee, it's going to be okay. We are all here, and it's going to be okay."

"Did… did I miss something?" Oliver asked.

Jurnee leaned forward towards Oliver and lowered her voice to a whisper. Well, a whisper by six-year-old terms anyway. "Do you even know what happens when you go into the rain, Oliver?" She looked around, as though voicing it even quietly might cause a monster to appear. "You turn into a monster!"

"I… I'm sorry, kiddo." He looked up at Zoe, and she could see there was more he wanted to say, but he stopped himself.

"Can you get up, Oliver?" she asked.

"I don't think I've ever felt so weak, and the pain in my back is brutal. And that's a lot coming from a guy who's been shot in the shoulder. I just don't remember ever feeling this weak."

This was bad. Real bad. Oliver needed medical attention or he might die. Zoe's worst fear was that he would pass back out and slip into a coma and never wake up. Most urgently, he needed an IV and to get that wound stitched closed. "You've lost too much blood and you're still bleeding." Zoe stood, her own vision blurring as she steadied herself.

"Zo? What's wrong?"

She brushed off her pants. "I'm fine," she said, even though she was the furthest from fine she had ever been in her entire life.

With a pained grunt, Oliver pushed himself up onto one elbow. "Okay, well, I can see the wheels spinning. What are you thinking?"

"The woman who lived in that house was an at-home healthcare nurse. I saw a makeshift surgical table and boxes of supplies, including an IV stand. I need to go back in, make it safe, and see what I can find to treat you. What you really need is a hospital, and we don't have one." Her jaw clenched tight as she shifted her gaze back to the house and the nightmare she had just barely escaped. Was she really about to do this?

"Zo, what's in there?"

"Something awful," she said evenly as she peered back out across the driveway. "I need my gun. Then I'll go back in the house, clear it, and we can all go in."

He followed her gaze. "I don't like the idea of you going back in there, but I especially don't think shooting a gun in there is a good idea." He pointed across the driveway. "Are we on Dee-Mac Road?"

Zoe nodded. "The rain was coming. I had to find cover."

Oliver shifted his gaze. "Those houses over there. That's a pretty good-sized subdivision. You start firing a gun and who knows how many might come running."

Zoe knew he had a point, but they didn't have a choice.

Oliver lifted a hand and pointed. "Look, there's a truck parked right behind the house – let's take it and go."

"You're assuming there's keys in the ignition. Let's sit you up so I can get a better look at your back." She knelt and pulled Oliver to a sitting position. "Are you dizzy?"

"Oh, yeah, dizzy like a drunk. Hey, are you going to tell me what the hell happened in there?"

She looked at Jurnee, who was standing next to her, petting Louie and pretending not to be paying attention, but six-year-olds were always listening. She motioned to Jurnee and shook her head. "Later, okay?" Retrieving the first aid kit, she removed the last piece of clean gauze and medical tape. She placed it on Oliver's back and pressed down firmly. "Jurnee, do you remember last time when you pressed really hard for me?"

Jurnee wiped her eyes on her sleeve. "Yes, but I already did that. It doesn't work."

"I know, but we are going to do it again, and this time I want you to press on it until I get back." Zoe ripped a few lengths of tape free from the roll and taped the gauze onto Oliver's back. "Okay, push hard."

Jurnee placed both hands on Oliver's back and pressed, puffing out both cheeks to show she was really pushing hard.

Oliver winced. "Good... job, kiddo," he managed through gritted teeth.

"That's it. Okay, do your best to push real hard just like that until I get back," Zoe said.

"Zo, I don't like this. Is there something in there that can hurt you?"

She shook her head. "No, it isn't like that. It's chained up. Look, I don't like it either, but don't worry. Just give me a few minutes."

"Chained up?" Oliver frowned in confusion but nodded.

"Oh, and if you feel like you might pass out again... well, don't. But if you do, lay down first. The side of your face is already starting to bruise from your last fall."

"Don't pass out and don't fall on my face – got it."

She didn't mean to sound so cold, but she couldn't allow herself to show just how scared shitless she was. Scared for herself, scared for Jurnee if she screwed this up, and most of all scared for Oliver.

She kissed him on the forehead and ran back to the workbench where she'd left her gun. She holstered the .357 and made her way back across the driveway with Louie on her heels. Glancing along the side of the house this time, she noticed the small rectangular basement windows were boarded shut.

Drawing in a steadying breath, she readied herself and crossed the kitchen into the living room where she'd noticed the bloody table, IV, and other medical supplies. Ignoring them for now, she made her way to the basement door, sure an infected or zombie version of Trent would leap out from some hidden corner and bite her. The thought had her trembling and sweating. The smell of rot hit her again, and her stomach threatened to heave.

Standing at the top of the stairs, she stood and listened. Two sounds were distinct; unfortunately, Zoe could picture them both perfectly. The louder sound was flesh being pulled from bone, along with chewing and grunting. The other was a hammer beating against a chain and stone. The boys wanted to be free of the basement. Free to find other sources of what the parasite demanded... human flesh, especially brains. She could go down there and end this now. Shoot them both. After all, that was the plan. Then maybe twenty or thirty zombies would show up outside, maybe even more.

Next to her, Louie let out a soft whine.

The noise in the basement stopped.

Zoe's breath hitched.

"We know you're up there," one of the boys said.

"We smell you. And when we smell *it*, the pain gets so much worse!" the other boy said.

With renewed urgency, the hammer began smacking the chain and stone floor again, twice as fast as before.

All she had to do was go down the stairs and start shooting before it was too late. Yet she couldn't bring herself to descend the stairs. Even knowing the boys couldn't reach her while they were chained, she simply couldn't go back down there. She closed the door, realizing only then that the door itself was solid wood. Even better, there was a large metal hasp on the door, which Trent must have put on as added protection. A large padlock hung from the hasp by its open shackle.

Zoe pulled the lock free of the hasp, flipped it closed, and locked it. She didn't like that they were down there right beneath her, but she liked it a whole hell of a lot better than going down there to deal with them. If – or, more likely, when – they broke free of the chain, the door would hold them long enough for her to deal with the problem. Shooting them through the door would be easier than going back down into that place.

She turned back to the living room and approached the area Minnie had used to do surgery on her daughter. On top of the entertainment center, opposite the couch and coffee table, sat several framed family photos. One of Minnie in her nurse's graduation uniform. One of Janis standing by a white Toyota Corolla with a bow on the hood. Another photo showed Trent and two more guys that looked similar, one older and one younger. Brothers maybe? The personalized frame read TRAVIS, TAYLOR, & TRENT – JUNE 2021. The photo itself showed a lake in the background, and each man was holding up a stringer filled with catfish.

Zoe turned her attention to the stack of boxes. Her hopes rose when she opened the first of several boxes of medical supplies

Minnie was hoarding. It seemed Minnie had been stealing medical supplies for some time. No nurse would have this much stuff on hand. Not even a home health nurse. "You were a bad girl, weren't you, Minnie?" she whispered. On an end table sat a suture kit. Minnie must have had it out to sew up her daughter's neck after she'd removed the parasite. In the supplies she found everything she needed to treat Oliver, starting with an IV bag, iodine, and antibiotics. Zoe was so elated she started to cry again, but this time she cried because for the first time in this godforsaken day, she had hope that somehow things were going to be okay.

CHAPTER 8
WE'RE ALL SHE HAS NOW

OLIVER DIDN'T REMEMBER how he ended up on a strange couch surrounded by pictures of people he didn't know. Just as unfamiliar was the smell. Pain shot through his back as he drew in a deep breath, trying to place it. He winced. The smell was a combination of spoiled meat and those Bath & Body Works candles Zoe always had around the house. He tried to push himself up but felt a twinge in his arm.

"Hey! Stay still or you'll pull it out," Zoe said, appearing from a doorway. The door swung back and forth behind her before settling into place.

Oliver looked down at his arm and the tube protruding from it. "You found an IV?"

"I found a ton of medical supplies. Including pain meds. How are you feeling?"

Oliver pressed his fingers into his eyes and rubbed. "Not sure yet. Back hurts a bit. But I feel... rested. Hey, what time is it?"

"Early. The sun isn't even up yet."

"It's morning? Jesus, how long did I sleep?"

"About fourteen hours." She sat two steaming mugs down on the end table. "Coffee?"

"Oh, hell yes." He started to push himself up again.

She reached down and placed an arm under his. "Let me help you. I sutured your back closed and I don't want you tearing it open again."

When Oliver sat up, his world didn't spin – for the first time since he'd blown up their house.

"How does that feel?"

"Actually, not bad." He reached and lifted the cup of coffee, held it under his nose, and breathed in. "Hey where's the kid?"

Zoe pointed to a pile of blankets atop an overstuffed recliner next to the couch. "I tried to get her to sleep in Janis's room, but she wouldn't leave your side. Louie's somewhere under there too. Anyway, I'm glad you're feeling better because we need to leave as soon as possible."

"Leave? Why? Zoe, what's happened? Where are the people who were in here, and why were you screaming?"

"You remember that?" Zoe asked.

He set his coffee down on the table and took her hand. "Of course. I've been hearing that scream over and over in my nightmares."

Zoe explained, starting the story all the way back in their driveway when they'd been forced to flee the horde of zombies that had invaded their home just before Oliver blew it up. She explained how she'd been forced to find immediate shelter, how Minnie and Trent pretended to want to help only to then try and feed her to what was locked in the basement. "I've never been so sure I was going to die. And if it hadn't been for Louie and Jurnee... I would have."

"Jesus, Zo. I'm so sorry. If anything would have happened to you... I'm just glad you're okay."

"A lot happened to me, Oliver. I'm not dead, but I'm far from okay. And what about you? Were you really going to run through the rain?"

Oliver met her eyes and nodded.

"And then what?"

"I was going to find you, save you."

She pulled her hand away from him. "By killing yourself?"

"Yes. If that's what it took."

"Not if, Oliver. It was raining, and you had made up your mind to die. What were you thinking?"

"Hey, what do you want me to say? That I was going to let you be in danger while I waited for the rain to stop? I would die a hundred times over if it means you get to live." He felt his eyes welling up. "So what? You want me to be sorry for that? Well, I'm not. If you die, we die. I don't want to live without you."

Zoe's eyes softened. "You think I don't know you would die for me? You think I don't know you love me?" She put her hand on his cheek and he closed his eyes, never wanting her to take it away. "But, Oliver McCallister, you can't think that way anymore."

"I don't understand. You want me to stop being willing to die for you? How does that work?"

Zoe pointed at the chair. "Easy. You think about her."

Oliver frowned.

"You don't get to live or die for only me now. Now you live for both of us, but if ever you have to choose, you choose her. Yesterday, when you were just about to run out those doors, you chose wrong. If you had failed to save me, what would have happened to her?"

Oliver's frown deepened. He didn't know what to say, but he knew she was right. When he heard Zoe scream, he didn't give Jurnee or what might have become of her a second thought. His only mission was saving the woman he loved, even if that meant he would die trying.

Zoe pulled her hand back from his face and ran her fingers through his red hair. She gave him a consoling smile. "You understand?"

Oliver nodded. "I'm sorry, Zo."

"I don't want you to be sorry, Oliver. I just want you to think about the unintended consequences, okay? When you pulled her from that car and brought her home, she became our responsibility. If something happens to us, she doesn't stand a chance." Zoe lowered her voice to a whisper and lifted her cup of coffee. "There's something else you need to know."

"What?" he asked, fearing something awful.

"Jurnee knows her mother died in that wreck."

"Shit. She told you?"

Zoe nodded, taking a sip of her coffee.

"What did you say?"

"I just hugged her and told her I was sorry."

Oliver sighed, realizing just how tunnel-visioned he'd been, unwittingly choosing to not only kill himself but essentially leave Jurnee for dead. He'd been selfish, and now he felt incredibly guilty.

"Even if her dad hasn't... well... you know, then maybe he is still out there somewhere, but I don't know how we'd ever find him. No time soon anyway."

Oliver picked up his cup and took a careful sip. "Oh my god, that's good," he said, returning the cup to the table. "Hey, didn't Jurnee say her dad was in the military and that he's far away? He could have been serving anywhere in the world when all this went down."

Zoe seemed to contemplate that, her expression taking on the same look he'd often seen when she was sitting at the kitchen table deep in her studies. "Oliver, I think we have to face the fact we're all she has now, which is why you can't go charging headfirst into danger at the first sign of trouble."

"But, Zo, I was only trying to..."

"Hey, I know what you were trying to do. And you can save me. Please save me, but just don't die doing it. Deal?"

Oliver nodded, a silence stretching between them as he took in Zoe's words: *We're all she has now.*

Five days now and no help. From what Zoe explained, their whole neighborhood had been destroyed. If this were a local thing, help would have come. This had to be happening all over the country, if not the world.

From the basement door, a low hiss found its way into the front room.

"Was that..."

"Yeah, one of the twins, I think. Though I suppose it could be Trent if he managed to get killed but not eaten. Whoever that one is, it isn't on a chain and it doesn't talk. I don't know, maybe one of the boys got off the chain but was wounded enough to die. I guess it's possible – when I escaped, Trent had gone for the hammer and was fighting them."

Oliver glanced across at the photos. "Those must be the twins, then? And that one must be the daughter?"

Zoe nodded somberly.

"And those guys?" he asked, pointing at the fishing photo.

"Well, the one in the middle, that's Trent and I'm guessing the other two are his brothers."

"So that guy in the middle might be the one on the other side of the door?"

"Yeah, like I said, him or the twins."

"I should go down there and shoot whatever isn't dead."

"You mean whatever isn't dead-dead," she corrected.

"Dead-dead? Yeah, I guess I do."

"I found a loaded magazine in the duffel bag and put it in your gun, but I couldn't get the empty one reloaded," Zoe said, pointing at a pile of folded clothes. There was a T-shirt, a flannel shirt, and a pair of jeans. Right on top was his holstered .45.

"Yeah, the spring is really hard to push. It's so much easier with a speed loader. There should be one in my bag. I'll find it later."

She eyed him with her too-familiar doctorly look that told him he was being assessed. "Well, you're in no shape to shoot anything anyway, and don't bother because we're leaving."

Oliver turned his attention back to the clothes. "Are those Trent's clothes?"

"Yeah, but you two were about the same size." Zoe sighed. "I couldn't find anything that would fit Jurnee. She needs shoes. We'll have to keep our eyes out for some clothes for her."

"Babe, are you sure we should go now? The windows are already boarded up. And honestly, this Trent guy did a better job than I did. That looks like old barn wood, and he attached it from the outside rather than the inside like we did. They won't be kicking their way in, that's for damn sure."

"Maybe, but we still have the problem of food, which there isn't much of here."

The mention of food made Oliver's stomach growl.

"And we would have to deal with the basement, which by the way smells far worse than up here. I know they fed a woman who broke down alongside the road to the boys, and I have a really bad feeling that after Janis died, they fed her to the boys too."

"Their own daughter?" Oliver asked in disgust.

"Yeah, I know, right?" Zoe pulled a sip from her coffee. "But look, it isn't even all the clean-up, the lack of food, the work that needs to be done, or the fact that you're in no condition to help. The truth is, I don't want to be here after what happened. I need to get the fuck out of this place."

Oliver appraised Zoe, his hunger replaced by a wave of guilt. He didn't know why he was blaming himself. He had only tried to do what he could to keep Zoe and Jurnee safe. He hadn't meant to get hurt. "Have you slept?"

"Some. I knew if anyone tried to get in, whether from outside or below, Louie would lose his mind, so I felt safe enough sleeping a little. Besides, I didn't have much of a choice. The drugs Minnie gave me have a lingering drowsiness effect. Thank god I'd only taken a couple sips of that tea. I hate to think what would have happened if I had ingested all of it."

"Don't think about it. We can't change anything about the choices we've already made or the what-ifs, so no use dwelling on any of it." The advice was as much for himself as it was for Zoe. If he let himself think about all the decisions he'd made up until this point, he could sit here second-guessing himself all day long.

The basement doorknob rattled.

He couldn't imagine how he would feel if he had been drugged and nearly fed to infected kids chained in the basement, but he was pretty sure he'd want to get the hell out of here too. "I see why you don't want to stay here. And if I know you, you've been thinking this through. What's your plan?"

"Plan? Same plan. Your plan. Go to the church and pray there's still a kitchen full of food. Then we load it all up and move on to your farmhouse mansion."

Slowly, Oliver lifted his right arm. The pain in his back felt somewhere between sharp and dull. He wasn't as sore as the time he got shot trying to repo a boat, but it still sucked, and he couldn't imagine firing a gun right now. "Um, Zo. I don't think I can shoot, which means I don't think I can be of much help to you in the church."

"I'll be fine. Besides, if it hadn't been for the broken windshield, I would have been at the church yesterday and you still wouldn't have been able to help. Also, Trent's got a double cab truck right out back. I already loaded all the medical supplies Minnie was hoarding and moved your bag of ammo from the bus to the truck."

"Are you fucking nuts? You shouldn't be going out there by yourself! There's a subdivision right across the street!"

Zoe set her coffee cup down a little too hard, causing Louie to growl and Jurnee to stir beneath her blanket. "Hey. Shit has to get done, Oliver. Besides, after a few hours, I'd slept all I could. What am I supposed to do, just sit here and watch you sleep? No television, no internet. I couldn't even find a radio. Other than a few houses with lights still on, I didn't see any signs of life. And I wasn't even out there that long."

Oliver knew his wife well enough to know he'd better let up. Her nerves were beyond frayed. "Zo?"

"What?" she snapped.

"You have done an amazing job, and I am so thankful. Without you, I'd be dead for sure. You saved my life." He motioned with his left arm, holding it out to her. "Come here."

She stood from the chair and then sat on the edge of the couch.

Oliver pulled her into him, wrapping his good arm around her. She buried her face in his neck. When she lifted her head, he kissed her. "I love you."

"I love you too." She looked down at his arm, then the IV bag. "Hey, let me pull that IV out."

He held up his arm and got a whiff of himself. "Do I smell as bad as I think I smell?"

Zoe smiled. "I dug you out clean clothes for a reason. The power is still on and the hot water works, but you don't get to shower yet."

"What? Why not?"

"Because I'm going first. I didn't want to chance being in the shower if one of the infected or undead showed up at the door."

"So I guess us showering together—"

"Isn't going to happen. And even if it were safe, I'm still pissed at you."

"Wait. What? Why... I thought we were good?" he stammered.

"You thought we were good?" Zoe huffed. "Hmmm" – she narrowed her eyes – "well, let's see, where do I start?"

There was slight playfulness in her tone, just enough he could tell they were going to be okay, but not enough he was going to push it. He waved her off. "Never mind. You're right. Get your shower. If any zombies show up, I'll give a shout."

But no zombies showed up, and finally it was his turn in the shower.

As he climbed in, Zoe came into the bathroom, her braids wrapped in a big bun and an oversized flannel hanging down to mid thigh. "Hey, don't run the hot water over your stitches. Actually, just let me wash your back. I don't need you messing up my work!" She grinned.

In the shower, Oliver bent forward, allowing the hot water to run over his head while Zoe washed his back. The hot water felt unbelievable, and he even felt his body loosening up as he washed.

"I put Neosporin on your foot too. It looks good, not infected or anything, but we'll want to put more on when you get out." She wrung out the rag and soaped it up again. "How does it feel?"

"Sore like the rest of my body. I swear, everything hurts. Like I've had the shit beat out of me."

Zoe gave him an ornery smile. "Or maybe like you stood next to an exploding house or were on a bus that smashed through a barn and wrecked into a tractor?"

"Something like that." He smiled back.

She shook her head. "Get rinsed," she said, retrieving a royal blue towel from the linen closet.

Oliver shut off the water.

Outside the bathroom, Louie growled.

A voice called from the kitchen. "Hey! Trent! Minnie! You alright? Trent? Bro?"

Louie barked.

"Shit!" Oliver whispered.

"Who's in there?" The sound of a pump-action shotgun racking a shell rang out.

Zoe gasped, turning and hurrying for the door. "Jurnee!"

"Zo! Wait!" Oliver tried grabbing for her, but he wasn't quick enough.

Outside the bathroom, the kitchen door swung open.

CHAPTER 9
T 'N' T

ZOE RUSHED from the bathroom only to come face-to-face with a bearded man in a Chicago Bears hat and stained Carhartt jacket as he burst through the kitchen door. "Trent!"

Louie was off the recliner, barking wildly as he crossed the room with ill intent, his teeth bared to bite.

"Louie, heel!" she shouted, knowing if he didn't, the man would be forced to shoot her dog to keep from being mauled.

Louie halted in a ready-to-pounce stance. He instantly stopped barking, but his growl of warning continued to rumble through the living room.

The man's eyes flicked from the dog to Zoe as he swung the shotgun up to point at her face.

Zoe felt her heart nearly stop as she flinched away, throwing her hands up in surrender. "Please, don't!"

"Who in the fuck are you, and where's my brother?" The man looked around, noticing Jurnee sitting up in the chair. He glanced down the hall then, over towards the bathroom Zoe had just exited.

Zoe's eyes followed his gaze to the bathroom. In the bathroom mirror, she saw Oliver pulling on the pair of jeans. He met her eyes and shook his head, warning her to look away. She knew that from the man's angle he wouldn't be able to see Oliver. She quickly looked back at the man. "It's okay, I can explain! There's been an accident."

"An accident! What accident, and who in the fuck are you?"

"Please!" Zoe begged, tipping her head towards Jurnee. "I have a little girl here."

"Who else is here?"

Louie barked.

The man aimed the gun at Louie. "Calm that mutt down or I'll have to shoot it."

Zoe lowered one hand and placed it on Louie's head. "Quiet, Louie!"

"Where's my brother? You better answer me right now, or things are going to go real bad for you."

She didn't know why she said it, but the words just came out. "In the basement. They're in the basement with Gene and Jack."

Zoe glanced back at the bathroom mirror. Oliver was standing shirtless behind the bathroom door. In his left hand he held his little handgun, the one he kept strapped to his ankle.

The man who Zoe now recognized to be either Travis or Taylor spun towards the hallway. "What do you know about my brother's kids?"

"I'm a friend of Minnie's. We both work for the same home healthcare company. They're helping my daughter and I. She said I could—"

"I said, 'What do you know about my brother's kids?'"

The man craned his neck to see as he took a step towards the hall. If he could see the basement door clearly, he would know it was padlocked, and Zoe didn't have a plan on how to explain that. Luckily, the doorway was on the right side of the hall, so she didn't think it would be easy to tell it was locked until he got closer.

"Well... I..."

A radio affixed to the man's belt chirped to life. "Taylor? You alright in there?"

Taylor pulled the radio from his hip. "Hold. I'm good. Still trying to figure out what's going on." He released the button, narrowing his eyes at Zoe.

The radio chirped again. "You need me?"

He glanced at Jurnee, then Louie, who was clearly on alert but at least obeying her. He settled his eyes on her. She was in a bra and underwear but at least she had Trent's oversized flannel covering her down to her mid thighs. She certainly didn't look like a threat. Taylor pressed the button again. "No. Stay out there with our guests until I call for you." He released the button and hung the radio back on his hip. "And you stay put," he said, lifting the shotgun again. He turned to his left, crossing the living room in several strides, shouting as he headed for the hallway. "Minnie! Trent!" The man glanced back. "They say why they were going down in the basement?" he asked, starting down the hall.

"I... I guess checking on the kids. They... they didn't say. But they asked me to stay up here." She couldn't think, but she needed to stall him and get him to turn back around away from the basement door until she had a chance to figure something out. "You're Taylor, and that was Travis, right? Trent told me about you guys," she lied.

Behind her, she caught movement as Oliver exited the bathroom and then hid behind the wall where the hallway met the living room. He was in front of her now, motioning for her to move back towards the bathroom.

There was no preventing what was about to happen. Zoe backed up just as Taylor stopped in front of the basement door.

"What the fuck?!" he shouted, spinning back towards Zoe.

Zoe was moving now, hurrying out of sight and back towards where Jurnee had been sitting in the overstuffed chair, but Jurnee was gone. She caught a glimpse of the little girl now hidden behind the chair with her hands over her ears and eyes slammed shut. For a split second she thought of joining Jurnee or running for the bathroom – but what about Oliver? What was he going to do? She needed her gun. Zoe scrambled for her .357 she'd left holstered in a yarn basket next to an overstuffed chair.

At the sound of Taylor's elevated voice, Louie lost it and began barking wildly. Zoe's new and more immediate fear was that as soon as Taylor appeared from the hall, he would shoot her or her dog.

The man was still shouting: "You locked them down there!"

Zoe yanked and pulled, but she couldn't get the gun out of the stupid holster.

Two shots in rapid succession. *Pop! Pop!*

Zoe whipped her head around just as the man appeared from the hallway, falling forward. The shotgun fired into the floor, recoiled, and flew from the man's hands.

Jurnee screamed from behind the chair.

Oliver stood with the small .22 extended in his left hand.

Taylor hit the floor, his body twitching like he was having a grand mal seizure, blood leaking from his temple.

She started to say something, but Oliver was already in motion. Hastily he dropped the .22 on the floor and darted for the shotgun, grabbing the barrel with his left hand. Desperately he tried to tug it free, but the twitching man was lying on the gun.

The urgency of Oliver's movement didn't register until Zoe heard the back door crash in and a man shout, "Taylor! What the fuck?"

Boots stomped across the kitchen floor.

Zoe scrambled over the chair for cover as she reached back into the yarn basket again to retrieve her gun.

The kitchen door flung open, crashing into the wall and knocking framed photos from their hangers.

Zoe peeked over the chair as the man, a spitting image of Taylor, locked eyes with her. He was taller, younger, built like a bodybuilder, and he was pointing a gun.

She raised her gun and pulled the trigger. The brain-jarring noise of her shot was so loud in her ears that she couldn't even hear his gun fire, but she saw the flashes from his barrel, the holes punch through the overstuffed chair in front of her, and feathers filling the air.

Then she felt it... the pain.

CHAPTER 10
THE LONGEST TWENTY FEET

FROM THE MOMENT Oliver made the decision to fire the .22 into Taylor's head as the man exited the hallway, everything happened so fast. He knew he only had seconds. Desperately, he tugged at the shotgun with his left hand but quickly gave up as commotion filled the kitchen.

He was back on his feet, barefoot and running for the door, all his instincts telling him he had to stop whatever was about to happen.

The door to the kitchen flung open before he could get there, smacking into the wall with a loud *wham!* Oliver caught a glimpse of the guy's extended arm pointing a pistol before the door swung back. But it didn't swing shut – it stopped abruptly in the open position on what Oliver knew must have been the man's boot.

Zoe fired the .357 with a resounding *boom!* that filled the small room.

Oliver tucked his left shoulder and collided with the kitchen door as the man returned fire. *Clack! Clack!*

Light burst through Oliver's vision as his own head bounced off the wooden door. Under the force of Oliver's weight and momentum, the door had no choice but to swing closed, and because the man on the other side had no idea what was coming, he went back with it.

The door design was called a double-acting door, meaning it swung through in both directions like saloon doors of the Old West. But this time the door didn't swing back into the kitchen – it stopped abruptly.

Oliver felt a pop through the wood, followed by a high-pitched scream. "Ahh! Fuuck!"

The man hadn't pulled his arm back in time. The appendage was pinned between the heavy wooden door and the doorjamb, and now it hung there, bent wrongly. Oliver realized the pop he'd felt was the man's forearm breaking.

Louie ran forward, barking and jaws snapping, ready to attack if the man made it through the door.

The man cried out in a tone somewhere between agony and rage, "You fucker!" His gun fell to the floor as he pushed back against Oliver, creating only enough of a gap to yank his broken arm back.

Oliver slid down the door, trying to maximize his leverage as he scrambled for the handgun. He didn't want to give the man a chance to push his way back into the room. Grabbing the gun, he repositioned himself, bracing his bare feet against the door. Then, lifting the gun with his left hand, he pointed where he thought the man might be and fired through the door. Wood splintered as round after round punched holes through the wood. Good god, his ears felt like they were bleeding.

Oliver waited, his gun trained on the door. He wanted to check on Zoe but was afraid to yell. He didn't think he'd hear her answer anyway, not through the ringing in his ears.

The pressure against the door eased. The man was no longer pushing, but he felt some kind of thumping on the kitchen floor. Footsteps? Maybe he was running away, or maybe it was a trick.

Cautiously, Oliver pushed on the door. It opened a couple inches and stopped. Oliver's breath hitched. Instead of pushing on the door, he let it rock back, reaching across his left arm to grab the edge of the door. Pain shot through his back as he stretched, but he ignored it.

He pulled the door open slightly and peeked through the gap.

The man was flopping on the floor. Oliver didn't see anyone else, so he climbed to his feet and pulled the door open farther. He'd shot the man once in the gut and once in the chest. The man, who Oliver now realized must be in his early twenties, lay there like a fish out of water, his mouth opening and closing, and his legs flexing – knees bending and straightening, heels scraping the tile.

Oliver pointed the gun, closed his eyes, and swallowed back the bile. He shot the man a final time.

Resisting the urge to heave up his coffee, he turned away from what he'd done and back to the front room. "Zoe!"

"I'm here!" she answered from behind the chair.

"Jesus, are you okay?" he asked, shuffling across the room.

"No! He shot me, Ollie," she cried.

The words echoed through Oliver's soul, and he felt his whole world crash down around him. "No!" He ran, crossing the living room and, with it, the longest twenty feet of his life. Oliver didn't make it a single step before his vision blurred with tears, their entire life together flashing before his eyes in milliseconds. The night they first met at the karaoke bar. Their beach wedding in Jamaica. When he'd brought Louie home after the miscarriage. Their first time picking out a Christmas tree. The damn thing had looked so much smaller in the field but oh how they'd laughed when it took up half the living room and pushed up against the ceiling of their small apartment.

"Zoe! Zoe!" he shouted, falling over the overstuffed chair to get to her. "Where?"

She was lying on her back with her eyes squeezed shut. "My side! Oh, Ollie, I'm afraid to look!"

Oliver wasted no time snatching up Zoe's flannel in both hands and yanking, snapping all the buttons to expose her bloody side. Using the flannel, he wiped the blood away.

Zoe winced.

Tears running like a river down his cheeks, he smiled. "Zoe, open your eyes."

"How bad is it?" she pleaded.

He leaned down and kissed her forehead. "The bullet only grazed your skin. It's a scratch," he said, laughing.

Zoe did not laugh. The tears flowed as she sobbed.

"Oh, babe. I'm sorry. I don't mean to laugh, I'm just so freaking relieved."

She shook her head. "It's not you. I just felt – well, it burns, and I thought... I'm just tired of this, Oliver! I'm tired!" She looked down at her side and pressed the flannel over it.

Oliver hugged her, pulling her into him. "I know. Me too." That was all he could say. It was all the consoling he could give her because at the end of the day he knew that, sick of it or not, until they found safety, true and real safety, every moment was life or death. "Hey, I don't think it even needs stitches."

She lifted the flannel again and looked. "No. It's barely bleeding. I'll just put some Neosporin on it and cover it."

"Can I open my eyes now, Oliver?" Jurnee shouted from behind the chair.

"Hey, we can't let her see them," Zoe said.

"Yeah," Oliver agreed. His relief that Zoe was okay was quickly replaced by the nausea he felt at having taken two lives. Not infected or zombies but real people. Then again, fuck those guys. They'd almost killed his wife. That was the reality of the new world, and that was all the rationalization he'd needed. Now that the adrenaline had passed, the pain was setting in. Pain in his head where he'd slammed it into the door, pain in his shoulder, and pain in his back. "But I can't drag them, Zo."

"I think it's time to leave," Zoe said.

Oliver nodded. She was right. "Keep your eyes closed, Jurnee – I'll come to you."

"Because of the monsters?"

Oliver's heart sank. "There are no more monsters. I promise. But just keep 'em closed, okay?"

"Okay."

Zoe climbed to her feet and motioned to her side. "I'll put a bandage on this. Meet me in the bathroom."

His heart was still racing as he knelt down next to Jurnee. "Are you okay, kid?" he asked.

Eyes pressed tight and lip quivering, her head bobbed up and down.

He pulled her into him and gave her a hug. "Hey, it's going to be okay – just keep those eyes shut." Taking Jurnee by the hand, he led her into the bathroom.

Zoe checked Oliver's stitches. "They're okay, thank god. Lucky you didn't pop a stitch when you hit that door. The side of your head is a bit swollen."

He grinned at her before pulling on a T-shirt. "Well, you always said I was hard-headed."

Zoe had found herself a clean T-shirt along with an oversized knit sweater. She donned both and zipped up her jeans, then froze. "Oliver?"

Oliver sat on the edge of the bathtub, pulling on his socks. "Yeah?"

"When Taylor was talking to Travis on the radio, Travis asked if he needed him to come in, and Taylor said no, wait outside... with our guests."

Oliver froze, suddenly recalling the conversation. "Shit!"

CHAPTER 11
THE BACK SEAT

ZOE SLIPPED her feet into her boots and turned to Jurnee. "Stay here with Louie – we'll be right back. We're just going to look outside. Then we're all leaving, okay?"

Jurnee sat atop the closed toilet, her head bobbing up and down. "Okay, maybe we can stop at the store and buy me some new shoes?" she asked, wiggling her little socked toes.

Zoe knelt down, pinched the little girl's toes between her thumb and index finger, and gave them a wiggle. "Yep, finding you some shoes is on my list."

Jurnee giggled.

"Louie, stay." Zoe followed Oliver out of the bathroom and into the kitchen.

"Be ready – I'm already a bad shot with the .45 in my right hand, but I'm an awful shot with it in my left," Oliver said.

She pulled the bathroom door shut behind her and then pulled the hammer back on her .357, keeping her finger off the trigger and the gun pointed down just like Oliver had taught her. They navigated past Travis's lifeless body and made their way across the back porch.

Oliver peeked out the busted screen door and around the side of the house. "There's a silver truck parked in the driveway. It's still running, but I don't see anyone. I'm going to check it out. Stay back and cover me."

Zoe assessed a sky full of burnt-orange clouds. Were the clouds slowly losing their color, or was it just wishful thinking? How long could asteroid dust stay in the atmosphere anyway? How long could parasites live up there? Did the cold keep them dormant and the strange slippery coating keep them protected until they fell from the sky? Could this go on for several more days? Or years?

Stepping out onto the stoop, she watched as Oliver approached the truck, then glanced across the street towards the subdivision. It was eerily quiet.

Oliver dropped down into a squat. "I see you in there! Come on out now!" He raised the pistol towards the truck.

"What do you see?" Zoe shouted, raising her own gun. Her heart was pounding, thudding in her ears.

"I saw something move in there, I'm sure of it. Hey! Whoever's in there! I'm not going to ask you again! Open the door!"

She didn't see anyone, but the windows had a tint on them. Slowly, keeping her eyes trained on the truck, she stepped down off the stairs and out from behind the house. A cold breeze bit at her cheeks and gravel crunched beneath her boots.

Inside the truck, something moaned.

Oliver glanced back at her. "Shit! Did you hear that? I think a zombie might be in there!"

"I heard it!" she confirmed.

"In the back seat! Something's moving!" Oliver trained the gun on the rear driver's-side window of the extended cab. "I swear, if you don't open the fucking door, I am going to start shooting!"

"Oliver, wait!" Zoe made her way around to the front of the truck.

Oliver glanced back at her. "Babe, what are you doing?"

"The window in the front isn't tinted – maybe I can see in!"

"Stay low! And keep your distance!"

Zoe squatted down, shuffling her feet as she scooted into position in front of the truck. She could hear the moaning now. Jesus, it did sound like an undead. Carefully she stood just enough to peek over the hood before dropping back down.

"See anything?" Oliver asked from the other side of the truck.

"Yeah, but..."

"What is it?"

She stood halfway up again, and this time she didn't duck back down. "Zo!"

"It's a foot. Well, feet."

"Feet?" Oliver repeated, standing up.

"Yeah, there are feet sticking up from the back seat."

Oliver approached the rear passenger-side door and reached for the handle.

"Be careful!" Zoe warned as she circled the truck and joined him.

Oliver hesitated. "If it's a zombie, shoot it before it gets out."

Zoe nodded, settling into her shooter's stance.

Oliver lifted the door handle, pulled it open, and backpedaled three quick steps. "What the shit?"

In back of the extended cab lay two people clad in pj's. Both were hog-tied and had silver duct tape covering their mouths. The man was face down on his stomach on the back seat, his feet jutting up. The woman lay twisted on her side on the floorboard, her fingers frantically trying to work loose the knots that bound her hands behind her back and to her feet.

"Mmmm. Mmmm."

"Nmmm! Nmmm."

"It's okay – we're here to help," Oliver said.

"Oliver, be careful – we don't know if they're infected."

He leaned in, whispering in her ear. "True. Keep an eye out, and I'll untie the woman first. Then we can get a good look at her eyes."

The two seemed to calm as they realized Oliver wasn't one of the men who'd tied them up.

Zoe kept watch as Oliver leaned into the cab and went to work untangling the knot binding the woman's hands and feet.

A loud bang, like a hammer hitting wood, drew Zoe's gaze to the subdivision across the street. Nothing moved except for smoke billowing from a house fire somewhere in the neighborhood. But the quiet was soon broken again, this time with the sound of glass shattering and an inhuman scream. Whatever was happening over there wasn't good.

"Hurry, Oliver," she warned.

Suddenly a car emerged from the subdivision, almost losing control as it tore north up Dee-Mac and then left onto a side road. Her eyes followed it across the cornfield as it built speed. It must have been going close to a hundred miles an hour. She couldn't imagine why or what awful thing had the driver driving so fast. Whatever it was reminded her they weren't the only ones fighting for their lives.

In the cab of the truck, Oliver finally freed the woman.

The woman rolled over and stretched her legs and arms. She looked to be in her fifties, but her makeup was a mess of tear-streaked mascara.

Oliver tried to help her with the tape.

"Mmmm!" she mumbled.

"I'm sorry. It isn't like the movies where you can just rip it off. I'm afraid if I did, it might tear your skin."

The woman slid out of the truck and stood up, pinching the corner of the tape as she tried to pull it loose. "Mmmm!"

Zoe recognized the woman. She was sure of it. "Here, let me help," she said, taking the opportunity to assess the woman's eyes. They looked as you would expect from someone who had been crying. But they weren't bleeding.

Zoe pressed on the woman's cheek and pulled ever so carefully. Slowly the tape came away.

"Howard!" she shouted, turning back to the truck.

"It's okay, Oliver will get him loose. What's your name?"

"Linda. Linda Jenkins," the woman said, keeping her eyes trained on Howard.

She knew she recognized the petite, short-haired woman. "Linda. You're the realtor I see on TV all the time."

"Yeah, that's me."

"Well, I'm Zoe. Are you hurt?"

Linda glanced back at Zoe, her eyes going wide as she screamed.

Zoe spun just in time to see a bearded man lunging for her. She scrambled back, lifting the .357.

The burly man turned with a sudden jerk, grabbing for Linda.

Zoe fired.

A gory combination of brain and blood sprayed out the opposite side of the man's head.

Linda was still screaming. Beyond the fallen man, silhouettes filled the backyard of the farmhouse as the undead moaned and ran towards them. Where in the hell had they come from?

"Oliver! We have to go!"

Oliver was still inside the cab of the truck, frantically working to free Howard from his bindings.

Across the road, more figures appeared from between the houses. They were spilling into the street, crossing it, and running up the driveway in a full-out sprint. From the back yard, more of the undead appeared. "Oliver!" she begged.

"Almost got it!"

Almost wasn't good enough. The undead were coming at them from both directions! They were going to get boxed in. Zoe couldn't shoot them all, and now there was no way to get back to the porch.

"Shit! Get in the truck, Linda!"

"What?"

"Get in the fucking truck!" She kicked the back door shut and jerked open the driver's-side door. Linda scrambled in and across the bench seat.

Zoe jumped in, pulled the door shut, and hit the lock just as the first of the undead slammed into the driver's-side door. He was lean, wearing a bullet-riddled North Face jacket. He slapped his palm against the window, his wedding ring clicking against the glass. Another, a young girl, leapt onto the hood.

Nope. Zoe knew where this led, and she wasn't interested in having the windshield smashed in and this thing falling into the cab with them.

She threw the truck into reverse and stomped on the gas pedal.

The girl fell backwards onto the driveway, jumped up, and gave chase, along with the rest of the zombies from the backyard.

The truck sped backwards down the gravel drive, batting down the undead like bowling pins.

From the back seat, Oliver shouted, "Zo! What are you doing?"

"The only thing I can think of!" She cut the wheel and slid out into the road, then threw the shifter into drive before the truck even came to a stop.

Bodies crashed into the side of the vehicle, immediately climbing into the bed of the truck.

As the undead tried to stand, Zoe stomped the gas.

Two zombies staggered back, falling over the tailgate and into the road.

Oliver was sitting up now, looking out the back window. "We still got one in the back!"

Zoe sped down the road, glancing in the rearview to find Howard was now sitting up too. His pale face was flushed red and his eyes were wide, hooded by thick grey eyebrows.

The undead crawled over the half-loaded truck bed of boxes and bags. When it reached the back of the cab, it stood. This undead was a young man, maybe in his twenties, wearing a torn Slipknot T-shirt. *Thump!* He punched the back window, lost his balance, and nearly fell.

"Zo, don't lose control of the truck because if we get stranded, we're screwed, but you need to slam on the brakes and then take off again – maybe we can throw this fucker from the back."

Howard tore the tape from his mouth. "Ahhh!"

Linda's pale face was etched with raw emotion. "Howard, honey, are you okay?" she begged.

Howard licked his lips and stretched his jaw. "Jesus, I... I don't know who you folks are, but thank you."

The undead wailed and punched the back window once more, but again it didn't break.

Zoe fastened her seat belt. "Seat belt, Linda!"

"Oh god!" Linda shouted, frantically fumbling with her seat belt before finally clicking it into place. She slapped her trembling hands on the dashboard, bracing for whatever came next.

"Everyone, hold on. I'm slamming on the brakes. In three, two, one!" Zoe smashed down on the brake pedal.

The truck screeched, throwing the undead into the back of the cab. Behind her, Oliver smashed into the back of her seat with a grunt.

She stomped the gas.

The undead guy staggered back, trying to keep his feet under him as he tripped over the boxes of god only knew what, before falling over the tailgate and smacking down hard on the pavement.

Zoe slowed to a stop and threw the truck in reverse.

"What are you doing?" Howard asked.

"Making sure he stays down!" Zoe shouted as the rear end of the truck slammed into the undead man just as he was about to gain his feet.

The truck bucked as the undead was pulled beneath the rear axle.

Zoe threw the truck back into drive and pressed on the accelerator. The rear wheels spun but the truck didn't move.

Howard slapped the back of the seat with a palm. "Great, now we're stuck! Why did you do that? We could have just left! We could have just kept driving!"

Behind them, dozens of undead filled the street, running towards them. Children and the elderly. Men and women. Some were fully clothed, others were partially or wholly nude. Some had shoes, while others ran with bloody bare feet slapping down raw and wet on the blacktop. But all shared a very distinct characteristic. Each had the same bloody eyes that burned with the same insatiable hunger. The sound of their pursuit was a cacophony of tortured moans and guttural snarls.

"It's alright, Howard, just stay calm." Oliver reached over the seat, pointing at the dashboard. "Zo, there are some buttons on the dash to the left of the steering wheel."

Linda's face was wet with sweat, her blond bangs slicked and pasted across her forehead, her eyes fixed on the side mirror. "Oh no. Please, they're coming!"

"We should have kept going!" Howard insisted.

"We're okay! Zo, push the button that says four high."

Zoe found the button and pushed it, engaging the four-wheel drive. Pressing down on the accelerator again, she felt the front tires grab. The rear end lifted up and dropped down with a thud. They were free and pulling away from the encroaching mob of undead.

Howard leaned over the seat, getting closer to Zoe then she would have liked. "Now, for god's sake, please! Just keep going!"

Zoe glanced into the side mirror as she sped up and pulled away from the horde. "We can't do that."

"What do you mean, 'can't?'" Linda begged, her breath ragged. Zoe thought the woman might be on the verge of a full-on panic attack. She could practically hear Linda's heart smashing against her chest like a load of bricks in a dryer.

Oliver placed his hand on Howard's shoulder. "Sit back, Howard. Everyone, just please calm down." He thrust a thumb over his shoulder. "The immediate threat is behind us. My name is Oliver – this is my wife, Zoe." Then to Zoe he said, "Go slow, and keep that mob following us. Broadway Road is just up ahead – turn there and we can turn around."

Linda shifted so she could see over the seat, her frantic eyes fixed on the mob of undead. "Keep them following us? Why would we want to do that?"

Zoe started to explain, but Howard cut in. "Now just hold on, son. I'm retired law enforcement and I'm telling you now, whatever you were going back for, forget it. We need to get out of here and find a safe place to hunker down. It won't be much longer before the military shows up in full force."

Zoe turned onto Broadway Road, keeping her speed at about fifteen miles per hour. Behind them, three more undead joined the mob – a severely obese man with a long grey beard, two middle-aged women, and another woman in a cycling outfit. The woman's bike helmet was still strapped to her head.

Zoe could hear the hope in Oliver's voice. "Really? You know that? How? Where are you getting that information?"

Howard scoffed. "Getting it? I just know our government won't allow this to continue. I'm sure our military is organizing right now."

Oliver's face fell in disappointment.

"Now listen," Howard continued, "those bastards that kidnapped us must have been watching us for some time. They learned when we went outside and what door we used, and they were waiting. I thought for sure if anyone even tried to get in, I'd be ready, but they were quick and heavily armed. They ransacked our house, trashed the whole place." Howard pointed towards the back of the truck. "All that shit scattered in the back of the truck, that's our stuff, stolen from *our* house. I smelled the gas and heard the flames when they lit it. Twenty years we lived there on White Oak Drive. Built it back in 2003 with my own two hands. Now it's all gone! Every goddamned thing we had. So what about those men? We go back for whatever it is you think you can't live without and we won't only be facing zombies, we'll be facing them. Linda and I got nothing to go back for – not anymore. Sorry, but we aren't going back down that road with those damn zombies filling the street, only to have to deal with those maniacs and whatever bad intentions they had planned for me and my Linda. We don't even know where they were taking us or how many more there might be!"

Oliver tried to interject. "But you don't understand—"

Howard cut him off. "No, son, I think it's you that doesn't understand. We aren't going back! That's final."

In the rearview, Zoe saw Oliver nodding along slowly. He was calm, too calm. "No. I do understand. See, we lost our home too and all we have left now is each other. But we aren't going back for stuff." Oliver pointed ahead. "Zo, speed up. Get just a little more distance between us and the horde then pull into that driveway."

Howard frowned. "We're stopping here? What the hell for?"

"Well, Howard, when Zoe pulls in, I'm going need you folks to get out. There's a house there. Maybe it's an empty one or maybe there is someone there that can help you. Looks like there's a car in the driveway. Maybe you two can take it if no one is home."

Zoe found Oliver in the rearview mirror and they locked eyes. She knew instantly where this could go, and with that one look she knew they were on the same page.

"What the hell are you talking about? You aren't leaving us on the side of the road with a mob of zombies heading this way!"

Zoe whipped into the driveway and stopped the car. Farther up the driveway sat a single-story ranch house. The windows weren't boarded up but the place appeared to be intact. There was an old Buick parked just in front of the garage. Maybe the couple would get lucky and find keys.

Oliver held up his hands. "Look, that's your choice. But we left a six-year-old back in that house when we came outside to rescue you and your wife. Oh, and by the way, before we killed both those men who kidnapped you, they were going to feed you to the zombies they have tied up in the basement."

The look on Linda's face turned to horror. "Feed us to zombies? Why would they do that?"

"Because their nephews had gotten sick and rather than put them down, they decided to chain them in the basement and give them what they wanted."

Whatever color was left in Linda's face drained away. "That's... that's disgusting!"

While Oliver was explaining, all Zoe could think about was the fact she'd left the back door open when she stepped out into the driveway. What if one of the undead went into the house? Jurnee had Louie and she was a smart kid. She would hide, but Zoe knew that wouldn't be enough. What if more came? What if the house was filled with zombies right now! Zoe gave Oliver her best *Get these people the fuck out of the car now* look she could muster.

Oliver nodded. "They're getting close, so if you want out, get out. But we're going back right now."

"Please, you can't leave us here," Linda pleaded.

Zoe looked at the older woman, realizing in that moment she hadn't heard a damn thing Oliver had said. She only cared about herself. "You have three seconds to get the fuck out of the truck before I turn around and go back for our little girl! One. Two."

Linda was sucking in breaths as if she'd just come up for air after being held under the ocean. "Please... wait!" she begged.

Waving his hand in desperation, Howard exclaimed, "Now just hold... hold on and let me think!"

"Three. Get out!" Zoe put her hand on the .357 but didn't draw it.

Linda gasped and scrambled to open the door.

Behind them, the zombies were getting dangerously close.

CHAPTER 12
SWIFTIE

OLIVER GLANCED down at the gun in his hand and then up at Howard. "You heard my wife, Howard. Last chance, better hurry."

The potbellied man's eyes flashed down at the gun and then back up. The mob of undead choked the road as they approached the driveway. "Close the door, Linda."

"What?" Linda moaned.

"You heard me, woman. We aren't getting out. Now, please, get us the fuck out of here. But don't go back through them, for god's sake! Go right! There's a side road that will loop back around!"

Zoe threw the truck in reverse and tore off, throwing gravel as she veered back onto Broadway Road, shifted into drive, and stomped it, throwing Oliver back in his seat.

Howard turned to face Oliver. "You didn't tell us you killed those men and that you left a little girl behind."

"Yeah, well, I tried, but you wouldn't listen. Now you know why we have to get back there, and I mean now."

"There's your turn," Howard announced as he pointed over the seat.

Zoe turned right on to the next side road. "Yes, I think this should go north until we reach a country road that runs east–west, right?

Which must be the one I could see from the driveway back at the farmhouse."

"That's... that's Warrick Road," Linda stammered.

Oliver could see the woman was visibly shaking as she did her best to try and compose herself. Clearly Linda was scared half to death. Oliver wasn't sure if it was because of what had just happened or what they were about to do. Either way, it didn't matter. All that mattered was getting back to Jurnee.

"There!" Linda pointed. "That's it. The crossroad coming up – that's Warrick Road. I drive down it every day to head into the office. Well, I used to, I guess – before... well, before." Tears fell from the disheveled woman's face. "It isn't bad enough we have to deal with whatever those nukes did to us, but now we have to worry about what the unsick will do. At least with the zombies, we know where we stand."

Zoe made the right onto Warrick Road, quickly building speed.

"Yeah, well this is where my dear wife and I don't see eye to eye," Howard said.

Zoe glanced up into the rearview mirror. "What do you mean?"

Howard twisted to the left and then right, stretching his back. "I'm not so sure this has anything to do with nukes – or an asteroid, for that matter."

Oliver frowned. Of course it had to do with the asteroid. "What? What are you saying?"

Linda dabbed at her eyes with the corner of her pajama collar. "He thinks this is all some government conspiracy – some disease like Covid, given to us intentionally to reduce the population."

Oliver placed his right palm on the seat and shifted to face Howard, realizing too late that it was a mistake. Pain shot from his back through his chest and down his right arm. He gritted his teeth, biting back the pain. "But... but the asteroid? The government couldn't have planned that?"

Howard huffed. "You're assuming there was an asteroid, but how do you know?"

Concern filled Zoe's face. "Oliver, are you okay?"

He met her eyes in the mirror, trying to play it off. "I'm okay, babe." He turned back to Howard. "C'mon, how else do you explain the emergency announcement, the flashes in the sky, the red rain."

"Yeah, I saw all that too, but I never saw an asteroid. How do you know this whole thing isn't some government population control plan gone wrong? Hey, are you hurt?"

Oliver shook his head. "I'm fine."

"No, he isn't fine," Zoe said. "Oliver, you're doing way more than you should with that puncture wound in your back."

"Puncture wound?" Howard repeated, his grey eyebrows bunching up.

"Right now, none of it matters. All that matters is getting to Jurnee."

As they crested a small hill, Oliver glanced across the barren cornfield. There in the distance was the brick house. He couldn't see the back door nor the front, only the north-facing side, the driveway, the big red barn... and undead. Only two that he saw, and not by the house but down at the end of the drive. His heart began thumping in his chest. *It's okay. It could be worse.*

Ahead, the road ended at a stop sign.

Oliver could feel Howard assessing him with his eyes.

"Do you have a plan, son?"

Lifting the gun from his lap, Oliver released the magazine, checked the rounds, and then shoved it back in with a click. He could feel his body becoming stiff, he was nauseous, and he would give anything for a handful of ibuprofen right about now. "When Zoe gets us back to the house, you two can have the truck and be on your way."

Linda spun to look at him. "You would do that? You would give us the truck?"

Oliver nodded. "It's all yours. There's another truck at the house. We'll take that one. That was our plan anyway. Hopefully those two zombies are the only stragglers and the rest are two miles down the road in the opposite direction."

Zoe pulled up to the stop sign.

"Okay, Zo, once you stop the truck, we'll get out and make for the back door as fast as we can, so get us as close as possible. Howard, Linda, you two lock the doors behind us and back out of here as fast as possible. Everyone ready?"

Howard looked hesitant. He placed a hand on Linda's shoulder and squeezed. "I think we can do a bit better than that."

"What do you mean?" Oliver asked, unsure where the man was going.

Howard spun around and looked out the back window into the bed of the truck and smiled. He glanced up at the sky and then said, "Stay put for a sec."

"Howard! What are you doing?"

Ignoring his wife's inquiry, Howard lifted the door latch and climbed out of the truck.

"Howard!"

The sky rumbled.

Great, just what they needed. It didn't look like rain at the moment, but Oliver knew the storms could materialize out of nowhere.

Zoe held up her hands. "What's he doing? We need to go!"

"Hold on, Zo." Oliver watched the man as he began rummaging through the scattered contents of the truck bed. After a moment, Howard smiled, unwrapping a blanket and lifting a long shotgun, a box of shells, and then something else that he tucked in his waistband.

For a split second, the man suddenly being armed made Oliver nervous, but as Howard climbed back in, he handed Oliver the shotgun.

"Hold this, please." Howard reached beneath his ample belly and produced a handgun, then he slid into the seat and slammed the door shut. "Remember earlier I told you those guys ransacked our place? Of course they would have taken my guns."

Oliver eyed the pistol.

"It's my standard-issue service pistol – Glock 22 .40 cal., and what you're holding is my Beretta 20 gauge. It's my bird gun. It's not really designed for defense, but I'm a crack shot," he said, smiling. "You get us in that driveway, and I'll cover you while you get your little girl into the truck. Then we'll all leave together."

"Howard! Are you sure? They said we could go." Linda's voice was panicked.

Oliver shook his head and held up a hand. "You folks don't have to do this."

"Nonsense. There are still good people in this world. You're good people. We'd be dead if not for you folks. I got your back. Now let's get your little girl."

Oliver nodded his thanks as he handed the shotgun back to Howard. "Let's go, Zo."

Zoe made the right turn back onto Dee-Mac Road and raced down the blacktop. Oliver felt his stomach rise and fall with the truck suspension as the vehicle nearly went airborne over a small rolling hill. As the entrance to the driveway came into view, he saw a middle-aged man in soiled sweatpants standing in the middle of the drive looking lost. *Okay, only one now – we can deal with one.*

"Oliver, he's right in the way!" Zoe said. Oliver could see she was gripping the steering wheel as if it were a ledge over a thousand-foot chasm.

"Zo, take a deep breath. You're okay. You just need to clip him with the corner of the truck."

Zoe blew out a breath. "Right. Okay." She aimed the corner of the truck at the zombie. At the last moment the zombie turned, his bloody eyes widening in excitement.

The corner of the truck's bumper connected with the man's knees, folding them sideways.

Out of the passenger-side window, Oliver watched the zombie, legs broken, pulling itself down the driveway, still pursuing them. The crawler was quickly overtaken by a teen with long blond hair and a bloody Taylor Swift T-shirt. *Where did she come from?* One of her shoulders was cocked oddly, all crooked, with what might have been a screwdriver handle sticking up from where her neck met her collarbone.

"Oh my god," Linda breathed.

"Yeah, what's with all these kids wearing band shirts? First Slipknot, now a Swiftie?" Oliver asked.

No one laughed. Sam would have laughed. Sam, his garbage route helper, but more, his best friend. Oh, how he wished things had gone different.

Up ahead, more undead appeared, this time from the barn. It was a woman and two men.

Howard pointed at the trio. "Not good!"

From the backyard, another three zombies: two women and a giant of a man in a pest control uniform.

Oliver's eyes were drawn to the man. He must have been close to seven feet tall. His white-collared shirt was bloodstained, and one eyeball hung loose from its socket. Even through the infection, the man had somehow managed to keep a ball cap positioned on his head that read WHAT'S BUGGING YOU?

Was that right? How would a zombie keep his hat in place?

"Oliver? What should I do?" Zoe shouted, nearing the end of the driveway.

"Stick to the plan. Get as close to the house as you can. If they get in the way, hit them. When you stop, I'm going to jump out, gun blazing!"

Howard switched the safety off the Beretta. "I've got five rounds in here, then I'll go to the handgun. Linda, stay in here and keep your door locked."

"Howard, please be careful. Ahh!"

Zoe swerved out of the driveway and onto the sidewalk, hitting a woman with brunette hair pinned in a bun. The woman's hands flew up as she vanished under the front end of the truck.

Oliver opened the car door and jumped out like he was back on the garbage route, going for a can to dump. A sinking feeling consumed him as he realized they'd left the back door of the house wide open. They couldn't have been gone much more than fifteen minutes, but if a zombie got in... Jesus. He wanted to take the five steps to the back door and go find Jurnee, but he knew they had to handle the undead first or they'd follow him inside. Zoe was already out of the truck too, and as the second zombie from the backyard came within reach, she fired the .357 only inches from the woman's face.

The side of the zombie's head burst in a spray of red mist.

On the other side of the truck, the Beretta fired. *Boom!*

Farther back in the yard, the tall exterminator had stopped. Now he stood still, watching.

As Oliver stepped forward to take a shot, something grabbed his ankle and he about shit himself. It was the woman Zoe had just run over.

The zombie used her grip on Oliver's leg and pulled, her head appearing from beneath the truck, mouth open and snapping.

Oliver reached down and shot her in the side of the head. When he looked back up, the exterminator was gone.

Zoe shouted. "Oliver! I'm out of bullets!"

He motioned to the door. "Get inside!"

Zoe froze, her eyes going wide. Even before she tried to warn him, he understood and spun. The teen in the Taylor Swift shirt was on him, reaching. Her lips were drawn back in a feral sneer; a string of syrupy drool hung from the corner of her mouth. Her dead eyes bulged with excitement. Reflexively, Oliver lifted his left hand to shoot, but he didn't see the side mirror until his wrist cracked painfully into it, knocking the gun from his hand.

"Fuck!" He raised his hands as the woman lunged in.

Boom! The top of the girl's head exploded.

Oliver jumped, looking to his left.

Howard stood on the opposite side of the truck bed. He dropped the Beretta off his shoulder and nodded.

Oliver nodded back.

Howard spun back towards the barn, unloading one round and then another into the woman who'd emerged with the two men from the barn.

More undead were crossing the road and sprinting up the long gravel drive, along with the crawler Zoe had hit with the truck. Worse, several more undead appeared from the woods behind the barn. Oliver knew there was another neighborhood over that way, and who knew how many undead could have heard the gunshots. "Go, Zo!" he shouted, and then turned back to Howard. "There's more coming! Too many! Come inside with us and we'll wait them out together."

Howard's eyes flashed to Linda, who was shaking like a leaf in the passenger seat. "No time!" Howard shouted. Turning, he fired the last round from his shotgun into the chest of an elderly man who didn't look capable of running as fast as he was. The blast dropped the runner face first into the gravel.

Oliver bent, snatching his .45 from the ground.

Zoe fled into the house.

The elderly man scrambled onto his hands and knees and leapt to his feet.

"Take care!" Howard said, hurrying around to the driver's side.

As dozens of zombies filled the driveway, a bad feeling filled Oliver's stomach, but there was no time to argue. He needed to hurry after Zoe. She didn't have any rounds in her gun, and he wasn't sure what might be in the house waiting for them.

"You guys be safe," he shouted back, then dashed across the back porch and through the kitchen door, locking the dead bolt behind him. The dead bolt no more than latched when the first undead slammed into the door. "Mmmm!"

From the direction of the living room, Louie was barking like a maniac. Oliver crossed the kitchen, catching up with Zoe. "Wait! You're empty. Let me go first."

Zoe nodded.

Pulling in a steadying breath, Oliver braced himself for what he might see. It wasn't a zombie he was most worried about – it was what one might have done to Jurnee. He shook the thought away, swallowed down his fear, and reached for the door. He stopped short, hesitating.

"What?"

Glancing around, he didn't find what he was looking for. Then his eyes fell to Travis's corpse. "I want a clear exit – a path of escape, just in case." Instead of pushing through the door, he pulled it open all the way. At first glance, he didn't see anything in the living room, only darkness. Turning his attention back to Travis, he kicked the dead man's foot, sliding it in front of the door and effectively propping it open.

Heart racing, Oliver stepped through the doorway.

CHAPTER 13
PEST CONTROL

STEPPING OVER TRAVIS, Zoe crossed the threshold behind Oliver. The first thing she noticed was the wretched stench. Fifteen minutes of fresh air, and now all she could smell was death and rot.

The second thing she noticed was how dark it was. The room was lit with a single lamp, shaded with a brown lampshade, intermingled with the natural light cast between the gapped boards covering the windows. The effect was eerie – creepy even. Zoe hated this place.

Glancing right, she could see the door to the bathroom was wide open. When they went outside, she'd left Jurnee and Louie in the bathroom with the door shut. To her left, Louie stood with his back to them, his attention on the basement door, barking and growling like a maniac. But there was no Jurnee.

"Louie! Come!" Zoe shouted.

Louie backed up towards them, not taking his eye off the basement door, a menacing growl emanating from his throat.

Puzzled, Zoe looked at Oliver, holding her palms up. She'd no idea what had gotten into Louie. From what she could see, the padlock was still clasped securely on the hasp. "Jurnee! Jurnee, where are you?"

"I'm over here!" Jurnee's tiny voice called from behind the over-stuffed recliner. The terrified girl peeked out from behind the chair.

Zoe exhaled, relief washing over her as she ran across the room. "Hey, it's okay."

"I heard a car! I thought you left us! Then the noise started!"

Tears spilled down Zoe's face as she reached for the girl. "Oh, honey, we would never leave you! Come here," she said, hugging her tight to her chest.

Something below them crashed.

Louie ran towards the basement door, barking wildly.

"It's alright, boy! Shhh."

Boom! The basement door shook in its frame.

"I can smell you up there!" a voice shouted.

Zoe looked at Oliver and shook her head. She didn't recognize that voice. It wasn't one of the kids, and it wasn't Trent. This voice was deep. Maybe one of the deepest voices she'd ever heard.

"I smell each one of you. Each one, the answer to my pain! The cure for my misery."

Boom! The door popped and cracked.

"Zoe! Is that Trent?"

"No. No way."

Oliver crossed the living room to the front door and peered out a small window set in the door. "Nothing," he announced, then ran to a window facing the south side of the house. He craned his neck, trying to peer down the side of the house through the gaps between the boards. "Shit!"

"What?"

"When Trent boarded this place up, he did it with two-by-fours from the outside."

"So what?"

"So that's smart. It means the zombies can't kick their way in like they did at our place. But he didn't do the same with the basement windows. I assume he secured those with boards from inside the basement. Maybe he did it that way so the kids couldn't kick their way out if they got off their leash."

"Oliver, what's your point?"

"My point is someone kicked the boards in from outside and they're in the basement!"

Boom! The basement door popped.

Oliver pointed at a box of shells on the table. "Hurry up and put some rounds in your gun."

Zoe grabbed the box off the table, drew her pistol from its holster, and ejected the spent rounds. Quick as she could she began shoving bullets into the cylinders of her .357. She wasn't practiced at loading a gun and fumbled several rounds, dropping them on the floor. "We should just go!"

"I'm not sure we can!" Oliver said, lifting his gun and taking aim at the door.

"Well, shoot it through the door before it gets in!"

"Jurnee, cover your ears as tight as you can!"

Jurnee slammed her hands over her ears.

Outside, a horn blew and wheels spun in gravel. A second later, the whole house shook.

Jurnee screamed.

"What the fuck!" Oliver shouted, spinning towards the kitchen. Through the kitchen door Zoe caught a glimpse of the silver truck sitting halfway inside the back porch.

Howard fired his handgun through the back window. She couldn't see Linda. Why wasn't she in the passenger seat?

Howard, his face smeared with blood, started to climb out of the driver's-side window.

Boom! The basement door came off the hinges.

Both Oliver and Zoe spun back towards the basement door.

A giant of a man emerged, ducking low to keep from hitting his head on the doorframe. He wore a pest control uniform and a ballcap.

"Shit. It's the exterminator," Oliver announced, taking aim.

"Oliver, shoot that thing!" Zoe shouted, loading the last two rounds into her .357.

Across the kitchen, Linda sat up in the passenger seat and screamed as she scrambled across the bench seat towards the driver's side.

One of the undead threw itself headfirst through the already busted passenger-side window. Frantically it reached and groped for the woman as she kicked and screamed to get away. "Help! Please help me!"

In front of Zoe, the big guy grimaced, his face stretched in agony as he broke into a run down the hallway. "I need to eat!" he shouted.

"Shoot!" Zoe screamed as she slapped the cylinder on her .357 closed.

Her first two shots went wide, but her third punched a hole through the man's collar.

He was so fast, and just like that he was within reach of Oliver.

Finally, Oliver fired.

She thought the shot hit the giant man in the head, but he didn't stop. The man's huge arms wrapped Oliver in a bear hug as he lifted him off the ground and carried him several more steps before slamming him into the wall. The drywall caved in with the force of both men crashing into it.

Oliver's gun flew from his hand.

The man held Oliver there, two feet off the ground, his massive hands around his throat. "I'm going to eat your fucking face!"

Hands trembling, Zoe lifted the gun and pointed it at the man's head. She stepped forward, ensuring she wouldn't miss... couldn't miss.

The man must have seen the movement. With a sudden motion he swung his hand out, backhanding the pistol from Zoe's hand.

The gun flew across the room, striking the television and shattering the screen. Pain shot up her arm with the force of the blow.

The man ignored her, his focus back on Oliver, his teeth snapping.

Oliver planted the palm of his hand on the man's forehead, knocking his cap off in an attempt to hold the zombie's snapping teeth away from his face.

"No!" she screamed, searching for the gun. But it was nowhere!

Everything was chaos.

Behind the chair, Jurnee was screaming.

Louie was on the man, biting his leg and pulling frantically, but the exterminator only ignored it, his focus solely on eating Oliver.

Linda and Howard were screaming from across the kitchen as Howard tried to pull Linda through the driver's-side window. From the passenger side, more undead were crawling into the cab.

Zoe caught movement in her peripheral vision. Glancing back down the hall, she saw two more shapes moving towards her, their chains rattling as they dragged across the carpet. The boys. And behind them, a third person appeared.

A very undead Trent.

CHAPTER 14
A NARROW VIEW

"ZO...EEE! GUN!" Oliver tried to shout. His vision was bursting in starry fireworks and his eyes felt like they might pop out of his head.

Zoe spun around, clearly not seeing his gun. Dammit, it was right there at his feet, but Louie was standing over it. But he couldn't say it. Couldn't breathe. Behind them, he could see zombies filing down the hallway. The lead boy was on hands and knees – half crawling, half dragging himself – but the others were quickly scrambling over him.

Oliver's arm was burning with the agony of trying to hold the giant man's head back. He was losing. He was losing, and there was nothing more he could do. He didn't want this for Zoe and Jurnee. She couldn't save him, and she needed to make the same choice she would expect him to make if the tables were turned.

"Bath... room! Go!"

What Oliver was asking had to register within a second, or they were as dead as he was about to be.

"Jurnee!" he tried to shout.

Zoe's face turned to horror as the switch from fight to flight registered. "Jurnee! Bathroom! Now! Run!"

Jurnee ran from behind the chair into the bathroom.

"Louie! Come!" Zoe ordered.

The dog released the man's leg and darted after Zoe into the bathroom.

As Zoe vanished, there was a concussive *BOOM!*

The exterminator's head burst apart. Oliver's hand shoved forward and he and the giant man fell.

Oliver went forward as the big, mostly headless man tipped over like a felled tree.

Oliver hit the ground, gasping for air. But there was no time to figure out what had happened. Glancing down at his hand, he found that, amazingly, his fingers hadn't been blown off. For the moment he was alive, and the moment was everything.

He scrambled, grabbing the .45 as he blinked back the water filling his eyes. On his hands and knees, he noticed a black pistol grip sticking out from under the coffee table – Zoe's .357. He lunged forward, grabbing it in his other hand. His vision wasn't perfect, but he raised the .357 and fired anyway. One of the boys dropped. Before he could fire again, there was another *BOOM!* Blood and brain matter splattered the entertainment center as Trent went down.

A hand reached under Oliver's arm, pulling him.

He flinched, ready to shoot the new threat when he realized it was Howard.

"Get up, man!" Howard shouted, but Oliver could barely make it out.

The crawling boy was just exiting the hallway.

Oliver fired, shooting him through the top of the head.

On unsteady feet, Oliver finally turned to look at Howard. The man was holding his Beretta in one arm and pushing Linda forward with the other. "We have to go!"

At first, the urgency didn't register – the zombies in the hallway were all dead – but then Oliver saw the undead piling through the opening in the porch and into the kitchen. "Fuck my life! Bathroom! C'mon!" He grabbed the handle to the door and shook it. "Zoe! Open up!"

Zoe flung the door open and the three piled in.

"Lock it!" Zoe shouted and then grabbed him and kissed him hard on the mouth. "I thought you were..."

Oliver handed her the .357. "I'm okay! Thanks to Howard," he said, meeting the man's eyes and nodding. Howard nodded back and then turned his attention back to Linda.

The woman was crying hysterically.

Zoe pointed. "Oliver, I can see the truck out this window."

"Window! Right!" The window was positioned above the toilet and looked barely big enough to climb through. Oliver straddled the toilet and lifted the window open, poking his head out. The truck was right there and – the best part – no zombies.

Behind him, something slammed into the bathroom door. Again and again. By now, Oliver knew how this went and what would happen in the coming moments.

"Zoe, please tell me you have the keys?" He needed just one thing to go right. *Please, God, if you're up there, don't be an asshole! Just give me one freaking thing!*

Zoe reached into her pocket and produced a set of keys.

"Right" – he smiled grimly – "let's go! Howard. You want to go first or last?" He thought it was only right to give the choice to the man who'd just saved his life twice in a row.

Howard pulled a handful of shells out of the pocket of his plaid pajamas and began sliding them into the shotgun, one after the other. "I'll go last and cover the rear."

Linda was still crying. Oliver realized that this wasn't the cry of hysterical fear – the woman was in pain.

"Linda, what is it? Are you hurt?" Zoe asked.

The wood panel on the door cracked.

"Zoe, we got to go now!" Oliver shouted as he climbed through the window headfirst. With the opening being kind of small, there was no easy way to do this and no time to be careful. He dropped the four or five feet into the grass and tried his best to sort of summersault, but nevertheless his head bashed into the ground and pain shot through his back, reminding him he'd been stabbed only a day ago. "Fuck me!" he cried through gnashed teeth.

Quickly, he stood, brushed himself off, and drew his handgun, surveying the area. It was still clear. Of course it was – the entire horde was trying to get into the bathroom.

Jurnee's little hand poked out the window next. She was holding Princess.

Oliver took the doll. "Got her, now hurry!"

Jurnee vanished back inside.

Zoe grunted and then feet in Mickey Mouse socks appeared out the window.

"Go ahead and lower yourself," he said, trying to sound encouraging.

"Oliver!" Jurnee cried. "Don't let me fall!"

Oliver holstered his gun, wrapped his left arm around the tiny girl, and lowered her to the grass.

Zoe sent Linda next, which made him incredibly nervous. Not that he wasn't worried about all of them, but he hated the idea of Zoe not getting the hell out of there right now.

Linda's feet appeared as she lowered herself, crying and mumbling, "Oh my god. Oh, my god, it hurts so bad!"

Oliver put his arm around the woman's waist and helped her to the ground.

Linda hit the ground and winced, falling back against the house.

Oliver had already noticed that the bottom of her pajama pants were blood soaked and her sock was stained in bright wet blood.

The woman gave him a desperate look.

"What happened? Were you bitten?" Oliver asked, offering her his hand to help her out of the way.

She took his hand. "Thank you, I... It's... I don't think..." The woman trailed off, her eyes frenzied and panicked.

He guided her over to the side. "It's going to be okay," he lied. "Zoe is a doctor. She will get you fixed up as soon as we're safe."

Louie appeared in the window next.

"Jump, Louie," Zoe commanded.

Louie hesitated, letting out a whine.

"Come on, Louie! Come on, boy!" Jurnee shouted as she slapped her thigh.

Louie jumped, landing in the grass beside Jurnee.

Finally Zoe slid out of the window, feet first and belly down, dropping gracefully to the ground.

Watching her, he realized he'd done it all wrong.

Howard appeared in the window. "Here, take this." He handed Oliver the Beretta, then stuck one leg out the window. Howard was a bigger man with an ample belly. Oliver realized the man might not fit out the small window.

"Hurry!" Zoe urged.

Howard tried to reposition himself and then announced, "No good."

Oliver shook his head and grabbed the man by the leg, preparing to pull if he had to. "Bullshit, no good!"

Howard adjusted and tried again. "I can't fit out this window. It isn't going to happen."

No way. Oliver couldn't accept that. "Well, fucking try harder! You can't stay in there."

Howard pulled himself back into the bathroom and stuck his head out the window. "Oliver, it isn't going to happen."

Linda let out a wretched sob. "Howard, please?"

Oliver shook his head. "Then I'll come through the front! We're getting you out!"

There was a loud crack of wood. "You can't! The door is failing – just please get Linda out of here."

The man had just saved his life. This wasn't right. It wasn't how this was supposed to go. "Zoe, get everyone in the truck!" Oliver said, backing away from the window.

From beyond the bathroom, the dead cried out with desperation.

"Howard. Lift the top off the back of the toilet and break the frame! Hurry! Smash the fucking frame!"

Howard looked at the wood window rails that framed the glass. Hope filled his eyes as he vanished back inside.

The window exploded outward, the toilet lid landing in the yard. Howard kicked the remaining components of the window rails out of the way. Inside the bathroom there was a crash. Hungry moans and cries of pain filled the tiny bathroom.

"Jump!" Oliver shouted, pulling the toilet lid out of the way.

Howard dove headfirst, landing on all fours in the grass and rolling.

Oliver grabbed the man, pulling him to his feet as the undead dove after him, piling out the window.

"Run!"

They half ran, half hobbled to the truck, both men climbing inside. Jurnee was in the front seat, already in the middle, and Zoe was behind the wheel with the truck running. Linda and Louie were in the back seat.

Oliver jumped in the front as Howard fell into the back. Before his door even latched, Zoe stomped on the gas, throwing sod and then gravel as she tore down the drive.

Behind them, the undead gave chase.

Tires squealed as Zoe slid out onto Dee-Mac Road.

In the side mirror, Oliver watched as the zombies fell away. Finally, they were together, safe, and free of this nightmare.

But if Oliver knew one thing about nightmares, it was that every time you close your eyes, there's a chance they'll come back.

CHAPTER 15
A WARM RAIN

LIKE A DOG on leash eager to stray, the old blue Chevy pulled to the right as Zoe sped down Broadway Road, the steering wheel vibrating in protest beneath her grip. The age of the truck was a mystery to her, but the odometer read almost 240,000 miles. Push an old dog too hard and it might lie down right in the middle of the road and refuse to get up. She eased up on the pedal.

She had to slow down anyway. A car, what kind she couldn't tell, was tipped up in the middle of the road with its undercarriage facing her. She maneuvered around it and sped back up, only to be forced to slow again. This time, she steered into the opposite lane to avoid the cab of a green semi that sat jackknifed with its trailer twisted into the ditch. The side of the truck read SAME DAY FREIGHT CO. Morbidly, she thought maybe it should read LAST DAY FREIGHT. And so it went. Speed up. Slow down. Navigate around an abandoned vehicle and speed up again.

The distance to the church would take fifteen minutes on a normal day, but they had departed normal days ago. Meanwhile, high above, the sky filled with burnt-orange clouds, and it began to rain. Zoe hated the rain, hated it with her whole soul. Scanning the dashboard, she searched for the wiper controls, fumbled the knob, and switched them on, imagining the wiper arms were destroying thousands of parasites as they slapped and slopped slippery red rain against the glass.

In the back seat, Linda sobbed quietly.

"Linda, what happened to your foot?" Zoe asked, glancing up to the mirror. Linda's face was drained of color and twisted in agony, sweat beading on her furrowed brow.

"I... I don't know. It all happened so fast. She just came right through... through the glass and grabbed me. I... I pulled away, but she wouldn't let go of my foot. I was kicking and kicking, trying to get away." Her words came between ragged breaths as she struggled to cope with the pain from her foot.

"Did she bite you?" Oliver asked.

"No. I... I don't think so. I think it was the window glass when I was trying to kick her away."

Howard shook his head. "Dammit, this is all my fault. When you folks left us, I thought it would be a good idea to reload my shotgun before we backed out. I figured that way, if we got stuck or something happened, I'd be ready. But they came so fast! They were all over the truck. Then one smashed through Linda's window. I tried to back away, but there were so many! They just kept coming and coming, filling the back of the truck. I had no choice. I aimed for the house and floored it."

Oliver's eyebrows raised. "You hit the house on purpose?"

"It was all I could think to do."

Zoe found Howard's eyes in the rearview mirror. She could hear the frustration and see the worry for his wife. "Howard, if it hadn't been for you, we might all be dead."

"She's right. You saved our asses back there," Oliver agreed.

Howard nodded solemnly.

"Listen," Oliver continued, "we're going to a church where there's a lot of food. We can load the truck full and then head to a place I know just down the road. It's a huge house with a steel gate, fence, and solar power."

Zoe could see the concern etched on Howard's face – he was focused solely on his wife. She said, "As long as the road doesn't get any worse, we'll be at the church in ten minutes. I'll get Linda's wound cleaned and bandaged."

Howard, his lips in a tight line, held Linda's hand. "Thank you. That sounds good."

"Zo's a doctor," Oliver said reassuringly.

She gave Oliver the side eye. "No, I'm not, but I am trained."

"Okay, practically a doctor."

The rain slowed just enough to make the wipers squeak as they dragged across the window. Zoe switched the wiper knob to intermittent. The wipers squeaked, paused, then, swoosh swoosh, pause. "Linda, is your foot still bleeding now?"

Linda sucked air through clenched teeth. "Oh god, it hurts so bad and my... my sock, it's so wet."

There was nothing around them but open fields. Up ahead, the road climbed over Highway 155. Zoe glanced back at the woman and pulled onto the shoulder. Was it her imagination, or was Linda even paler than before? Pale as a ghost.

"What are you doing, Zo?"

"I need you to take over so I can look at Linda's foot. If she's bleeding bad, I don't want to wait. We need to get pressure on it now." That was the truth, but it wasn't the whole truth. Something was niggling at her to get a look at that wound.

Oliver gave a reluctant nod. "Well, we can't get out, so start climbing."

Zoe shifted the truck into park and turned to Jurnee, next to her. "Okay, you two scoot this way while I climb over."

Jurnee giggled and shuffled towards Zoe, who climbed over both Jurnee and Oliver.

Oliver looked down at Jurnee. "Well, unless you want to drive, we better switch, kid."

Jurnee laughed again. "I can't even see out the window, Oliver!"

"Right. Come here." He smiled and helped her to climb over him.

Oliver checked the side mirror and pulled back out onto Broadway Road.

"Okay," Zoe said, turning to face the back. "Louie, lay down."

Louie lay down on the seat.

"Good boy." She gave Louie's head a rub, and he licked her hand. "Okay, the first thing we need to do is get your foot elevated. Can you lift it up here and rest it on the back of the seat?"

"I'll try. It hurts so bad and it's burning."

Linda leaned back and lifted her leg up, resting her heel on the back of the seat. Her sock was blood soaked and dripping, along with the cuff of her plaid pj's.

Initially, she thought Linda had cut her foot, but now she understood the cut must be above the ankle for her pant leg to be so bloody. "I'm just going to lift this up so I can have a look."

Linda nodded and winced.

Zoe lifted the bloody cuff to reveal what she'd feared most. What the little voice inside her had been trying to warn her about. Linda had been bitten.

Linda grabbed Howard's hand, slamming her eyes shut and squeezing as if she were in labor. "Ohhh! Is it bad?"

The bite itself was horrific. A whole chunk of tissue was missing on the anterior of Linda's lower leg just above the ankle. There was clearly tendon damage, and she was pretty sure the yellowish patch at the back of the wound was the woman's fibula. Of course, none of that mattered. Linda was now infected.

Howard saw it too, and the blood drained from his face.

"Howard? Is it bad?"

Mentally, Zoe did the math. The moment Linda must have been bitten to the moment when she climbed out the bathroom window couldn't have been more than – what? – five to seven minutes. They'd been driving another five minutes or so.

Howard squeezed his wife's hand. "It's... it's going to be okay."

Linda opened her eyes. Zoe saw it then. They were pink. Not the

I've-been-crying pink, but the bad pink – the pink that would soon start leaking blood.

"Then why are you looking at me like that? Oh, Howie, you never were any good at lying to me. Don't lie to me now. How bad is it?"

Oliver looked at Zoe, his face questioning.

She shook her head.

Pressing his lips tight, Oliver dragged a hand down his face.

Outside, the wipers slapped back and forth as rain fell steadily from an uncaring sky.

Zoe tried to think what to say, even though they all knew there was nothing she could do for the woman. "Since the bed has a cover on it, I... I packed all the medical supplies in the back. But maybe there is something in here we can use. If we can tear the sleeve off my sweater, we can get pressure on the wound and at least stop the bleeding."

Tears glistened in Howard's eyes. "Thank you, but that's okay. Can you pull over, please?"

Oliver glanced up in the mirror and then over to Zoe.

She nodded.

"Howie? Please tell me? It's bad, isn't it? I don't feel right. My stomach hurts and I'm hungry. I... I don't think that's right. It doesn't seem right."

Oliver pulled onto the shoulder and put the truck in park. Zoe watched as he discreetly drew the .45 from his holster and set it in his lap.

"Come here, boy," Howard said to Louie, slapping his thigh.

Louie looked up at Zoe. "Go on," she urged.

Louie climbed onto Howard's lap.

Howard scooted towards his wife, and Louie jumped down on the other side and lay back down.

Howard pulled his wife's bloody pant leg down and lifted her foot off the back of the seat. "Hey, do you remember that vacation we took to Cozumel?"

Linda frowned. "Howie, we've taken lots of trips to Cozumel."

"I know, but I'm talking about the very first time."

"I remember. It rained the whole time."

Howard smiled, clearly fighting back tears. "That's right. It rained, but it was a warm rain. We were sitting under a cabana on the beach just watching it pour. Then you asked me—"

"I asked you to... to dance with me." Linda placed her hand on her belly and winced.

"That's right," he said, chuckling. "I thought it was silly. It was a downpour and there was no music, but you didn't care. You stepped right out into the rain and held out your hand."

"And you took it and followed me... Ahhh!" Linda shouted, suddenly bending forward. "My stomach!"

Louie barked.

No longer able to restrain himself, Howard's eyes overflowed as he took both her hands in his. "You remember what you said while we danced?"

Linda swallowed, bloodstained tears spilling down her cheeks. "I said... the world could end right now and it would be okay because I never... never felt safer than in your arms."

"And ever since that very first time twenty years ago, on every vacation we've taken... when it rained, we danced."

"Howie, I'm so hungry. I can smell it all around me."

Very slowly, Oliver lifted the gun from his lap and twisted in his seat.

"I know, my love." He let go of one of Linda's hands, reached across her lap, and lifted the door latch.

"What...what are you doing?" Linda asked.

"Well, it's raining out and I was hoping you would dance with me?"

Zoe tried to hold back tears that refused to be restrained. Through blurry eyes she watched Linda hold her husband's gaze as realization set in. The pained expression was gone now, replaced by a look of longing.

"I would like that very much." Linda pushed the car door open, placed her good foot onto the pavement of the road, and stood.

Howard slid towards the door.

"Howard?" Zoe said.

Howard tucked his service pistol into his pajama pants. "Thank you both, but it's time Linda and I went our own way."

Oliver's eyes were pleading. "Are you sure you want to do this?"

Swinging his feet out of the truck, Howard leaned out, rain speckling his face. Then, as if it was an afterthought, he glanced back at them and smiled. "Sometimes all we can hope for is a safe place to die."

CHAPTER 16
OCCUPIED

IN THE REARVIEW MIRROR, Oliver watched the silhouettes of Howard and Linda become one as they swayed back and forth. A moment later, they faded into the rain.

Next to him, Zoe stared out the passenger window and cried softly.

Little Jurnee held Princess close to her. "Are you okay, Zoe?"

Zoe sniffed and wiped her eyes on her sweater. "I'm okay."

"Are you sad because they went into the rain?"

She forced a smile. "Yes, something like that."

"Why did they go?"

Despite her apparent effort, Zoe let out a sob. "I..."

Oliver glanced down at Jurnee. "They made a choice to go. But we can't make that choice. The rain is bad, and you can never, ever go in it. Okay?"

Jurnee nodded. "I know, and Princess knows too."

Zoe dabbed her eyes on her sleeve. "Is that what we're doing, Oliver?"

"What do you mean?"

"Looking for a safe place to die? Is that all that's left?"

"Zoe, don't talk like that. We'll find a safe place to live. This can't last forever. Maybe Howard was right. We just need to hunker down and wait it out."

"Until what? Until we're forced to escape through another window? If it isn't the undead, then it's the living! It's only been five days, and already the world has become a desperate place. What will it look like a month from now?"

Oliver navigated onto the shoulder to get past a black Grand Cherokee that had apparently veered head on into a yellow Corvette. "Howard and Linda weren't like that. There are still good people in the world."

"Maybe there are, but how will we know? I can't wait until I'm drugged to find out!"

"I don't know what you want me to say."

"I don't know either, but you're right that Howard and Linda were good – and now they're de..." – she glanced down at Jurnee – "gone because of us."

"Wait a minute! You can't be serious! I gave him the truck and told him to go!"

Zoe crossed her arms over her chest. "But we made them come back with us!"

"No. That isn't true! They had a chance to get out and go to that abandoned house, but they chose to stay!"

"That wasn't a choice! I tried to force them out when those damn dead things were right on us. They probably wouldn't have made it up the driveway before they were overtaken!"

Oliver screwed up his face. "You're blaming yourself for this? Zo, listen to me. They made decisions. We made decisions. Whether the decisions turn out to be good or bad isn't the point! The point is the intent. You never intended this to be the outcome. Just like Howard never intended that stopping to load his shotgun would turn out the way it did!"

"I just can't stop thinking if I'd only..." She shook her head. "First Angel and now Linda and Howard."

Oliver slapped his palm down on the steering wheel. "You can't think that way! You can't see the future. We made decisions we thought would save Jurnee – would save ourselves! Remember this, if you hadn't pulled into that driveway and smashed into that barn, Linda and Howard would have had no control over how they died. Because of you, they got to spend their last moments doing the one thing that meant the most to them!"

As they crossed the overpass of Highway 155, the rain slowed to a drizzle. Oliver slowed to a stop on the overpass.

"What are you doing?"

"Just looking." As far as he could see to the north and south, cars lined the road – all of them appeared to be either wrecked or abandoned.

"Look, those are people down there." Zoe pointed to what must have been a couple dozen people dodging in between cars as they ran towards them in a dead sprint.

"They must have seen our car." They were high up on the overpass, but the fact the people were coming gave Oliver the creeps. He pressed on the gas and continued on.

Oliver pointed ahead. "That's our turn, and the church is only about a mile or two farther."

"Unsicker Road? I never knew it was called that."

"Maybe that's a good omen." Oliver made the right turn as the memory of the last time, when he'd been coming from the other way, flooded back. Jurnee had been bitten in the back, and this was the exact place he'd stopped to check on her. He swallowed dryly, remembering just how scared he'd been that she was infected.

"Well, we could use something good right about now."

"Are we almost there?" Jurnee asked. "Because I sure am hungry!"

A huge, brick-sized lump sat in Oliver's stomach. He couldn't imagine eating anything, but then again it must have been close to noon by now, and they hadn't eaten anything today. "Just a little farther and we'll get something to eat."

"And Louie too? I bet he's hungry."

Oliver put on a smile, fake as it was. "I bet you're right. He's always hungry."

They went down a small dip and across a creek. Oliver pointed. "That wasn't there last time." The guard rail was broken and a car sat upside down in the bed of the creek; only the bottom of the car and wheels were sticking up out of the fast-moving water. They climbed the small hill, and the church came into view. "Oh, that's weird."

"What? What's weird?" Zoe asked.

"My garbage truck. It isn't there."

"What do you mean it isn't there? Are you sure?"

Oliver turned into the parking lot. "Of course I'm sure. I left it right there, half under the carport. Look" – he pointed – "you can even see damage where the truck bed hit the roof."

"Okay, so what? You think someone stole it?"

"Maybe, but you'd have to know how to drive it, plus it overheated so bad I'd be surprised if the heads weren't cracked." Oliver drove towards the porte cochere. "Shit!"

"What?"

"I busted the glass out of the front door, but look – it's boarded up."

"The windows too!" Zoe pointed.

Two broken stained glass windows were covered from the inside. Oliver couldn't be certain, but it sure as hell looked like the top of one of those dining room tables from Fellowship Hall had been fastened over the window from the inside.

"Damn, someone beat us here. Let's drive around the building and see how many cars are back there. Maybe we'll be able to determine approximately how many we're dealing with."

"Dealing with? Oliver, shouldn't we just move on? We don't know these people – they might not be welcoming."

"Yeah, I mean we could just go down to that house I told you about. But like Howard said, there are still good people out there. I don't see what it hurts to ask. Besides, wasn't it nice to have someone watching our backs? I mean, you always hear about safety in numbers and, well, maybe there's something to that." Oliver navigated to the back of the building. There were several new vehicles in the lot, including a few trucks and a white panel van.

Jurnee was sitting up on her knees. "Look, Oliver! There's Mack!"

The big red-and-white garbage truck was sitting in the very back of the lot.

Zoe laughed. "Mack? You call your truck Mack?"

"Hey! I don't know why that's funny! Mack is as good a name as any – besides, it says so right on the grille."

Zoe looked down at Jurnee. "Maybe he should call it Big Mac," she said, snorting.

Jurnee giggled. "Weeellll, it is awful big, but it sure doesn't smell as good as a Big Mac!"

"Oh, you two have jokes about poor old Mack." Oliver found himself smiling. It didn't take away the lump in his gut or the uneasiness he felt about what he was about to do. Still, the laughter felt right somehow, nervous as it was.

He pulled back around and parked under the porte cochere. "Let me go knock and see what's up."

"Like hell. I'm going with you." Zoe lifted the handle and pushed open her door.

"Alrighty then," Oliver said, pushing open his own door. "Jurnee, you better stay here."

"Not again!" Jurnee's bottom lip started to quiver.

Honestly, Oliver couldn't blame her. She'd been left in the bus and then left in the house, but he already wasn't happy Zoe wanted to go, and he sure as hell wasn't going to put Jurnee in front of that door until he knew it was safe. "Listen, if we leave Louie in here alone, he will get lonely and cry, so you have a big job to do. You've got to keep him calm while we go talk to the people staying here. But I promise, we won't go inside without you, and you'll be able to see us the whole time."

"Can he come up here with me... so he won't be scared?"

"Sure." Oliver climbed out. "Slide over towards me."

Jurnee scootched over into the driver's seat.

"Come on, Lou!"

Louie jumped over. "Good boy, now sit."

Louie sat, his face plastered with a big shit-eating grin.

"Okay, watch us through the window, and we'll be there at the door and then right back." With his back to the church door, Oliver drew the .45, checked the mag, and holstered the gun.

Zoe made her way around the truck, and together they approached the door to the church.

"Well, here we go." Oliver made a fist and rapped on the wood now covering the busted-out glass.

A small wooden panel about the size of a Kleenex box slid open.

"Hello there, we're—"

The barrel of a shotgun jutted out towards Oliver's face.

CHAPTER 17
ATTACKING TEAM

BY THE TIME ZOE GASPED, Oliver had grabbed the barrel of the gun and yanked, ripping it through the opening in the door.

"Hey! You can't do that!" a voice shouted from the other side of the door.

Before Zoe could understand what was happening, Oliver grabbed her and pulled her off to the side.

Inside, there was a commotion, and someone was shouting for help. It sounded like a young boy.

"Oliver, what did you do?"

"Reacted."

She pushed herself back against the wall. "This is bad!"

"Yeah, no shit, but I thought... I thought he was going to shoot."

Another voice, this one older. "I don't know who the hell you are, but you just fucked up, pal!"

"I... I'm sorry," Oliver shouted.

"Sorry! You knock on our door then attack us and you're sorry?"

"I reacted! I saw the gun and thought you were going to shoot."

The voice lowered, and Zoe realized the man was talking to someone else. "Chad, dammit – what did I tell you? This is exactly why you don't go shoving your weapon out the slide. He could have shot you dead! You think that wooden table is going to stop a deer slug?"

"I'm sorry, Uncle Fred. I won't do it again."

"Damn right you won't. You've just shown me you aren't ready for this. Now go get your dad and the others. Tell them we got a problem."

"Yes, sir," Chad whined.

"Fred? Fred, listen, my name is Oliver, and I'm with my wife, Zoe, and we have a little girl in the truck. I promise we aren't here to cause trouble."

From inside, Zoe heard the distinct sound of a slide racking back and a round being chambered. "Yeah? Well, you got a funny way of showing it. Step in front of the door where I can see your eyes. You try anything and I'll shoot you dead where you stand. Do you understand me?"

"I won't try anything. Please, just don't shoot."

Zoe had an incredibly bad feeling about this. "Oliver, I don't know."

"It's alright, Zo," he reassured her. "I just want to talk to him." Holding the shotgun by the barrel he stepped in front of the door.

"The woman too!" the man ordered.

Oliver held up a hand, telling Zoe to stay put. "If I'm not infected, you can trust she isn't either or she'd be trying to kill me."

Damn him. He was doing it again. Putting himself in harm's way. Like him getting killed would somehow keep her safe. She stepped in front of the door.

In front of her, a man's hazel eyes filled the viewport. They were narrowed and skeptical as they studied her and Oliver's eyes.

"This belongs to you," Oliver said, slowly lifting the shotgun with the stock facing the door. He slid the stock into the viewport, and the man on the other side quickly snatched it back through.

"Well, good for you. You aren't infected. Now get your asses back in that truck and move on down the road before I change my mind."

Oliver stood there with hands up, trying to think what to say next.

The man's eyes narrowed. "If you're thinking about pulling that piece, you better think twice because you will not make it."

From beyond the door, another voice approached. "Fred, what's happened? Chad said someone snatched his gun!"

"I got this under control, Tommy."

"Is the guy out there now? Is he infected? Shoot his ass!"

"He isn't infected. And I'm not shooting unless he gives me a reason."

"He already gave you one when he snatched my boy's gun out of his hand."

"He gave it back and he's sorry."

"Sorry!" Tommy shouted. "He attacked my boy!"

"He didn't know he was a boy. And what the fuck was Chad doing sticking his gun out there anyway? I told you that kid had no business with a shotgun. You're ice fishing on two inches, Tommy! It ain't no good! Use your head and put yourself out there – someone sticks a gun in your face, what would you do? I know what I'd do, and you're damn lucky you still got a kid."

"You're unbelievable! The times we're living in, it's kill or be killed! You're worried about Chad, but you're going to be the one to get us all killed. One of us getting shot ain't enough for you? Jerry's all fucked up, might not make it, and you want to go being neighborly!"

"I got this under control – now shut your big fucking mouth!"

Oliver cleared his throat. "That garbage truck parked out back. That's my rig from when I was here a few days ago."

"What?" Fred asked.

"The garbage truck out back," Oliver repeated.

"What the hell's that got to do with the price of fish?" Tommy asked.

Zoe, hands still held up, muttered under her breath, "Oliver, what are you doing?"

"Look, I'm just saying, I was here a few days ago when all this started. I fought a bunch of the undead. I had to escape in the church bus."

"So what? You want your truck back? Hell, take it and leave," Fred said.

"No... no, I just... Look, we came back here hoping to find a safe place to hole up and maybe some food. I know the kitchen was well stocked."

Tommy scoffed. "This guy serious? Yeah, well, we don't need no trash man! We can take our own garbage out. And what food we found here is ours. Now, my brother has been way more accommodating than I'd like. You best get on, because I'm not asking again! I've served ten years on active duty and made three tours. I will shoot you and that pretty wife of yours and not think twice about it. If you want that truck back, assuming it's even yours, you're welcome to it. The keys are in the ignition, but it ain't going far with a blown radiator hose."

"Fred? Fred, what's happened?" a woman called from somewhere farther inside.

"Just stay back, dear. We got this under control."

"Whatever's happening, you need to hurry. Dad's awake. The bullet hole isn't bleeding very much, but he's moaning something awful! I don't know what to do!"

"Shit," Tommy cursed. "I'm coming. I got a bottle of Jack and some ibuprofen we found on that last run – might take the edge off."

Fred still had his eyes trained on them. "You folks see we've got our own problems to deal with. Now you take care." With that, the viewport slammed closed.

"Wait!" Zoe shouted. "Don't give him alcohol, especially if he's bleeding. That will only make it worse! Where was he hit? Did the bullet pass through, or is it still in him?"

The moment hung silent.

Oliver lowered his hands. "Dammit! I think they're gone. Come on, let's try the house."

Zoe turned to follow. Behind her, she heard the viewport slide open.

Fred's voice called through to them. "Hey! You talk like you know something about gunshot wounds."

Zoe turned back towards the door. She could hear Tommy's muffled voice next. "Fred, what the fuck are you doing?"

"Shut up, Tommy." The man's eyes flashed back to Zoe. "Well? Do you?"

"I'm a nurse practitioner." She wasn't really, not yet, but she didn't think these guys would be asking to see her license. "I also have a bunch of medical supplies in the truck."

"Zo," Oliver said, giving her a careful-what-you-tell-them look.

"Look," Zoe said, hooking a thumb back towards Oliver and the truck. "If you let us in and give us some food, I'll help your friend. I work in the Bloomridge Hospital emergency room. I have pain meds, bandages, and IVs in the truck."

Fred's eyes disappeared from the port, and Zoe could hear a conversation taking place behind the door, but she couldn't catch all the words. Then Tommy started shouting. "Fuck that guy! She and the kid can come in, but he stays outside!"

Zoe approached the door. "Hey! It doesn't work that way! You want my help, we all come in and we all get fed."

"Fred, I don't like this," Tommy warned.

"Look, I don't know how bad your friend's wound is or how much blood he's lost or if I can even save him. But I know this. Without medical treatment, he's probably going to die."

Oliver started for the truck. "Zo, let's go."

"Hold on, Oliver." She was so close to convincing them, and she wasn't ready to give up now.

Inside, she heard Fred say, "Medicine and treatment for Jerry for some food and shelter seems like a pretty good deal to me."

Tommy was adamant. "You're crazy if you let them in here."

"What then, Tommy? Are you going to go back and tell my wife we could have saved her dad but you were too pissed-off over some bullshit?"

"Zo! Get in the fucking truck, now!"

Zoe spun, ready to rip into Oliver. She had these guys. They were going to open the door! "What's your deal, Ol..." She froze, eyes wide.

Three undead, all teen girls in matching soccer uniforms, were sprinting towards them at full speed.

Oliver yanked open the driver's-side door.

"Oh god!" Zoe shouted. The girls were still halfway across the parking lot, but they were moving quick.

"What is it? What's happening?" Fred shouted from the viewport.

"They're coming!" was all she could get out.

Behind her, the door opened. Zoe turned back to see a grizzly bear of a man rush out the door. He looked like that character Hagrid from *Harry Potter*. Behind him, a smaller, clean-shaven man with a crew cut appeared; he was wearing fatigues and holding the shotgun Oliver had passed back through the viewport.

Zoe stopped and drew her pistol, taking up a shooter's stance.

"Jurnee, cover your ears!" Oliver shouted.

Zoe and the two men opened fire, dropping all three of the undead teens at thirty yards.

The barrel-chested man looked down at Zoe. "They probably heard those gunshots all the way in Groveland and Libbyton. They'll just keep coming! Come on, let's get you all inside."

By his voice, she knew that was Fred. So the guy in camo with a crew cut, currently sneering at Oliver like he wanted to kill him, must be Tommy. "You didn't draw your gun! Do you always just stand there and let your wife do the shooting?"

Zoe wanted to defend Oliver, but when he didn't answer, she thought maybe he didn't want them to know he was injured.

Fred was quick to speak up. "Knock it off, Tommy."

Tommy poked his tongue into the side of his cheek and spit

tobacco juice on the ground. "Yeah, whatever." He shook his head and went inside.

"He'll be alright. He just needs to get to know you. Come on, let's get your little girl inside." He glanced into the truck's cab. "Well, hold on now. Is that a pit bull? We never agreed to a dog."

Zoe froze. "Well, that's Louie, and he's part of our family. He's also immune to the parasite and saved my life more than once. We'll take our chances out there if we can't bring our dog."

Fred held up his hands. "Immune, huh. Is he friendly?"

Zoe nodded. "Of course. Unless he has a reason not to be."

"I think my Martha is going to like you." Fred looked around nervously. "Come on, we better hurry – we can't be out here with our asses flapping in the breeze."

Oliver opened the tailgate and lifted the bed cover. "Are you the pastor?"

"Me? Aw, hell no. But on occasion we attend this church. Truth is, no one's seen Pastor Tut or his wife, Sandi, and we don't expect we will anytime soon. They were away on vacation when all this went down."

Fred helped her grab the two large boxes containing medical supplies while Oliver helped Jurnee down out of the truck.

Zoe paused just before she entered. "Hey, uh, Fred?"

"Hmm?" he asked, turning back to her.

"You don't have a bunch of undead chained up in there you're planning on feeding us to, do you?"

Oliver shot her a look like she was crazy.

"Young lady, that's a pretty morbid question."

"Would you be surprised if I told you it wouldn't be the first time?"

"I would. But if for some ungodly reason I were about to do just that, I suppose I wouldn't tell you."

Zoe froze – half in the door, half out.

"For Pete's sake, I was joking." The man smiled through his thick beard, but when he caught Zoe's look, his smile slipped. He glanced at Oliver, his bushy brows knitting together like two caterpillars about to crawl away. "But clearly you weren't. Look, whatever happened, I'm sorry for that, but you're safe, and remember, it was you who knocked on our door. Now, I got a hurt friend and he needs your help. Besides, I want to hear about this parasite theory of yours."

"It's no theory. It's reality." Satisfied as she could be given the circumstances, Zoe crossed the threshold just behind Oliver and Jurnee.

The foyer was stacked with boxes and other supplies. She set her armload on a box next to the coat rack.

Across the way, a door stood open to a room labeled FELLOWSHIP HALL. Curious faces crowded the doorway, whispering to each other. In the middle of the group stood a young boy with crossed arms and teary eyes. Behind him, an even angrier Tommy stood with a hand on the boy's shoulder.

Under normal circumstances, meeting strangers didn't bother Zoe. It was her job. But normally the sick and injured came to her. This was different – she needed help from these people as much as they needed help from her. She slipped her hand into Oliver's, and he squeezed it reassuringly. Glancing up, she hoped to find the same reassurance in his eyes she'd found in his touch, but Oliver looked awful. In fact, she didn't think she'd ever seen him look so bad. He was pale and his eyes were dilated. They'd been so busy fighting for their lives that she'd forgotten he was badly injured.

Fred closed the door behind them and barred it with a length of four-by-four. He picked up one of the boxes of medical supplies. "Well then, let's get you introduced to everyone."

CHAPTER 18
HEY, YOU DON'T LOOK SO GOOD

ONCE AGAIN, Oliver marveled internally at just how quick-witted Zoe had been under stressful conditions. In hindsight, grabbing the gun and yanking it through the window might have been a mistake, but in truth he'd been scared shitless. Not just scared for himself, but for Zoe and Jurnee too. Grabbing the gun had been a reflex. He was actually pretty lucky the kid hadn't shot him.

Tommy was staring at him like he wanted to punch him in the face. That little shit kid of his was a spitting image of the guy and giving him the same look.

"Come on out here, everyone! Meet our new guests." Fred turned to Zoe. "Doctor...?"

"Just Zoe is fine." She smiled, turning her attention to the boxes of medical supplies. She squatted down and began consolidating what she'd need into one box.

A short and portly older woman rushed towards them. "You're a doctor?"

Zoe stood. "Well, not exactly, but I've nearly finished my nurse practitioner program."

The woman took Zoe's hand in hers. "I'm Martha. Fred is my

husband. Oh, we need you so badly! My father was shot in the leg and is in horrible pain."

"I understand. If it's okay, we'll save the rest of the introductions for later. Right now, let's get your dad some help. Can you take me to him, please?" Zoe knelt and picked up the box.

"Of course! Thank you, dear!" Martha said, leading Zoe and her armload of supplies into Fellowship Hall.

Three children ran from the doorway and surrounded Louie and Jurnee.

"Can we pet your dog, Mr. Oliver?" asked a young boy who looked to be a little older than Jurnee.

"If it's okay with your parents – his name is Louie."

A man in a sharp suit with a woman in an equally nice dress approached. The woman was very pretty and looked like she could have been Zoe's sister but much older – maybe by a decade, but Oliver couldn't be sure.

"Fred, what's happened?" the man in the suit asked. "We heard gunshots?"

Fred held up his hands. "It's alright, folks. We had to deal with a few of the sick, but the danger has passed."

Tommy broke his hateful stare at Oliver just long enough to offer his thoughts. "There must have been a few soccer practices going on in Libbyton the day this all went down. I swear those three make no less than ten soccer players we've had to deal with since coming to this place. That's gotta be the whole team."

"I see – well, hello," the sharply dressed man said, offering his hand to Oliver.

The act of gripping the man's hand in his own right hand sent a shock wave of pain through Oliver's back and chest. For a brief moment, he thought he might puke on the man's designer shoes. But the wave was just that and passed quickly, though he felt dizzy and didn't know how much longer he could stand.

"I'm Raymond, but you can call me Ray. This is my wife, Aneesa, and these are our kids – our youngest, Sean, he's five. Our daughter, Trinity—"

"She's seven going on twenty-five." Aneesa laughed, holding out her hand to shake Oliver's.

Trinity rolled her eyes. "Mom, can I pet Louie?"

"You know better than to interrupt, young lady. Now just hold on."

"Sorry, Mom."

Aneesa smiled apologetically and then nodded to the tallest of the three kids. "And this is Craig, our oldest."

The boy's hair was braided down in a cool zigzag of cornrows, and he was sporting a Colorado Buffaloes Sanders jersey. "I'm ten." The boy cautiously held out his hand towards Louie and then froze, unsure.

Oliver nodded. "It's okay. He loves kids. Just prepare to be licked."

"He's really big, but he's the nicest! Right, Louie?" Jurnee said, planting a big kiss on the side of his head.

Louie returned the gesture with a big lick down her cheek.

"Louie!" Jurnee laughed.

Aneesa laughed too. "Okay, for heaven's sake, pet the dog."

Louie was even more excited than the kids as he went to work licking while his nub of a tail wagged uncontrollably.

"Sorry, he's just so happy to see the kids."

Aneesa waved him off. "Honestly, they've been getting bored over the last couple days. Maybe this will entertain them for a little bit."

"How long have you folks been here?"

"We arrived – what, Ray – three days ago? We had been visiting friends in Bloomridge when everything happened. It's a long story, but things went really bad at our friend's place, and we had to make a break for it. We were trying to get home to River City, but blocked roads forced us into the country."

Ray nodded. "Then there was the gas situation, or lack thereof.

With no gas stations open, I was sure we wouldn't make it, and when we saw this church, well... I'm just grateful for this place and these good folks for taking us in."

A very pregnant young woman with striking blue hair pulled back in a ponytail appeared from behind the others. She was wearing yoga pants and cowboy boots and gave a shy wave. "Hi. I'm Melissa, and I'm here with my husband," she said worriedly. "Except he's not here right now. He's out foraging with the others."

The entire room started to spin. Oliver managed to stay upright, but this time he extended his left hand to shake Melissa's. "What do you mean, foraging?"

Fred nodded. "That's what we call it when we send others out to look for supplies. We've also sent a two-man team to recon north and another team to recon south."

Tommy looked the part of a soldier, but the burlier and hairier man, Fred, spoke and carried himself in a way that told Oliver he was military as well. The older man was confident and experienced, and it only took a few moments of seeing and hearing how the others reacted to Fred to understand he was clearly the group's leader.

Tommy jutted a finger towards Oliver. "Yeah, you see, around here, people have to pull their weight. For example, we don't stand there and do nothing when others are shooting zombies. You know, like you just did!"

Oliver tried to clear his throat. Fuck. He really was starting to hate this guy.

Aneesa frowned. "Hey, you don't look so good. Are you okay?"

All the adrenaline that had kept him going over the last couple hours had drained away, the tunnel closed in, and Oliver felt himself fall.

CHAPTER 19
A GODSEND

THE DINING HALL had been converted into a combination of storage and dining. It had probably been full of tables at one time but now only four round tables remained. They were pushed together and surrounded by chairs while the rest of the chairs had been stacked against one wall. As they crossed the large room, Zoe realized this wasn't their final destination. Martha was leading her to another door on the north side.

"That door in the back leads outside to the rear parking lot. The door over there leads directly into the kitchen. This door empties into a hall lined with classrooms." Martha pushed the door open. "We've converted the classrooms into sleeping spaces for the families staying here. My dad is this way."

Zoe followed, hugging the box of the supplies against her chest. "You all have managed to collect a lot of supplies. Have you managed to find any medical supplies?"

"Oh, yes, but only some basics. The men said they checked a Walgreens in Libbyton, but it had been ransacked. There was some stuff there, but nothing any of them recognized."

"What have you been giving your dad so far?"

"Just Tylenol, but it's barely taking the edge off."

She followed the woman across the hall to another closed door with a sign that read Classroom 1.

Martha opened the door. "Dad? It's me. I brought someone here to see you."

"Ugh. To see me? Who? What for?" the man croaked.

The room was dimly lit with the window completely covered. The only light was from a battery-operated LED lantern.

"We lost power two days back, but the boys had collected a whole bunch of flashlights, candles, and battery-powered lanterns while they were out. Let me turn this light up and bring it closer so you can see better."

Jerry was lying on his left side atop a church pew with a throw pillow beneath his head and a crochet blanket covering the rest of him, except his socked feet, which were sticking out the bottom. The man looked to be in his mid to late seventies. His hair was grey and disheveled, and he hadn't shaved in days.

"Hello, Jerry. My name is Zoe."

"What?" the man hollered, and it was then Zoe noticed the hearing aids and realized he was hearing impaired.

"She's a doctor, Dad!" Martha shouted.

"A doctor, you say?"

Zoe sat the box down on a small kid-sized desk. "Jerry, I'm Zoe," she said again, this time louder. "I'm here to look at your leg."

"Oh, well, I got a damn bullet in it!"

Zoe smiled at the man and lifted the blanket off of him. "You seem like a nice enough guy. May I ask, who in the heck would want to shoot you, Jerry?"

Jerry laughed.

"Well, go on and tell her what you did, Dad."

Jerry's smile turned to a cringe. "I sort of shot myself."

Zoe raised her eyebrows.

Martha waggled a finger. "Nothing 'sort of' about it. He shot himself. This fool insisted on riding along with the boys on a supply run. While Adam and Jesse were loading up, the sick attacked. Thankfully there were only a few, and the boys were able to deal with them. My lovely father decided to draw his pistol and help, but before he could get his gun out of the holster, he shot himself."

Jerry lay there pantsless with a bloodstained Ace bandage wrapped around his thigh and secured with silver duct tape. "Oh, alright, Matty! You've had your fun," he said, waving a hand at her. "Does it even matter how the bullet got in there? We just need to get the damn thing out."

"Well, maybe. Maybe not. I need to remove this bandage and have a look." Zoe retrieved scissors from the box and began to cut the bandage away. "What caliber was it, Jerry?"

"Ruger .22."

"Well, that's good. A smaller caliber should mean less damage. How bad did you bleed?"

"Oh, I don't know, it bled pretty good at first but not for long."

She nodded. "Good."

In Jerry's upper thigh was a small hole surrounded by bruising. The hole itself looked irritated and possibly infected. "The femoral artery runs just to the inside of where that hole is. If the bullet would have gone a couple inches closer towards your groin, you might not be here right now."

"Lucky shot," Jerry groaned.

"I'm assuming no exit wound?"

"Nope it's still in there, alright."

"Are you still standing to go to the bathroom?"

"Yeah, I can walk, it just hurts."

"Stand up for me." Zoe put her arm under Jerry's as he turned and lowered his feet to the floor. "One. Two. Three."

"Ohhh!" Jerry moaned.

"What does the pain feel like?"

"Ahhh. Like I got shot in the leg!"

"Any sharp or shooting pain down your leg?"

"No. It's just sore as all hellfire!"

"Obviously, I can't take an X-ray of your leg to see if it is broken, but I don't think it is. Let me help you sit."

Jerry plopped down on the bench. "What about the bullet? You gonna dig it out? Give me something for the pain first, would you?"

"I'm not going to dig the bullet out of your leg."

"What? But I thought... Well, you can't just leave it in there."

"Actually, I think that's exactly what we should do. There are plenty of people who live out the rest of their lives with a bullet still inside them."

"But... but won't I get lead poisoning?"

"No, that is highly unlikely. The more likely scenario is your body will build fibrous tissue around it as you heal."

Martha's face was a visage of concern. "Dear, are you sure it's okay to leave a bullet in there?"

"Truthfully, I would feel much more comfortable if I knew where the bullet had traveled to and what internal damage it might have done. But on the other hand, he hasn't lost that much blood, and I don't think his leg is broken. I know what you see on TV, but this isn't the Old West. Remember when I said how close the femoral artery is to that hole? With no way of knowing how far that bullet went and in what direction, it would be a really bad idea to go digging around in there."

Jerry frowned. "So we can't do anything?"

Zoe reached back into her box of supplies. "Now, I didn't say that. My more immediate concern is infection. I'm going to clean the wound out with an antimicrobial wound cleanser. It isn't going to feel good. After that, I'm going to assess. If it starts bleeding badly, I may need to pack the wound. If not, I'll get it covered with a fresh bandage. I have ibuprofen with me, and you have Tylenol. We can alternate between the two and see if that manages the pain. If not, I have something stronger, but if I give it to you, you'll be out of it. Also, I would really like to start you on an antibiotic, but I don't have any. I do have an idea where we can get some, though. Maybe the next time the guys make a run?"

Martha wrung her hands. "Of course. We'll talk to Fred as soon as we're finished here."

"Okay, Mr. Jerry," Zoe said with a smile. "Let's get you back on your side."

Zoe and Martha eased the man down onto his side, and she went to work.

Zoe cleaned the wound the best she could, seeing no visible sign of the bullet – but then she didn't expect to. Thankfully, it only bled a little. Next, she bandaged the wound and gave Jerry four ibuprofen. "I want you to try and stay off that leg for a few more days. Let's let the muscle and tissue heal before you start walking and flexing those damaged muscles."

"Stay off my leg? How am I supposed to go to the bathroom? It's all the way down the hall."

"The place I want to send the guys to look for antibiotics should have some crutches or a walker. If we can find you something like that you should be able to get around okay."

Jerry grumbled, reluctantly nodding his agreement.

Martha gave Zoe a hug. "Oh, you are a godsend."

CHAPTER 20

THE BEST PART OF WAKING UP

THE SUN SHONE yellow and warm as Oliver watched Sam bang a blue Rubbermaid onto the lip of the hopper and then lift it, shaking out its contents. It must have been a Wednesday because they were in the alleys, and Wednesdays were alley day.

She smiled her most mischievous smile. "Remember the time that dickwad on Deadwood Lane filled the bottom of his can with melted lead so it wouldn't blow away?"

"I remember!" Oliver laughed, happy to see his best friend. But his smile slipped when he glanced at the sky and noticed a fat crimson cloud had blotted out the sun like a splash of blood over an otherwise perfect canvas of blue.

"That asshole's can must have weighed fifty pounds empty." Sam laughed and then coughed and choked something up. She spit a bloody glob into the hopper.

Something wasn't right. This wasn't right.

"You remember, Ollie? I got pissed and crushed the shit outta the guy's can with the hopper blade." Sam laughed again, but the laugh was all wrong and wet. She cleared her throat. "When I got done with it, the metal can looked more like a shiny manhole cover than a garbage can! I set it right back in its place. Ha-ha! We taught that prick."

Oliver looked down and realized he was holding a garbage can too, but his was red. The garbage in the hopper was red. The sky was red. He glanced over at Sam – she was still laughing, laughing so hard she was crying. Red tears leaked from her eyes.

"Remember when the guy called in to complain? You had my back all the way. You told base you'd forgotten the can was in the hopper and accidentally ran it through. You wouldn't even let me pay you back for the cost of the prick's can when they deducted it from your paycheck."

Oliver lifted his can, but when he dumped the Rubbermaid's contents into the hopper, maggots poured out. They covered the wad of Sam's bloody spit. This wasn't right. None of this was right! The maggots changed, growing larger right before his eyes. Tentacles burst from the vile creatures, flailing wildly as mouths opened from one end of their bodies to the other.

Sam wasn't laughing now. "Why didn't you have my back when the rain came?"

"What? But I did! I tried!"

"No! You let me go back for the doll. You, Oliver McCallister!" Sam pointed an accusing finger, leveling it at Oliver's face. "Why didn't you have my back when I was so hungry? Why? WHY?"

"Sam! Please, I... I'm sorry!" Oliver shouted. He tried to turn back to face her, but her arms wrapped around him from behind.

"You didn't have my back, but I'll have yours! I'll have yours."

He tried to throw her off his back, but he couldn't shake her. She bit down, tearing a whole hunk of skin and muscle from his back.

He dropped the can and spun around to face her.

Sam was chewing a mouthful of his flesh. The side of her head was smashed in and her whole head was cocked wrongly to one side. Blood spilled from her head wound, running into her mouth only to spill back out as she chewed. Sam shouted at him through a full mouth, spitting bits of flesh as she spoke. "You did this to me, Oliver! My best friend, and look at what you've done!"

Above them, the sky opened up, and rust-colored rain fell in heavy sheets.

Sam pushed him backwards.

"No, Sam – don't!" Oliver felt himself tip back over the lip of the hopper, felt himself slip down the shiny wet metal and into the hungry parasites. "Sam! No! Please!"

He woke up with a jolt, his arms flailing. Hot pain shot through his back.

"Oliver, it's alright!"

"Sam! I'm... I'm sorry!" he shouted. Gasping in ragged breaths, he felt a light touch on his chest. A hand, warm and gentle.

"Oliver, you're okay! It's me! It's Zoe. You're safe."

The room was dark, lit only by a single candle. "Where? Where am I?"

"We're at the church. This was one of the classrooms. This is our room. Fred assigned it to us."

It was all coming back to him. "Right. The burly guy." He swallowed and tried to blink away the fuzz.

"You were having a nightmare."

"Yeah, that was fucking horrible."

"Want a drink?" Zoe asked.

"Thanks." He nodded, realizing he was lying on a church pew, but he had no memory of lying down. He swung his feet off the bench and started to push himself up.

"Hey, go slow – you already took a nasty fall. Luckily, Ray was standing close enough to break your fall or you might have busted your head open."

As he righted himself, the world around him steadied and he felt okay. "Ray? Right, I remember. He and his wife were introducing themselves, and then that asshole Tommy was talking shit. Did he hit me?"

Zoe laughed. "No. No one hit you. You fainted."

He raised his eyebrows, rubbed his knuckles into his eyes, and stretched. "Oh, well, shit. How long have I been out?"

"Since yesterday."

Oliver blinked. "What? Yesterday?"

She handed him a glass of water. "Hey, you needed the rest."

"What about you?" he asked, pulling a sip and sloshing it around in his mouth.

"I've been busy taking inventory of the supplies and setting up an exam room. Did you meet Melissa?"

"Melissa? No, I don't think so."

"She's nineteen and very pregnant. Her boyfriend is Adam. You wouldn't have met him because he was out on a supply run when we got here. She only has two weeks before she's at full term."

He suspected he knew where this was going. "What about the guy who got shot?"

"You mean Jerry, the guy who shot himself? He's Martha's dad."

"Shot himself?"

She told him the story. "Honestly, with what we've been through, we're lucky the same thing hasn't happened to one of us."

"How many people are staying here?"

"Well, let's see," she said, ticking off fingers as she went. "You have Fred and Martha and Fred's brother, Tommy, plus his kid, Chad. Then there's Ray and Aneesa and their three kids. Then there's the two carpenters, Scott and Chris. They're the guys who secured this place. Scott's a short white guy, older and balding, maybe in his fifties – he's always telling funny jokes – and Chris is a younger guy, really shy. He's – oh, what do you call it – Scott's protégé?"

"You mean apprentice?"

"Yeah," she said, laughing. "You'll know him when you see him. He's much younger, Black with long dreads, and really tall and thin, like six-six."

"You realize you just described Snoop Dogg?"

"Yeah, kinda. Snoop in his twenties maybe. Okay, then there's the pregnant couple, Melissa and Adam, and Adam's buddy, Jesse, who always smells like pot. Jesse's a sweetheart, but at some point his supply is going to run out, and I worry he may struggle."

"Does he look like Snoop Dogg too?"

"Nope, more like Ed Sheeran."

"Right, one looks like Snoop and one smokes like Snoop but looks like Ed – got it."

"Right," she said, chortling. "Oh, and finally, there's this kid Aaron. I don't know much about him except that he's a sweet kid. Really shy, though. I think he might be on the autism spectrum. He looks like he's only fifteen or sixteen. I asked how he was connected to this place. Turns out he isn't. He was sitting by himself outside when Fred and Martha got here. Anyway, that's sixteen, plus the three of us, and Louie makes twenty. When Melissa has her baby, that'll make twenty-one."

"Speaking of Jurnee and Louie, where are they?"

"They're playing with the other kids. Tag or hide-and-seek. I don't know who's having more fun, Louie or the kids."

"You're just letting them run around on their own?"

"Yeah, Oliver, this place is the most safe I've felt since this whole thing started. Scott and Chris have the doors and windows buttoned tight. No zombies are getting in here. Besides, someone is always on watch duty. They take turns and work in shifts."

"Makes sense." He vaguely remembered the short carpenter and his much taller apprentice. He grinned. "Did you say zombies? You're calling them zombies now?"

"Look, I admit I was in denial, but after we escaped from the house, I came to the conclusion that, medically speaking, they are in fact the definition of a zombie."

"It's fine. You were wrong, I was right. I got it. We don't need to dwell on it."

She narrowed her eyes at him and shook her head. "Whatever! Oh, hey, despite what you put your body through yesterday, my stitch work looks really good. You just need to take it easy for a few days. How is your foot doing?"

"My foot? Oh, I had forgotten all about it. Don't feel any pain at all sitting here, but my back is still sore as heck."

"I bet it is." A bottle rattled, and Oliver noticed her dump something into her hand. "Now hold out your hand."

Oliver did as he was told. "Sure thing, Doc."

Zoe dropped four pills in his palm. "You're a smart ass, you know that? Take those but eat first so you don't burn a hole in your stomach. You got to be starving."

He was in fact starving. He didn't know what time of day it was, but he knew he hadn't eaten anything the day before. "What am I having for breakfast?"

"Well, breakfast was four hours ago, but here's an energy bar to hold you over." Zoe tore open the packaging and placed the bar in his hand. "Then maybe you can join everyone in the hall for lunch."

"I wonder if it is even possible to get coffee here?"

"Possible?" She gave him the biggest smile he'd seen from her in days. "They keep two pots going all day long."

Oliver grinned. "Well, that's something." He took a bite of the energy bar. It wasn't very good, but he was so hungry he didn't care. "How are they treating you here?"

"They're treating us great, Oliver, and for the first time since all this started, I feel like I have a purpose other than surviving. Later today, they're making a supply run to Sunny Acres. I still remember the combo to the med room, but they're going to try and grab both med carts and bring them back here too. They'll probably be locked too, but Scott will be able to break into those."

He was glad to hear Zoe was feeling good about this place, and he was getting the feeling she wanted to stay here. They hadn't discussed it, but he knew his wife and knew she wouldn't be happy unless she was helping others. Yet part of him was feeling unsettled. This was supposed to be a stop for food on their way to the mansion down the road.

"Hey babe, one more thing," she said in that voice that told him he wasn't going to like whatever it was she had to tell him.

"What is it?"

"Try to get along with Tommy, okay?"

"Why would you have to tell me to get along? The guy was a dick."

"Well, if someone rushed the door and yanked a gun out of your kid's hand, you'd be upset too, right?"

"My kid wouldn't be shoving a shotgun barrel out a peephole into someone's face. I thought I was about to get shot."

"I'm just asking you to try and make amends since we're all living under one roof. I mean, put yourself in his shoes."

"Zoe, the plan wasn't to stay here." Oliver stood up from the bench and stretched. It took him a second to straighten completely. His whole body felt stiff, especially his upper back.

"I know it wasn't, but plans change. Who says there's anything better down the road? Don't you think we'll be safer in a group rather than on our own?"

God, he hated it when she used logic and sound judgment. Couple that with the fact she looked absolutely stunning – even now, with her braids pulled up in a twisted mess, clearly exhausted and stressed, she was hard to resist. And besides, all he had was a feeling. If being here made her feel safe and gave her purpose in this crisis, he owed it to her to try.

"Hey, where are you going?" she asked.

He was going to go find a cup of coffee, but now, looking at her, he figured coffee could wait. "Nowhere." He leaned in and kissed her. Then easing himself back down onto the pew, he let his hands slide down her shoulders and onto her hips.

"Ollie, what are you up to?"

"Well, Jurnee and Louie are occupied. So, I was hoping to be up to no good." He pulled her hips gently towards him. This was literally the first moment of safety and solitude they had shared in almost a week. Also, the first opportunity for make-up sex since he'd come clean and told the truth about his after-hours side hustle repoing for Georgie.

Zoe narrowed her eyes. "You think so, huh? Well, we're in a church, Oliver."

He unbuttoned her jeans and pulled them down off her hips. "I think god has other things to worry about."

Zoe pulled her foot free of her jeans and placed a knee on the pew, her own hands finding his zipper.

Oliver arched up, ignoring the pain as he pushed his jeans and underwear down and kicked them away.

Pressing her lips into his, Zoe swung her other leg over him and pushed him back against the pew. Their tongues tangled, and he felt her hands sliding through his hair. His own hands found her hips again as he guided her onto him.

They made love, both doing their best to stay as quiet as possible despite the door being closed. He needed this connection to his wife... they needed this.

After, she sat atop him, her head on his shoulder and his arms wrapped around her. At some point their shirts had come off and now with her bare chest against his, he could feel her heart pounding.

"I love you, Zo," he whispered, still trying to catch his breath. "With every ounce of my soul. I love you."

She lifted her head and looked him in the eyes. "You know what? I already know that."

He smiled. "Well, just in case you had any doubt."

"I'll never doubt that, Oliver McCallister. And I hope you know I feel the same. A million times the same."

"Only a million?"

She slapped his shoulder.

He winced.

"Shit! I'm sorry! Did it hurt?"

Oliver laughed. "It's fine."

"Hey?"

"Yeah?"

"How did making love to me feel?"

Oliver immediately recognized this was an important question.

She wasn't looking for him to say, "Oh, it felt great." This was deeper, more significant. He felt a wave of anxiety ripple through him. He didn't want to get this wrong. *Think! Dammit! How did it feel?*

"Ollie?"

"Yeah, sorry just thinking. Well, it felt honest."

"Honest? Meaning other times it felt fake?" Zoe narrowed her eyes, staring at him intently, her vulnerability evident in her expression.

"No, I... I mean I didn't have to feel like I was keeping something from you. I was fully there in the moment, you know? And because of that, I felt like we were connected in every way."

Her eyes softened.

In the moment and with little thought, he decided to take a chance on asking his own question, hoping it wouldn't spoil the moment. "Hey, do you forgive me for lying to you about repoing?"

Zoe didn't answer right away – she just stared into his eyes as if searching his soul.

Fucking stupid to ask that now, he scolded himself. Why couldn't he just leave it alone? When she was ready to forgive him, she would tell him, right? But he hated that it was still there in the back of his mind, this awful elephant in the room. They were already going through this horrible thing, and he didn't want this—

"You know what?" she asked, quietly interrupting his self-deprecating thoughts.

"What?"

"For me, making love to you felt like it used to before you decided to keep a secret from me. It's the way I want it to always feel. You said honest, and honestly, I think that was the perfect answer." She put her hand on his scruffy cheek. "I forgave you days ago. After you blew up our house and nearly got yourself killed doing it."

"Really? Well, you could have told me that."

She smiled a rare smile. Rare because this was her ornery smile and also his favorite. This was the smile he'd fallen in love with all those years ago. "I could have, but it was so much more fun watching you squirm – besides, you deserved it."

He grinned back at her. She was right, he had deserved it. "Actually, I wasn't trying to blow myself up, you know."

"Right… just our house."

"No, just the thirty or so zombies occupying it."

"Well, I didn't want to clean up after all those guests anyway, so problem solved. Besides, we're here now, and until something changes and we get word on what's going on in the rest of the country, we should stay here. They make supply runs, I can get things I need for research, and at the same time I can help take care of the others."

"And how do I fit into this?"

Zoe climbed off of him and began to dress. "Well, I think you should give yourself a few days to rest and heal. Get to know everyone. I've only just met them. I'm still trying to get their names straight."

"And then what?"

"Then you can pitch in. I don't think there's a shortage of things to do around here." She passed him his jeans.

"Right. And the first thing I'll get to know is my way to the coffeepot."

CHAPTER 21
THE CREEP

A WEEK into staying at the church, Zoe found herself standing in her makeshift lab, staring into the large mason jar of liquid containing the parasite Minnie had removed from her daughter's neck. Zoe had found the jar in a kitchen cabinet of all places and decided to pack it in the truck with the other supplies to study later. On the table in front of her was a book titled *The Parasite Field Guide*. It wasn't a medical journal and didn't offer much on medical treatment of parasites, but it was the only thing on the subject Tommy could find in the Groveland Library. Even though this wouldn't have been her first choice of subjects to study, she was learning a lot. She turned from a page on the zombie wasp to a new chapter on worms.

"Doc?" a voice called from the doorway.

Zoe turned to find Tommy, fresh back from a supply run and holding a lighting rig in his arms as he entered the room. "Still staring into that creepy-ass jar?" he asked.

Zoe nodded. "Yeah." But in truth she found it less creepy and more fascinating. Despite knowing that her resources were limited, something inside her drove her to want to learn all she could. "You can just set that down on the table here."

"Hey, I see you're reading the parasite book I found. Is it helping?" Tommy asked as he went to work setting up the light.

"Yes, I'm learning a lot. Thanks again. Turns out the world of parasites is incredibly vast and complex."

"Right," Tommy said, glancing back at the jar. "Would you call those tentacles?"

"They appear to be. But I'm not sure of their purpose."

Tommy leaned in close, peering into the jar. "This thing. It attaches itself to the back of the neck. Then those tentacle things creep all the way into your brain."

"Makes sense. I didn't remove this one, so I can't say exactly how or where, but it seems to me like it attaches to the brain stem and then, yes, perhaps those tentacles find their way into other parts of the brain. I was told that when it was removed, the host and the specimen died."

Tommy drew back from the jar and stepped closer to Zoe, eyes still on the jar. "No. I wasn't asking. I think that's what it does."

Zoe nodded. "Yeah, I mean it's controlling the dead somehow," she said, wishing she could remove one herself. She still had so many questions. What drew these things to humans? What was exclusive to human brains that the zombie parasites were drawn to? As far as Zoe knew, the chemical compounds present in a human brain – such as serotonin, dopamine, and acetylcholine – were present in other mammals as well.

So then what? Well, humans had a more complex neural network than animals, giving them higher cognitive abilities. And wouldn't higher cognitive abilities make humans the perfect host? Perhaps the complexity of human thought processes, emotions, or consciousness produced a distinct energy signature that attracts the zombie parasites. Maybe what the infected were "smelling" was the energy signature of the human brain itself.

Okay, but why eat the brains? What were they doing with the brain matter? It had to be more than simply digesting it. Besides, a dead human couldn't digest anything. So then what? She knew too that they ate more than just the brains, though brains seemed to be the primary target. She was way out of her depth, but she couldn't help wanting to understand how this damn thing worked. Real research needed to be performed, and she hoped like hell there were scientists hidden away somewhere trying to figure this out. Right now, all she had were her theories.

Tommy's shoulder brushed hers, pulling her from her thoughts.

"Earth to Zoe. Did you hear anything I said?"

"Sorry. Uh, yes."

Tommy laughed. "Um, no you didn't. That's okay. Look, these lights are battery powered. I was able to get you a few extra batteries, but once they go dead, there'll be no way to recharge them until we can talk Fred into letting us fire up the generator."

"Thank you. I'll keep that in mind." She took a tentative step to the side, trying not to be obvious, but she didn't like him touching her.

"You flip this switch here. This way for low and this way for high." Tommy stepped close to her again, reaching around her to demonstrate the switch operation. His lips were close to her ear. "So, where's your trash man?"

Zoe bristled. "Oliver is talking to Fred, but he'll be checking in any minute," she said, sliding to the side and turning to walk away.

Tommy grabbed her by the elbow. "Hey, I don't get what you see in that guy. You two just don't make sense."

His touch wasn't forceful, but it wasn't welcome either. She jerked her arm away and moved to the other side of the table. "And where is your wife, Tommy?"

"Karen? Oh, we live in Libbyton, but she works in a heavily populated area in River City. Chad had just left for school when the announcement came over the radio. I knew the bus route and managed to pull him off the bus before the rain started. It was a close call, but it all happened so fast. After that, there was no way I was going to risk trying to get into River City. Not with all that rain and the world around us going crazy." Tommy started to make his way around the table.

Zoe clicked the switch, and the LED work light swelled to a bright glow, illuminating the room. She didn't need the light right now, but she did not like being alone in a dim room with Tommy. "Have you gone to look for her yet?"

"No," he said, shaking his head sadly. "I wanted to, but I don't see the point. Especially after hearing the reports back from our scouts. Half the city burned, and the other half is overrun by zombies. I'm sure Karen is either dead or... well, undead."

Zoe pretended to fidget with the light position, wishing he would just go away.

But Tommy wasn't going away, and now he was back on her side of the table. He placed his hand on top of hers.

She yanked her hand away as if she had just noticed a spider crawling on it. There was no mistaking it now. This creepy bastard was coming on to her.

Tommy shook his head in disappointment. "Hey, you don't have to be afraid of me. I'm the last guy you should be worried about. In times like these, you need a real man, a man that can protect you."

That's it. She'd had enough of this shit. She spun on him. "A real man? Tommy, do you know the difference between you and Oliver?"

He started to open his mouth, probably to make some smart-ass comment, but she cut him off. "Oliver would have come back for me no matter how dangerous. No matter what the odds. You left your wife out there alone."

Tommy's demeanor changed like a switch being flipped. "You think it was that easy for me? I have a kid to protect. What happens if I go into River City looking for my wife and get myself killed? What about Chad?"

Zoe could respect that logic. She had to. After all, it was the same thing she'd lectured Oliver about back at the farmhouse. But there was one big difference. "But now your kid is here with people who can take care of him if something happens to you. How can you stand not knowing? Your wife might be out there hoping and praying her husband will come get her... come save her."

Clearly, Tommy thought this was going to go a different way. "What? Look, I already told you. There's no point. Karen is gone."

"But you don't know that. So instead of looking for your wife, you're here alone with a married woman you barely know trying to come on to her – trying to tell her how strong you are, how you can protect her, when you didn't even try to find your own wife."

Tommy's face flushed with anger, and he started to open his mouth, but she wasn't finished.

"One thing I know about my husband is that he would come for me – did come for me. And you're right, he's not a trained military man like you, but he loves me and would go to the ends of the earth to find me and make sure I was safe."

Tommy's reddened face drew up in anger, and he stepped towards her again. "You think I wouldn't have gone back for her if there was any chance she was alive?"

Tommy was a big guy, muscular and lean, and for a second she thought he might actually hurt her, but despite her sudden fear she stood her ground. "What I think is that you should leave before Oliver gets back."

Tommy's anger faded and he smiled. "You got me all wrong. I just want you to know you're safe as long as I'm here to protect you."

"I swear if you don't leave... I'll tell him you tried to—"

"Tried to what? I don't know what you're talking about. I just came to bring you a light. But instead of being grateful, you make these wild accusations. You go ahead and tell whoever you want, and we'll see who ends up on the outside."

"Just go, please."

"Sure. I'll go. But soon enough you'll see that I'm right. The only ones who are going to survive this world are the ones who're trained to survive and kill. Well, those and the ones they choose to protect. So ask yourself what that means for you and that husband of yours." Tommy turned and started for the door.

Zoe opened her mouth to shout something, to ask if that was supposed to be a threat, but Tommy turned around and started towards her again. The worst things flashed through her mind. He was going to do something! He was going to hurt her. She started to backpedal.

"Oh, I almost forgot. I brought you something else. Something I thought you might appreciate." He reached into his cargo pocket, producing a gallon-sized zip-top bag folded in half, containing something opaque and smeared with blood.

She let out a breath and inhaled, allowing herself to breathe again, curiosity replacing her fear. "What the hell is that?"

"I hear you complaining all the time about needing more samples. Well, it just so happens I came across a zed standing on the front lawn of a house I was coming out of. I was just about to smoke the fucker when I realized there was something strange about it." Tommy dropped the bag onto Zoe's worktable.

"Strange how?" she asked, moving to the other side of the table to create distance between her and Tommy as she pulled on rubber gloves.

"Strange that it didn't attack me. For that matter, it didn't even seem to notice me. But its face was all contorted and twisted up, and its arms were stretched out to the sides. The damn thing was shaking like it was having a seizure standing up. It started making this horrible screech. And it just went on and on, never pausing to take a breath. I mean not that the undead would breathe, I guess. Anyway, suddenly, I heard two more zeds at my one o'clock. They came running from across the street. I thought they were coming for me, but they ran to the one making all the noise."

Despite the fact that Tommy disgusted her and less than one minute ago she wanted nothing more than for him to get away from her, she now hung on his every word. "What did they do?"

"Do? I don't know. The one doing that crazy screaming wrapped its arms around the others, like it was hugging them."

"Hugging them?"

"Yeah, I know, right? But about that time, I noticed another zed at about my five o'clock appear from around the corner of a house in a dead run. Whatever this thing was doing, it was somehow drawing others to it." Tommy smiled a dark smile. "I can't say why because I shot the two fuckers from across the street in the face. Then I shot the one crossing the yard before he made it to the screecher. When I turned my attention back to that thing, I swear it was looking right at me and it was pissed. I pulled the trigger. Four dead. Well, dead again. I looked around and didn't see any more so, assuming you might want to take a look, I cut this out of the back of the screecher's neck. Earlier when I said they attach themselves to the spine and those tentacles go into the brain – well, like I said, that wasn't a question."

Zoe's mind reeled. "Was it attached to the spine? Where did the tentacles go exactly? Could you tell?"

"Look, I wasn't trying to analyze the fucking thing, that's your job. In the moment I thought about you and thought you might appreciate it is all." Tommy's face flushed, which seemed to irritate him. "You're lucky I was willing to cut open the back of a zed's neck and pull out whatever the hell that thing is. I was exposed and I was in a hurry. I pulled, and those damn tentacles slipped out like wet noodles."

Zoe tried to puzzle out what all this meant. "But what was it doing?"

"Beats the shit out of me. Like I said, that's your job to figure out, Doc. And before you ask, don't worry, I'm okay. I had gloves on. Oh, and by the way, you're welcome." Tommy spun on his heel and exited the room.

Part of her wanted to ask Tommy more questions, but the bigger part of her was just glad he was gone.

Even before she opened the bag, she could tell this one was bigger. Zoe used forceps to remove Tommy's specimen from the zip-top bag, placed it in a plastic tub, and rinsed it with a bottle of water. Then, laying it out on the table, she compared it to the one in the jar. This one must have been a full two inches longer, giving it a total length of six inches. The tentacles were longer too, maybe eight inches total. But it wasn't only that this specimen was bigger – it was different. Minnie's sample had opaque skin with raised lines that reminded Zoe of scars. The lines were evenly spaced across its back, a couple centimeters apart and perfectly straight. Tommy's specimen also had raised scar-like lines, but they were arranged in spirals.

Zoe couldn't be sure, but she didn't think a few extra days of growth would change the straight lines into spirals. And that wasn't the only difference. Tommy's sample had twelve tentacles. The one in the jar only had eight. She thought maybe when Minnie removed it from her daughter's neck, the tentacles had been torn off, but there was no sign where four more might have been attached. Its shape was oddly different too. Tommy's was thicker near the tail end, reminding Zoe of the leopard gecko she'd had when she was a young girl. Her pet gecko, Teddy, had this sort of fat, bulbous tail. However, the specimen in the jar tapered down evenly to a point.

Zoe rolled the parasite over and examined what she guessed was the mouth, which ran the length of the body. Using a pair of long tweezers, she opened the mouth, revealing row upon row of shark-like teeth. However, they were narrower than shark teeth, with tips that were needle sharp.

Unless in only a few extra days the parasite went from appearing like the one in the jar to literally changing its stripes and shape, growing four more tentacles, and nearly doubling in size, this was not the same organism.

CHAPTER 22
DUMB BABY

JURNEE SAT ON A CHURCH PEW, holding Princess on her lap, with Louie on one side of her and Trinity on the other. On the floor sat little Sean, the youngest of the kids by a whole year. He was pushing little cars around on the floor, making engine noises. She and Trinity watched the two oldest boys, Craig and Chad, punch each other in the arm to see who flinched first. She didn't get it, and she hoped no one punched her in the arm. She also didn't like Chad. He was really bossy and mean, and not just to her but to Trinity too. He said he hated girls, and he was always stealing her turn when they played board games.

Trinity was nice though. She was a year older than Jurnee. She wanted to be a ballerina, and she could really spin too. Except she didn't call it spinning, she called it... Well, Jurnee couldn't remember what she called it but it wasn't spinning. But it sure looked like spinning.

Jurnee didn't know what she wanted to be when she got older, but not a ballerina because spinning made her dizzy, and once when she was dizzy she walked right into a wall and hit her head. Maybe she would be a doctor like Zoe.

"Ouch!" Chad shouted, rubbing his arm.

"You flinched," Craig announced triumphantly.

"You cheated!" Chad said, his face flushing red. "You all saw! He's a rotten cheat."

"You better watch who you're calling a cheat," Craig said, stepping towards Chad.

"Uh-oh, Princess, Chad's getting mad. We better go." She slid down off the pew. "Come on, Trinity, let's find another game to play. Louie, you can come too."

Chad turned away from Craig, focusing his attention on Jurnee. "What did you call me?"

"I didn't call you anything!" Jurnee said, feeling like she might cry. She didn't like the way he was yelling at her or the way he was looking at her.

"You know, playing with dolls is for dumb babies!" Chad announced as he snatched Princess from Jurnee's hand.

Jurnee's eyes snapped wide. "Hey! Give her back! Give her back now!"

Chad held the doll high above her head and laughed. "Maybe I'll pull her arms off. I bet they pop right off like grasshopper legs!"

Jurnee started to cry. "You better not! You better give her back right now!" She didn't want them to see her cry, but she couldn't help it.

"Give it back, Chad!" Trinity shouted.

Louie stood up and barked in disapproval, his fur bristling as he faced Chad. His eyes, normally gentle and warm, were focused on the doll.

Jurnee jumped, trying to get Princess, but she couldn't reach, and it only made her cry more. He was going to hurt her. He was going to hurt Princess. "No!" she shouted.

Chad laughed harder, taking Princess by both arms.

"No! No!" Jurnee was shaking her head back and forth. She hated Chad, she hated him!

"You heard her, Chad. Give her the doll back," Craig said.

"Or what?" Chad sneered.

Craig made a fist. "Or this time I won't punch you in the arm."

Chad narrowed his eyes and stared at Craig for a long time.

All Jurnee could think was, *Chad's going to do it, he's going to pull Princess's arm off.* "Please give her back!" Jurnee wailed.

Craig walked closer to Chad and punched a fist into his palm.

Chad pushed Princess into Jurnee's arms. "Here! Take your stupid doll, dumb baby. And stop that crying before you get us all in trouble."

Craig put a hand on her shoulder. "I promise, Jurnee. He won't touch her again – will you, Chad?"

Chad crossed his arms. "Whatever."

Trinity hugged her. "It's okay, Jurnee – my brother won't let him hurt you. Hey! I know, let's play Twister! Have you ever played?"

Jurnee wiped her eyes on her shirt and shook her head.

"That's okay, we can teach you. It's easy! Right, Craig?"

"Sure, let's get it set up." Craig crossed the room to the shelves and returned with a big polka-dot mat.

"Twister?" Chad made a face. "I'm not playing Twister. Let's play hide-and-seek."

"No." Jurnee hugged Princess tight to her chest. "I'm not playing with you ever!"

Louie moved closer to her, pressing his side against hers, not taking his eyes off Chad.

Craig spread the Twister mat out on the floor and said, "I have an idea. Chad, how about you go hide, and we won't come look for you."

Jurnee clutched Princess tight to her chest with one hand and patted Louie on the head with the other. She wished Chad would go hide and never come back.

CHAPTER 23
CHANGE

ZOE FOUND OLIVER WITH FRED, Martha, and a few of the others in Fellowship Hall. After the weird run-in with Tommy and an hour spent comparing parasites, she wanted to get out of that room for a while, but more, she didn't want to be alone. She half expected Tommy might be there with Oliver and the others but was happy to see he was nowhere in sight. The small group sat around a radio listening intently to a voice that was naming states, one after another. "Alabama, Tennessee, Georgia, and Mississippi. That's it, folks. The only states we haven't heard from are Hawaii, Rhode Island, New Jersey, and Connecticut. Now I don't know about Hawaii, but it's safe to say those states on the East Coast are overrun and we just haven't heard from them yet. And with that, I can say with certainty that forty-nine of our fifty states are lost to this insanity."

"What's going on?" Zoe asked.

Oliver nodded towards Aaron. "Tommy found this shortwave radio on his last supply run and Aaron was able to get it working using a car battery. This kid is something else."

Aaron smiled nervously, not looking up from his current project – reassembling some sort of electronic device that, in its current deconstructed state, Zoe didn't recognize. His words came out as a quiet mumble. "Connecting the radio to the battery was quite straightforward. Of course, fixing the radio in the first place was more involved."

Ray and Aneesa were at the table too, along with Jerry, who sat sideways, one elbow leaning on the table, his wounded leg stretched out and propped up on another chair, a single crutch resting across his lap.

Zoe nodded towards the radio. "What's the host saying?"

Fred cleared his throat. "I'm afraid it isn't good. This guy is in Utah, just south of Provo, and calls himself Radio Mike. He has a setup that allows him to broadcast all over the country, Canada too. But even more importantly, others are communicating with him. Apparently, this thing isn't isolated to Illinois or even the Midwest. It's spread into every state he's heard from."

"Except Hawaii," Martha chimed in, sounding hopeful.

Fred shook his head sadly. "Sorry, dear, that isn't what he said. He said he hasn't heard from Hawaii, but that doesn't mean the same thing isn't happening there – in fact, I would guess not hearing anything is a bad sign."

"But we don't know for sure," Aneesa said.

Fred conceded. "Fair enough. We don't know for sure, but I wouldn't plan a trip to Hawaii on the chance it hasn't hit there. Not without more information."

Jerry pushed himself back in his chair, adjusting his leg. "Whether Hawaii is infected or not, I think we can assume help isn't coming. No time soon anyway."

Zoe forced a smile, pushing away thoughts of spending what could be months under the same roof with Tommy. She bent and gave Oliver a peck on the cheek.

"Hey, listen!" Ray pointed at the radio. "Someone's talking to Mike!"

"It... it doesn't make sense. We've been tracking eleven of the biggest asteroids ever discovered, and none of them pose a threat. The next one set to pass even remotely close to Earth is Apophis in 2029 and then again in 2036."

"Who's talking to Radio Mike?" Martha asked.

Fred shook his head and held up a hand for silence.

The sound of Radio Mike's palm slapping a table filled the airwaves. "Which supports my point – this could not have been an asteroid! Over."

"No. You're wrong. This wasn't our government!" the man said, sounding offended. "It came in through our blind spot. You see, only about three-quarters of the sky is captured by sky surveys. The asteroid was spotted by an amateur astronomer about three days before the event. Our NASA team had been tracking the anomaly since then. Over."

"You're telling me an asteroid, never before seen, magically appeared within three days of striking our planet? Why would the government wait until the last minute to tell us? How was this not all over the news? Over."

"Because until three hours before impact, it wasn't on a collision course with our planet. Over."

Silence filled the airwaves. Finally, Radio Mike said, "Dr. Willis, are you saying the asteroid changed course? Over."

A soft click preceded the scientist's somber voice. "I'm afraid that's precisely what I'm saying. Over."

"And how do you explain that? Over."

"If you asked me the day before, logic would have dictated the asteroid was struck by another, smaller asteroid, forcing it off course, but now... Now, I don't know. The odds of something striking the asteroid at the exact point when it was in its closest proximity to Earth is hard enough to believe, but combine that improbability with what's happened and, well, I just don't know anymore. Over."

"I'm here with Dr. Reggie Willis from NASA's Center for Near Earth Object Studies. And we're talking about the truth behind the asteroid. Doctor, I'd like talk about what NASA and our government are doing now, and what about the rest of the world? Over."

Silence.

"Doctor? Over."

Dr. Willis's voice was full of a sudden urgency. "I'm... I'm sorry, but I have to go."

"Doctor, please, wait. I have so many questions! Has anyone from NASA been in contact with the president? What's the status on a cure? What is NASA doing now? Over."

Dr. Willis laughed, but there was no humor in it. "NASA? There is no NASA. Not anymore. I... I'm sorry. I have to go. Something's happening."

"Doctor? Doctor, are you there? Doctor, if you are still listening, call me back. For everyone else out there... I guess we know more than we did, and on that note, I think it's time for a piss break. But never fear, fair listeners, I'll be back in five. Until then, stay safe and dry and beware of the sky. This is Radio Mike, signing off."

Around the table, the faces were crestfallen as everyone sat in stunned silence. The words *There is no NASA. Not anymore* echoed through Zoe's mind.

Fred was the first to break the quiet. "Well, so much for my theory the government was behind all this."

Jerry rubbed the back of his neck. "Sounds like an alien attack to me."

At that, chatter broke out amongst the group, everyone offering their own theories and counter theories. Zoe's mind reeled with questions of her own. Was Jerry right? Could this have been aliens? Some intentional attack on their world? It was all too much. First Tommy's creepy behavior and now this.

Oliver's brows furrowed. "Hey, is something wrong?" he asked her.

"Just been busy and needed to come up for air."

"You want some coffee or water?"

"A bottle of water would be great."

Oliver pushed his chair out from the table and reached into a cooler. "It isn't cold, but it's wet!" he said, smiling as he handed her a bottle. "Hey, are you sure you're okay?"

Zoe took the bottle, twisted the cap, and took a long pull. "I'm good." She shrugged off her backpack and set it down on the table. This pack had become her medical kit, and she was now used to carrying it wherever she went. This time, however, she had a surprise to show everyone.

From the pack, she removed the jar with the original parasite and set it on the table. Then she removed a clear plastic candy container with Tommy's specimen inside and set it next to the jar.

"Okay. I recognize the one in the jar. But is that another one?" Martha asked.

"A second parasite?" Fred interjected, before Zoe could answer.

Oliver's face crinkled in confusion. "But I thought you only had one?"

"Tommy brought me another one," she said, tapping the plastic lid.

The whole group leaned in, peering into the two containers.

In one, the parasite filled the entire mason jar, with its tentacle-like appendages pooling into a pile at the bottom of the jar like a pile of worms. Its flesh was the color of nicotine-stained teeth. The other parasite filled over half of an old Costco M&M container, but it lay twisted, with the mouth side against the plastic, murder-sharp teeth showing.

"Is that a mouth?" Martha breathed, her face horror-stricken.

Zoe nodded. "Some form of one, yes."

"Then those sharp bony things are..."

"Teeth," Ray finished.

"They certainly appear to be, but I'm not so sure if they are meant for chewing. I think they're for attaching."

Aneesa's face drained of color as a shaky breath escaped her lips. "Attaching... attaching to what?"

"I don't know, maybe the brain stem. What I really need to do is remove one myself."

"You've got to be kidding. How would you propose to do that?" Fred asked.

Zoe had been thinking about the answer to just that question. "Well—"

"Well, we aren't bringing one in here!" Martha insisted.

Zoe nodded. "I understand the concern, but if it is true they die with the host, I would only be removing a dead one. At least I could learn where it attaches, and maybe I can even figure out where those tentacle things go."

Everyone began talking all at once.

Fred pushed his chair back and stood, holding up a hand for silence. "Hold on! Everyone, quiet now!"

The others fell silent and turned their attention to Fred.

Over the course of a week, Zoe had gotten to know Fred. He was the complete opposite of Tommy. Though they were brothers and both had served in the military, Fred was much older and much less full of himself. He had that leadership quality about him. From what she understood, he hadn't demanded to be in charge, nor was he voted in; he just was the de facto leader of the group, and everyone accepted it. She accepted it too. Fred was a good man. A good leader.

Fred asked, "Doc, would learning where and how these tentacle things attach impact our survival?"

"Well... I don't know. Maybe we'll learn a way to get them to release the host."

Fred pointed at the jar. "I see. But you already said the host died when this one was removed."

"I did, but I still don't know why. I mean, if the host is already an undead, that makes sense, but what about the ones who are infected but still alive? Maybe those are the ones we can save *if* we can find a way to remove this thing."

Martha's face lit up. "Oh, what about medication? You know like that pill they give people when they get tapeworms?"

Jerry took a sip from his cup of coffee. "Somehow, I don't think a tapeworm pill is going to fix this."

Martha's face fell.

Zoe held up her hands. "Well, not so fast. I've been thinking the same thing. In fact, for early infection, a drug to eradicate the parasite may be the ultimate fix. But even for known parasites, the effectiveness of a medication varies greatly, and there isn't one drug that targets all parasites. For some parasitic infections, there's still no treatment available. Even to begin to understand the effect of drugs, I would first need to have them and then need to test them on recently infected people. And if they didn't work, I'm not going to be able to create a new drug to test. That's far beyond my capability." Zoe could see the words hit home in the crestfallen faces around the table. "Our best bet is to let me remove one and see what we can learn."

Everyone looked to Fred, who in turn looked at her, seemingly contemplating. "Again, I'm going to ask you, Doc, what could you learn that will change the actions we need to take to survive?"

Zoe hesitated and then answered honestly, "I don't know. I guess it depends on what I learn."

"I see. I can also see the drive in you to figure this out. But our main priority has to be survival. I won't support bringing an undead or infected into this building, not even a truly dead one. The risk is too great, no matter the potential reward. Honestly, I'm not crazy about those samples being here, and I'd like to slap the shit out of my little brother for bringing another one in here without talking to me first."

"I'm sorry. I assure you I didn't ask him to."

"No. Don't be sorry. I'm sure you didn't. That's just Tommy." Fred let out a long sigh. "I'm sorry, Doc, but I'm afraid you'll just have to study those and learn what you can."

That wasn't what she wanted to hear, but it was also a logic she couldn't argue with. That didn't mean she was ready to give up either. She needed to rethink this. Once she could ensure safety, she could make her case. For now, she would study and learn what she could from what she had. "I understand your concern. I'll see what I can learn from these."

"Excuse me, dear. But why do they look so different?" Martha asked.

"Great question. I think we may be looking at a male and a female."

Jerry's already wrinkly face scrunched up like an old prune as he leaned in. "How can you tell?"

"Well, I can't. I might be completely wrong. They could also be different organisms of the same species. But based on my analysis of their exterior and what Tommy told me he saw out there, I have to believe they are in some way different and not just the same organism in different stages of life cycle."

All eyes leaned in, shifting between the jar and the container. Even Aaron stopped his work, seemingly fascinated by the two specimen parasites.

Fred cleared his throat. "There's also something else you should see. We noticed the oddity yesterday, but we think it started a few days back when Scott was on guard duty. He reported that around 2:00 a.m., he heard a loud screech from way off in the field. When it didn't stop, Scott woke me up. I tell you it's the creepiest thing I've ever heard, and it just went on and on. But we couldn't see the source, and then finally it just stopped." Fred moved towards the hallway and motioned for the others to follow.

Zoe's heart began to race. Based on Tommy's description of the zombie with the outstretched arms, she had the feeling she was about to be shown something incredible.

Oliver and the others pushed their chairs out from the table.

Jerry waved a hand. "You all go ahead. I've seen it. I'll stay here with the kid and rest this leg."

"This way," Fred said, as he led them towards the rear exit of Fellowship Hall.

Zoe whispered into Oliver's ear, "What's going on?"

Oliver took Zoe's hand in his. "I can't explain it. You need to see it."

A chain wound through the door bar and then through metal

eyebolts that had been added to the frame only to loop back through the door bar again. The chain was secured with what Zoe knew to be rock-climbing clips. Fred removed the clips from the chain and pushed open the back door. Tipping his head to the sky, then looking left and right, he stepped out into the rear parking lot, motioning the rest to follow. "Come on. The coast is clear."

Fall wind whipped across Zoe's face as she glanced around the parking lot, observing several cars, Ollie's garbage truck, and a clear sky. What was she supposed to see?

"Over there, in the field." Fred offered Zoe a pair of binoculars. "It's easier to see with these."

Zoe lifted the binoculars. She didn't see anything. Then she felt Fred's hand on the binoculars, gently guiding them. "Right about there. Do you see them?"

Far off in the field, a group of undead huddled as if they were crowding together to share warmth. But she knew better. "What the hell?"

Fred huffed, "What the hell is right. This morning, I watched several stragglers cross the field to join the mob. I can't tell what they're up to. It reminds me of a football team crowding around the QB to call the next play. You think they're plotting something?"

"No. Not plotting. Well, not in the sense we communicate, but I... I don't know."

Aneesa fidgeted with her bracelet nervously, her voice quivering as she spoke. "Not in the sense? What do you mean?"

"It's like I told you," Tommy said, appearing from the doorway. "There's a zombie in the middle of that pile. And that screech you heard was one zombie calling in all the others. I'd bet my life on it. Fred, you remember I told you I saw another group like that one gathering together in the Walmart parking lot in Libbyton? So that's three that we know of. There's the one that I broke up, Walmart, and now this!" Tommy pointed at the field. "We need to go on the attack before it's too late! Now, I've been thinking about this. I've got a sniper rifle and plenty of ammo. I could pick them off from here."

Fred crossed his arms over his barrel chest and shook his head. "Dammit, Tommy. I already told you that's a bad idea. Use your head. You shoot one and the other forty or fifty come running right at us."

"Shit, I could kill half of them before they got to the parking lot."

"We aren't fighting them just for the heck of it. Resources are limited and we need to save ammo for when we really need it. For the last time, we aren't attacking them just to do it."

Martha nodded in agreement. "Just this once, listen to your brother, Tommy. Firing a gun when we don't have to is a bad idea."

"Anyway," Fred said with apparent annoyance as he turned his attention back to Zoe, "I understand you don't know why they're gathering like that, but I was hoping you might have some theories."

Zoe studied the group of undead. It was strange that they would huddle up in the middle of a barren field. She thought back to what she'd learned in the *Parasite Field Guide*. Parasites could force their host to perform numerous activities. They could even get them to commit suicide in some instances. "I think—"

"For all we know," Tommy interrupted, "they're over there planning something. Some sort of collective attack. They're probably strategizing their advancement right now!"

"No," Zoe said with certainty. "They aren't strategizing some military attack."

Tommy shot her an incredulous look. "How can you be so sure?"

"I know they look like us, but remember, they're only the host. They're dead. It's the parasite controlling them. We need to think about this more on a subconscious level. Parasites don't plot and strategize. They operate with an instinctual response, guided by their genetic programming and evolutionary adaptations."

"What the hell does that even mean?" Tommy asked.

Zoe motioned to the field. "Look out there – I don't know why they're gathering. But one thing's for sure. They're evolving and, whatever this is, it must have something to do with the next stage of the parasite's life cycle."

They all stared into the field, soaking in the words, until finally Aneesa, eyebrows bunched in a combination of confusion and horror, asked, "Evolving? Evolving how?"

"I... I'm not a scientist, I'm studying to be a nurse practitioner. This is all very much out of my depth. But I'm sure of this. Something has clearly changed."

CHAPTER 24
HIVE

AROUND OLIVER, everyone was talking all at once.

Despite having already seen the mob of undead earlier, Oliver took his turn with the binoculars, watching as the mass of zombies pushed and swayed in a tangled mass, like a mosh pit at Ozzfest. It was like the undead were trying to push their way into the center of the group.

In the back of Oliver's mind, a tiny part of him had questioned if there had even been an asteroid. They were told an asteroid was coming by an announcement on the radio, followed by flashes in the sky, but no one had seen it. He wasn't much on conspiracy theories, but it had made him wonder. Not now, though. After Radio Mike had talked to the guy from NASA, he was convinced more than ever that whatever was happening wasn't from this world. "It's crazy to think this could all have started with an asteroid."

The chattering stopped.

When Oliver let the binoculars drop, all eyes were on him.

"Oliver, even after what we all just heard on the radio, are you saying you don't believe it was an asteroid?" Fred asked.

"No. Not at all. I mean I know we can't say with one hundred—"

Tommy laughed. "Oh great, another conspiracy theorist. Go on, trash man, what do you think it was? Let me guess, the government? You and my big brother ought to get along just fine. Two peas in a fucking pod!"

"No... that's not what I said." Oliver frowned, unsure how the conversation had spiraled out. "I just... Well, it's just crazy to think an asteroid created that."

Fred nodded. "Hell, up until that little conversation with Radio Mike, I thought it might be a terrorist group, or some global plan to control the population."

"Here we go!" Tommy said, throwing his hands in the air.

Ray nodded along. "I was right there with you, Fred. But I guess if that NASA guy is to be believed, it was an asteroid after all."

"What NASA guy?" Tommy asked.

"Long story. I'll fill you in later." Fred motioned to Oliver to pass the binoculars. "Still, whatever the source. I don't think this is random. Asteroids don't just turn on a dime at the last possible second."

Martha put her arm around Fred's waist. "I don't know about you, but I feel better knowing we didn't create this."

Fred squeezed Martha close to him. "Don't be so sure that's better, dear. If our government had created this, maybe it would be easier to figure out how to uncreate it. But now, we're truly dealing with the unknown."

Oliver exchanged looks with Zoe, noticing she was quietly chewing at her lower lip in nervous thought. Oliver knew the look. She wanted to say something and was building up the nerve. He nodded his encouragement to her.

Zoe took a breath and held up a hand. "Everyone, please. Look, I wasn't going to push this issue, but after seeing this, I feel it is even more important to perform as much research as possible. We need to understand what is happening now to understand what comes next."

Fred scratched at his beard. "You still think bringing an undead or infected in here is going to give you answers that are worth the risk?"

Tommy waved his arm in a broad stroke. "If I had a frag and I could get close enough, I could take out that whole hive with one swipe."

Fred pinched the bridge of his nose and sighed. "Tommy, you don't know what you're talking about, so how about you just stop talking."

"If Mom was still alive, she wouldn't stand for you talking to me like that."

"Well, Mom isn't alive, and for god's sake, you're thirty-five. Grow the hell up."

Tommy took a step closer to Fred. "How about you go straight to hell!"

Oliver was really trying not to hate this guy, but Tommy was the perfect combination of an egotistical asshole and a maximum douchebag.

Fred ignored his little brother, turning his attention back to Zoe. "I'm sorry, Doc, but the answer is still no. But here's what we can do. I want round-the-clock surveillance on this... this whatever the hell it is."

"Hive," Tommy snapped.

"Christ, Tommy, call it whatever you want. I don't care." Fred turned to face Zoe head on, his body language indicating he no longer wanted to talk to his little brother. "We have a viewing port in the door. We'll take turns and make this part of our standard surveillance."

Oliver could see Zoe's disappointment – hell, anyone paying attention could.

"Look at it this way," Fred went on, "if you were to walk around this building and stare out across the empty fields and down the road as far as the eye can see, you wouldn't see any other hordes gathering like this."

Zoe's brows furrowed. "Okay, but what does that have to do with research?"

"You have a gathering of undead right here in your own backyard."

"Hive," Tommy corrected.

Fred closed his eyes and took in a calming breath, choosing to somehow ignore his brother. "You said it yourself – something is happening. So, take advantage of the opportunity to study them from a distance. I suppose time will tell us what they're up to."

Oliver took Zoe's hand again and gave it a gentle squeeze.

"Okay," she conceded and nodded her agreement.

From across the soccer field, far to the left and much closer than the mass in the middle of the cornfield, a zombie turned in their direction.

Aneesa pointed. "Look at that man. I thought he was heading for the crowd in the field, but he turned towards us."

Fred lifted the binoculars to his eyes. "He's definitely coming this way."

Tommy took position at his brother's side, and Fred passed him the binoculars. Tommy scanned the field. "Oh yeah, he's on to us. Even with the hive we saw earlier at the Libbyton Walmart, there's still plenty of zeds that don't seem interested in grouping up, plenty that will still run you down. We had to do a smash-and-grab at the hardware store, and I mean they were coming."

"That raises the question of why some group up but not all," Zoe said.

The man on the soccer field tilted his head back, sniffing at the air. He started to run towards them.

Tommy pushed the binoculars at Fred and drew his side arm. "He smells us now! I'll pop him when he gets within range."

Fred placed a hand atop Tommy's pistol and pushed it down. "Don't. Gunfire might draw the others from the field. Alright. Back inside, everyone."

Back in Fellowship Hall, the group gathered around the tables, except for Ray and Aneesa, who headed off to the kitchen to begin preparations for dinner. Oliver had learned Ray was a chef after eating a meal of coq au vin the night before. Ray had explained that, traditionally, French peasant food didn't include young hens as those were saved for the wealthy. Instead, peasants often had to make do with old roosters. Hence the name coq au vin. Ray specialized in creating mouthwatering dishes from the less desirable cuts of meat – "garbage meats" like the old rooster the French used or scrap meats given to slaves during slave times. Ray explained the key to coq au vin was slow cooking it in wine to break down the old muscle tissue. As everyone complimented the amazing dish, Ray chuckled humbly and explained that since they had no old roosters, this really wasn't coq au vin. It was just chicken cooked in wine. Whatever it was, Ray could throw down, and Oliver was here for it.

It had been two weeks since the asteroid, with no end to the crisis in sight. Power was out but they had gas, food, and community. Other than that asshole Tommy, it wasn't so bad. Maybe Zoe was right after all. These were good people, they were safe, and Jurnee seemed happy having other kids to play with.

Louie bounded into the room and nuzzled Oliver's hand with his snout.

"You need to go out, boy?"

Louie whined.

"Alright." He pushed his chair back. "I think I'll take Louie out front and then go help Ray in the kitchen – maybe I can learn something."

Tommy pushed his chair back too. "Negative on helping Ray. You can play sous chef later. I think it's time you started pulling your weight around here."

"Ease up, Tommy – the man has been healing," Fred said, lifting his coffee mug and pulling a sip.

Tommy held up his hands. "Ease up? The guy seems alright to me. Look, Oliver, you want to sit around here, or do you want to get into the action? Jesse and Adam have been making supply runs and rotating for guard duty. Scott and Chris have been working maintenance and making this place as secure as possible, plus doubling down on guard duty. Ray and Aneesa have been cooking most of the meals. Martha and my loving brother here have been sorting supplies, planning, and helping keep watch. Even your old lady is doing her doctoring stuff. I get that you needed a few days for your back or whatever, but you've had them. It's time to get mobile."

"Hold on a second," Zoe interjected and Oliver could see she was pissed. "As the resident medical expert, I don't think a week is an adequate amount of time to heal a severe puncture wound. I only just took the stitches out this morning."

"Well, Oliver, what do you think? You tired of sitting around here sucking off the teat of the group?"

"Tommy!" Martha scolded.

"Kid, don't listen to my brother," said Fred. "You take the time you need. Supply runs are dangerous, and you need to be able to move and move quick."

"Which is the reason my big brother doesn't go. Bum knee and all."

"I was wounded serving our country, you ass."

Tommy held out his hands defensively. "Look, Oliver, it isn't that bad. We take the panel van and load up on beans, bullets, and Band-Aids. We're in and out. We'll do a short run to a gas station in Groveland to start with, and we're back in an hour to an hour and a half, tops."

Zoe was giving Oliver "the look." He was clearly supposed to decline.

"Even old Jerry went out with me before he shot himself in the leg."

Jerry nodded. "I did indeed. But tell the truth, Tommy. I stayed in or near the van. I didn't go inside. If you don't feel like you can hustle, better pass, son."

"Oliver, you need more time," Zoe insisted.

He actually felt pretty good. A little stiff, but it wasn't all that bad. And Zoe had him taking an antibiotic for almost a week now just to ensure there was no infection. Going on a supply run might do his mental health some good. For years, he'd been outside every day running the route. He'd even kept up with his after-work trail runs when he'd started working his side hustle for Georgie. It wasn't uncommon for Oliver to get off the route early, go on a five-mile run, then pull a repo job all before heading home for the night. Besides, Zoe had asked him to try and get along with Tommy, and this would give him some alone time with the guy.

"Yeah, I feel good. I mean, why not?"

Tommy smiled. "Hooah! Roger that!"

Zoe narrowed her eyes and set her water bottle down hard. "Oliver, can I talk to you for a minute?"

"Sure. Come with me while I take Louie out?"

As the two walked towards the front of Fellowship Hall, Tommy shouted after them. "I'll meet you back here in five. Don't let her crack that whip on you, Oliver."

As they ventured out into the foyer, they heard the kids laughing from the daycare room, which had been converted into a game room. The room was already kid friendly, and Carpenter Chris had done a great job making it even better, with storage for all of the board games, puzzles, and toys grabbed during supply runs. Like Fellowship Hall, the room had skylights, allowing the kids to see without the need for battery-powered lights.

As they walked past the door, little Sean shouted, "Right foot blue!"

Oliver peeked in to find Jurnee and some of the other kids locked in a heated game of Twister.

He chuckled, and they moved on to the front door, where Jesse stood guard. The young man wore jeans, a backwards ballcap, and a Glock on his hip. "What up, Doc?" Jesse asked. He looked half asleep, but he might have just been really high.

From what Oliver could tell, Jesse was a good kid. On the other hand, Jesse was standing guard and probably shouldn't be high when he was supposed to be ensuring the safety of the group. He was about to say something but thought better of it. He'd talk to him later. "If it's all clear, we'd like to take our dog outside," Oliver said.

Jesse peered out the viewport. "Clear skies and no undies that I can see."

"Undies?" Oliver asked.

"Undead – I call them undies for short." He beamed a bright smile, clearly proud of his original nickname. "I see you have your gun. That's a good deal. Just try and stay where I can see you, Mr. McCallister, and shout if you need me. I'll come running."

"Will do."

Jesse knelt and gave Louie a scratch behind the ear. "You like that, boy? Sure, you do!"

Zoe hesitated, looking around. "You're alone?"

Glancing up, Jesse said, "Yeah. Scott and Chris are busy on some project and Melissa isn't feeling good, so Adam's spending some time with her."

"Isn't feeling good? I better check in on her after we take Louie out."

Jesse stood back up, unlocked the door, and pushed it open.

Louie bolted out the door and ran across the parking lot to a patch of grass between the concrete lot and the road.

They stood under the porte cochere. Wind whipped from the west, blasting them in the face. Zoe crossed her arms over her chest. "Oliver, I don't want you to go with Tommy."

"What? It's okay, Zo. My back isn't that bad and my foot isn't even sore anymore." Oliver noticed her shivering and quickly removed his flannel and draped it over her shoulders.

"Hey, what about you? You're going to freeze out here."

He pulled the flannel around the front of her and rubbed her shoulders. "I'll be fine. Now, what's up? Why don't you want me to go? I know it's dangerous, but whether we're on our own or with a group, we all have to pull our weight. I can't sit around here and play it safe while others risk their lives every day to bring us supplies."

"No. It isn't that. I mean, I hate the idea of you going out there at all, but I understand."

"Then what is it?"

"I just don't want you to go with Tommy."

"But didn't you ask me to make nice with the guy? What better way to do that than to go on a supply run with him?"

"I know what I said, but I don't like him."

"Zo? I get it, the guy's a dick, but he's also a trained soldier, and you were right – if we're going to stay here, we all have to get along."

"Tell them you need more time."

"I don't get it. Is there something you aren't telling me?"

She nodded. "Yeah... Tommy is reckless, and I just don't trust him. I... I don't want you to go."

"Alright, but if I tell him no, we need to be ready to collect Jurnee and our things and leave. They aren't going to let us stay here if I don't start pulling my weight. If you're good with leaving here right now, then I am too."

"Fred wouldn't do that. They all said you didn't have to go if you weren't ready."

"I guarantee Tommy is going to have a fit, and if we do stay, he isn't going to let up. And I'm telling you now, I'm not dealing with it. He starts in, and I'll tell him to go fuck himself. After that, we're probably going to have to leave, so be ready."

"No... no, I don't want to leave. We can't. Melissa needs me, and this is best for Jurnee too."

Oliver turned in a slow circle, keeping an eye out. "If you want to stay here with these folks, I get it. And besides, you're right, they need you. I know you, Zo. You won't be happy if you aren't taking care of others. Thanks to you, Jerry is on the mend and Adam won't have to deliver a baby by himself. Not to mention you got me all fixed up." He grinned, but the smile seemed lost on Zoe. She looked like she might burst into tears. "Look, it's only an hour. I'm expected to start contributing. I need to go."

Louie ran past them and right up to the door, his nub of a tail wagging. A single bark echoed beneath the porte cochere demanding entrance.

Oliver motioned to the stocky pit bull. "Looks like someone's ready to get back to their game of Twister."

"Ollie, please be careful. Don't trust him, okay? He isn't your friend."

He would understand if Zoe were concerned about him going out there to face the undead. Hell, he would even understand if she were against him going for that very reason alone. But to be solely focused on Tommy seemed odd.

They started for the door. "Zoe, what's the deal? I know the guy's a dick, but I've worked with plenty of dicks in my time. What's going on?"

"Nothing. I know you have. The guy just gives me the creeps, okay?"

"Oooo...kay? I'll be careful."

CHAPTER 25
FAMILY FEUD

AS ZOE and Oliver approached the doorway to Fellowship Hall, she could hear a heated argument taking place between Fred and Tommy. She and Oliver paused, exchanging glances as Tommy's voice rose to a yell.

"I swear, you think you know everything! Well, you're wrong! And even if you're right, this place is so secure it could withstand a hundred of those things trying to get in. But I'm telling you, they won't bother!"

Fred shouted back, "You aren't telling me shit because you don't know shit!

Something banged. It sounded like a chair falling over. "I don't know shit?! You were in the military like fifteen years ago!"

"You know, Tommy, for some who was just dishonorably discharged, you sure have some nerve."

Oliver nodded towards the door. Zoe nodded back, and they both walked into Fellowship Hall.

"You know my case is going up in front of the DRB for review! I'm getting it overturned."

"Yeah? Well, I wouldn't hold my breath. Not after—" Fred stopped short, noticing them enter the room.

Fred and Tommy stood next to the tables, their faces only inches apart and beet red with anger. On the opposite side, Jerry still sat with his leg propped, appearing cool as a cucumber. Martha and Aaron were gone now, and it was just the three men remaining.

"What's wrong, guys?" Oliver asked.

Tommy glanced over, yanked a chair out, and threw himself down in it. "Don't worry about it. The grown-ups are talking."

Zoe opened her mouth to tell Tommy that if anyone was acting like a child it was him, but then she caught the look from Oliver – the look that told her to just leave it alone. So instead, she drew in a long, calming breath. One thing they'd always had was the ability to be the calm to each other's storm with a single, shared look.

Fred rolled his eyes, sat down across from Tommy, and crossed his arms. "It's alright, Oliver. My brother and I are having a spirited debate is all. As you might have noticed, it's getting colder each day. It's only mid-October now, but it's already dropped below freezing the last couple nights. By late October, we could see snow. The problem is that with no electricity, we have no heat."

"Except that isn't true!" Tommy interjected. "There's a massive Cat genny on the north side of the building. On our supply runs, we've been filling five-gallon gas cans and stockpiling them in barrels. We must have three or four hundred gallons stored out there by now, and I know where to get more!"

"So, what's the argument?" Zoe asked.

"My idiot brother wants to fire up the generator." Fred pointed at the exit door at the back of the hall. "But what happens when that mob of undead standing in the field hears a genny running? Or, for that matter, other undead that we can't see?"

"I only want to test it out! Make sure we can get it up and running! We can't wait until it's subzero only to find out it doesn't work!"

"I said no. Not until I know what is happening with that group of undead."

Tommy leaned forward. "You know what, Freddie? The only one

who made you in charge was you. But I'll tell you this. We can't live here through the winter without heat. Whether we test it today or ten days from now, we have to get that genny running. Now, while you've been sitting around playing General Know-It-All, I've been out there getting us the shit we need to survive, so maybe you ought to listen to what I have to say for once."

Fred sucked in a breath, and Zoe watched him swell with anger. She could have sworn the man grew three inches in that single breath. "That's right, Tommy, because that's your job... gopher. So why don't you make your point and then get your ass back out there. The bathrooms are low on toilet paper." Fred flipped a folded piece of paper across the table like he was dealing a playing card. "Here, Martha made you a list."

Tommy snatched up the list. "Fuck you, Fred. The point is this. I've been out there plenty, and never once has a zombie attacked our van unless we were in it. When we're in a store, they ignore the van and come for us. I'm telling you, they don't care about engines running unless there's a piece of meat sitting on top of it. They go for the smell."

Fred slapped one of his big palms down on the table with a smack of finality. "And I told you no. Noise might draw them close enough they'll smell us. Not today, and not until I understand what's happening in that field."

"Whatever! Don't come crying to me when it's ten below and we can't get that genny running!"

"It's a Cat – it'll run when we need it to!"

Tommy bolted up, flipping the chair onto its back. "Let's go, trash man," he said, storming off towards the door.

Fred turned away from his brother, focusing his attention on Zoe and Oliver. "Sorry you had to see that."

Oliver leaned in and gave Zoe a kiss. "Back in a jiffy."

"Oliver?"

"Yeah?"

She wanted to say so much. Things like, *Don't go. Don't take any stupid risks. Don't trust that jerk, Tommy. Remember that time you just had to go to the neighbors, and you ended up running a nail through your foot? Think about us. We need you.* But Oliver knew all those things, and saying them now wouldn't change the fact he was going. Instead, she said, "I love you. Hurry back."

Oliver kissed her again. "I love you too."

It wasn't until she watched him disappear from the hall that a sinking feeling filled her stomach. Was it always going to be like this? Was she always going to have to worry?

CHAPTER 26
SUPPLY RUN

"HEY, Tommy, I need to swing by my room real fast," Oliver said, cutting right towards the classrooms.

"The van's parked at the side entrance. I'll pull around and pick you up out front."

"Sounds good." Despite how he felt about Tommy and the fact Zoe said not to trust him, she'd also asked him to get along, and he was going to try his best to do just that.

Actually, he was kind of excited to get out and be of some use. His foot didn't hurt much anymore, and his back felt pretty good. More than anything, he wanted to see a town – any town. Since barely making it out of River City the day everything went down, all he'd seen was from his own yard. That and country roads. Zoe had told him how wrecked their neighborhood was and about the plane crash a few streets over, but he'd been unconscious for all of it. He was eager to see a town for himself, even if it was only the size of Groveland. Thinking back, he realized that when he'd gone through Groveland on his way home, he'd seen the gas station getting ransacked, houses burning, and a woman being eaten on the sidewalk. If memory served, the gas station was on fire. Oliver wasn't sure what they could hope to salvage from there, but he didn't care – he was just glad to be going out.

Entering his room, he retrieved the Beretta shotgun Howard had left him and an extra magazine for the .45. He stuffed the mag in his jeans pocket, grabbed a box of buckshot from his duffel bag, and headed for the main entrance.

"Hey, Mr. McCallister. Back again?" Jesse asked. "Whoa, looks like you're going out for more than fresh air."

"Yeah. Hey, Jesse, those coats and jackets hanging on the rack behind you – do they belong to anyone? I mean, anyone here?"

"Oh. No. I think they've been here since before."

"Care if I grab one?"

"Knock yourself out, bro! *Mi casa es su casa*."

"Thanks, Jesse." Oliver grabbed a windbreaker and a long navy peacoat off a coat hook. The grey windbreaker fit perfectly, but the peacoat was a bit large. Better too big than too small, though. "Hey, Jesse?"

"What's up?"

"Are you sure you should be smoking while keeping watch?"

Jesse nodded sagely. "I understand, but honestly, I am so focused right now. I promise you got nothing to worry about with me, Mr. McCallister. Undies don't stand a chance of getting in here on my watch."

Outside, a horn honked.

"What the fuck?" Oliver winced. "Why would he honk?"

Jesse slid open the slide and peered out. "In case you haven't figured it out yet, Tommy is a real dickhole. I hate going on supply runs with him. That's why I mostly go with Adam."

"But you have gone out with Tommy?"

"Yeah, and no matter what goes down, Tommy does what Tommy wants."

Well, that isn't reassuring, Oliver thought.

Jesse unbarred the door and pulled it open. Turning back to Oliver, his face became stone serious. "Trust me when I say I'm not the one you should worry about. As long as I'm alive, no undies are getting in here, and that's a promise. Now, you be safe out there, Mr. McCallister."

Oliver smiled and patted him on the shoulder. The look in Jesse's eyes showed him all he needed to see. "Thank you, Jesse."

Oliver opened the van door and climbed in.

Tommy shifted the van into drive and accelerated from beneath the porte cochere to reveal a partially cloudy sky. "'Bout time. Now, are you boys ready for some fun?"

You boys? Oliver frowned, immediately glancing back over his shoulder.

In the back of the work van, young Chad sat on the floor, his back leaning against a rack of hanging utility baskets. A twelve-gauge pump shotgun sat across his lap. "I'm ready to blast some Z, Dad!"

"Hooah!" Tommy shouted. "Heard! Understood!" He paused, smiling into the rearview mirror.

"And acknowledged! Right, Dad?"

"That's my boy!"

Oliver couldn't believe Tommy had thought it was okay to bring his twelve-year-old son along on a supply run. "Tommy, are you sure you should be—"

"Sure I should what?" Tommy glared at him. "Are you going to tell me how I should parent now?"

"No. I just don't think—"

"Good. Leave the thinking to me. Listen, this is our reality now. How is my son going to survive it if I don't teach him?" Tommy hooked a thumb over his shoulder. "Chad has been shooting since he was eight."

"Last year, I shot a twelve-point buck! It was a tough shot too! Right, Dad?"

Tommy laughed. "Sure was! Every bit of a hundred yards and through a thicket no less."

Chad beamed.

Up ahead was a crossroad – left for Groveland, right for Libbyton. Go straight, and another mile or so down the road was the farmhouse mansion Oliver had wanted to go to. "Tommy, you ever scavenge farmhouses?"

"Dangerous business. Folks who live in the country are even more likely to be heavily armed and supplied. If they weren't caught in the rains, they're still holing up at home. I try to avoid them. Why?"

"There is a big one up the road. I used to drive by it every day on the way to work."

Tommy glanced over, eyeing him.

Suddenly Oliver felt like he'd said too much until Tommy's stone face slipped and he started laughing. "You're talking about old man Meyer's place? Bad idea, Oliver. Benson Meyer owns over half the farmland in the surrounding five counties. He's a shrewd businessman, a gun enthusiast, and basically hates people. I guarantee you if he survived this, no one is going onto his property and living to tell about it."

Oliver felt the disappointment press down on his shoulders like a carry-out barrel full of sloppy wet trash. If he were honest with himself, he knew why he had been fixated on the farmhouse mansion. In his favorite zombie book series, *Mountain Man*, the main character, Gus, had found a mansion atop a mountain overlooking Halifax. It had a stone wall and solar too. This farmhouse was supposed to be his Halifax mansion. A place with power, safety, and an endless movie selection. A safe place for the four of them to wait this thing out in some semblance of comfort.

As they approached the crossroad, Oliver was pulled from his thoughts when Tommy unexpectedly turned right towards Libbyton, rather than left towards Groveland.

"Tommy, I thought we were going to hit the gas station in Groveland?"

"Honestly, Oliver, I just said that so that pretty wife of yours wouldn't worry and she'd let you come along. I got us a better mission. Besides, that gas station has nothing left to offer. What didn't burn up in the fire has been picked clean."

An uneasy feeling filled the pit of Oliver's already sinking stomach. "So, what's the plan?"

"Well, for one, we can't have you going on supply runs dressed like that. You see what we're wearing?" he said, pointing at his own jacket.

"Not sure how camouflage is going to help much in town."

"Not the camo, Oliver. The material. Most of mine is military-grade body armor made with Kevlar. Now I couldn't get this for Chad, and I can't get it for you either. But you see what Chad's wearing?"

Oliver nodded. "Brown bib overalls with a heavy camo jacket."

"Right. Point is the material. That's Carhartt. They make some damn good gear. It isn't Kevlar but it's a heavy canvas. Zed can't bite through that shit. And I happen to know where there's a large supply just waiting to be claimed."

"Zed" was Tommy's nickname for zombies. Oliver recognized it from some popular zombie movies. When Tommy used the term, it sounded ridiculous, and he could just see Zoe rolling her eyes at the very unscientific name. *Shit, Zo, what have I gotten myself into?*

"I got the idea from touring in Iraq. You see, the Taliban used whatever they had on hand to armor their vehicles." Tommy barked out a laugh. "We called it farmer armor. Step one of our mission is to secure and outfit you in some Carhartt farmer armor."

Oliver was also quite familiar with Carhartt. On the garbage route, he would don the heavy gear only on the coldest of Illinois winter days. The stuff was durable as hell and kept you warm too, but it wasn't very conducive to hustling. He would usually start off wearing the thick jacket over bibs in the early morning, then strip the gear off as he warmed up.

"Well, don't you want to know where?"

"Oh, right. Farm and Feed?" he guessed.

"Yeah, that's right. Farm and Feed carries a ton of it. Gloves, hats, you name it. So first stop is we get you some better gear. And what the hell is on your feet?"

Oliver glanced down. "Trail running shoes."

"For what? I hate running. Look, you're going to want to ditch those go-fasters for some military or at least a more durable boot that protects the ankles."

Oliver frowned. He understood Tommy's logic, but the last thing he wanted on his feet were heavy boots.

"If all you do is run, you can't hold muscle mass. Besides just looking at you, I can tell you don't have a frame built for speed. You're too big to be very fast. Honestly, you could stand to put on some muscle. So, what's the point? Running is for people who can't lay off the fat cakes. Is that your problem, Oliver? Can't lay off the sweets, so you have to run to keep from blowing up?"

Oliver started to respond but Tommy just went on listening to himself talk.

"Shit, I haven't run more than a ten-minute warm-up since basic training. I mean you look fit enough, you just need to bulk up. Free weights is where it's at. Just look at my boy back there." Tommy nodded into the rearview mirror. "He's in wrestling and football, plus lifting with me. The boy's put on ten pounds of pure muscle. Show him, Chad!"

"Dad, I got my coat on," Chad whined.

"Well, trust me, those two-a-day workouts are working."

"So what's the plan?" Oliver asked, wishing he would have made any excuse not to come along. Zoe had had a feeling about this trip. He should have listened.

"You look like you're about to dump a load in your pants. Listen, I wouldn't have brought Chad along if I didn't know I could keep him safe." Tommy slowed to navigate around an abandoned SUV as they passed under Highway 155 and approached a stoplight. "The thing is, there are lots of those dead fucks roaming around, so we need to be smart. Last time I was over this way, right across from Farm and Feed, dozens were grouped up in the Walmart parking lot just like in the field back at the church. What I'm saying is, once we're inside, you can't go shooting your gun unless you absolutely have to."

"But, Dad, you said I would get to shoot some zombies!"

Was it wrong that young Chad's whiny voice made Oliver want to duct tape the little shit's mouth shut? And for Christ's sake, these were people – human beings! Undead but still, did he miss the part where this had turned into a sport?

"You will, son, but I only let you bring your shotgun as a precaution."

"Then how am I supposed to shoot them?"

Tommy smiled over at Oliver and then glanced into the rearview mirror. "Pull back that tarp, son."

Oliver twisted in his seat as he watched Chad scramble over to the back of the van and throw back a blue tarp.

"My bow! You brought it!"

"Ha-ha! That's right! I'll get you within twenty yards of zed, and you can take a shot." Tommy's face became serious. "But you can't tell Uncle Fred."

"Don't worry, Dad. I won't! Scout's honor, I won't!"

"What about you, Oliver? Can you shoot a bow?" Tommy asked the question doubtingly, as if he already knew the answer was going to be disappointing.

In fact, Oliver could shoot a bow, though he hadn't in several years. But there was a time when, like many in central Illinois, he bowhunted deer. Then he got shot in the shoulder. After that, pulling a bow back was painful. So instead, he picked up a new hobby in trail running. Soon, hunting became more of a memory than a thing he did.

Before he could answer, Tommy shouted, "Hold on!" as four adults ran into the street.

For a split second Oliver thought they might be alive, but when they turned to face the van, it was horrifyingly clear they were not.

Oliver slapped his hands onto the dashboard, bracing himself.

In the middle of the road stood a woman and three men. All four were covered in blood and guts, their faces stretched and twisted, their eyes wide, dead, and unblinking. They ran straight for the front of the van.

"The trick is, you don't want to slow down too much, or they'll climb on or punch through the window, but you can't go too fast, or they might break the grill and bust the radiator. You sorta want to give them a firm nudge just hard enough to knock them out of the way."

"Yeah! Hit 'em, Dad!" Chad shouted.

Tommy hit them alright, and when the undead woman jumped up at the last second, Oliver thought for sure she was going to come through the windshield. Instead, her head thumped into the glass like a hollow melon as she deflected off the hood.

In the back of the van, glass rattled and clinked.

"Just like that!" Tommy shouted.

Chad laughed.

Oliver unclenched his ass cheeks in relief.

Tommy shook his head, a stupid smirk plastered across his visage. "You should see your face. Pale as a ghost! Well, get used to it. That was nothing. They run at the van all the time. But the funny thing is, I can leave the van running and as long as we aren't in it, they could care less, except to know that we must be inside whatever building we're parked in front of."

"Wait, you mean infected but not dead, right?" Oliver peered into the back of the van, trying to trace the clinking glass sound.

"No. I mean the undead ones. They can't talk or think like we think, but they have instincts. Now, if you get an infected but still alive, well, sky's the limit on those fuckers. They got a gun, they'll shoot it, a truck, they'll chase your ass with it. But I haven't had to deal with an infected for five or six days. My theory is the ones that were infected initially are all dead. I think after a time they all die and become zed. Maybe they get so miserable they kill themselves, or maybe the disease just kills them. I can't say."

In the back, Oliver observed three utility baskets full of wine bottles, each with a rag sticking a few inches out of the neck. "Tommy, are those wine bottles—"

"Molotov cocktails!" Tommy proudly interjected. "Made 'em myself. I like to use a combination of gas and oil! Sticks to whatever it hits better and burns longer."

"Hey, Dad? Maybe we can throw one at a zed or maybe at that group of zombies at Walmart!"

Tommy chuckled. "Good thinking, kiddo, but I don't think we want to try getting that close."

As they navigated down Libbyton's main street, it looked as though a war had taken place. Cars – burnt out, wrecked, or just plain abandoned – littered the road and front yards. Many houses were destroyed; others were boarded up, and some of those had clearly been broken into and ransacked, either by the living in search of food or by the dead in search of the living. Lawns were littered with trash and debris as if the town had been hit by a tornado.

Tommy wasted no time, driving as fast as he could while bobbing and weaving between cars and the larger debris. The undead were everywhere, running down sidewalks, zigzagging into the streets, sprinting from house to house as they sniffed at the air. Their behavior reminded him of a panicked crackhead on alley day, pacing back and forth and digging through the trash to find a rock he was sure he'd lost but had never had in the first place. But it wasn't crack the zombies were looking for.

Tommy ignored the undead, making sure to keep the van moving fast enough that they couldn't catch up. "I told Zoe about my theories too. Hey, how did you meet her, anyway?"

"What?" Oliver asked, understanding the question but not understanding why he was asking.

"Zoe? How did you meet her? A pretty girl like her – a doctor. Just wondering how you, a trash man, hooked up with a girl like her. She seems a bit out of your—"

Somewhere nearby, a gun fired.

Despite the gunshot being way too close for comfort, Oliver

welcomed the interruption; it saved him from having to tell Tommy to mind his own business. The questions were weird and out of place.

Tommy waved off the gunshot. "That's pretty much normal. Either an infected with a gun or someone trying not to get killed. Listen, when we get to Farm and Feed, there's no telling who might be there. For sure, zed will be there. Possibly infected too. Like I said, I haven't seen any lately. Oh, and there could be other survivors like us trying to find supplies."

Other survivors? That would be good. Maybe others had more info on what was happening. "Have you talked to any other survivors?"

"Fuck no! Don't talk to anyone. Your job is to keep your head down, get the shit we need, and beat feet back to the van. The best thing we can do is give others a wide berth. They don't want to get shot and neither do you. Anyone tries to talk to you, shoot them."

"What? Just like that?"

"Yeah, just like that. What? Are you going to ask them to let you examine their eyes? Or maybe you plan to stand there and hold a conversation with them to see if they're infected? I sure as shit know I'm not. They get within my personal space, and I end them with two to the head." For emphasis, Tommy placed his index finger against his temple and pretended to pull the trigger. "This is reality, Oliver. You don't survive by being the nice guy. The nice guy dies every time. Out here, this is a war for survival."

Chad laughed. "My dad's been in gunfights."

Oliver's bad feeling only solidified with every word Tommy spoke. Tommy's logic was: be the first to kill, and you can never go wrong. That was certainly one way of approaching it, but it wouldn't be Oliver's way. He wouldn't be shooting anyone he wasn't sure was infected unless they gave him a reason to. And maybe in the end, Tommy would be right and being the nice guy would get him killed, but the alternative wasn't something he could live with.

One thing was for certain, in the future, he would not be going on supply runs with Tommy, even if it meant leaving the church to go back out on their own. Fred would just have to decide if having a medically trained professional was more important than sending Oliver out with his psychotic brother.

"Enough about that – tell me about you and Zoe?" said Tommy.

"No. I don't think so."

"Excuse me?" Tommy's demeanor flipped like a switch as he shot Oliver a cutting glance.

"I... I just want to focus on the plan. We're almost there."

Tommy stared at him for a moment that stretched into an awkward silence. The guy wasn't even looking at the road.

"Car up ahead," Oliver announced.

"No shit," Tommy replied, slowly turning his gaze back to the road.

They passed through a four-way stop; on their left was a car lot and to their right a Jimmy John's. Both looked like they'd been bombed. Farther down they passed a Gold's Gym on their right and a large distribution center on their left.

Tommy didn't share his plan for Farm and Feed, but he didn't ask any more questions about Zoe either. Clearly, Oliver had pissed the guy off. But that was fine – the silent treatment he could handle.

They made the turn, and about a mile down the road, Farm and Feed appeared on the left. Across the street was a Walmart. Both parking lots looked like the demolition derby at the state fair, minus the mud and spray-painted numbers on the destroyed vehicles. But what caught Oliver's attention was a group of undead crowded close together near the edge of the Walmart parking lot. "The mosh pit," Oliver breathed.

"The what?" Tommy followed Oliver's gaze. "Oh. Yeah, they're still there just like in the field. Well, don't worry about them. Last time I was here, I just kept my distance. So far, they're only focused on the one in the center of the crowd."

The crowd seemed in constant motion as they pushed and pulled. It was as if each of the undead were trying to get to the center of the crowd. "There must be, what, fifty or sixty people there?"

"No less than a hundred I'd say."

"I want to see, Dad!" Holding on to the two bucket seats, Chad worked his way to a standing position. "Oh wow! Can we shoot some of them and see what they do?"

Tommy made the turn into the Farm and Feed parking lot. "No, son. Not until we're done here, but maybe before we leave. I'd like to see what would happen myself."

Oliver did not want to see what would happen, but he kept his mouth shut, deciding instead to have that argument when the time came.

In the Farm and Feed parking lot, several undead took notice of them.

"They're coming." Oliver pointed.

"No shit, Sherlock. Don't worry about them. We're going around back." Tommy sped around the building. In the back, a huge area was fenced off with a tall hurricane fence and razor wire. This was where Farm and Feed stored materials that could be kept outside – things like cow mats and horse troughs. "When I pull up to the gate, jump out and push it open."

"It looks motor-driven. You sure it's going to push open?"

"Hell, yes, I'm sure! Inside the back door is a toggle that switches the gate from auto to manual. There's no power, smart guy, so I switched to manual last time I was here."

"Okay, but then how do we get back out?" Oliver asked.

"Shit's sake. You think too much. Didn't I tell you to let me do the thinking?" Tommy sighed. "Look, by the time we get in, get what we need, and beat feet back here, most if not all the bastards will have wandered off. If any are still hanging around, we'll light 'em up, open the gate, and be gone before more can engage."

A dozen "what ifs" popped into Oliver's mind as his pulse quickened.

"Now, if you're satisfied, get your ass out there and, once I'm inside, close the gate and throw the latch!" Tommy must have noticed Oliver's expression. "Don't worry – you've got plenty of time if you hustle. Plus, you got those go-fasters on, right? Well, go fast."

Oliver glanced up at the sky. This check had become instinctual in an apocalyptic world where a single raindrop could end your life. Seeing it was still clear, he jumped out and pushed the gate. It didn't swing open but rather rolled sideways like a giant pocket door.

From around the building, dozens of undead appeared, running as fast as their undead legs could carry them. Their moans and grunts echoed off the building walls, but they didn't sound like in the movies. The undead moans were cries of agony – their grunts pained expressions of misery. The parasites inside them tormented them with cravings. Their only promise of relief was to feed on the brains of the living.

A chill ran up Oliver's spine. Grimacing at the anguished sounds of the undead, he motioned Tommy to hurry through. He just wanted to get the gate closed as fast as he could.

Tommy eased forward like he hadn't a care in the world, finally clearing the gate and pulling forward beneath a covered portion of the building where customers would pull up to show their receipt to the yard attendant.

Oliver quickly pushed the gate closed and secured the hasp.

"See that chain?" Tommy called. "Wrap it around the hasp and clip it back to itself with the carabiner."

Oliver did as instructed. The undead slammed into the fence and began to climb.

"Don't worry about them, they can't get past the razor wire."

Oliver glanced up, watching as a fast-climbing teen neared the top. He would have thought that since the dead didn't feel pain, they would fight their way through the wire but as he watched, he understood. It wasn't the pain but rather the puzzle they couldn't get past. The undead boy couldn't think to be careful. Instead, he clutched the wire in an effort to pull his entire weight up and over. The razors cut deep into the boy's hands, severing a few fingers. With no fingers and with no way to grip, he fell hard onto the concrete.

"Jesus," Oliver breathed.

"Yeah!" Chad cheered. "That's what you get! Dad, can I try to shoot one through the fence?"

Oliver backed away from the fence.

Tommy opened the rear of the van, retrieving a crossbow for himself as Chad grabbed his compound. "Yeah, why the hell not," he said with a smile. "Go on – get yourself set up and I'll let you take a shot, kiddo. Look there, see that fat chick? She'd be a hard one to miss. But remember, it only counts if you punch that arrow through her head. Now, it won't be easy to thread an arrow through the fence with her head bobbing around, so take your time and breathe just like I taught you."

Oliver reached inside the van to retrieve his shotgun.

Tommy grabbed him by the arm. "Hold up, Oliver. Listen, seeing how the front doors are busted, there are bound to be a couple zeds inside. You can't go firing that thing in there or you might bring all the dead from here to downtown right through the front door, including that mob across the street, and if you think there's a lot of zed on the other side of that fence you ain't seen nothing compared to what's inside that Walmart. Shit, I won't even go over there."

"What are you asking me, Tommy? I'm not going in there with my dick in my hand."

"Settle down. Of course not. Look" – he pointed at Oliver's shoulder holster – "you got your side arm just in case, but a .45 won't be quiet either. Maybe leave the shotgun in the van. Just take your side arm, but you got to do your best not to freak out and start shooting. I mean, shit, I got my boy here and I'd rather not have an army of these things to contend with. We get in, we get out. You're going to want your hands free anyway to load up all the gear you need. So take the pistol but shoot it only if you absolutely have to."

At the back of the van, Chad had donned a quick release, clipped it onto the bowstring, and drawn back, presumably taking aim at the woman.

Tommy pointed at the woman. "Alright, big man, take your time and breathe, just like I taught you."

The thirty-something woman gripped the fence with soiled fingers and broken nails, staring hungrily from the other side. A wedding ring void of the diamond still clung to her finger as she reached up and started to climb. Her dirty blond hair was a rat's nest of tangles that covered a face streaked in mascara and blood. She could have been a mom in her once white fleece and pastel yoga pants now stained with a mix of bloody dirt, body fluids, and the rain itself. Oliver imagined the blonde dropping the kids at school before heading to the Starbucks across the street for her morning caramel macchiato thingy.

Chad pulled the release.

The arrow flew true, sparking off the fence before punching through the crazed woman's right eye. Her head snapped back and she fell away from the fence.

"Yeah! Attaboy! I saw that spark and thought your arrow deflected!"

Oliver's stomach lurched as he quickly turned away from the sickening celebration. This wasn't a sport to him, and it never would be.

Chad was laughing triumphantly. "No way! I got her right through the brain pan! Can I shoot another one? Can I, please?"

"No. Not right now. But get an arrow knocked and keep your head on a swivel when we go inside. And, Chad, you stay right next to me the whole time. Understood?"

"Yes, sir!"

As Oliver tried to collect himself and not vomit on his shoes, Tommy and Chad walked past him towards the back of the building. Tommy stopped and called back over his shoulder, "You better toughen up if you're going to have any hope of surviving this, Oliver. I mean, for fuck's sake, how can you protect that pretty wife of yours if you can't even stomach killing something that's already dead?"

Oliver felt a flush of anger wash through him, but he held it down. What did this asshole know about him, his wife, or what they'd been through? He wanted to say so much. No. That wasn't true either. He didn't need to explain himself. What he really wanted was to tell Tommy to fuck off. Instead, he asked, "What's the plan, Tommy?"

Tommy turned back to him, his crossbow held down at his side and his own pistol holstered on his hip. "There are some shopping carts just inside. Get one and head to the hunting section. It's inside to the right. Get yourself a bow and a bunch of arrows. The carbon fiber ones, not the aluminum ones. Grab a couple packs of broadheads, preferably one hundred grain." Tommy frowned. "You do know what broadheads are, don't you?"

Oliver gave a slight nod.

"Good. Get a quick release too. If you don't know how to shoot a compound, you could grab a crossbow and some bolts. I imagine even you can shoot one of these," he said, holding up his own crossbow. "But whatever, just be quick. Nock an arrow and then head across the store to the men's section and as fast as you can grab your Carhartt gear and some boots. Might want to grab some for Zoe too. Not that she'll be needing it for supply runs, but if I can't convince my stubborn brother to turn on the genny soon, it's going to get real damn cold, real damn fast. Meet us back at the van when you're done. By then, I should have everything on my list. And, Oliver, I will only say this one more time. Do your best not to shoot your gun. If I hear gunshots, I'm getting Chad to the van before I come looking for you. Don't make me come looking for you. Understood?"

"Yeah. I got it," Oliver said. Tommy had to know splitting up was stupid, but Oliver didn't care. He wasn't going to argue and give the guy more fodder to call him a coward. Besides, he couldn't wait to get away from him.

Tommy nodded. "Well then, let's go shopping."

CHAPTER 27
THIS IS REALLY HAPPENING

ZOE SET THE M&M container containing Tommy's parasite specimen next to the one in the mason jar and turned on the battery-powered LED work light. She readied a tray of surgical instruments Tommy had brought her from one of his trips to a prompt care in Libbyton, then donned a disposable mask and surgical gloves.

Tommy, she thought, feeling her stomach knot. What was she thinking, letting Oliver leave here with that asshole? She should have told the truth about Tommy trying to come on to her. But she knew exactly why she hadn't. Tommy she could handle. But if she'd told Oliver, he would have just gotten upset and either said something to Tommy, which wouldn't have gone well, or he'd have demanded they leave. And that was the real crux of it. She didn't want Oliver upset because she didn't want to leave. She wouldn't leave. These people needed her, and if she was being honest with herself, she needed them too. Taking care of others was where she thrived. Plus, she felt safe here. Well, safe as she had felt since all this started.

Fred was the ying to Tommy's yang. The opposite side of the coin. He was a vet too, but he was a sweet man. The perfect leader for this group. And his wife, Martha, was like the mother hen. Then there was Aaron – he was so gentle and shy, but he could fix anything. The kids were all getting along so well and keeping each other entertained. The other men had all fallen into their element. Scott and Chris spent a lot of time reinforcing the building, working on interior projects, or taking their turn standing guard. Ray was an amazing cook. How he did what he did with what they had was mind boggling. Plus, over the last week, Zoe had become quite close with Aneesa and Melissa. And any day now, Zoe would be delivering Melissa's baby!

Knowing all that she knew, Zoe couldn't possibly leave now, and that's why she hadn't said anything. In hindsight, she knew she should have told Oliver and just stood her ground if he had a fit. That decision was eating at her insides. Especially after she heard Fred and Tommy arguing. Fred mentioned that Tommy was dishonorably discharged from the military, yet Tommy had told them he was still active. Next time she had some alone time with Fred, she planned to ask about that. Something about Tommy was wrong; she could feel it.

Carefully, she unscrewed the lid on the mason jar and picked up a pair of forceps.

Louie let out a soft whine.

"It's alright, boy, this one is dead-dead. Besides, what are you worried about? They don't like dogs." She gripped the parasite with the forceps and very carefully began to lift it from the jar. She'd gleaned all she could from studying through the glass of the mason jar. Now that she had adequate lighting and proper tools, plus the other sample from Tommy, it was time to probe deeper. She wondered if she could find sex organs and identify if one were male and the other female. She'd also like to get a better look inside its mouth at those strange teeth.

Jesse burst into the room. "Dr. Zoe!"

Zoe jumped, dropping the forceps, and with them the parasite, back into the jar. "Jesus Christ, Jesse!"

"I'm sorry. I didn't mean to scare you but..." His eyes found the jar and fixed on the parasite it held.

"But what? What is it?"

"Whoa! That's the thing, right? The thing that makes them zombies?"

Zoe glanced at the table and back to Jesse. "Yeah. These are the parasites."

Jesse marveled, his eyes wide. "Whoa, that's mental. They said one might not be the same as the other. Man, seeing them side by side, they sure do look different."

"Jesse, did you need something?"

"Oh, right. Sorry. It's Melissa, she's having pain. Contractions, I think."

"What? When did this start? Did her water break? How far apart are the contractions?" She removed the forceps from the jar and secured the lid.

"I… I don't know. Adam came to relieve me and then we heard Melissa shouting from their room. Adam shouted for me to go get you as he ran back to their room."

By the time Jesse finished the sentence, Zoe had already ripped off her rubber gloves and tossed her backpack of medical essentials over her shoulder. She hurried out the door and down the hall. Melissa and Adam were staying in the church nursery, which was equipped with a mother's room, allowing Melissa a private restroom. If this pandemic continued, the new mother would be in the best place the church had to offer for her and the baby.

Zoe ran into the foyer and around the corner to another hall with double doors propped open. She ran down the hall, past doors with brass plates that read KITCHEN, MAIN OFFICE, RESTROOMS, MOTHER'S ROOM, and finally, NURSERY.

Zoe pounded on the door. "Melissa? Adam? It's Zoe."

The door opened and Adam appeared. His normally smooth face was creased with worry. "Zoe, thank god! Come in."

Melissa half lay, half sat on a futon, pillows propped behind her back. Her blue bangs only highlighted the painful grimace on her face. "Zoe! My water broke!"

"Okay. You're okay." Zoe shrugged the pack off her shoulder and set it on the floor. "How far apart are the contractions?"

"I don't know!" she cried. "I've been having them all morning, but I wasn't sure if they were false labor pains like last time, so I didn't want to bother anyone until I was sure. Well... I'm... I'm sure now!" Melissa groaned, slamming her eyes shut and clenching her jaw.

"I know it hurts, but try and breathe like we practiced."

Adam glanced at his watch. "Five minutes from the last one."

"Five minutes?" Zoe repeated. Braxton-Hicks or prodromal contractions were typically not especially painful, nor were they consistent.

"I knew when I saw the discharge and the pain got really intense, this must be the real thing. It's the real thing, right?" Tears spilled down Melissa's cheeks.

"Yep. This is the real thing." Zoe dug through her bag, retrieving a fresh pair of rubber gloves. "But it's okay," she said, hiding her own nervousness behind a reassuring smile. "I just need to check and see how far dilated your cervix is."

She remembered from clinicals that a fully dilated cervix is about the width of a bagel. Eight centimeters is about the width of an orange. Melissa was somewhere in between, approximately eight to nine centimeters.

Melissa's face bunched up and she groaned. "I want to push."

"No. Don't push! Not yet, mama. I want you to breathe just like we practiced." She glanced over at Adam, who looked panicked. He needed a job. "Take her hand, dad. You know what to do. Guide her through the breathing."

Adam did as instructed and sat down next to Melissa. Together they started taking long, steady breaths.

"That's right. In through the nose, out through the mouth. In through the nose, out through the mouth."

The contraction seemed to pass. "Good job, mom. That's exactly what you need to do. Until you're fully dilated, we're going to avoid pushing by breathing the way we practiced."

"This is it, isn't it? It's really happening?" Adam asked.

"It is. But not yet. Baby could come anytime over the next few minutes or hours."

Adam nodded nervously as he brushed Melissa's hair from her face.

Zoe stood and removed the gloves. "Rest as much as you can between contractions. Breathe together when the next one comes. I need to get Martha and maybe Aneesa too – we'll need clean water, towels, and a few other preparations, but I'll be right back."

As Zoe moved to the door, Adam followed. "This is really happening here in a church. Not in a hospital but in a church."

Zoe smiled, putting on a face that was much more confident than she felt. She had seen births, was trained in prenatal and well-woman care, but she had never delivered a baby. Unless a nurse practitioner obtained a degree as a certified midwife, they wouldn't, under normal circumstances, be performing delivery. But these circumstances were anything but normal. "Adam, you're her rock. And we're going to get through this."

He nodded his head, looking paler than dead coral.

"Hey, it's okay. Women were giving birth long before there were hospitals, and there are still plenty of women having home births today."

"Yeah... I know you're right, I just... I don't know what to do."

Zoe laughed. "You get the easy part. Keep her as comfortable as you can, hold her hand, and do your breathing together. You're going to be a dad soon!"

"Right. A dad!" He smiled nervously.

Zoe hurried back towards her room to grab a few more things. She also wanted to tell Aneesa and Martha what was happening and recruit one of the women to be an extra set of hands.

As she passed by the game room, Jurnee appeared with Louie at her side. "Zoe?"

"Hey there," she said.

"Can I ask you something?"

"Sure, hun, but I'm in a big hurry, okay?"

"Well, I was wondering why Chad got to go with Oliver but I couldn't. The other kids said it was probably because Chad was older."

"What? What do you mean Chad got to go?"

Jurnee nodded. "Uh-huh, with Oliver and his dad."

This has to be a mistake. "Jurnee, are you sure?"

"Yep. He was in the game room with us when his dad came and got him. Is it because he's older?"

"Jurnee, I'm going to be very busy for a while, but when Oliver gets back, we'll find out, okay?"

"Okay. Come on, Louie. We better get back in there before we lose our turn!"

The feeling Zoe had about Tommy and this supply run was growing worse with every passing minute. She changed her route to Fellowship Hall, wondering if Fred and Martha knew about Chad.

CHAPTER 28
THE BLUE FALCON

FOR SOME REASON, Oliver expected the Farm and Feed to look like it had the last time he'd ventured into the store. Not that he expected to be greeted by the friendly staff in red vests, but he hadn't prepared himself for the ransacking the store had endured. Aisles were littered with goods, and some of the shelves had been turned over. From what he could see – which wasn't much, given the only light was coming from a few skylights and the glass windows at the front of the store – the place was trashed.

The Farm and Feed was big, like a hundred thousand square feet big. Oliver couldn't see the front of the store, but he could feel a breeze. Plus, he remembered seeing the broken windows and doors when they'd passed through the parking lot. There was nothing keeping the undead he'd seen out front from coming right in through the front door. Hopefully most of them had followed them around the building and were wandering around out back.

Oliver began to navigate his cart towards the sporting goods section, giving a final glance back at Tommy and his little shit of a kid. Tommy held his crossbow at the ready, panning it back and forth, illuminating aisles this way and that way. Tommy's crossbow had a flashlight mounted to it? A fucking flashlight? Little Chad stood behind his dad, his own bow held up and ready to draw.

Tommy made some hand gesture Chad seemed to understand, and he switched to his father's right side. Tommy nodded to Oliver, pointing to the sporting goods section before creeping forward up the aisle.

Oliver turned away, vowing to himself to find a flashlight.

As he headed off to the right, he decided to leave his cart for now. He would grab it when he passed back through on his way to the clothing section.

Hurriedly he made his way past a rack of mountain bikes and tipped-over canoes. When he reached the bow section, there wasn't much left. Also, even though his bullet-wounded shoulder had been healed for a long time, it still bothered him, and he didn't think with his more recent back injury he stood any chance of drawing a bow.

Okay, a crossbow then. Down the aisle he found a couple left on the rack. It was really dark at this end, but his eyes had adjusted to the point that he could see well enough. There were even some arrows, or rather bolts. He found broadheads too. Okay, so which one to pick? Well, that was the problem – he'd never shot a crossbow. Actually, he wasn't even sure how to cock the thing. It looked like you stepped on a handle thingy sticking out the front, and then you must use something to pull the string back to lock it into a drawn position.

Oliver sighed. No time to figure this out now. He grabbed the most expensive one, plus bolts and broadheads, and made his way back to his cart. Glancing around, he didn't see Tommy. Come to think of it, Tommy never mentioned what was on his list, so he supposed the guy could be anywhere.

Across the store, something crashed.

Oliver jumped. "Tommy?" he called into the shadows. But there was no answer. "Shit." Quietly he made his way back to his cart and placed his items inside. He crossed the store to the clothing section, taking longer than he would have liked, as he had to continuously maneuver the cart around and sometimes over items in the aisle.

On an end cap he found LED flashlights. Snagging two, he tore open the packages, illuminating one and stuffing the other into his coat pocket before moving on. In the pet care aisle, he found there was still plenty of dog food. On his way back, he would grab a bag for Louie.

As he approached the clothing department, he could see this wasn't going to be as simple as finding the section he wanted and grabbing his and Zoe's sizes. Racks were overturned, with clothing and abandoned shopping carts strewn across the floor. Then he smelled the stench of rotten flesh and froze, sweeping the flashlight beam across the piles of clothes.

There! Bodies.

Slowly he crept closer. Several people lay twisted in the heaps of clothing, their heads cracked open and emptied, their bowels spilled and spread all over the place. Oliver exhaled a heavy breath, reaching beneath his peacoat to pull his T-shirt over his nose. "Fuck me." He didn't want to dig through this mess to try and find clothes. If Tommy had been here before, why hadn't he told him what to expect?

From the corner of his eye a blinking blue light drew his attention. He whipped around but didn't see anything. Oliver crept forward, deciding he'd cross the mess and see if the next aisle looked any better.

There! He saw the blinking again. This time he was sure of it. But when Oliver spun to find the source of the light, he only spotted a small boy, younger even than Jurnee. The little guy was standing about twenty yards away at the opposite edge of the clothing department. Unsure what the light had been, Oliver frowned, keeping his own light hidden as he glanced around before turning his attention back on the boy. It was dark so he couldn't tell if the boy was hurt, only that he was wearing sweatpants and a matching zip-up hoodie.

Oliver knelt onto one knee. "Hey, buddy. You okay?"

The little boy took a few unsteady steps towards him, his shoes lighting up with each stride. *Blinky shoes?* Oliver lifted the flashlight, illuminating the child's face, and gasped. One side of the boy's face was bloody and torn open, an ear was missing, his bloodshot eyes were clouded, and he was as pale as a sun-bleached fence post.

The little guy let out a tortured squeal, "Reeeaaawwww!" and charged.

"Oh, come on!" Oliver backpedaled. Infected or undead, the last thing he wanted was to brain a toddler. He'd already crushed a teenager's skull the first time he'd visited the church, and every time he closed his eyes to go to sleep, he could still see the bat connecting with the kid's head, could still feel the reverberation of crushing bone.

Blue lights flashed from the toddler's shoes as he stomped forward, slipping and falling in a tangle of clothes and guts.

Seeing the opening, Oliver lunged for an abandoned shopping cart, yanking it between himself and the kid. As the boy came within reach, Oliver flipped the cart upside down, atop the kid. The weight of the cart bashed the boy over the head and knocked him onto his bottom, pinning him inside.

The boy hissed. Placing his palms above his head, he started to stand.

"No, you don't!" Oliver said, tipping a clothing rack onto the cart.

With the kid pinned inside the upside-down shopping cart, Oliver exhaled a relieved breath. Before returning to his search for clothing, he stood there a moment to make sure the boy couldn't get out.

The little guy moaned, his mouth snapping open and shut, his little teeth click-clacking together over and over. He pushed and stomped, his tiny shoes flashing, but no matter how hard he tried, he couldn't lift the cart. Thank god the parasite didn't seem to be giving the undead superhuman strength.

Finally satisfied that the boy was trapped, Oliver was ready to resume his search when gunfire erupted from across the store. *Clack! Clack! Clack! Clack!*

"What the fuck?" The shots came from the back of the store where they'd entered! Oliver drew his .45, abandoning his cart of goods as he ran for the exit. Something must have gone horribly wrong for Tommy to start shooting.

As he ran down the back aisle, shrill cries and moans filled the front of the store. The undead were coming in from the parking lot!

More gunfire echoed through the darkened store. The first set of shots were definitely inside the store, but the last three sounded like they came from out back in the yard. What the hell was happening?

Boom! Boom! Boom!

That was either Chad or Oliver's shotgun! Either one would had to have been retrieved from the van.

Oliver ran through the rear door and across the shipping department to the exit leading into the yard. He wasn't sure what to expect, but it didn't matter. Tommy and Chad must be in serious trouble to have resorted to shooting. Had the dead somehow opened the gate and come in through the back? But if they'd gotten inside the store, shouldn't he have passed by their bodies?

These questions spun through Oliver's head as he stepped into the yard, pistol raised.

What he saw, he couldn't comprehend at first.

From his right, the van sped towards him with Tommy behind the wheel and Chad in the passenger seat. "Whoa! Hey!" Oliver shouted, waving his arms, expecting Tommy to stop and pick him up.

Something flew from the driver's window high over his head – something on fire! Glass shattered behind him. *WHOOMP!*

Instinctively, Oliver ducked his head, feeling the heat on his back even before he turned to find the entry back into the building blocked with flames.

"Tommy!" he shouted again, but Tommy didn't stop. The van sped on, picking up speed.

Oliver looked to find the gate was pushed all the way open, but how? What the hell? "Tommy! Wait!"

Tommy looked into the side mirror, smiled, and gave a "so long" nod with a two-finger salute.

With that single look, Oliver's world came crashing down. "Tommy! You motherfucker!" he screamed.

Everything became horrifyingly clear. Zombies wouldn't have rolled the gate open all the way even if they had broken the latch. They would only have pushed it open enough to get clear. No. This was intentional. Tommy had opened the gate on purpose. The shooting must have been to kill the stragglers so they could open the gate safely. Or to bring a horde to the gate. Tommy had set him up! That son of a bitch had been planning this all along!

Tires squealed on pavement as the van batted down any undead in its way before vanishing around the side of the building.

Thirty yards away and just inside the gate, an undead man in a red Farm and Feed vest pushed himself to his feet and groaned. The throaty croak was like a war cry for the dozens of other undead that had been watching the van. He might as well have shouted, "Guys, there's one over here! Fresh meat!"

They spun back towards the gate, all eyes fixed on Oliver.

Oliver glanced back at the growing wall of flames. "Fuck me!"

Shrill screams of excitement echoed across the yard as the crowd of undead surged through the open gate.

CHAPTER 29
RADIO MIKE

ZOE FOUND FRED, Jerry, Aneesa, Raymond, and Martha sitting around the table, playing cards and listening to the latest from Radio Mike. At the back of Fellowship Hall, Carpenter Chris leaned one shoulder against the door frame, peering out the viewport with binoculars.

"Well, hey there, Doc. Pull up a chair and we'll deal you in," Fred offered.

"Yeah, and you can deal me out!" Jerry announced, tossing his cards onto the table.

Martha laughed. "Oh, Dad! Don't be a fly in the ointment."

"Easy for you to say when you haven't lost the last dozen hands straight!"

Zoe nodded towards the radio. "Anything new?"

Raymond shrugged. "Nothing we don't already know. Radio Mike is talking about a group of zombies huddled up just like ours."

Fred reached over and adjusted the antenna. "Yeah, but ours are way out there in the middle of the field, and apparently old Mike's are right in his backyard, a literal stone's throw away. He's speculating they're performing some sort of strange breeding ritual. Maybe pairing off in the center of the group for some hanky-panky."

Aneesa pulled a face. "Eww!"

Zoe shook her head. "No, I don't think that's what's happening. I mean, it could be something to do with breeding, but I don't think they're—"

"Having an undead orgy?" Jerry announced.

Martha choked on her coffee. "Dad!"

Zoe smirked. "I was going to say 'mating.' Anyway, in other news, Melissa is in labor."

Martha sat the coffee cup down, her face going serious. "What? I knew she wasn't feeling well but, labor? Already?"

"Well, she's less than a week from full term. I was hoping to have a bit more time, but—"

Martha pushed her chair back and stood. "Say no more. I'll be right over."

Aneesa tossed her hand of cards into the center of the table. "Count me in too!"

"Thank you, both. Before we head over to Melissa, there's one other thing."

Fred's bushy eyebrows bunched together. "Well, that sounds serious. What is it?"

Zoe took a deep breath. "Has anyone seen Chad?"

Martha's brows knitted together. "Chad? Isn't he with the other kids?"

Zoe shook her head. "No. It seems Tommy took Chad with them on the supply run."

Martha's hand went to her mouth and her eyes welled up. "Dear god, no."

Fred slapped his cards down onto the table. "How could he be that stupid? Are you sure?"

"No, not one hundred percent, but Jurnee said she saw him leave with his dad and wanted to know why she couldn't go too. I was hoping you might tell me it was a mistake. Any idea why he would take Chad along?"

"Because he's an idiot!" Fred shouted. "Martha, so help me, when he gets back here, he's going to wish he'd stayed gone."

Martha looked at her watch. "Didn't he say they'd only be gone an hour or so?"

Jerry nodded. "They've already been gone for just over an hour. They shouldn't be much longer."

"Something's happening!" Radio Mike announced, pulling everyone's attention back to the radio. "After almost three days, the crowd of undead are dispersing!"

Jerry spun his finger at Fred. "Turn it up!"

Fred adjusted the volume.

"Oh, Jesus! The zombies have turned towards the back of the house! They're sniffing at the air. Shit! They're running this way! I… I still can't see what's in the center! There are too many." A shotgun pumped in a shell. "Whatever happens next, I've locked the mic button so you'll all be with me!"

Glass shattered and the moans of the undead filled the airwaves. "Wuuuaaaaaaa!"

Martha gasped.

Boom! Boom! Boom!

"Come on, you sons a bitches! I got two-by-sixes nailed across every window and door, and I'm holding a full flat of buckshot! You want to dance with old Mike? Well, we can dance like Lionel Richie! All night long!" *Boom! Boom!*

In the background, Zoe could hear the wails of the undead as more glass shattered and they beat against Radio Mike's walls and door. Beneath the chaos was the sound of Mike starting to hyperventilate, along with the mechanical click of shells sliding into the shotgun's receiver.

Ray shouted at the radio. "Oh no, Mike! Get out of there. Go hide or make a run for it through the front! Doesn't the old guy have a car?"

The hungry undead hissed and squealed as if they were being tortured.

The sound of two more blasts came through the radio. Then

another three. Between the cries of the undead came the frantic mechanics of more shells feeding back into the gun.

"He said he had a flat of buckshot? How much is that?" Jerry asked.

"Like two hundred and fifty shells!" Fred answered, leaning closer to the radio. "Listen, he's reloading again."

"If his boards hold, maybe he can make it." Jerry's face was full of hope, but as Zoe glanced over at Fred, she could see the man was crestfallen.

Suddenly Radio Mike began shouting between frantic gasps for breath. "Wait! I see... I see... something! It's right there! No... Wait! That isn't... isn't right! That can't be right!" *Boom! Boom! Boom! Click.* "Oh pleeeeease!" the man cried.

The pounding and moaning stopped. There were no more sounds of shells sliding into the receiver, no pump action of the shotgun. For a brief moment, there was only the sound of ragged breath and whimpering.

In Fellowship Hall, no one moved or dared to speak. Each person was frozen, eyes on the radio even though there was nothing to see.

Finally, Aneesa whispered, "What is it? What does he see?"

Through the radio came the creak of nails wrenching from their hold, followed by the groan of wood bending to its limit until finally cracking and snapping.

Radio Mike screamed.

"Mike!" Ray shouted at the radio.

But Mike's scream was swallowed by another scream – an inhuman scream. The horrid sound filled the airwaves, drowning out everything else. It was unlike any noise Zoe had ever heard. It was anguished and at the same time angry – a desperate plea for something it had to have. The sound grew and grew until suddenly there was a *pop*!

Then... static.

CHAPTER 30
NEVER EVER LOOK BACK

ASS-CLENCHING FEAR THREATENED to seize Oliver by the testicles, but he didn't freeze up. Instead, he turned and ran. His last glimpse was of the potbellied Farm and Feed man in the red vest and Wranglers being overtaken by a crowd of undead as they poured through the open gate.

Oliver thought the overtakers were probably in their teens or twenties. These were fast fuckers. The fittest of the group. He could feel the hair on the back of his neck stand at attention. Any second, the first hand would snatch hold, then others, dragging him down onto the ground. He was so fucked!

All he could do was run through the yard, between the rows, praying to stay ahead long enough to come up with a plan. There had to be another way out of the yard. A man gate. Some kind of emergency exit. But then what? Even if he found it, they'd follow him right out into the open, and he'd be doomed!

Think! What about a ladder leading onto the roof? Maybe. But even if there was one, they would climb up after him. What would he do then?

He cut right, up an aisle of decorative paving stones, heading towards the back of the building. There had to be another door leading inside. But even if there was, it might be locked. If it was, there'd be no time to shoot it open and way too many of them to turn and face. Behind him he could hear shoes scuffing on the concrete, hungry snarls, and desperate whines. He knew better than to look back. You never *ever* look back.

Maybe if he circled the whole yard, he could make his way back to the gate, run through, and shut it.

He reached the back wall of the building and turned left down another aisle. This one was lined with terracotta pots, plastic pots, foam pots, any freaking kind of pot you need, yet not a single door. But then there it was, a plain grey door. An emergency exit, not like the bigger double doors in the shipping department. But would it open? If he stopped to try and it didn't open, he was dead. Even if it did open, he might not be able to make it through before they grabbed him. But what choice did he have?

Still gripping the .45, Oliver spun as he slid to a stop in front of the door. He raised the pistol and shot the first zombie in the right eye socket, blowing a fist-sized hole out the back of its head. The bullet kept going, hitting the next zombie in the face, and both went down.

He kept shooting, getting off five more shots. He was a horrible shot with a .45, but you didn't need to be good when the target was only an arm's length away.

The first of the five rounds went into a woman's face, and then he hit an older man – first through the mouth and then in the forehead. Another girl, younger than the man, dropped next, then he somehow missed his shot at a small Asian man in a navy blue chef's uniform, despite being only inches away. As he fired again, he realized he knew that guy. Well, not on a first-name basis, but he was the guy who made the amazing sushi at his and Zoe's favorite takeout place across town.

With his free hand, Oliver turned the knob and yanked.

The door pulled open just as a man in a police officer uniform grabbed his collar and lunged in to bite.

Oliver twisted like he was trying to shake a tackle, pressed the gun against the man's cheek, and fired.

The undead officer fell back into the groping crowd as Oliver slipped inside the store. He wanted so badly to pull the door shut, but undead hands seized hold, pulling it wide.

He ran down the back aisle, jumping over anything in his way.

Oliver could run for the front of the store and make his escape into the front parking lot, but what then? Try and find a car? But what if it didn't have keys, didn't start, or was locked? He remembered the first time he and Jurnee had escaped the church. Yeah, he'd be fucked, that's what. And how many zombies might be out there just waiting? No way. He had a better plan.

The undead horde behind him crashed and smashed their way forward, relentless in their pursuit of an easy meal. The faster Oliver ran, the more his fear of being eaten was turning to rage. "C'mon, you sons a bitches!"

As he made his way along the back aisle, he once again approached the shipping department and the exit back into the yard. Smoke was pouring in from the back of the store. He didn't slow as he ran past the right turn that led back to the yard. Back to the very spot where he'd been betrayed. A quick side glance revealed the entire shipping department was now engulfed in flames. But going through the rear exit and back into the yard wasn't part of his newly developing plan anyway.

Oliver headed back to sporting goods. But this time he wasn't gearing up to fight zombies with crossbows. What Oliver needed was dependable transportation. Transportation he didn't need a key to and didn't have to worry about starting.

Oliver holstered his pistol. The mountain bikes and canoes were just up ahead. Behind him, he could hear the undead, noisier than a pack of bloodhounds on a scent as they crashed into and over everything in their way.

As Oliver sprinted into sporting goods, he noticed an endcap of golf supplies. There was a golf bag, clubs, and best of all, several fifty-count containers of recycled golf balls. Doing his best not to slow, Oliver snatched one of the containers, raised it above his head, and slammed it into the floor next to him.

The plastic container popped as the beautiful sound of golf balls bouncing across the floor filled his ears.

Despite knowing better, Oliver risked a glance back just in time to see the first few zombies fall, creating an instant pileup of undead.

He stopped at the bikes just long enough to snatch hold of the first adult-sized mountain bike he could get his hands on – a blue Mongoose. It could have been polka-dotted with tassels for all he cared. This was no time to be picky.

Behind him, products crashed into the tile floor as the undead jockeyed for position, each hoping to be the first to get to him, the first to split his head and taste their reward.

Hands on the handlebars, he cut left, running up an aisle towards the front of the building.

There was too much shit in the way to ride, so he zigged left, then right, up another aisle, hoping the distance he created and the zigzag pattern would help him lose the undead until he made it to the front of the store.

But he could feel them behind him and, worse, he could hear their cries as they ran up both adjacent aisles. "Shit!" Oliver announced through gritted teeth.

The undead were overtaking him.

CHAPTER 31
THEY GOT HIM

FOR A MOMENT, everyone stared silently at the radio.

Ray's eyes were saucers. "What just happened?"

Fred looked shell-shocked. He swallowed dryly and licked his lips. "I... I don't know." He turned, looking back over his shoulder and across the Fellowship Hall. "Chris! How's our group doing out there? Any changes?"

The tall carpenter hunched down, pulling the binoculars to his eyes, and stared out the viewport. "If you're asking if there's an undead horde of zombies about to attack the door, the answer is no, thank god. Our group is still huddled up halfway across the field. No change."

Martha breathed out a sigh of relief. "That's good."

Fred scratched at his beard. "Good? No, I don't think so. Folks, disturbing as that was, we just learned something very important. We know that group is going to disperse, and when they do, they may well attack us. Now, maybe, just maybe, we're far enough away from our horde that they'll wander off in a different direction."

Ray nodded. "Right. I think that makes sense. I mean, Radio Mike had them right in his backyard. Our horde is several hundred yards away."

"But what did Mike see?" Aneesa asked.

"I don't know, but whatever he saw scared the hell out of him," Fred said.

Jerry pointed at the radio. "Whatever it was got through Mike's fortified windows."

Teary-eyed, Martha moved to stand behind Fred, placing her hands on his shoulders. "And that scream! I don't ever want to hear that again!"

Fred turned to Zoe. "Doc, any thoughts? I mean, medically speaking. Any idea what that could have been?"

Zoe stared at the radio, replaying the horrible sound over and over in her mind, unfamiliar yet familiar. She glanced up to find all eyes were on her.

"I... think... I mean... It could have been the one that screamed to call the others to it in the first place. Maybe it's... changed somehow?"

"Changed? Changed how?" Jerry asked.

"I've no idea. Maybe it's multiplying. Whatever it's doing, it's something awful."

Fred nodded solemnly. "Roger that. Listen, people, when Tommy and Oliver get back, that's it. No more supply runs until we see what happens. Chris, don't take your eyes off that mob, and if anything changes, I want to know ASAP. I'll bring a chair over there in a minute and help you keep watch. Doc, any thoughts on why ours hasn't broken up yet?"

At the mention of Oliver, her thoughts went elsewhere. What if they didn't get back before the groups broke apart? What if he was out there dealing with whatever in the hell was at the center of the hordes?

"Doc?" Fred repeated.

"What? Sorry."

Fred pressed his lips into a tight line, causing them to vanish beneath his beard. "Doc, it's going to be okay. Tommy and Oliver are going to be fine. There's been no sign of a gathering over by Groveland. You'll see. They'll be back any minute."

Zoe nodded, but Fred's words offered little comfort. She wouldn't feel better until Oliver walked back through the door.

"I was asking you what the reason would be our horde hasn't broken apart yet?"

Zoe exhaled. "Right. Well, my guess is our group hasn't finished whatever it is the parasite is driving them to do. Could be our horde formed a little later than Mike's, or maybe it's the climate. It's warmer in Utah this time of year, right? If they're breeding more parasites, then maybe ours haven't finished developing yet."

Aneesa's face contorted and her body trembled as if she'd been struck by a cold chill. "Some giant cocoon is in there, waiting to hatch demons?"

"We don't know what it is any more than we know why the hive hasn't broken up yet. Honestly, it could be a number of reasons – climate, duration, maybe something to do with the hosts themselves – but since I don't understand their purpose, it's hard to speculate."

"I guess we just pray when it breaks up that it goes away. Until then, we stay inside and out of sight. I'll let Scott know we shouldn't work on any projects that require hammering. We don't want to give them any reason to come this way."

Zoe nodded, glancing around the table of mournful faces. "I'm so sorry about Mike, but I better get back to Melissa. Will someone please let me know when Oliver returns?"

Fred nodded, "Don't you worry, I'll make sure you're informed the moment they get back here."

Over the next hour, Zoe closely monitored Melissa, timing contractions and checking Melissa's cervix for dilation. In between, she went through all her supplies for a fourth time. She found herself obsessing about all the things that could go wrong. It was easier than the alternative: worrying about Oliver.

Aneesa and Martha did their best to help Adam keep Melissa

comfortable by frequently wetting washcloths, placing them on her forehead, and breathing along with the couple. They'd even found a yellow smiley face stress ball among the toys for Melissa to squeeze.

Adam placed his hand atop Melissa's. "You'll be holding our little boy soon, babe!"

"Jonathan!" she moaned. "We're naming him Jonathan!"

Adam's eyes went wide as he glanced between Zoe and Martha, over to Aneesa, then back to Melissa. "Jonathan? I thought you hated that name." He glanced over to Zoe. "It... it was my grandfather's name."

Melissa dropped the stress ball and snatched Adam's hand. "I said Jonathan, didn't I? It's— mother fuuuaaaaa!!" she screamed as she squeezed.

Adam's eyes flashed to his hand, his own face contorting into a painful grimace. "Alright! Jonathan! The baby's name is Jonathan!"

"I want to push!" Melissa cried.

"Not yet, mama. I want you fully dilated before we start pushing. Breathe like we practiced. We aren't going to rush this!" There was a good reason Zoe didn't want her to start pushing. Pushing too hard too soon could cause complications like premature swelling or even tearing that could require surgery or, at a minimum, stitches. Zoe was prepared to suture if she absolutely had to, but performing surgery to repair serious vaginal damage was not something she was ready for.

Adam started breathing. "Hee, hee, hoo. Hee, hee, hoo."

Melissa joined him, and the contraction passed.

That was when they heard the shouting from outside the room. It sounded like Fred, and he was yelling. Then she heard what she was sure was Tommy's voice.

"You hear that? What's happening?" Zoe asked.

"That's Fred and Tommy. He must be giving him hell over taking Chad with him. I'll go check on them," Martha said, hurrying out of the room.

Just knowing Oliver and Tommy were back gave Zoe some instant relief, allowing her to let go of the worry she'd been holding on to in the back of her mind. She blew out a breath. Now she could fully focus on the task at hand.

Another contraction came and went.

Behind her, the door opened and Martha's shaky voice said, "Zoe? Can you come here, please?"

Zoe glanced over her shoulder and frowned. Something was wrong. She checked Melissa's cervix again. "Okay, mama, you're doing great. Keep breathing through the contractions." Zoe stood and smiled down at Melissa. "I'll be right back. We're so close!" She turned away, her smile slipping.

Outside the room, Tommy and Fred stood toe-to-toe, each seething.

Zoe's eyes darted back and forth between the two men. "What's happened? Where's Oliver?"

Fred glanced over, his expression changing from rage to regret. "Tell her, Tommy."

"Tell me what?" Zoe asked, feeling her stomach knot and her heart drop.

Tommy turned to face her. "Zoe, I'm sorry."

"Where's my husband?" she demanded.

"We were in the Farm and Feed and he panicked. I told him not to shoot his gun! I... I don't know why he did it!"

"Farm and Feed? In Libbyton? You were supposed to be in Groveland!" Fred shouted.

"Where is he?" Zoe screamed, feeling the whole world close in around her.

"He didn't make it! They got him, Zoe. Oliver is gone."

CHAPTER 32
AUTOMOTIVE

A RAY of red-tinted sunlight spilled through the Farm and Feed's broken front windows. These days, red was Oliver's least favorite color. It represented everything this world had become. Rain, blood, and death. But right now, he'd give anything to make it to the red sunshine. Freedom from his undead pursuers was right there, if only he could reach it in time.

But he couldn't, and he knew it.

The exit and windows beyond the cash registers were beacons of false hope. It was impossible.

When he broke from the aisle, so did the undead. Hands reached, groping, forcing him to turn right just before checkout.

Oliver collided with a shirtless undead man.

The man squealed in excited desperation, his teeth snapping so hard they must have cracked. The man's discolored tongue poked out as he opened wide to try again. This time, when his jaws snapped shut, he bit down on his tongue, severing it. The chunk of tongue hung by a sliver of flesh. The man paused, reached up, and pushed it back into his mouth, then swallowed. His crazed eyes blinked. He squealed and lurched forward again.

Oliver held firmly to the bike, shoving the man back, knocking him onto the ground, only then realizing the man's flesh was missing from his left side, starting at his hip and extending all the way up to his chest. As the man tried to stand, a large rope of intestines spilled out and uncoiled, dangling down to the man's knees, while above, his rib bones were exposed in a stack of pinkish-white Lincoln Logs.

"Fuck!" Oliver breathed as hands seized his oversized peacoat from behind, pulling it down. Oliver let go of the handlebars with one hand, letting the coat slide off as he ran forward. Once his arm was free, he switched, letting the other arm slide out, as more hands groped at him from behind. Teeth clacked near his ear as a zombie let go of the coat and lunged in.

Another darted in and bit down on the back of Oliver's triceps.

"Ahhhh! You son of a bitch!" he shouted, jerking away. Adrenaline-fueled fear surged through him and he screamed like that woman from the *Psycho* movie, shoving the bike forward. He'd no idea where he was going, only that all his instincts were telling him to get away!

A woman jumped at him from a side aisle. He juked to the side and she missed him entirely, belly-flopping onto the floor and tripping up some of the others behind him.

To his left was the paint department. Nothing that way but a colorful palette of death. Ahead was automotive. Automotive! You didn't have to come through the store to get to the automotive desk! There would be an exit that way for sure.

Oliver saw a man door that led into the automotive repair area. The door was closed. *Shit!* He couldn't risk the door being locked. If it was locked, he was dead.

To the right of the door there was a counter with an open window. Above the counter was a roll-up security gate made of metal rods like you might see in a mall when stores are closed, but the gate wasn't all the way down. It was half open! But he couldn't get over that countertop with the bike. Damn! He'd really wanted that bike. He'd dragged the damn thing halfway across the store!

With only one choice, Oliver let go of the bike, took three

running steps, and dove onto the counter. His gun fell out of his holster, slid across the countertop, and fell on the other side, skittering across the floor.

Pushing himself up, he grabbed the handle on the roll-up gate and pulled.

The metal-tubed gate rolled down and bashed into the countertop, locking into place.

For the first time since he'd come into the store, Oliver got a good look at the horde chasing him as the tidal wave of flesh smashed into the gate.

There were so many more than he'd thought, dozens upon dozens. From his position atop the counter, he could see over the crowd. They were filling the store, spilling in through the front and filling the aisles.

In the back of the building, smoke was pouring in from the shipping department and flames were now crawling up from the doorway towards the ceiling.

As the word "doorway" popped into Oliver's mind, his heart skipped a beat. The door! He spun, his eyes flicking to the door separating auto repair from the rest of the store and himself from the undead. The door handle rattled as the thumping of fists echoed from the other side.

Thank god! The door was locked. And thank god he hadn't chosen to try the door.

Oliver slid down off the counter and scanned his surroundings, trying to find his gun. He rubbed the back of his arm where the woman had bitten him. Fortunately, she'd been unable to bite through his windbreaker and long-sleeve shirt, but damn if it didn't hurt.

He looked back at the countertop roll gate as the undead shook it violently. The gate was made for security, but he doubted it would hold for long with dozens of undead pulling and slamming themselves into it over and over. A few were even attempting to climb it. How much weight could the mechanism hold?

"Hey," a voice called.

Oliver froze, trying to see in the dimly lit area. He was behind an L-shaped counter capable of serving both customers from the store side and walk-ins from outside. Behind him was an employee-only area that might have led to a parts area or break room. Opposite the counter was a waiting area with a flipped-over coffee table and a smashed concession area, the remnants of which were scattered all over the floor. Across the lobby was a shattered glass door leading outside and another door leading into the garage. To the right of that door, a hallway led out of sight to what he guessed were restrooms.

And it was from somewhere down that dark hall the voice had called to him. It had called, hadn't it? Or was he losing his shit?

Behind him, the moans of the undead raged on, the security gate shaking wildly. He needed to get the hell out of here.

Scanning the area again, Oliver used his foot to push busted computer screens, clipboards, and scattered office supplies out of the way. The urgent need to run tugged at him but he didn't want to be weaponless either.

"Hey, over here!" the voice shouted again.

Oliver jerked his head up and leaned out over the counter. "Where are you?"

"Back here, in the hall."

"Come out!" Oliver shouted back, his eyes returning to the floor.

Behind him, something popped. He spun to see part of the ceiling above the roll gate collapse. It was only drywall and insulation, but clearly the barrier wasn't going to hold for long. Looking for something to use as a weapon, Oliver scanned the area. Then he remembered that he was the biggest idiot on the planet. He had a gun in his ankle holster – his little .22 deuce-deuce.

"I… I can't!" the voice called.

He knelt down and drew the pistol.

Oliver exited from behind the counter and made his way around towards the hall.

"Here!" the man shouted.

Oliver could barely make out the silhouette of a man sitting on the floor. Behind him, a wheelchair lay turned over. "Shit."

"I'm in a real mess and I need some help, pal."

Next to Oliver was the door into the repair shop, and behind him, the busted glass door that exited into the parking lot. Somehow, Oliver knew it was only a matter of moments before more undead ventured in from the parking lot. Everything inside screamed for him to run. But he couldn't leave a paralyzed man lying on the floor to become easy pickings.

Oliver rushed forward, grabbing hold of the man's wheelchair with his free hand. "Okay, but we have to hurry!"

"Oh god, thank you!" The man's voice cracked with emotion. "I've been sitting here starving to death for what, three? No, four days!"

"It's alright," Oliver said, feeling the sense of urgency tug at him as he stepped over the man. How was he going to do this? He'd have to get the man to a car and pray it had keys. "I'll get your chair flipped back onto its wheels and we'll get you out of here."

"Thank god you came along... smelling so good – so sweeeet."

Oliver halted, sucking in a sharp breath. Before he could jump back, the man lunged , snatching Oliver by the ankles and jerking.

Oliver's feet came out from under him and he fell hard onto his side, his elbow taking the brunt of the fall. "Mmmmauh! Christ!" he moaned.

The man tugged, scaling his way up and onto him.

It all happened so fast. But despite the fall, he was still holding the little .22.

The man's face appeared in front of Oliver's. His red eyes were crusted with dried blood and his bewhiskered lips were drawn up in a feral sneer.

Oliver held the man only inches from his face as he fought to place the gun against the old man's head.

Beyond the hall, metal twisted and the undead screamed as if they sensed their chance for a meal was about to be stolen.

Sour breath washed over Oliver's face. "Finally! You've no idea the pain! No idea how I've suffered!"

Oliver pressed his lips tight and slammed his mouth shut. He didn't even want to breathe – didn't want to take any chance he'd get infected when he shot the man. Pressing the barrel to the old man's head, he pulled the trigger.

There was no report. The gun had jammed.

CHAPTER 33
WHAT HAS TO BE DONE

FROM ACROSS THE lobby Jurnee screamed, "Oliver!" Tears fell down Jurnee's face as Zoe's whole world fell apart. She hadn't even seen the little girl standing there. Hadn't known she'd heard Tommy's words: *Oliver didn't make it. He's gone.*

Zoe blinked. "Gone... What do you mean, 'gone'?"

"He panicked, Zoe. The damned fool lost his shit. There was nothing I could do."

Zoe slapped Tommy across the face. She didn't think about slapping him; it just happened. She slapped him once, then she slapped him again. Her hands were flailing now – uncontrollably flailing. Someone was screaming, "You're wrong!" It was her – she was screaming.

Tommy raised his hand and made a fist. She wanted him to do it – to punch her. She slapped him again.

"Fred, you better get this bitch!" Tommy warned.

Fred was on Tommy now, dragging him back.

Jesse was there too and then Raymond, both standing in front of her, their faces full of heartbreak. No. No, this wasn't real, it wasn't happening!

Tommy and Fred were yelling at each other.

Aneesa was next to her now. "What's happened? Tommy, what have you done?"

"Oh sure, right away it's what have I done? The guy freaked out and shot his gun. They were all over us in seconds. I couldn't help him. I had to get back to the van. Back to Chad."

Fred pushed Tommy back. "And for god's sake, why in the hell did you take Chad on a flipping supply run into Libbyton?"

"That's my boy and I'll raise him how I see fit. He's got to learn!"

Zoe collapsed onto her knees. Beyond Fred and Tommy, Jurnee stood holding Princess down at her side as she sobbed uncontrollably. This wasn't right. None of this was right. "No," she whispered. "No... No!"

Everyone quieted, turning their attention to Zoe.

"Come here, Jurnee."

Jurnee ran to Zoe with Louie right on her heels.

Zoe held out her arms as the little girl collided into them. She closed her eyes, squeezing her tight to her chest.

Between hitched breaths Jurnee whispered in her ear, "Chad said Oliver got eaten by zombie monsters because he didn't listen to his dad."

"I... I don't know what happened, but I... I don't believe that." Zoe stood back up, keeping Jurnee's hand in hers. "Tell them how you tried to come on to me, Tommy. Go on, tell them. And when I turned you down, you decided to take Oliver on a supply run! Not yesterday! Not tomorrow! But the very same day I told you no!"

Through Melissa's door came a long groan of active labor.

Fred ran a hand over his face. "It's true, isn't it? Jesus, Tommy! You didn't learn your lesson in the last go-around? Getting dishonorably discharged and facing a potential court-martial isn't enough, you start it again?"

"You better shut up, Fred. You know I didn't force that girl to do anything she didn't want to do!" He threw his hands up. "That's what they do. They get embarrassed and they want someone to blame!"

Zoe had felt it earlier in the day when Tommy was alone with her in her room. Felt that he might try to force himself on her. She told herself she was overreacting, but it was all true. "Oh my god! You're a monster!"

"You don't know what you're talking about!" Tommy shouted.

Louie growled a low rumble.

Zoe stood up a little taller. She knew exactly what this man was, and she wouldn't cower from him. "I don't know if my husband is dead or alive. But I know that, whatever happened, you're a liar. Now, I'm going back in that room and delivering this baby, and when I'm done, I'm going out there to find out what happened to my husband."

"I already told you he's—"

"Shut up!" Zoe stared daggers at Tommy, wanting him to feel all her hate. "You better pray I don't find out you hurt him." Zoe turned to leave but then stopped and turned back to Fred and Martha. "I know Tommy is your brother, but you need to understand something. I won't stay here under the same roof as him. Not for even one more night. As the leader of this community, you need to decide because if this poor excuse for a human isn't gone when I get back..." She let the words hang in the air, but she didn't wait for Fred to respond, nor did she try to read his face. "Jurnee, come with me."

Jurnee wiped her eyes on her sleeve and took Zoe's hand.

"You're taking her in there?" Fred asked.

Zoe paused but she didn't turn back. "You've been so worried about the monsters out there that you failed to see the one standing right in front of you. Jurnee stays with me, and so does my dog."

Aneesa cleared her throat. "We won't be staying either... not if he does."

Martha looked as though she'd been struck. "Aneesa?"

"I'm sorry, Martha." Aneesa's gaze fell to Tommy as she cut him a disgusted look. "I won't stay here another night as long as Tommy is here."

Tommy was shouting again. "You got your nerve! I told you all what happened."

The shouting continued, but Zoe barely heard it. Holding Jurnee's tiny hand in hers, she turned away and walked back towards Melissa's room. In her soul, a mix of emotion swirled like a funnel cloud about to touch down. Inside... she was dying. But she wouldn't collapse into an inconsolable heap. She wanted to, but she wouldn't allow it. Something about this didn't feel real. Maybe she was in denial or maybe she was in shock... or maybe she just knew what had to be done.

Zoe took a deep breath and opened the door.

CHAPTER 34
SUNSHINE ON A DOG'S ASS

OLIVER LAY on a cold tile floor. An infected man paralyzed from the waist down and soaked with urine and shit had managed to not only take him to the ground but then to climb atop him.

Beyond the crazed man, the metal roll gate shook violently.

Still holding the small .22, he pulled the trigger again and again, but it was no use. It wouldn't fire. "Piece of shit," Oliver grunted through gritted teeth. He dropped the gun and placed both hands on the man's shoulders, holding back his snapping jaws from biting him in the face.

The man stopped biting and punched Oliver in the forehead. "If I can get in there! If I can break it open, I can eat it all. Then I can go to the calling! Then she will have me. No more pain! It's calling for me! Calling for me!!"

Oliver bent his leg, planted his right foot wide and out to the side, shifted his shoulder, and lifted his hips, bucking the man off of him.

The man grabbed him, holding onto his shirt, but Oliver tore away, scrambling backwards and then onto his feet.

"No! No, you can't!" the man cried, crawling towards him, dragging himself by his arms. "The calling! The pain! I need you!"

Oliver turned and ran back down the hall towards the broken

front entry in a near panic. A glance to the left was all he needed to see he was about to be fucked. The corner of the roll gate was torn away and the first of the horde, a male zombie, was squeezing through, pulling himself over the counter. *Stupid!* Oliver scolded himself. What was he thinking? Outside, shadows moved past the windows towards the broken front door. Oliver only had one option left. Hastily, he pushed open the door to the repair shop and stumbled through.

The door had a lock on the knob. He frantically thumbed the button, locking the door as he identified the first of several problems. The upper half of the door was glass. He spun back around, and that's when he noticed his next and more pressing problem. A large man in a blue mechanic's uniform was sprinting directly at him, full speed ahead.

It was all Oliver could do to force himself to stay put and stand his ground until the last possible second.

The big mechanic was a full-blown undead zombie. He could tell not only by the half a dozen bullet holes in the guy's torso, but also by the way it ran at him. There was no thought behind the thing's bloody eyes, other than to feed. Oliver knew the undead wouldn't square off for a fight because once dead, zombies didn't think that way. Instead, it would simply bowl him over.

At the last second, Oliver juked right, nearly colliding with the workbench.

The zombie smashed into the window, shattering the glass as momentum carried it forward.

Oliver grabbed the closest thing he could find, which happened to be a large ratchet from the workbench.

As the undead mechanic stood and pulled itself back through the upper part of the shattered door, Oliver cracked him over the back of the head. Once. Twice. Then again. He could feel the crunch of bone through the handle of the rachet.

The zombie turned its now deformed head towards Oliver. Its

black hair was matted on one side and pushed deep into its dented skull.

"What the hell, die already!" Oliver begged through clenched teeth as he reared back for another swing. But before Oliver could strike another blow, the zombie let out a grotesque gurgle, dropped to his knees, and fell on his face.

Another zombie with a displaced toupee hanging down over one ear was frantically climbing through the broken window.

Oliver's first thought was, *What the hell is holding that chunk of hair on this guy's head? Is it tape or some kind of glue?* Then his next and more important thought was to attack before the thing made it inside, but what would be the point? More were coming, and they would keep coming. Instead, he used what little lead time he had to scan the repair shop. He needed a car and a way out. Or a way out and then a car.

Closest to him was a silver Ford pickup truck, but two of the four tires were off the vehicle. In the next bay, a red Kia was on a lift. It appeared to be in the process of an exhaust replacement. The third bay was empty, and in the fourth a brown sedan was pulled over a pit with the hood up. Who knew what the mechanics had been doing with that one – a tune-up perhaps. *Well, shit!* he thought, running towards the opposite side of the repair shop. All the garage doors were shut, but at the far end was another man door. His only choice left was to flee out the door and hope he could find a car before being attacked and eaten alive. Awesome.

Behind him, zombies piled through the broken door window.

As he crossed the third bay, something caught his eye. "Oh sweet, sweet Jesus!" he breathed, cutting right towards the back wall.

Oliver's dad used to say, "Even the sun shines on a dog's ass now and then." Well, it appeared the sun was finally shining on his.

Left of the tire-changer machine, against the back bench, stood a black Trek commuter bicycle. It was as if it had been placed there just for him. Suddenly he felt a strange mix of stupidity and vindication. Stupidity for nearly having died dragging that mountain bike halfway across the store only to have to ditch it to survive, and vindication for having found this one. The bike was still a good idea.

Oliver made a beeline for the bike, grabbed it, and headed for the man door, his lead on the pursuing zombies slipping. As the door swung open, several terrifying thoughts invaded his mind but none more terrifying than being consumed by the horde on his heels. *Dad, if you're up there, this old dog could sure use some more of that sunshine.*

As Oliver crossed the threshold, he quickly glanced up into a clear afternoon sky. No rain. Without further hesitation, he ran forward into what would be the east side parking lot. There was no sign of the undead either. Finally the break he needed. Running forward, he leapt onto the bike and stomped down on the pedals. Stealing a glance back, he saw zombies falling over each other as they piled out the door, first onto their hands and knees, then on their chests and faces. Others clambered over the fallen, stomping them down as they tried to stand.

Pedaling with all he had, Oliver quickly created distance between himself and the horde.

As he rounded the building, heavy dark smoke wafted across the parking lot, creating a smoke screen.

Oliver had no choice. He pedaled into the smoke, reducing his visibility to only a few yards. As abandoned cars appeared from the smoke, he weaved, steering his bike around them. The toxic smoke burned his throat, and it was all he could do to not cough. Quickly, Oliver unzipped the top of his windbreaker and pulled his shirt up and over his nose.

He hadn't planned it this way, but now he realized the smoke might be a blessing. The zombie horde would surely lose sight of him and hopefully through the stink they would lose his scent as well.

When Oliver broke from the smoke, he was on a small road that led out of the Farm and Feed parking lot. To his right were several prefab storage sheds lined up in rows. Beyond that was the Walmart parking lot. To his left was a grassy area, and beyond the grass were the backs of several businesses, including a gas station, a family restaurant, and a fast-food chain.

What he didn't see were zombies. He glanced back, half expecting the horde to break from the smoke, but none appeared.

Once he cleared the storage sheds, he glanced back towards Walmart and did a double take. Strangely, the undead mosh pit was nowhere in sight. Oliver frowned; he could see the whole parking lot. He wasn't mistaken. They were gone.

He bet Tommy had taken Chad over there to shoot at them or throw gas bombs. Great. Now they could be anywhere.

Oliver pulled onto North Libbyton Road, turned right, pedaled a block, and then turned onto West Courtland. Walmart and Farm and Feed were on the north edge of town. The church was several miles to the southwest on the opposite side of Libbyton, but he had no plans of cutting through town. That would be suicide. Instead, he would have to skirt around the edge.

Six miles, maybe seven. If he pushed hard, he could be back to the church in thirty minutes. As Oliver made his way down West Courtland, he passed an urgent care and then a fire station. After that, he passed a few barren cornfields lining both sides of the road. All that remained were short stalks jutting up from the soil – a reminder of summer gone, but more, a reminder of what might never be again.

Oliver pedaled through the gears, building speed. Soon, his immediate fear of being zombie lunch faded, and his thoughts drifted to Tommy. The images played over and over in Oliver's mind. The van racing past. The firebomb. Tommy's smug salute as he left him for dead. The more the images played, the angrier he became; the angrier he became, the harder he pedaled.

It was all clear to him now. Probably should have been clear before. Tommy wanted Zoe. He brought Oliver along to get rid of him. That was his plan the whole time. In Tommy's twisted mind, he thought if Oliver was out of the picture, he could take Zoe for himself. Maybe she would be distraught. Maybe Tommy would weave some story about how he tried to save Oliver. Zoe would be grieving and vulnerable. "Oh, I'm coming, Tommy, you son of a bitch! I'm coming!"

Hate welled inside Oliver, pulling at his guts like a swallowed fishhook being yanked. Never had Oliver felt this way about another man, but as he turned onto Veterans Road, he knew he was going to kill Tommy or die trying.

Heading south across Jackson Street, Oliver passed the Circle Lake apartment complex on the right. The apartments were made up of several four-story complexes set around a small lake. Like the rest of Libbyton, the complex looked as though a hurricane had swept through. Some of the windows were boarded up, others were busted out, and one complex had partially burned. Twisted and decomposing bodies littered the grounds. It was no wonder the smell of death hung in the air. From somewhere deep within the complex, someone screamed. Whoever that someone was, they were being attacked. He couldn't see them, and he sure as hell wasn't going in there to investigate – not after the man with the wheelchair.

Down by the water, movement caught his eye as four, no five, people broke into a run. But they weren't running towards him – they were sprinting for the complex, drawn by the blood-curdling scream. Oliver shifted gears and pressed on.

His next turn took him away from town. Just up ahead, he would pass a large mobile home park and then a farm that, when the season called for it, sold pumpkins and Christmas trees. If the asteroid hadn't happened, he and Zoe might have stopped there this weekend to pick up some pumpkins for the porch.

Oliver could only imagine how Zoe must be feeling right now. How devastated he would feel if the tables were turned. *Please don't believe him, Zo. I'm coming.*

Lost in thoughts of her, Oliver didn't see the ambush.

As he passed by the main entrance to the mobile home park, a wiry man in a leather jacket stepped out from behind a fenced-in dumpster and threw something.

Oliver flinched, jerking the handlebars as the object struck him hard in the shoulder. At his sudden yank, the front tire bit into the curb, the wheel folding like a taco. Oliver's world went upside down as he went over the handlebars.

"Ha! I got you now!" the man's voice called.

Oliver lay sprawled on the grass along the shoulder of the road.

Footsteps on pavement closed in. As fast as he could, he scrambled onto all fours and then his feet.

The disheveled man looked crazed; his bleeding eyes were wide as he sprinted towards him from across the street. Oliver blinked and glanced at his shoulder, fearing the worst, but there was no visible injury.

When he glanced back up, he realized the man wasn't looking at him, he was looking at the ground to his right.

Quickly he scanned the ground along the edge of the road.

There, lying next to the curb, was the cause of his pained shoulder. It was a... a throwing axe? The black axe had a curved blade on one side and a spike on the other. The fucker had hit him with a throwing axe?! Since it wasn't stuck in his shoulder and he wasn't gashed open, obviously he'd been hit with the flat top or maybe the bottom of the handle.

The man dove for the axe.

Oliver knew he couldn't get there first, so instead he grabbed the bike. Lifting it high above his head, he smashed the bike down on the back of the man's head.

The man cried out, reaching for the axe.

Oliver stomped on the guy's hand and snatched up the axe, reared back and swung, burying the blade in the back of the man's skull right where the parasite bulge was.

The man collapsed onto his stomach as a mix of yellowish-green fluid and blood gushed from his neck wound. He didn't move again.

Oliver sat down on the curb, catching his breath as he rolled his shoulder forward and then backwards. It didn't hurt too bad now, but he could tell it was going to be a mess tomorrow – assuming tomorrow was still in the cards. He glanced at the bike. The front tire was blown and the rim was folded. What the hell was he going to do now? *Stay calm,* he told himself. *As long as you're still breathing, there's still a chance.*

There was probably a car inside that trailer park – along with a hundred zombies, or more infected like this asshole. Christ, he didn't even have a gun. Glancing up the road, he supposed he could wander along, hoping to find a working car before the next something tried to eat him. No transportation, no gun, and little hope. His heart sank down into the pit of his stomach and a wave of despair washed over him.

At that moment, oddly enough, he thought of Howard and the last thing the man had said before he stepped out into the rain. *Sometimes all we can hope for is a safe place to die.* Later, Zoe had asked him, *Is that all we can hope for... finding a safe place to die?* But it wasn't until right now, when he felt all hope was lost, that he truly understood what Howard had already known. It wasn't about finding a safe location. Where you die doesn't really matter at all. Howard knew this.

If he was going to die, then so be it, but he didn't want to die like this; not out here – not alone. His safe place to die was with Zoe. "It isn't over yet. So... suck it up, get off your ass, and figure it out, asshole."

Oliver stood and spun in a slow circle, then he looked down at his trail shoes. "Remember that crap you gave me about not having boots, Tommy?" He reached down and worked the throwing axe loose from the dead guy's spine, wiped it on the grass best he could, and slid the handle through his shoulder holster. It fit well enough and would be easy to get to if he needed it.

Feeling a renewed sense of determination, Oliver did the math, figuring if he abandoned the roads and cut across the fields, he was maybe only three to four miles from the church. *Twelve-minute miles, and I'll be back at the church in thirty to forty-five minutes. Just an easy run across some fields. Nothing to it... as long as I don't get eaten... and it doesn't rain.*

Oliver stepped back onto the grass and gazed south. Behind him, a noise from deep within the trailer park caught his attention. Gunshots, screams, and pained cries from the hungry were all quickly becoming the norm at this point, but this was something else.

He peered back across the road and down one of the shadowed streets, quietly listening for the sound to return.

First, a twisting of metal, then a scraping like steel on concrete. There, almost as far into the trailer park as his eyes would allow him to see, a mobile home rocked side to side. It had only moved a little, but he was sure he'd seen it. Everything went still again, quiet as death. Oliver stared into the trailer park for what seemed like an eternity. So long that he began to question what he thought he had seen.

Urgency to get back tugged at him. It was time to go, but as Oliver stepped towards the field he heard it again and spun. There! Near the trailer he'd been so sure he'd seen move, a car was pulling forward. No, not driving. The SUV shifted, sliding sideways, forced out of the way by what appeared in the road.

Oliver blinked, trying to fathom what he was seeing. "What in the ever-loving fuck..."

CHAPTER 35
DIRTY DUNCAN

"ALRIGHT, mama, it's time to work! On your next contraction I want you to bear down and push!" Zoe glanced over at Jurnee, who sat across the room with eyes big and curious. Louie lay at her feet, eyes closed, ears twitching along with each contraction. This wasn't the preferred timing or method for a six-year-old to learn about birth, but you couldn't have paid Zoe enough to leave Jurnee outside with that maniac Tommy. At least the angle was such that Jurnee couldn't see the birth itself, but Zoe could see the curiosity building on the girl's expression as she looked up from her doll.

Zoe had explained to Adam and Melissa why Louie and Jurnee were in the room. But their consoling expressions had told her they'd heard the shouting and knew what had happened. When Zoe couldn't find the words to say more, Aneesa had chimed in and backed her up, agreeing that either Tommy had to go, or they would all be better off finding somewhere else to wait this out.

Thankfully, the yelling outside faded. A few moments later, the lights flickered and then came on.

"What the hell?" Adam said, glancing around. "Do you hear that? Dammit! Tommy must have gone back outside and turned on the generator. Listen. You can hear it running! Fred's going to lose his mind!"

Zoe couldn't worry about that. She was just thankful she no longer heard Tommy's voice shouting in the background. Difficult as it was, for now she had to compartmentalize her thoughts of Oliver and the whole situation into a mental box and lock it away. This moment with Melissa had to be her whole world. Melissa was now fully dilated. A new life was coming and Zoe owed it to little baby Jonathan to be her best.

As the contraction came and went, Melissa held Adam's hand and pushed. Minutes passed. Twenty, then thirty. Melissa's blue bangs were wet and slicked back with sweat and she looked exhausted. "You're doing great. I see the top of his head, Melissa!" When the head didn't retract, Zoe knew it wouldn't be long. Then came more yelling from outside.

Fred's voice first: "You stupid bastard! I've been looking everywhere for you! You shut that genny off right now before you get us all killed."

A brief quiet.

Fred shouted again. "What the hell is wrong with you? Did you hear what I said?!"

"Oh, no," Martha said, rising from her spot on the other side of Melissa. "That doesn't sound good. I'll be right back. Let me calm those two down."

Aneesa wet a rag and wrung it, then dabbed at Melissa's brow. "Martha, maybe you should stay here."

"Nonsense," Martha said. "Let me tell these boys to quiet down or take all that shouting somewhere else. I'll be right back." She vanished outside.

As the door swung shut, Zoe heard Fred say, "What's wrong with you?! Are you even listening to me?"

Zoe assessed Melissa again. "Alright, Melissa, we're going to get you into position. Adam, help me scoot her down. Aneesa, can we get another towel here and one here?"

"I feel another contraction coming!" Melissa shouted.

Outside, Fred shouted, "You're pointing a gun at me?!"

A gun fired and Martha screamed.

Melissa tensed as another contraction hit her, then shouted and pushed.

The gun fired again. Zoe blocked it out, staying focused on Melissa. "Push, Melissa, you can do it! Give him his eviction papers!" From the corner of her eye, she noticed Aneesa run across the room and shove the slide bolt into place.

"That's it!" Zoe announced. "The baby's head is crowning, Melissa! Breathe! Relax and breathe!"

"I feel like I want to push!" Melissa shouted.

"I know you do, but don't. I want you to blow out instead. Keep blowing out! We want baby to deliver gently. The head is out! Wonderful job! Again blow out and let your body do the work now," she encouraged.

Another contraction came and went. Supporting the baby's slightly cone-shaped head, Zoe forced herself to stay in the moment as she observed the baby already had a scalp covered in a mess of matted black hair. With the baby's head delivered, she felt for any sign the umbilical cord had wrapped around his neck but felt nothing. As his shoulders completely cleared, Zoe found herself holding little baby Jonathan. He was limp and silent. Quickly but carefully, she flipped him over in her hand and began vigorously rubbing his back, then flicked her finger against the bottom of his foot.

"Is he okay?" Melissa cried.

A moment passed, silent and terrifying, but then...

Baby Jonathan sucked in a little breath and let out a cry.

Melissa started crying.

"You did it! You did it, Melissa!" Zoe exclaimed, tears spilling from her eyes.

"He's perfect," Adam said as Zoe laid the new baby on Melissa's belly.

Zoe glanced up at Aneesa, now standing on Melissa's opposite side, but she wasn't looking at the new baby. Her eyes were fixed on the door.

"My baby!" Melissa cried tears of joy as she looked upon her little Jonathan for the first time. The baby wailed the healthy cry of an infant with strong lungs.

"Here," Zoe said. Laying a soft blanket over baby Jonathan, she cleaned him off a bit before tucking it around him.

"Is the door locked?" Zoe asked Aneesa quietly.

Aneesa nodded.

Another gunshot, farther away this time.

"Raymond is out there! My kids are out there!" Aneesa said, her voice cracking.

"I know. But please don't go out there, Aneesa. From that tray, hand me those two plastic zip ties," Zoe said, trying to get the woman focused and keep her from running out that door. If Aneesa went out that door, Zoe knew she would never see her again. She felt it with all her soul.

Shakily, Aneesa handed her the zip ties one by one. The woman's eyes flashed towards the door as she bit at her lower lip. "Please? Oh god, what's happening?" she whispered.

Zoe cinched the zip ties she'd scored from Scott tightly around the baby's umbilical cord about two inches apart. "Adam, do you want to cut the cord?" she asked, offering him the scissors.

Adam shook his head, his eyes darting from the baby to the door. "No. You do it!"

As Zoe prepared to cut the cord someone screamed in the distance. This time it was a man. She looked at Jurnee to tell her to cover her ears, but the little girl's hands were already pressed tight to her head. "Louie! Stay with Jurnee!"

"That's coming from the lobby! I think that's Jesse!" Adam said, starting for the door.

Clack! Clack! The screaming stopped.

"Do not open that door, Adam!" Zoe warned, pausing with scissors in hand. "You have a baby and a girlfriend who need you right here!"

Adam swallowed. His eyes were wide and fixed on the door. "What the fuck is happening out there?!"

I don't know," Zoe said, glancing at the back corner of the room, where a door led from the nursery into a more private mother's room. "Does the mother's room lock?" she asked as she cut the cord and turned her attention back to Melissa.

Aneesa bolted for the door.

"Aneesa!" Zoe tried, but it was too late. The woman slapped open the lock and pushed open the door.

Adam ran to the door and pulled it shut, locking it once more.

Zoe closed her eyes. "Dear god, Aneesa." She wished she hadn't gone, but if Jurnee were out there, wouldn't she have done the same?

Adam crossed back over to Zoe and pointed at the door leading to the mother's room. "Yes. It locks from the inside and has a keyed dead bolt."

Outside, Aneesa screamed, and Zoe opened her eyes.

Another shout, "Tommy! No!" It sounded like Jerry.

Another shot. *Clack!*

"Why is he doing this?" Adam shouted.

She didn't say what they both already knew. Tommy wasn't out there defending the occupants against an attack of zombies. He was executing everyone. It made no sense. Had he lost his mind and gone completely insane? "I don't know, but we aren't done here and now I'm going to need your help."

"What do I do?"

"Melissa is about to pass the placenta. Can you prepare clean washcloths?" Zoe's medical memory kicked in, and she remembered that afterbirth was the critical and final stage of birth. It was important that the afterbirth be passed in its entirety. She would need to examine the placenta to ensure it was fully intact, and somehow they needed to hurry because there was no telling what Tommy might do next.

"After the placenta passes, I want to get Melissa cleaned up and as comfortable as possible." In truth, Zoe had another motive. She wanted to make sure Melissa didn't need sutures. There was some blood, though not an alarming amount, and she guessed the baby to be somewhere between seven and eight pounds, easing her concern of serious vaginal damage, but until she could see, she couldn't be sure.

"Of course," Adam breathed and went to work soaking and wringing clean washcloths.

Three concussive booms roared out from somewhere deep within the church.

"Shotgun!" Adam announced. "Sounded like it came from Fellowship Hall! I think someone's firing at Tommy?"

Jurnee bolted up and ran towards Zoe. Adam grabbed her. "I'm scared!" she said.

More shots echoed from somewhere deep within the church. Silence followed.

"I know. We're all scared, kiddo, but your mom is still working, okay? You're safe, stay right here next to me," Adam said, standing off to the side of the futon. "Look, Jurnee. Look... at my... my baby."

Zoe placed a hand on Melissa's belly and pressed lightly.

Without warning, Tommy shouted through the door. "You think you can hide from me? I can smell you in there! Each one is so sweet. Sweet and creamy." Tommy laughed. "What's that, fresh blood? Oh-ho, there's a new one! Tender, fresh, and brand new!"

Jurnee screamed. Louie growled and then barked at the door.

Melissa pulled little Jonathan closer, her face horror stricken.

Adam drew a pistol from his waistband and took up a shooter's stance in front of the door.

Suddenly, everything became clear. "Jurnee, take Louie and get in that room now! Run!"

"Come on, Louie!" Jurnee shouted, running for the mother's room.

Zoe didn't know how it had happened, but sometime in the last thirty to forty minutes, Tommy had become infected. "He's infected," Zoe warned. "Be careful standing in front of the door – he has a gun too!" She turned her attention back to Melissa.

When Zoe saw the umbilical cord lengthen she realized the placenta had separated from the uterus. Pulling gently on the cord while holding the uterus with her other hand the afterbirth passed easily, and Zoe was able to capture it in a large bowl.

Zoe gave the placenta a cursory glance, remembering the shiny side was called the Shiny Schultz – she only remembered that because the opposite side, which was jagged and dark maroon, was called the Dirty Duncan. In nursing school, she and her classmates had found the name humorous and spent far too much time laughing at Dirty Duncan jokes, but here and now she found no humor. Upon examination, the placenta appeared to be intact. Hastily now, Zoe went to work rinsing and inspecting for any major tears in the vaginal wall. When she found nothing in need of stitching, she breathed a sigh of relief.

Tommy's deranged voice came through the door again. "Be a good girl, Zoe! Be a good girl and come join Aneesa. I have so much to eat now. But I've never felt like this, never been hungry like this."

The building shook.

"Did you feel that?" Adam asked.

Zoe nodded that she'd felt it. It was like a truck had hit the other side of the building.

Through the door, Tommy shouted, "The others are coming in from the field now. But I'm not sharing. No fucking way! I did the work. It should all be mine."

"Tommy, think about the kids!" Adam shouted. "Your own kid is out there. You don't want to let anything happen to him."

Tommy's voice went instantly calm, reduced to an urgent whisper. "What? What's that, Adam? Hooah, sweet, gooey Adam. What happened to Chad? Chad didn't want me to hurt like this! Chad understood! Why don't you understand?" He was shouting again, his fist pounding against the door.

Adam looked over at Zoe, his eyes knitted in confusion. But she wasn't confused. She knew exactly what he'd done. And if there was any doubt remaining, Tommy's next words confirmed it all.

"They're dead! I. Shot. Everyone!"

Adam's face twisted in horror as he adjusted the gun in his grip. He took two steps towards the door, squaring up right in front of it.

Around them, the building's walls shook again.

"This place won't hold them out long," Tommy warned and started mumbling again. "I have to fill it up, that's all. I have to fill it up and the pain will stop. But my stomach! Ugh! The pain! I can fit more! I have to. Eat them like the others. Eat fast! Eat. Eat. Eat it all!" He was shouting again. Then through the door Tommy whimpered, "Make this easy and just let me the fuck in!"

Zoe glanced over at the mother's room, making sure Jurnee and Louie were safe inside. "Adam, help me get Melissa up. We need to get her and baby Jonathan to the—"

Tommy let out a scream of rage, followed by the staccato burst of four more gunshots.

Adam staggered backwards.

Zoe could hear the bullets hitting the wooden door, and at first she feared Adam had been shot. Adam must have thought so too because he scanned his body, checking for any sign of a wound.

But when Zoe scanned the door for holes, she found none.

"You bastards!" Tommy shouted. "You think this door can keep me out? Keep me from what's mine?" He laughed. "I'll just get a bigger gun."

CHAPTER 36
TWISTED FLESH

BY ANYONE'S STANDARD, Oliver wasn't a fast runner, but then trail running wasn't like road running. Particularly trail races that went to ultra distances, which was anything over a marathon distance. For Oliver, that meant a lot of power-hiking or walking with purpose. This was especially true over rugged terrain and on hills. No matter how much he trained, he would never be the fastest guy on the trail. But winning races wasn't what drew him to long-distance running. Through pushing himself further and further, Oliver had found that he possessed a single bad-ass attribute – his ability to suffer. To date, he had run six one-hundred-mile trail races, and he'd finished every one. In his last hundred miler, it had rained two inches and a portion of the trail flooded. The flash flood was unsafe to cross. The course had to be rerouted during the race. It had taken Oliver thirty-three hours to finish, earning him last place.

But dead last was fourth place. Fifty-two other runners had toed the start line, but overnight forty-eight had dropped out due to the storms and the soul-sucking mud on the trail.

After the race, it had taken him weeks to recover. He'd lost half his toenails, had blisters on every toe and both heels, and was chafed in every crevice of his body. But he was one of only four that survived the suck and finished the race.

Oliver's normal strategy was to let the terrain dictate his pace – normally. But today was anything but normal.

Oliver was running full-out as fast as he could push his body to go across a freshly plowed cornfield. He moved at a rate of speed that would raise his heart rate to max thresholds, have him gasping for air until he eventually seized up in cramps. He could only hope that wouldn't happen before he crossed the three or four rolling miles back to the church.

So on he ran, like his life depended on it. And after what he had just seen in the trailer park, maybe it did! He glanced back, hoping not to see... *it*. Thank god he didn't. Maybe it hadn't noticed him. The important thing now was getting back to the others and warning them. If that thing came from the middle of one of the zombie mosh pits like back at the church, Zoe, Jurnee, and everyone else were in grave danger, and they didn't even know it. And where else could it have come from? It was too much of a coincidence that on the same day the group of undead at Walmart disappeared, this *thing* appeared. If he hadn't seen it for himself, he wouldn't believe it.

He couldn't see the church yet, but somewhere to the south, Oliver thought he heard gunshots. He stopped only briefly as he tried to slow his breathing enough to listen. More gunshots – he was sure this time. Then several booms from a shotgun. Could those shots have come from the church? Were they under attack?

As Oliver crested the top of a small rise, the church came into view. He half expected to see something awful, but from this distance all appeared quiet. Far to the southwest, a couple miles beyond the soccer fields, the rolling fields hid the mass of zombies and the secret they held within. He hoped to see them – to know they were still there or maybe that they weren't and had instead wandered off in a different direction – but no luck from this vantage point.

Oliver jumped the ditch and crossed the road, hurrying into the field on the other side. "Two more miles! Suck it up!" he told himself.

As he drew closer to the church, he heard a hum growing louder and louder. At first, he didn't understand what it was, but the closer he got, the more it sounded like an engine.

"Son of a bitch!" Oliver shouted through ragged breaths. Tommy had turned on the generator. Why would Fred let him do that?

With a little over a mile to go, Oliver felt his body fighting him to slow. His heart rate was cranked into the red. This was not how he ran on the trails. But then he saw something that knotted his gut and kicked his adrenaline into high gear.

The mosh pit of zombies appeared from the low spot in the field, running like an undead battalion of soldiers set to seize a castle as they rushed towards the church.

Then he saw *it* among them – the thing they had been hiding or... creating? It was all wrong. It moved all wrong, with human body parts that didn't belong where they were. He'd only caught a brief glimpse of *it* deep within the shadows of the wooded trailer park, hiding a truth he wanted so badly to be false. Now there was no denying it.

Jesus Christ, this thing wasn't one human – it was many humans. Under the light of day he was sure, but how many people made up the tangle of flesh he didn't know.

From this distance he judged the monster to be at least nine feet tall and running on all four... legs. It was hard to see from this distance, but the legs were too big to be human. He guessed each appendage must have been made up of several human legs, four or maybe five! It had what Oliver thought was a head, but it too was bigger. Dear god, it looked like several heads stuck together. And the rest of it was some horrible collage of twisted bodies. It galloped along behind the horde like a newborn colt still trying to find its rhythm.

As Oliver stepped into the side parking lot, the zombie horde reached the back of the church just ahead of the monster that followed.

He couldn't imagine they had enough firepower in the church to defend against this.

More gunfire rang out from the church.

Someone was shooting from inside! Oliver crossed the parking lot, hoping and praying the zombies didn't come around the building before he made it inside.

He glanced at the noisy generator as he ran past it and the dozens of fuel barrels lining the side of the building. He couldn't believe Tommy's dumb ass had fired up that generator!

Oliver figured his best course of action was to go in the front, find the others, and quickly convince them to leave everything behind and make for Tommy's van and the truck, which were both parked out front. They had to get out of here right now!

He reached the front door, prepared to frantically pound on it to get Jesse or Adam to open up, but the door was ajar. Pinched between the door and the frame was a foot wearing a familiar Chuck Taylor. "Jesse?" Oliver called quietly as he pulled open the door.

Jesse lay in a pool of blood, his head smashed open, most of his brain missing. "Oh, god, Jesse." He glanced back over his shoulder. The van was three strides away. Through the passenger window he saw the barrel of his shotgun sticking up. Quickly, Oliver ran back to the van, grabbed the Beretta and hurried back inside.

He entered the church and closed the door, not bothering to lock it.

Farther inside the church's lobby he found Fred sprawled out face down on the floor; a few feet away lay Martha. Both appeared to have been shot, and Martha's head had been... Jesus. Oliver turned away, feeling like he might be sick. He wanted to scream for Zoe.

Beyond them, he caught a glimpse through the open door of the game room. Several of the children lay motionless; red stains spread out across the Twister game mat. Oliver ripped his eyes away before he could see any more. That was the last place he'd seen Jurnee! She was playing Twister with the others. "Jurnee," Oliver rasped, his eyes spilling over. "Zoe! Jurnee!" he screamed, no longer caring who or what heard.

He raised the shotgun and spun in a slow circle, rage and pain building in him as he cried out. “Please god! If you’re real! Please!” he begged, dropping onto his knees. “Zoooeeee!”

CHAPTER 37
THERE NEVER REALLY WAS A CHOICE

"WAS THAT? IT COULDN'T BE!" she gasped, a storm of emotion erupting inside her. "Did you hear that! That sounded like... that was Oliver!" Zoe ran past Adam towards the door.

"Wait, Zoe! Don't open that door! I... I don't think that was him," Adam warned.

She reached for the door lock. "I know my husband's voice. I know that was Oliver!"

"But what about Tommy? We've no idea where he is!" Adam begged.

"Exactly! I need to warn Oliver!" She glanced over to the futon where Melissa lay with the baby on her breast, her own exhausted eyes wide with fear. Zoe took a breath. What was she doing? She couldn't put them at risk. "Take Melissa and the baby into the mother's room and lock yourself inside! Jurnee, stay with Adam!" She looked at Louie, and for half a second she considered taking him, but she knew that if Tommy came back, he'd shoot her dog and not think twice about it. "Go with Jurnee!" she pointed.

"What about you?" Adam pleaded.

"Just do it! Hurry!"

Adam went to work gathering his wife and baby into the mother's room.

As the mother's room door slowly swung closed, Zoe glanced back, meeting Jurnee's tear-filled eyes. In the time it took for the door to swing shut, Zoe's mind filled with doubt. This was the wrong decision. She should be behind that steel door. She should be choosing to do everything she could to live for that little girl. That's what she would have expected Oliver to do. She'd told him as much. "You don't get to live or die for only me now. Now you live for both of us, but if ever you have to choose, you choose her." That's what she'd said.

Now, in this dire moment, the ultimatum she'd laid down seemed silly. There were never going to be easy choices between those you love. There was only ever going to be a single choice. You choose to save those you love and pray you don't die trying.

Behind her, the door latched and she heard Adam lock the dead bolt.

Outside the room, she heard Oliver scream her name again.

Zoe opened the door and leaned out. "Oliver! Oliver, we're in here!"

Oliver appeared from around the corner, sprinting towards her! "Zoe! Oh, god! I thought..." He grabbed her, pulling her into him. His body was wet with sweat, his normally shaggy red hair slicked back, and he was gasping in ragged breaths. "What the hell happened here?"

"Tommy happened! He's infected!" She stepped back from his embrace. "Hurry, get inside!"

"What? Infected?" He glanced past her. "And Jurnee? Please tell me she's..."

"She's in here with me! She's safe, Oliver!"

"Safe. Thank god, but none of us are safe! We got to go! The monster and the horde from the field are right outside!"

Zoe shook her head, not understanding. "Monster?"

From the direction of Fellowship Hall came a fracturing of wood.

Oliver's eyes widened. "We have to go now!"

"Right. I'll get the others!"

As Zoe started to turn, movement caught her eye from a shadowed office across the hall. Before she could scream a warning to Oliver, Tommy rushed forward from the darkness and punched Oliver in the side of the head.

"No!" Zoe shouted, lifting her own gun to shoot.

Tommy was too quick. He grabbed her gun as she pulled the trigger.

The round fired into the ceiling.

Tommy's eyes were blood crusted, his overshirt was gone, and all he wore was a blood-soaked white tank top stretched over his grotesquely swollen abdomen, which distended well beyond any semblance of normal.

He backhanded Zoe across the face.

Fireworks exploded in Zoe's vision, and she felt herself fall.

CHAPTER 38
AMBUSHED

OLIVER HAD NEVER BEEN HIT SO hard in the head in all his life. As he hit the floor, a gun went off and Zoe screamed, his own shotgun sliding away and out of reach.

Oliver turned back in time to see Tommy strike Zoe hard across the face.

Zoe screamed as she went down.

The fear and pain fell away, replaced by a surge of raw rage. Oliver kicked the side of Tommy's ankle, sending one of the man's feet into the other.

Tommy went down, but he landed atop Oliver's legs. "I'm going to break your head open, Oliver!"

From the room beyond, Oliver heard Louie going nuts.

The shininess of Zoe's nickel-plated revolver flashed in Tommy's hand as it swung towards Oliver's face.

Oliver managed to get his hand up in time to block most of the strike – but not all of it.

Warm blood spilled into Oliver's left eye as Tommy reared back for another swing.

In the moment, it felt like time slowed down. Zoe was trying to stand and shouting something into the nursery.

From the rear of Fellowship Hall came the sound of cracking wood. Oliver imagined the giant zombie thing ramming into the back of the building over and over. Above him, Tommy, with his high-and-tight crew cut and twisted visage, snarled down at him, his bloody teeth exposed. As Oliver stared up at the man, he could see the bits of flesh and smeared brain matter coating Tommy's teeth, like he'd been eating a can of lard mixed with raw ground beef.

The gun came down again.

This time when Oliver raised his hand to block the strike, he was holding the throwing axe. He hadn't even remembered drawing it from his shoulder holster.

The axe handle caught Tommy's wrist.

Oliver jerked it sideways, ripping the gun from Tommy's hand, his confidence surging as the gun clattered across the tile. He tried to swing for the man's neck but Tommy straight-jabbed him in the mouth. Oliver's head rocked back and bounced off the floor, his mouth filling with blood.

"You're weak, Oliver. You smell like fear and sweets!" Tommy snarled.

Oliver blinked, trying to see through his watering eyes. He flinched, bracing himself for the next hit as he frantically and blindly tried to swing the axe at Tommy's face.

He felt Tommy's hand seize his wrist and jerk him forward, slamming his forehead into Oliver's already bleeding eyebrow. Pain exploded in his head as he fell back, dropping the axe.

Tommy didn't let go of his wrist, jerking him forward again.

Oliver could barely make out the fuzzy visage of Tommy's fist as it careened towards his face in a wild arc. He slammed his eyes shut, tried to lean back and turn his face, bracing for another blow.

Instead, Tommy shouted, releasing Oliver's wrist.

"You mangy bastard, let go!"

Oliver opened his eyes to find the blurry image of Louie, jaws locked on Tommy's forearm. The blue-nose pit bull shook the man's arm wildly, as he squatted back, pulling him away from Oliver.

Oliver blinked away the fuzziness as he searched for the gun.

Tommy punched Louie in the ribs over and over, trying to free himself. "You son of a bitch!" he screamed. But the more he fought, the harder Louie shook and the louder he growled. Louie was doing his best to rip Tommy's arm from its socket.

The gun had slid too far away and there was no time left. Tommy stopped punching and reached for the axe with his free hand.

Oliver knew he couldn't let the man get a swing in with that axe, so he lunged and grabbed the handle with both hands.

"Get him, Louie! Don't let go, boy!" Oliver shouted as he ripped the axe from Tommy's hand.

Behind him there was a loud crash followed by the moans and screams of the hungry. In front of him, Tommy sat across his legs, pinning him to the floor, his arm bucking wildly as he reached forward with his now free hand, groping for purchase to pull Oliver to him. Tommy's blood-caked mouth opened and closed, clicking and biting.

"You should just give yourself to me! There's nowhere to run!"

Oliver reared back with the axe and swung, planting the spiked end of the hatchet into Tommy's eye socket.

The man sat there, his one red eye staring at Oliver, his body shaking as Louie continued to shake his now limp arm. Louie tugged a final time, and Tommy tipped over onto his side.

There was supposed to be some feeling of vindication, some witty last words. But after what Tommy had done to them, to his own family, Oliver couldn't find any words.

From Fellowship Hall, tables and chairs crashed. And he could hear the double doors burst open.

"Oliver! Get up!" Zoe screamed.

Louie let go of Tommy and ran forward, prepared to defend Oliver against whatever came around the corner.

But what appeared from around the corner wasn't the undead but a very much alive Fred.

Oliver shouted. "Fred! I thought you were—"

"Not dead yet! Now, get up and move!" Fred ordered. The man was practically dragging one leg and holding his hand over a bloody gut wound.

Frantically, Oliver kicked Tommy away and scrambled to unsteady feet, scanning the floor for the shotgun and the .357. Oliver snatched up the Beretta and kicked the .357 towards Zoe.

From the lobby came a throaty groan that sounded like an army of bullfrogs croaking in unison.

At the end of the hallway, the monster emerged.

All frantic motion stalled as Oliver and the others fixed their eyes towards the lobby. Up until this point, Oliver had not frozen up once, but the sight of this thing up close and under the artificial light of the hallway stopped him in his tracks, fear seizing him.

The low bullfrog groan continued rumbling through the walls of the hallway like a souped-up engine beneath the hood of a Mustang. The thing had three heads, each fused to the other at the back. Each head faced a different direction and all of the faces appeared vacant, eyes fixed in death like a cadaver on the slab. As it ducked low to clear the double doorway into the hall, one face stared absently down at the floor, one looked to the left, and one up and to the right. Pointing towards Oliver was the top of the three fused heads. In the center was a dark hole. "What the..." he breathed.

It was only when the hole stretched open to expose row upon row of shark-like teeth that Oliver realized with frightening horror he was staring into its mouth. The image of the parasite in Zoe's jar and its long tooth-filled mouth popped into Oliver's mind.

Long misshapen arms, fused together as if melted into each other, gripped the door frame with twisted hands – too many hands.

The zombie monster pulled itself forward, the rest of its patchwork body coming into view.

Oliver flinched back as the creature announced itself with a jarring high-pitched howl, reminding him of the coyotes he'd heard on trail runs at dusk.

In response, the three faces changed, animating like they were ripped from death. Their eyes suddenly bulged as if they would bust, their mouths went freakishly wide, too wide... and in unison they screamed.

CHAPTER 39
AMALGAMATION

ZOE'S ELATION at seeing Fred alive was quickly replaced by shock at the sight of the creature entering the opposite end of the hall. Her medical mind immediately worked to put the pieces together to rationalize what she was seeing.

This was an amalgamation. A merging of hosts – yes. But was it also a fusion of the parasites themselves? A section from the *Parasite Field Guide* about roundworms flashed into Zoe's mind. The accompanying photo wasn't of a single roundworm, but of over a thousand of the microscopic worms conjoined into a single tower capable of being seen with the naked eye. The worm tower's only purpose is to reach high enough to latch on to a passing beetle, where the worms would then invade the body, wait for the beetle to die, and consume the microbes that grew inside the carcass.

As the monstrous zombie amalgamation cleared the hallway doors, it stood tall on its rear legs, a towering colossus of decay and despair. Faces contorted in eternal agony throughout its twisted form, each one a testament to the undead the parasite had consumed.

Fred was still halfway down the hall and moving too slow.

"I'm going!" Oliver ran towards Fred, calling back, "Hold the door open for us!"

Zoe held the door wide as Oliver reached Fred and got an arm around him.

Behind them, Zoe could make out the shapes of bodies still mostly whole but now twisted together to make up the torso of the creature. A shoe and a piece of torn denim hung from one of the legs – legs configured in groups of three or four and somehow congealed together, then stacked atop another group of more twisted legs.

The once-separate corpses had become intertwined, their flesh melding and mingling until they formed this singular, towering monstrosity. As it stretched upward, Zoe saw a face half concealed in the fleshy goo of the creature where she might expect to see ribs.

Why? What was its purpose? Size had to be part of it. The parasite Tommy had brought her was different from the first one she'd seen in many ways. For one thing, it was much larger. Looking at the amalgamation before her, she wondered if this was a necessary step for the larger parasite species. Perhaps it simply didn't have enough room to grow in a single human. Then what of the other parasites already occupying the humans it merged with? Were they a sacrifice, or were they working as a collective?

Of course, her questions would be moot if she didn't live past the next few moments. "Oliver! Fred! Get out of there!"

Oliver shuffled towards her, urging Fred along. "Go, Fred!" he shouted, lifting the shotgun as he stooped next to Tommy's dead corpse.

"Oliver, what are you doing? Hurry!" she shouted.

Louie stood his ground, barking up at the creature as Fred hurriedly limped past her and into the nursery.

"Louie, come!" she ordered.

The amalgamation screamed again as it fell forward onto all four sets of legs.

Louie continued to bark warnings as he backed towards her and Oliver.

Oliver jerked the axe from Tommy's eye socket, pulling free the man's eyeball and optic nerve along with it.

From behind the amalgamation, zombies appeared, frantically squeezing around the sides of the imposing creature. The first zombie to get past the creature was holding something. At first sight, she thought the round object was a ball. What would a zombie be doing with a ball? Then she realized with stark horror that it was a head – Aneesa's head. The zombie dropped into a squat and began to beat Aneesa's head on the tile floor in an effort to crack it open.

Zoe's hand went to her mouth as she tried not to vomit at the macabre scene playing out before her.

The amalgamation's three heads spread apart, its mouth opening ever wider as sickening screams echoed off the corridor walls. The amalgamation charged forward as more and more zombies crowded the hall.

Oliver grabbed her, pushing her back into the nursery. "Go! Go! Go! Louie! Come on, boy!"

Louie shot past them into the nursery.

Oliver threw himself against the heavy wood door, slapping the bolt into place.

On the opposite side, the amalgamation wailed and the undead crashed into the door.

Fists pounded against the heavy wood. Then something denser. Zoe couldn't stop the image of an undead man smashing Aneesa's head into the wood door over and over from popping into her mind.

Oliver's eyes darted around the room. "When that thing gets to the door, we're fucked!"

Zoe pointed to the mother's room. "We can go into the mother's room with the others. The door is steel." She snatched her backpack off the floor and slung it over her shoulder. Some of her medical supplies, as well as the *Parasite Field Guide* were inside – she'd have to leave everything else behind.

"Is there a window in there?"

"If there is, it's boarded up," Zoe said, beating her fist on the door. "Adam, open the door! I have Oliver and Fred!"

The door swung open. "Fred! Oliver! Where's Tommy?"

Zoe motioned her hand towards the nursery door. "Tommy isn't our worry now! There's an amalgamation on the other side of that door along with a hallway full of zombies! We have to get out of here."

"Amal... what? Where will we go? How?" Adam's eyes filled with panic. "Melissa can't leave!"

Oliver passed his shotgun to Fred and rushed past her into the mother's room. Before he could get to the window, Jurnee threw her little arms around his leg. "Oliver!" she cried. "Oh, I'm so happy you're okay!"

In the nursery, Louie barked at the door. From the hallway, the amalgamation screamed from an array of once human vocal cords, now a raspy harmony of grotesquery, desperate and depraved.

Behind her, Oliver said, "I'm happy you're okay too, kid." He turned to Adam and rushed to a covered window. "We've no choice. Melissa, you'll have to move – and not only move, but we're climbing out this window."

Adam pulled a face as he glanced over at Melissa, who was sitting in an overstuffed chair holding their newborn. "You can't be serious, Oliver!"

Outside the small room, the wall to the nursery shook and bowed in. The sound of crunching and popping filled the nursery.

"It's coming through the wall!" Fred shouted.

Zoe watched in horror as Oliver desperately pried with the hatchet at the thick wooden tabletop covering the window. The repurposing of the Fellowship Hall tabletops into window coverings had given Zoe a feeling of safety – a feeling that no amount of zombies could break through. Now that feeling was flipped on its head as she realized that same chunk of wood was holding them prisoner.

"We need to break the screws and get this window open now! Everyone, get in here and lock the door!" Oliver shouted.

Zoe turned her attention back to Fred. The man had been shot multiple times, including at least once in the gut. He stumbled across the room, dragging a pink plastic school chair in one hand, still holding Oliver's shotgun in the other.

"Fred, what are you doing? We have to get inside!"

Fred waved her off and dropped himself heavily into the chair. He lifted the shotgun and pointed it towards the door.

"Fred, no. Please! What are you doing?"

"Buying you time. Look, I'm already dead, Doc. There's nothing you can do for me."

Zoe didn't believe that. Didn't want to believe that. If they could just get out of here, she could stop the bleeding and treat his wounds. She knew she could.

The wall shook again. The baby blue drywall cracked.

"We have to go now. Get up, Fred! Once we get out, I can—"

"Tommy bit me."

Zoe felt her heart sink. "Oh no, Fred. I'm so sorry."

Fred's lips quivered and he closed his eyes. "My Martha... What Tommy did..." He choked on the words, unable to finish. He opened his eyes and looked at Zoe. "Even if he hadn't bitten me, I wouldn't go. There's nothing for me without her. You two. You still have each other and there's a baby in that room!"

"Fred..."

Fred coughed and spit crimson on the floor. "You know, for the last thirty years I lived with the fact I lost men in Desert Storm. The ambush started with an improvised explosive. They died. My friends died... and somehow, I didn't. I never knew why I was spared. Now I've lost my Martha..." He looked up at her, his face steeled in determination, "Please, Doc, let me do this! I'm meant to do this! Now go! Get in there and shut the door. I'll hold them as long as I can."

The wall flexed in again, but this time the drywall gave way as the amalgamation of hands punched through, gripping the drywall and the metal two-by-fours within.

Zoe gasped.

"Go now!" Fred ordered, aiming the shotgun at the strange

collage of twisted hands as they gripped and yanked the metal two-by-fours apart.

Zoe ran inside the room. As she turned back to pull the door closed, Fred shouted, "Well, come on, you son of a bitch," and fired at the amalgamation.

The first shot was deafening.

She slammed the door and locked it.

From beyond the steel door, Fred fired more shots in rapid succession.

Boom! Boom! Boom! Boom!

Behind her, Oliver stopped hacking at the window. "Why? Why didn't he come?"

"He didn't want to. He wanted to give us more time."

The amalgamation screamed and the whole building shook. Fred shouted something, but she couldn't understand.

Zoe reached for Jurnee and covered her ears with her palms.

Beyond the door, Fred screamed.

For a brief second, everyone froze. Their eyes locked on each other – all of them saying so much without saying anything.

Finally, Oliver went back into motion. "Adam, help me!"

Oliver had managed to break loose one side of the wooden covering just enough to get his fingers beneath and pull. "It's moving!"

Both men wedged their fingers behind the repurposed table, grabbed, and pulled together.

Zoe listened as, beyond the door, the nursery filled with cries from the undead amalgamation and zombies. There were no more gunshots, no more shouts or screams from the living.

Fred was gone.

CHAPTER 40
A FOOTSTEP FROM FREEDOM

"ONE! TWO! THREE! PULL!" Oliver shouted as he and Adam jerked back on the wooden table. "Again! One! Two! Three! Pull!"

Next to the steel door, the monster's arm burst through the drywall.

Jurnee screamed as Louie ran forward, jumped up, and bit the cluster of arms. Jaws locked on, Louie dangled there, growling and shaking his body back and forth.

"Louie, let go!" Zoe ordered.

"Everyone, get away from the door!" Oliver shouted, turning his attention back to the window. As he went to pull again, his eyes caught Melissa's. The exhausted woman looked terrified as she held her newborn to her chest. He looked at the others. Little Jurnee's eyes were saucers as she screamed. Zoe was ushering Jurnee away from the door as Louie released the monster's arm and dropped back to the floor. Twisted hands and arms ripped and pulled at the wall as the undead creature's head tried to force its way inside.

The small mother's room filled with the smell of shit, body odor, and death.

They had to get out that window. It couldn't end like this. He couldn't fail them.

When its head didn't fit between the steel two-by-fours, it reached in again – a foot, two feet, three feet – the mishmash of arms swiping back and forth.

Oliver's eyes found Adam's. No words were exchanged as the two men pulled in unison. The room filled with the primal roar of two desperate men putting everything they had into one singular physical task, but the damn board wouldn't break loose of the window.

There was no more time! No time to chop, no time to pry, no other way. Zoe wedged herself against them, sliding her fingers beneath the board next to his. Oliver met her eyes, planted his foot against the wall and the three of them leaned back, and pulled with all they had.

Behind him, the thing's arms retracted, grabbed the metal two-by-fours, and pulled. The metal creaked and twisted as it tore the wall apart.

The tabletop let out a cry of resistance as screws creaked and snapped. All at once, the tabletop let loose and the three of them fell back.

Dull red light poured into the room, illuminating the undead monster pressing itself through the wall. Its heads and twisted arms were fully inside the room now as it struggled to force the rest of its hodgepodge body through the gap.

Oliver stood and pulled Zoe to her feet as the wall flexed and groaned. The monster wailed, its rotten breath filling the small room. It must have known how close it was because it went into a sudden frenzy, pressing itself forward with a renewed sense of urgency.

Behind the wood covering was a slider window big enough to step through, and beyond was a darkened sky and the sound of falling rain.

At first, Oliver's heart sank, but quickly he realized the window faced out beneath the massive porte cochere. Okay, things could be worse. And if he'd learned anything about this new world over the past couple weeks, he'd learned that as long as they were still alive, things could always be worse.

Oliver unlocked the window and slid it open. He stuck his head out and looked both ways. The van and truck were right there.

Zoe handed him Jurnee. He lifted her through the window. "Run to the van and get inside! Louie, go with Jurnee!"

Louie barked and jumped through the window.

Melissa handed Zoe her baby. With help from Adam, she managed to step up onto the window ledge. Oliver was there and took her hand, then her arm.

Behind them, drywall dust filled the air. Oliver glanced back to see the hungry undead pulling at the edges of the torn wall, trying to squeeze in around the monster, all of them hoping to be the first to feed.

Zoe passed him the baby. Oliver turned and passed the baby back to an anxiously waiting Melissa. Oliver turned back in time to see the wall implode.

"Zoe!" he shouted as the monster and countless zombies surged into the room.

Zoe reached.

Oliver grabbed her hands and fell backward, using his weight to jerk her through the window. The drop was only a couple feet but he landed hard on the concrete, Zoe falling atop him.

As Zoe rolled off, Oliver grabbed the .357 from her hip holster and jumped to his feet. "Adam!"

Adam was a fit guy, only in his early twenties. He leapt onto the window ledge and jumped. Well, he tried to jump, but as he went up onto the balls of his feet, hands seized him by the back of his shirt.

Adam's eyes went huge. "No! Noooo!" he shouted, trying to fight forward.

He was right there – only a footstep from freedom.

Oliver lunged forward.

Adam's eyes were desperate. He couldn't get free. The undead were pulling him back. One hand, then two, then four. Behind him, the amalgamation bellowed.

Melissa was screaming now.

As Adam began to fall back into the mob of undead, his eyes found Melissa, turning from desperate to apologetic.

In that split second, the young man knew he was going to die.

Oliver reached up, seizing the man's wrist. Adam returned the gesture, desperately clasping onto Oliver's wrist as if they were two Vikings shaking hands.

As Oliver planted his feet on the window sill, he leaned back with all his weight and let out a roar as he pulled. "Ahhhh! Let him goooo!"

A zombie's face appeared next to Adam, mouth open in a vicious snarl. Oliver didn't think – didn't measure the risk. There was no time for thought, only action. No time to think about the fact he was holding the .357 in his left hand but was right-handed. No time to consider this was Zoe's gun and he'd rarely shot it. And no time to consider Adam's face was only inches away from the zombie's mouth.

Oliver's only thought was, no, this man could not die like this. He raised the gun in his left hand, pointed, and fired. The crack of gunfire drowned out the screams, as the thunderous roar reverberated beneath the porte cochere. The bullet hurtled forward with lethal velocity, its trajectory arrow true.

In an instant, the air was filled with the acrid scent of gunpowder and decay. The round from Zoe's .357 struck the zombie's head with devastating force, tearing through flesh and bone with brutal efficiency. The impact was immediate and catastrophic.

For a brief moment, the zombie swayed precariously on unsteady legs. Then, with a final, shuddering convulsion, it fell forward against Adam's back.

Using his own weight and the weight of the dead zombie as it fell into Adam, Oliver pulled with all he had.

Adam was jerked forward, his T-shirt tearing away as he fell out the window and into Oliver.

Both of them went down in a heap of twisted limbs and rotted flesh. In addition to the one Oliver had shot, two more zombies fell out the window with them: a heavy-set balding man and a young woman in a bloodstained dress shirt and business skirt.

"Go! Take our truck!" Oliver shouted as he shoved the woman off of him and fired into her face. *Boom!*

Not even in a fully standing position, he immediately twisted around to shoot the balding man in the back of the head. But the position he fired from was weird and he missed the man's head from only two feet away as the gun bucked in his hand.

Frantically he fired again. The sound reverberated across the parking lot. This time he missed the head but hit the thing in its shoulder.

The zombie was on its feet now.

He fired again, blasting a portion of the man's jaw off.

Oliver felt like his ears were bleeding. Through his ringing ears, he thought he could faintly hear screaming from the cars.

The zombie dove forward again, its bloody eyes full of excitement despite its devastating wounds.

He pulled the hammer back, aimed, and fired. This time a chunk of the undead's skull burst apart in a spectacular spray of brain and dark blood.

Stealing a glance back at the window as he turned to run, Oliver saw more zombies jumping through the window onto the ground and falling over each other. Behind them, the monster filled the window, its heads twisting as if searching – searching for him. Then it screamed – all of it screamed. Every mouth throughout its twisted body screamed. Oliver could feel its rage. Its heads tipped down, extended through the window, and stretched apart. Teeth and more teeth. On the ground, the zombies were getting to their feet. He was fucked! He wasn't going to make it! He was...

Above him, a familiar wine bottle with a fiery wick sailed past.

The Molotov cocktail smashed into the window frame in a bright explosion of flame.

Oliver turned back to the vehicles to find Zoe standing next to the van holding a lighter and a second bottle. He couldn't hear her words but could read her lips. "Run, Oliver!"

Melissa was already in the truck and Adam was rounding the front of the vehicle.

Zoe threw the second bottle of fuel, smashing it at the feet of the pursuing zombies. Oliver scrambled forward as the two zombies ran through the fire, undeterred in their pursuit.

Oliver waved his hand wildly, motioning Zoe to start the van. He stole a glance back. The church wall was on fire, the window completely engulfed, but the monster was gone.

By the time he made it to the van's side door, the engine rumbled to life and Oliver dove inside.

He found his feet and peered out the side door to make sure the old blue Chevy started and Adam was with them.

Zoe stomped the gas, tearing out from beneath the porte cochere with Adam on their bumper. Behind the Chevy, dark shapes gave chase, framed by the quickly spreading fire. But the zombies were losing ground and falling farther behind by the second.

Satisfied, Oliver let out a relieved breath and looked at Jurnee. She was sitting next to Louie, still hugging Princess tight in her arms. "You okay, kiddo?"

She dropped her doll on the floor and threw herself into Oliver's arms. Her voice was barely a whisper, or maybe his ears hadn't settled from all that gunfire. "Tommy said horrible things. I'm sure glad you're okay, Oliver."

Oliver felt his eyes blur as he did his best to swallow down the emotion. "I'm sure glad you're okay too, kiddo."

They sped across the front parking lot towards the north side of the building, the blue Chevy behind them. Oliver cleared his throat and called up to Zoe, "Hey, how did you know about Tommy's Molotov cocktails?"

Zoe glanced up in the mirror. "You can thank Jurnee for that idea."

"Huh?" Oliver asked, eyeing the little girl. She retrieved Princess and sat back down on the floor and put one arm around Louie. The pit bull's tail wagged excitedly as his tongue licked out.

"She was curious, handed me one, and asked what it was. Then I saw the pack of cigarettes and a lighter sitting in the console tray."

"You're fucking amazing!" Oliver said, completely awestruck at his wife's ability to think on her feet.

Jurnee let go of Louie and placed both palms over Princess's ears. She pulled a face that was somehow half disappointed and half stern. "Oliver! How many times have we talked about this?" she scolded. "You know that's the worst one."

Oliver held his hands up. "Sorry, kid."

Jurnee shook her head.

If Oliver could have found it in him to laugh he would have, but as Zoe prepared to pull out onto the country road, all Oliver could think about was the dead friends they were leaving behind and the church full of zombies... And that... that nightmarish creation.

Oliver reached up to close the van door, glancing back at the church one last time. "Zo! Stop!"

"What? Why?"

"I'll be a son of a bi—" Oliver stopped short and glanced at Jurnee. "Look!" He pointed back at the north side of the church, where the yellow generator sat rumbling beneath an awning.

"What is it? I didn't see anything... oh... oh my god!"

There, next to the generator, stood the silhouette of a familiar young man.

"That's Aaron! What is he doing out there?"

"Yay! Aaron!" Jurnee cheered.

Oliver shook his head. "I don't know, but we have to get him."

Zoe swung the van around and raced back towards the generator. Adam didn't follow – instead, he pulled out onto the country road with the two zombies that had cleared the window following.

Oliver pointed. "That's good, they're following Adam, but let's hurry so we don't lose them. You'll have to pull onto the curb to get under the awning."

Zoe pulled up, guiding the van over the curb and into the grassy area just beneath the edge of the awning.

Aaron hurried over, stepping over a dead zombie that lay face down next to the genny, and started to climb into the van.

"Wait, Aaron!" Oliver ordered.

Aaron froze, his face an expression of worry.

"I'm sorry, but we need to know if you're okay?" Zoe asked.

Oliver held the .357 but he didn't point it as he stared into the young man's eyes – eyes that appeared to be clear.

"I believe so, actually," Aaron replied. "Can I get in?"

"Were you bitten?" Zoe asked.

Aaron shook his head.

Oliver scanned the boy's arms and clothes for any hint of the red rain. "And what about the rain? You didn't let the rain get on you, did you?"

"No, actually."

"Okay. Good." Oliver smiled. "Well, get in here, kid."

Aaron climbed in, sat next to Jurnee and Louie, and began to rock back and forth.

Oliver reached above the boy's head and lifted one of the Molotov cocktails from the basket.

Zoe gave him the side eye. "Oliver, what are you doing?"

That thing was still in there, along with who knew how many undead. "Making sure nothing in that church gets out." He lit the cloth and tossed the bottle out the passenger side door in a high arc, smashing it into the blue plastic barrels of fuel. "Drive!" he shouted, slamming the van door.

Zoe took off across the lot and tore out onto the country road.

Oliver climbed into the passenger seat and leaned forward, staring into the side mirror. For a moment, he worried the flames would burn out before melting through the barrels and causing a reaction, but when they were less than a half mile down the road, the north side of the church exploded in a fantastic mushroom cloud of flame.

It was little solace, but at least the friends they'd made at the church could all rest now. And whether they knew it or not, they had been avenged.

CHAPTER 41
THE FARMHOUSE MANSION

ZOE'S EYES flicked to the side mirror to reveal a vista of flame as the church's ceiling collapsed and the building folded in upon itself in utter devastation. Up ahead, the two zombies chasing Adam had fallen behind, but still they ran on, undeterred by the hopelessness of their pursuit. As she passed the man and woman, the one closest looked over, making eye contact. He was a middle-aged man, average in height and build. There was nothing remarkable about him other than the excitement in his bloodstained eyes and the fact that he was undead.

The burning church grew small in her rearview mirror. Over the past week, this place had started to feel like a new kind of normal. Zoe had found purpose in helping those in their tiny community, and most of all, she'd felt as safe as possible given the circumstances. Now it was all gone, their new friends – Aneesa, Raymond, and their kids! Martha, Jerry, Fred. Jesse, Scott, and Chris! All of them – dead! She didn't know how to process it. She wanted to scream – to collapse in a heap and give up.

All in a single day, she'd thought her husband was dead and found out he was alive, delivered a baby, and then lost so many of her new friends. She thought of Fred and what he'd said. And now she wondered – why were they allowed to live when so many others died? Fred's decades-old question would be her burden to carry. Tears stung at her eyes, making it hard to see the road. Inside her, a mix of emotions swirled. The unfairness of it all. Why? Why?

"Zoe? Are you okay?"

That was the dumbest question anyone had ever asked her.

"Sorry. Of course you aren't. Zoe, I don't know how you did what you did. Delivering a baby while Tommy was... And thinking I was, well—"

"Don't say it. Please, don't," she begged. "I'm sorry I just don't ever want to think about that."

"I understand. Still, you did it. Despite it all, you did it." He reached for her, squeezing her hand.

She forced a smile. But she didn't feel like anything was over. She didn't feel safe. Not for her, not for them, certainly not for baby Jonathan. "Oliver, what the hell are we going to do now?"

Oliver nodded up ahead. "Flash your lights. When we get to the stop sign, pull alongside Adam. We're going to the big farmhouse up the road, the one I told you about. Hopefully we can get in and get Melissa a safe place to rest."

"A safe place? Until the next attack," she said bitterly.

"Zoe, I know you're hurting. I am too. But this is the best that I got. Even if we wanted to keep on driving, we couldn't. Not yet. Travel won't be any safer. We don't know where to go, and we aren't stocked with enough firepower or provisions for a road trip. So we find a new place and we hunker down. Maybe then we can plan on how to reach Alexis, your parents, and my sister. But for now, that big farmhouse is perfect."

She knew Oliver was right. They couldn't go storming off into the night without a plan and with only the clothes on their backs. They needed safety, and Melissa needed rest and time to heal. "Okay, let's try," Zoe said, glancing into the rearview mirror again. Aaron continued to rock back and forth. Long blond curly locks covered half his face, a face that was fixed in a pained expression. "Aaron, what were you doing outside by the generator?"

Aaron didn't stop rocking as he pushed his bangs back out of his eyes. "Tommy made me come with him. He knows I am quite adept at mechanical technologies. Of course I was interested. But I didn't know Tommy would get attacked! Actually, the generator started easily. Of course, I didn't hear the zombie over the sound of the engine, and my mother doesn't allow me to bring my authentic hand-forged sword outside of my bedroom. Of course, she would rather I leave it in its sheath, but I often take it out and practice. Of course, she doesn't know that."

Zoe asked him gently, "Can you tell us what happened to Tommy?"

Aaron rocked harder. "I saw the zombie bite Tommy on the back of his wrist. Tommy screamed but, without my sword, I thought it best to hide, so I ran behind the generator and crouched down. When I finally stood to look around, the zombie was dead, and Tommy was gone. By now it was raining. Of course, I couldn't go in the rain, so I hid behind the generator again next to some of the fifty-gallon barrels. I heard gunshots, people screaming, and zombies." Aaron's face screwed up as if he were in pain. "The church is on fire. Where's Martha?"

Zoe shared a look with Oliver. Aaron was autistic and was clearly showing signs he was in distress. Telling him Martha was dead might put him over the edge. "Aaron, right now we're going to find somewhere safe and warm."

"Do you think the fire hurt Martha?" Aaron asked.

Zoe didn't understand. Was he asking if Martha was able to survive the fire?

He banged his back into the wall of the van. "I just hope she didn't suffer. I hope none of them suffered."

So he did understand Martha was gone. "Aaron, I know for sure she didn't suffer. No one suffered."

Aaron nodded, continuing to rock forward and back but slower now. "That's good."

Zoe eased the van along the driver's side of Adam's pickup truck.

Oliver couldn't risk rolling the window down so instead he pointed at Adam then at himself, then up the road. Even from her vantage point she could see the stress and worry creasing Adam's face, but he nodded his understanding.

Zoe maneuvered past the vehicle.

Adam pulled off the shoulder and followed.

Slowly they made their way down the country road towards Oliver's farmhouse mansion. "What do we do if it's still raining when we get there?"

"I suppose we'll wait."

From the back, Jurnee's tiny voice said, "I sure hope we don't have to wait long because I got to pee."

"It's barely raining, I think it will pass soon." Oliver pointed at a patch of woods surrounded by a barren field. "Hey, it's just up ahead on the left, see there."

Just off the road, the driveway led to a bridge that crossed a fast-flowing creek. On the opposite side of the bridge stood a tall wrought iron gate. Zoe turned in and pulled up to the gate, taking in the massive brick home. It had a huge four-car garage stretching across its south side. There was a second story above the garage covered in solar panels, while a third story topped the rest of the large structure. Four tall brick chimney stacks jutted skyward from various parts of the roof. As she took in the behemoth and its high privacy fence, Zoe had to admit to herself, this house would be the perfect place to lie low and prepare for what came next. White smoke bloomed from one of the chimneys – even from inside the car she could smell the wood fire. "Oliver, I thought you said the gate was open and that a car had crashed up the driveway? And look! There's smoke coming from one of the chimneys! This place is not empty!"

Oliver dragged a hand down his face. "I know," he admitted.

"You know? What do you mean you know?" she asked, sensing

he wasn't telling her something. "You know because you see the smoke too, or you already knew?"

Oliver closed his eyes, drew in a breath, and sighed.

"You knew!" she accused.

Oliver held up his hands defensively. "I didn't want to say this before, but Tommy told me there was an elderly man who lived here. One guy, Zo. One guy and all that house." His voice wavered with uncertainty as he gestured towards the darkened silhouette of the house looming in the distance.

Zoe's voice quivered with a mix of surprise and frustration. "Why... why wouldn't you tell me this before?"

She watched him shift uncomfortably, avoiding her gaze as he scratched the back of his neck. "I didn't want you to freak out about what I'm about to do is all," he admitted, his words coming out in a rush.

Confusion furrowed Zoe's brow as she tried to make sense of the situation. "And what is that exactly?" she pressed, her voice tight with apprehension.

Oliver pointed out the windshield. "The gate is damaged. It's clearly been hit and it isn't even locked. I'm going to open it and we're going to drive in, then I'll knock on the door. I just hope like hell he is a decent guy and allows us to stay here."

A surge of panic coursed through Zoe's veins at the thought of Oliver putting himself in danger. "I don't think you should go up there. What if he shoots you? Look, there's a call box right there. Let's see if he answers," she pleaded, her voice trembling with fear.

Oliver shook his head stubbornly, his jaw set in determination. "No. It will be easy for him to just tell us to leave when he can't even see us," he countered, his tone resolute.

Frustrated, Zoe sighed. "But what does seeing us have to do with it?"

"He'll see we are good people," Oliver insisted, a glimmer of hope in his eyes.

Zoe couldn't help but scoff incredulously. But she couldn't be mad either. After all, this was one of the many things that attracted her to him in the first place – his optimism and his ability to see the best in others even in a world gone to shit. A wry smile tugged at the corners of her lips. "Ollie, people don't see that you're a good person from a glance – and besides, you look like hell." Her gaze flicked pointedly to the bruises marring his face.

A flush of embarrassment colored Oliver's cheeks, his shoulders sagging under the weight of Zoe's scrutiny. "Wow, thanks," he muttered sarcastically.

Zoe softened at the sight of his discomfort. "You know what I mean. Your upper lip is swollen twice the size it should be and you have a knot the size of a golf ball on the side of your head. Do you feel nauseous? I'd be surprised if you didn't have a concussion."

Oliver dismissed her concerns with a wave of his hand. "Thanks, Doc, but can you stop examining me for a minute and focus on the plan?"

Glancing back through the rain-coated windshield, she felt her stomach churn with unease. "You're calling this a plan?" In truth, she didn't like this. She didn't like this at all.

"Let's just try. If he absolutely won't help us, we'll find somewhere else to go."

She gave Oliver her best pleading look. "At least try the call box? Warn him we're coming in and we mean him no harm?"

After a moment of contemplation, Oliver nodded in agreement. "Alright, I'll try the call box first, just to give the guy a heads-up that we're coming in and that we're not a threat."

"Good idea," she murmured, a flood of relief washing through her.

Oliver narrowed his eyes. "Did you just try and trick me into thinking that the call box was my idea?" he asked, trying to force a smile. He leaned forward and gave her a kiss, then winced. "Son of a..." She watched as he pulled down the visor and lifted his upper lip to reveal two deep punctures.

"You're lucky your teeth didn't go all the way through your lip – I mean, I'm not examining you or anything, just an observation. One friend to another, you probably could use a couple stitches."

"I'll pass!" he replied.

"Well, good because I have nothing to stitch you with anyway. It all burned up. By the way, you think if we are lucky enough to get inside, you can manage not to blow this house up?"

Oliver narrowed his eyes. "What are you saying?"

"Nothing. Just that, you know, you blew up our house and, well, you exploded the church."

He raised his eyebrows. "Now hold on, the house is on me but you're the one who lit the church on fire first. I just finished off what you started. And before you say anything, Farm and Feed wasn't my fault! That was all Tommy."

"Farm and Feed?" she gasped, cupping a hand over her mouth. "Oliver McCallister! You burned down the Farm and Feed too?"

"Oh shit. I forgot I hadn't even told you about that yet," he said, wincing. "But no. No, ma'am, I did not burn down the Farm and Feed! Tommy started that one." Oliver pushed himself back in his seat and crossed his arms defensively.

Zoe held her hands up. "Whatever you say. It's your story. Speaking of stories, want to tell me what happened out there?"

While they waited for the sky to clear, they traded stories and took stock of what they had in the van to barter with, which wasn't much. "Anything in the truck that might be helpful?" he asked.

"No, unfortunately I unloaded all the medical supplies the day we arrived," she said, adjusting the climate controls on the dash.

"Right. And my bag of ammo was in our room," he said with a sigh.

Zoe and Oliver retreated into their own thoughts while, in the back, Jurnee lay with her upper half on Louie as if he were her very own bean bag chair. She played with Princess and chatted with Aaron.

As they sat in silence Zoe's mind went to where it had often gone during the rare quiet moments over the past two weeks. She thought of her parents and, even more, she worried about her childhood friend, Alexis. She realized it now. There was no one coming to help them and losing so many new friends only moments ago only increased her need to know if Alexis was okay. She knew the chances weren't good for Alexis and even worse for her parents since they lived in a heavily populated area. Still, she wanted to know – had to know.

The group at the church had given her a brief illusion of safety. She would have been content to stay there for a while. She could have just told herself that things would get better, that help would come – at least for a little while. But now... now she knew that was all bullshit.

Oliver leaned forward and peered up through the windshield. "Alright, no more clouds, so wish me luck." The door to the van creaked open and Oliver jumped down onto the concrete drive, hurrying around the van and over to the call box.

Zoe glanced up to the sky. It wasn't enough to simply wait for the rain to stop. They had to wait for clouds to pass completely since even one stray drop of rain from the sky could mean death. She rolled her window down enough so she would be able to hear what Oliver was saying. As she cranked the knob, she noticed the cuff of her bloodstained shirt. Glancing from her wrist to her waist, she realized for the first time that she had the remnants of childbirth staining her clothes. She lifted her hands. She hadn't even had a chance to wash them. Had all of this really just happened?

Oliver punched the button on the call box, drawing her from her thoughts. "Hey, if there's anyone in there, my name is Oliver. I have my wife and little girl with me. Also, another family with a newborn baby just delivered an hour ago. We're good people, we just need some help."

He took his finger off the button and waited. No one answered. Lifting the collar of his windbreaker, he turned back towards the van, lifted his hands, and shrugged, then thumbed the button again. "Look, we're coming in and we mean you no harm. We just need some help." A few more seconds passed and nothing. Oliver shook his head as he walked towards the gate. "Not answering." It looked like he started to reach for it then paused. Instead of grabbing it he touched it with the back of his hand, quickly jerking his hand away.

Zoe gasped. "What's wrong?"

Placing both hands on the wrought iron, he pushed one side of the gate open. "Nothing," he said, glancing back. "I just didn't want to find out it was electric after I grabbed hold."

"Hey, are we still going in? Maybe no answer is a sign."

"For all we know, the damn thing could be broken," he said, pushing open the other side before turning back to Zoe.

She supposed that was true.

Pausing at the van, Oliver said, "I better touch base with Adam before we go in."

Zoe lifted the door handle. "Good idea. I want to check on Melissa and baby Jonathan too."

Making her way around the van and over to the passenger side of the vehicle, she found Melissa asleep in the back seat with the baby on her chest. "How is she doing?"

Adam tried to smile, but it didn't stick. "She's okay – they both passed out as soon as she lay down."

It was all Zoe could do not to climb in and take the pulse of both Melissa and the baby. "I can only imagine how exhausted she is."

Oliver reached through the window and gave Adam's shoulder a squeeze. "What about you? How are you holding up?"

"Still trying to wrap my mind around what just happened, but yeah, I guess I'm okay." Adam nodded at the house. "Of all places, why did you bring us here?"

"You know who lives here?" Zoe asked.

"Everyone knows Benson Meyer. He's about the most hateful person you'll ever meet."

Zoe crossed her arms. "Really?"

Oliver held his hands out. "Look, we're here, and I honestly think it's best we try."

"Just be careful, Oliver. This guy didn't get rich through his generosity. I hear he's a shrewd dude, owns half the county, and... well, just look." Adam pointed towards the woods to the right of the bridge.

Zoe hadn't noticed the sign nailed to the tree when they'd pulled in. In large white letters on a red background were the words NO TRESPASSING! VIOLATORS WILL BE SHOT. SURVIVORS WILL BE SHOT AGAIN.

CHAPTER 42
OLD MAN MEYER

OLIVER WATCHED Zoe pinch the bridge of her nose, her frustration evident. "Are you kidding me, Oliver? Let's just move on!" she exclaimed, her voice tight with irritation. He could see the tension etched in her features, the worry lines around her eyes deepening.

He tried to sound confident, crossing his arms and standing his ground even as doubt gnawed at the edges of his resolve. "He won't shoot me for knocking on his door."

Adam glanced in the rearview mirror at Melissa and the baby, his concern clear in his tone. "Maybe not, bro, but why risk it?" He ran a hand through his hair, glancing nervously at the tall privacy fence surrounding the property and the iron gate that even in its now open position looked unwelcoming, like two sentries keeping guard.

Oliver gestured to the fence and the solar panels glinting in the evening sunlight. "Look at how secure this place is, and it has solar panels, which means electricity. Look, it's worth asking. If he says leave, we leave," he insisted, trying to convey the sense of hope he felt. He needed them to understand, to see the potential he saw.

Zoe shook her head, a worried frown creasing her forehead. "I have a feeling, and it isn't a good one." Her voice was low and she hugged herself, as if trying to protect against her unease.

Oliver stepped closer to her, softening his expression. "Yeah, I know, but I have a feeling too. Please, babe, we're just going to ask," he said gently, placing a hand on her shoulder. He looked into her eyes, silently pleading for her to trust him just this once.

After a long moment, Zoe sighed and gave a reluctant nod.

"Alright then – Adam, just stay behind us until I talk to the guy," he instructed.

Adam nodded nervously. "Alright, but I sure hope you know what you're doing."

They returned to the van, and Oliver could see Zoe's hands trembling slightly as she gripped the steering wheel. She eased the vehicle forward through the gate, her apprehension palpable. Behind them, Adam mirrored their movements, his eyes darting around nervously as he cleared the gate.

The moment Adam was through, he jumped out of his vehicle and ran back to push the gate shut – one side and then the other. The heavy clang of the gate closing sent a chill through Oliver, but he pushed the feeling aside, focusing instead on the task at hand. *It's just one old guy,* he told himself. Then, taking a deep breath, he steeled himself for whatever came next, hoping this gamble would pay off.

Zoe continued forward, steering the van up the long driveway, which ended in a circle with a flagpole in its center.

Oliver pointed. "Go past the house and pull off to the side where the pavement goes back towards the garage."

Zoe pulled off the circle and onto the driveway leading to the garage.

"Okay. Wish me luck," he said, lifting the door latch.

Zoe reached for his arm. "Oliver!"

"What is it?" he asked, seeing the worry in her eyes. Zoe had always said the eyes were the windows to the soul, and he felt like in this moment he could see into hers. He knew she wanted to tell him not to do this, to beg him not to knock on that door. Their eyes were locked, anchoring each other to the moment until finally Zoe said, "I love you."

He forced a smile. "I love you too. Hey, it's going to be okay," he reassured her, squeezing her hand before climbing out of the van. "I'll be right back."

"Oliver, wait!" Jurnee exclaimed.

"You too!" Oliver said, leaning back in.

Jurnee was sitting next to Aaron as he slowly rocked back and forth. Louie lay on Jurnee's other side – the dog appeared to be asleep, but Oliver knew better. The pit's ears gave him away as they perked up and twitched.

"What is it, kiddo?" Oliver asked.

"Don't go away again!" she begged, her eyes welling up.

"Hey, it's okay." He smiled. "I'm just going to knock on the door. I'll be right back."

Oliver approached the house with his hands held up high so he wouldn't look like a threat. He glanced from the front door to the shuttered windows. He didn't see any sign of life, but he could smell the wood fire from the chimney.

He stole a glance back. Both Zoe and Adam watched him, their eyes wide with worry.

At the steps, he hesitated, something Zoe said resonating. *People don't see you're a good person by looking at you.* So assuming the guy answered the door, how would he convince him? Well, honesty might be a good place to start. As he steeled himself to step forward, above the front entry a door opened on the balcony.

Oliver stepped back and peered up.

A frail-looking elderly man stepped from the doorway – he was holding a rifle against his shoulder. "Not one more step! Turn your ass around, get back in that van, and get on down the road," the old man barked, his voice steady and authoritative.

"Listen, please, we need—" Oliver began, his voice wavering with desperation.

The man slid back the bolt on the rifle and shoved it forward with a menacing click. "Don't care what you need, and I'm not going to ask again. I'll give you to three and you best be heading back the way you came. Get on now!"

Behind him, Oliver heard Zoe's urgent plea. "Oliver! Get back in the van!" she begged, her voice high-pitched with fear.

"One!" the man counted, his grip on the rifle tightening.

"Sir! I have a—" Oliver tried again, his hands shaking.

"Two!" the old man shouted, one eye closing as the other looked down the sight.

A commotion behind him caught Oliver's attention. He spun around just in time to see the van's side door slide open. Aaron stepped aside as Jurnee jumped down onto the driveway.

"Jurnee! No!" Zoe screamed, but she couldn't get out of the van fast enough to stop what was about to happen.

"Three!" the old man yelled.

Jurnee ran towards Oliver, her face determined and fearless.

"No, Jurnee!" Oliver turned, desperately motioning for her to go back.

In his mind, it all played out in a split-second flash of gunfire.

The man shot.

Jurnee stepped in the way.

Princess fell to the ground as the bullet meant for Oliver ripped through the little girl.

But in real time, Jurnee wasn't even holding Princess as she threw her little arms around his leg and hugged him with all she had. "No. No!" she screamed, tears flowing.

Zoe was out of the van now, running towards them.

Above them, the man stared down, the three-count having come and gone with the rifle never firing.

Jurnee pulled her face back from Oliver's pant leg and looked up at the man. "Don't you shoot Oliver! Don't you know anything?" she screamed. "My mom's gone forever, and I don't know where my dad is!" Tears streamed down her face.

Above them on the balcony, the grey-haired man opened his

other eye, pulled his face away from the sight, and stared down with a questioning expression. “What’s this?” he asked, his voice gruff and suspicious.

Zoe, now by Oliver’s side, called up towards the man, her voice trembling slightly. “I’m sorry,” she said, cutting a pleading look at Oliver as she took Jurnee by the hand. “We’re leaving! Come on. Get in the van, we’re leaving right now,” she repeated, her voice firmer, trying to pull Jurnee towards the van.

Oliver turned back to the man, his hands still raised in a placating gesture. “I’m sorry. We’re going,” he said, trying to convey sincerity through his tone and body language.

The man narrowed his eyes, suspicion deepening the lines on his face. “That little girl doesn’t belong to you? You family to her?” he asked, adjusting the grip on the rifle.

People don’t see your good, Oliver reminded himself. Be honest and bare it all. “I found her when this all started. We’re all she has.” He kept his hands raised, palms outward, trying to appear as non-threatening as possible. “Look, sir, we just need some help.”

“Help? I’ve heard that before. You think you’re the first to try?” the man snapped, still pointing the gun at them. He nodded towards the truck. “Who you got in the truck back there?”

Pain twinged through Oliver’s shoulder, reminding him of another time there was a gun pointing at him and the searing lead bullet that followed. He stopped again, this time very slowly lowering one hand to point at the truck. “We have a woman, Melissa, and her husband, Adam.”

The old man eased forward a little more, craning his neck to get a better look. “I don’t see no woman. I see a man,” he said, scrutinizing the truck.

“Melissa is in the back seat, sleeping. She gave birth less than an hour ago,” Oliver explained, his voice steady despite the tension knotting in his stomach.

Zoe and Jurnee stood next to the open side door of the van, but they hadn't gotten in yet. Zoe's eyes darted between Oliver and the old man.

"And who else you got with you in the van?" the man demanded, his tone sharp and mistrustful.

"That's Aaron. He's a good kid," Oliver said, his voice calm but his heart pounding. "We aren't trying to hurt you or take anything away from you. We just need help. You know what's happening out there?" He hoped his sincerity would reach the man.

"I know enough. I can't help you. Now you all best be on your way," the man replied, stepping back towards the open French doors, his eyes hard and unyielding.

Oliver's shoulders sagged in defeat. He turned back towards the van, feeling the weight of their dire situation pressing down on him. Suddenly, Jurnee's voice cut through the air. "Mister, you're mean! Everyone knows you're supposed to help people who need help."

"Get her in the van," Oliver said, still feeling his heart thudding against his chest. He'd known by the look in Meyer's eyes just how close he'd come to being shot.

Zoe held Jurnee's hand. "Come on, Jurnee. Climb up."

Jurnee wiped her nose on her sleeve and looked up at the old man. "Mister, don't you have grandkids?" she asked, her voice innocent but piercing.

"What did you say?" the old man asked, his voice suddenly hollow, as if struck by a painful memory.

Oliver glanced back. Meyer was back standing at the railing of the balcony, staring down at them with a vacant expression. His brow was bunched up in deep wrinkles.

"She's sorry. We're going. Jurnee, get in the van," he said sternly. He looked back at Adam and shook his head.

Adam nodded and shifted the truck into reverse.

"But, Oliver, I don't want to go. I want to stay here. I'm hungry, and I have to go to the bathroom!" she whined.

Oliver was next to her now. "I know, and I promise we'll stop somewhere soon. Everyone just get in," he said, looking back up at Meyer. He didn't want to take his eyes off the old man.

As Jurnee and Zoe climbed into the van, the old man blinked and shouted. "Don't any of you move!" He backed across the threshold and vanished back inside.

Zoe exchanged a look with Oliver.

Oliver took her hand. "I thought he was really going to shoot me. You were right – let's get the hell out of here."

Zoe swallowed and shook her head. "No. Wait. He isn't going to shoot, or he would have already done it."

"You sure about that? Because I felt pretty damn sure he meant every word."

Zoe glanced down at Jurnee and then back up and nodded. "Didn't you see the look on his face? Something Jurnee said resonated. I'm sure of it. Let's just wait – maybe he's bringing us something to eat." She climbed back out of the van to stand next to Oliver.

A moment later, the front door creaked open. The man still held the rifle, but he was no longer pointing it directly at them. He was a short man, thin but wiry. His posture had softened, and his expression was more weary than angry.

Behind them, Adam was already backing up and slammed on the brakes; the tires chirped on the concrete, drawing all their attention. He killed the engine and rolled the window down. "Shut off the van!" His voice was urgent but he didn't shout.

He was looking back in his side mirror and pointing.

"What? Why?" Oliver frowned, not understanding.

Meyer lifted his chin and pointed to something beyond the closed gate, something out in the field.

But then Oliver saw it, the same thing they all saw.

"Oliver, is that...?" Zoe started but trailed off.

Zoe was closer to the open door of the van. "Quick, kill the engine, Zo."

She climbed back in, reached over, and turned the key.

With the vehicles silenced, everything around them went still. From far out in the field came a familiar low croak followed by a sharp scream as if someone was being tortured. Oliver swallowed dryly. It was so far out he couldn't tell if it was coming towards them or moving away. "It... it's another one of those things!"

In the van, Louie pushed himself against Jurnee and whined.

"You know what that is? You've seen it before?" Meyer asked. But before anyone could answer, the old man started coughing.

Oliver was no doctor, but he didn't need to be to know Meyer's cough wasn't right.

Meyer pulled a handkerchief from his back pocket, held it over his mouth, and hacked.

Zoe's face took on a look Oliver knew all too well, and suddenly her eyes held a storm of questions. "Sir, are you okay? That cough sounds bad. I'm a doctor, and I might be able to—"

Meyer pulled the handkerchief from his mouth and quickly folded it. "I don't need no damn doctor!" he snapped. "Now I asked you if you know what that is?"

Zoe nodded, a shadow of concern passing over her face. Seeming to concede, she glanced back to the field. "Actually I do. It's an amalgamation."

"An amalga what?" Meyer asked.

"It's when the zombies group up and then sort of congeal together," Oliver started but as he tried to explain it he realized it wasn't so easy to put into words.

"To what end?" the old man asked, his frown deepening.

Zoe stepped forward. "We don't know, but we think it has something to do with the parasite infecting people."

"A parasite? That's what's in the rain?" he asked.

Oliver nodded. "That's right. Look, we best leave now. Before it comes any closer. So far I haven't seen one move very fast. But we were attacked by one in the church down the road and I'll tell you this, if that thing takes an interest in your place, I'm not so sure that gate will keep it out."

Meyer stared past Oliver, his attention on the van. Oliver glanced back to see Jurnee's little face peeking around the corner of the open side door.

"Look, Mr. Meyer, once we go I'll be sure and—"

Meyer interrupted, his attention back on Oliver. "You know my name? How?"

Oliver hadn't meant to say the man's name. He shrugged, playing it off. "Heard it from some of the others at the church, that's all."

"At the church," he spat. "You heard of me and still you came here?"

Oliver nodded.

From the truck Adam said, "Oliver, what are we doing, man?" His voice was near panic as his eyes flicked between Oliver and his side mirror. In the back seat, Melissa had sat up and was holding baby Jonathan with his little head resting on her shoulder.

"Mr. Meyer, I'll be sure and shut the gate when I leave. With any luck, that thing is far enough out it won't notice us but if it does, we'll lead it away from your place." Oliver turned to climb in the van.

"Oliver, do we have to go?" Jurnee begged.

Oliver nodded. "Yeah, kiddo, we do, but it's going to be alright."

Jurnee's little shoulders dropped and she moved back to sit down next to Louie.

Meyer looked from the field to the truck and finally to Jurnee. "Dammit!" he cursed, just loud enough to be heard. The old man was shaking his head, seeming to struggle with some internal decision. "Now just... just hold on!"

His hand on the sliding van door, about to slam it shut, Oliver froze. "Sir, we really need to go now."

Meyer dragged a hand down his face and cleared his throat. "You aren't going anywhere."

Oliver exchanged a glance with Zoe, who looked about as confused as he felt. "I... I don't understand."

Meyer's gun was pointing down at the ground now. "Well, for god's sake, you heard the little girl. She needs a bathroom and she's about as skinny as a stick of straw. You ought to at least get her belly full before you go gallivanting off to who in the hell knows where. And what about them? You're just going to drag them around the countryside with a new baby and all, not knowing where you're going, not having a plan at all?"

"I... um. Well." He looked at Zoe. She cupped a hand over mouth to hide her smile but her eyes gave it away.

"Jesus Christ! Well, are you coming in or are you just going to stand there looking dumbstruck? Or maybe you want to invite that thing from the field onto my property while you're at it," he grumbled.

Oliver couldn't believe it. His tongue knotted, trying to find words. "I... a... we, um, have a dog too."

"I ain't goddamn blind, son! Bring your dog. Shit, might as well, you brought half a village with you anyway."

"Alright, well, thank you, Mr. Meyer," Oliver said, gesturing to Adam.

"Yay!" Jurnee shrieked. "Come on, Louie! Come on, Aaron!" She jumped back to her feet and darted out of the van with Louie in tow.

Adam was out of the truck now and helping Melissa.

Zoe leaned in and gave him a kiss on the cheek. "Nice job, babe."

"Nice job?" he asked, watching Jurnee as she ran past Benson Meyer and onto the porch. "I don't think I did anything at all."

"Oh, I wouldn't be so sure about that."

Oliver raised an eyebrow. "How's that?"

"I think you showed him, Ollie, and I think he saw." She smiled and squeezed his hand. "Hey, I better help Adam with the baby."

As Zoe hurried off to assist Adam, Oliver watched old man Meyer reach for the door. Just as he did, Meyer glanced back, and Oliver saw it – hidden just beneath the old man's silver, bewhiskered face was the slightest hint of a smile. It was faint, but unmistakable.

Oliver thought of his friends – Jesse and Fred, Raymond and Aneesa, and Sam too. Then he thought of Howard and what he'd said to him: "There are still good people in this world."

For the first time in a while, Oliver felt a flicker of hope. He took a deep breath, letting the tension of the past few minutes slowly ebb away. Through the gate he saw only an empty field now, void of monsters. Maybe they had a chance here, a real chance. He watched as Zoe helped Melissa inside, and he felt a surge of gratitude and renewed determination.

"Oliver, you coming?" Zoe called back to him.

"We're going to be okay," he murmured to himself.

"Oliver?"

"Yeah, of course." He smiled, and with a final glance at Meyer, he followed his family into the house.

EPILOGUE – AN EYE FOR AN EYE

A CONCUSSIVE BLAST shook Tommy into consciousness. For a moment, he was back in the desert. Had he been hit? What was it, an IED? But then as hunger ripped through his stomach like hot lead, he was reminded that the only reason he existed was to feed. Not even the worst starvation should feel this way, but it did.

The hallway was choked with smoke, the crackle of fire, and the moans of the dead. He lay face down on the ground. Zombies scurried past him like soldiers on the hunt. He peeled his face from the coagulated mess on the tile floor and rolled onto his side. Something was wrong with his eye. He pushed his index finger into an empty cavity where his eye used to be and swirled it around in the empty socket. More pain. He winced and grunted. Try to remember. Something else. Something more. The pain he felt in his eye was connected to pain radiating behind his nose and into the back of his throat.

A young undead girl tripped over him. She scrambled for her feet and followed the others through a door labeled Nursery. From the other side it sounded as if the whole place was being pulled apart.

"Nursery," Tommy croaked as he pushed himself up. A memory

flashed through his mind. He'd had Zoe right there. Delicious Zoe. Then Oliver was here. Somehow, he'd made it back to the church.

It all came back in a flood. The fight. Zoe fell, then Oliver. He'd been about to kill the man! Then somehow... wait. He remembered the throwing axe. Oliver had spiked him in the fucking eye! Then that was it. Everything had gone dark. Maybe the spike had hit a nerve and he'd passed out from the pain.

In his hand-to-hand combat training Tommy seemed to remember the distance from the front of a man's eye to his brain was about two inches give or take. The spike on that axe was every bit of three inches. "You had the angle all wrong, Oliver," Tommy muttered as he found his way to his feet. Swallowing down a mouthful of bile and blood he fought his way, not towards the nursery, not to her, but instead through the crowd of undead. For now, he wasn't dead, not yet. Soon, maybe, but not yet.

Around him the roof began to collapse in fiery chunks. Tommy staggered out of the hallway and back into the lobby. Next to Jesse's broken skull lay Chad's shotgun. Tommy snatched it up as above him the whole structure began to collapse.

Running forward, Tommy dove out the front door and rolled across the concrete.

From the building, she screamed as she burned. Tommy didn't know what she was, only what he was to do. He was to consume and consume and when she or one like her called, he was to join. On an instinctive level he understood he wouldn't be summoned to the calling until he had become one of the undead.

Once an undead, he could be one of the lucky chosen to join her. But if not, he would simply go on consuming. He would do better, eat more, and when called again, maybe then he would be one of the chosen.

Tommy felt the back of his neck. A small lump no bigger than his thumbnail had already started to form there. In time it would get much bigger. For now, he was still alive and he had control of himself to some degree. But the pain and the cravings that went along with it were undeniable. The creature living inside him would not be denied. There was no voice in his head. No communication with the thing controlling him but still he felt all too clearly what it wanted and if there was one word to describe what it was commanding of him, it was this. "FEED!"

"I know!" he shouted, his hands pressing against his bloated guts. He'd eaten so much already. The three kids plus Chad. Then Jesse, Ray, and Martha too. He'd had to leave Fred to deal with Jerry, but the old man's fragile skull cracked open easily. He'd only been able to kill Aneesa, but before he could claim the prize some other zed fuck ran off with her head. Scott had been clever and shot himself in the head before he could get to him. What a waste. He'd wounded Chris but before he could crack his skull open, the guy managed to lock himself in the walk-in freezer in the kitchen.

Even after seven brains' worth, his stomach was still racked with sharp, stabbing, hot poker pangs of hunger. "Ahhhh! HUA!" Tommy shouted, setting his one eye to the north as he watched the supply van grow smaller and smaller. The van didn't turn towards Libbyton or Groveland; instead it crossed the road and continued north towards old man Meyer's place.

"Of course," Tommy said with a smile. "I spy with my little eye."

Another wave of hunger pain ripped through his insides.

This time, Tommy buckled over at the waist. When the wave of pain lessened, he righted himself, tipped his head back, and sucked in a breath through his mangled sinuses. He could smell them in the air, sugary and sweet. The scent only made the pain that much worse.

Tommy stepped out of the parking lot and into the road as the rain that created him soaked his white undershirt, turning it to a rust color. He couldn't run with so much in his gut and his stomach on fire. But as long as he still lived and the ability to decide was still his, he would place one foot in front of the other and by god he would have his revenge. "I'm coming for you, Oliver. You owe me! An eye for an eye, and a belly full of fat cakes!"

ACKNOWLEDGMENTS

Book two in the Wrack and Ruin series is a wrap! I hope you enjoyed reading it as much as I enjoyed writing it. Ever since I was in my teens, I wanted to write a zombie book. I even tried once but, alas, I was too young, too busy with life and all the things, to really commit to my writing.

Now years later, this is my seventh book. One might think that by now my process is like a well-oiled machine but in truth, my style of writing is anything but formulated. When I start that first sentence, I have little idea where my characters are taking me, and that's the part I really enjoy. As I write, the plot and outline unfold internally as the story progresses. Long ago and far away, I wanted to be one of the organized – one of the cool kids who plotted it all out. My brain simply doesn't work that way, and by the second chapter my characters were taking me to places far outside the outline. But that's the magic bit. The moment in my writing when an idea strikes and I say, *Shit! Will that work?* And then you make that critical decision to run with it – to see it through to end. *Oh, man! If this doesn't work, I'll have to delete the sentence, the last page, the last chapter!* THAT is what I love! The feeling of trepidation as I step off the cliff, write into the void, and pray there's water at the bottom, rather than a pit of spikes. I truly believe this is where my best writing happens.

For example, in this story I learned more about delivering a baby than I would have ever imagined. I really had no idea that was coming until my characters arrived at the church and found a very pregnant Melissa. I asked myself, *Can I do this? Can I write Zoe delivering a baby in a way that is believable?* Once I decided yes, then came more internal questions, *How can I raise the stakes? How can I put Zoe in the direst of situations?* And well, you know the rest...

Okay, that's the secret sauce, but it is only part of it. After I get the story that far I need experts. Whether it be a midwife who has delivered dozens of babies (thank you, Christine Knapp!), someone to check for unconscious bias, a scientist to check my tech references, or medical experts to check the first aid being administered, I know I can count on Kristen Tate at the Blue Garret. Kristen leads my editing team and contracts whatever help we need to make the story as true and accurate as possible. From the bottom of my heart, thank you, Kristen! I am so grateful to get to work with you on our seventh project and I look forward to many more!

A special thanks to my advanced reader team, JC, Mandy, and Kamy, who passionately commit to reading my book very quickly and with little notice. They find the tiny things we all miss, make me better, and their response to my stories gives me encouragement!

And to you, the readers, who take the time to not only read my work but also review it. Reviews are incredibly important to authors, and I appreciate each and every one. Thank you so much!

Finally, to the two most important women I've known in this life. My wife, thank you for supporting my journey. I know it isn't always easy to sacrifice the time I've spent pursing this alongside a full-time career, but despite this you have been there the whole way. And my mom, the woman who read a book a day for years, it seems so unfair you passed away so young. You have influenced my writing journey greatly and I know you would have enjoyed my stories. I miss you.

Otto Schafer
July 16, 2024

ABOUT THE AUTHOR

Otto Schafer grew up exploring the small historic town in central Illinois featured in his award-winning God Stones series. If you visit Petersburg, Illinois you may find locations familiar from the books. You may even discover, as Otto did, that history has left behind cleverly hidden traces of magic, whispered secrets, and untold treasures.

Otto and his loving wife reside in a quiet log cabin tucked away in the woods. When he's not writing, he can often be found running along the forest trails near his home, lost in a tangle of thoughts he can't wait to rush back and put on paper.

Currently, Otto is working on his popular zombie apocalypse series, Wrack and Ruin, continuing to captivate readers with his vivid storytelling and imaginative worlds.

Check out my website and blog: www.ottoschafer.com
Connect with me on social:
Instagram – www.instagram.com/ottoschaferwriter
Facebook – www.facebook.com/ottoschaferauthor
TikTok – www.tiktok.com/@ottoschaferauthor

ALSO BY OTTO SCHAFER

A history hidden from the world. A truth long sought, but better left unfound. Will two teenagers survive the magical secrets they unearth?

Oak Island, Nova Scotia. Breanne Moore blames herself for her mother's tragic death. So when her archaeologist father is invited on an exciting new dig, she's determined to tag along and keep him safe. But as the mystery leads them closer to the island's secret, Breanne's dreams are filled with visions of a strange boy she's never met… and a world of flaming carnage.

Petersburg, Illinois. Sixteen-year-old Garrett Turek is the unofficial leader of his fellow outcasts. Grappling with a volatile relationship with his stepfather, he avoids his home life by helping an eccentric accountant restore a historic Victorian house. But when he and his crew stumble upon a crusty journal in the basement, Garrett uncovers a dead president's key to a secret world-saving society.

As Breanne and her dad seek clues to a treasure hidden deep beneath the surface, they trigger a dangerous magic that should have stayed dormant forever. And when Garrett closes in on the truth, he'll question everything he thought he knew and find trust in a girl from far away as they prepare to battle a dangerous foe.

Can the two would-be heroes fulfill a powerful prophecy and save the planet from destruction?

The Secret Journal is the first book in the sensational God Stones YA contemporary fantasy series. If you like unusual pairings, well-researched historical backgrounds, and heated suspense, then you'll love Otto Schafer's coming-of-age adventure.

Destiny awaits those brave enough to turn the page!